Praise for
THE BLOOD-DIMMED TIDE

'Most accomplished and, with its unusual combination of
wholesomeness and horror, highly enjoyable. Let us hope
that John Madden, retired though he may be, happens
upon another corpse before too long'
Spectator

'Airth is good at describing landscape and the
different ways in which people relate to it . . .
The natural world is a vivid presence here, and
often a metaphor for mood; Rennie Airth has
an emotional and sensual precision. His darkened
lanes are less like the pastel colours of cosy crime
and more like the mean streets of quite another thriller'
Times Literary Supplement

'Spine-chilling horror . . .
terrific story full of period detail'
Guardian

'Well worth the wait.
Airth has written another first-class police procedural'
Independent on Sunday

'*The Blood-Dimmed Tide* shows what can be done with
the crime novel when good plotting, excellent character-
isation and a fine sense of place are given their head'
Birmingham Post

THE
BLOOD-DIMMED
TIDE

RENNIE AIRTH was born in South Africa and worked for a number of years as a foreign correspondent for Reuters. *The Blood-Dimmed Tide* is the second novel in his Inspector Madden trilogy. He lives in Italy.

Also by Rennie Airth

RIVER OF DARKNESS

THE
BLOOD-DIMMED TIDE

Rennie Airth

PAN BOOKS

First published 2004 by Macmillan

This paperback edition published 2005 by Pan Books
an imprint of Pan Macmillan Ltd
Pan Macmillan, 20 New Wharf Road, London N1 9RR
Basingstoke and Oxford
Associated companies throughout the world
www.panmacmillan.com

ISBN 0 330 48472 9

5 7 9 8 6 4

A CIP catalogue record for this book is available from
the British Library.

Typeset by SetSystems Ltd, Saffron Walden, Essex
Printed and bound in Great Britain by
Mackays of Chatham plc, Chatham, Kent

To the Mooreheads – Caroline,
and John and Boo – in gratitude.

The blood-dimmed tide is loosed, and everywhere
The ceremony of innocence is drowned

W. B. Yeats
'The Second Coming'

PART ONE

1

ONLY CHANCE brought the Maddens to Brookham that day.

Earlier, they had driven over to Reigate to attend a luncheon party and in the normal course of events would have returned directly by the main road to Guildford. But the fine weather had tempted them to break their journey in order to climb a narrow bridle path that led up the steep slopes of Colley Hill to the top of the North Downs.

It was a walk they had made many times before – the view from the crest was justly famous – and for more than an hour they had strolled arm in arm in the late summer sunshine, pausing now and then to gaze out over a wide sweep of southern England, a patchwork of fields and hedgerows and woods extending to the distant horizon.

A land at peace in that year of 1932.

By the time they returned to their car, however, the afternoon was well advanced and they had found the main road clogged with slow-moving Sunday drivers out for a spin. It was then they had decided to make a detour and to return home by quiet back lanes.

Madden had driven with one eye on the road ahead and the other on the darkening sky. A bank of clouds had been massing in the west for some time, and although the harvest was over and the haymaking done, a hailstorm now would do costly damage to crops of vegetables still ripening in the fields.

Glancing up through the windshield, he might have driven past the line of cottages without noticing anything was amiss if Helen hadn't touched his arm.

'John! Look—'

They were passing through a small hamlet called Brookham, still a few miles from home. A group of men had gathered in front of one of the cottages in the row. Some were in the garden, others outside the fence. An air of expectancy hung over them.

Madden stopped the car.

'What is it, do you think?' Helen was a doctor and her first thought had been that her services might be needed.

Madden made no reply. The scene struck a chord in his memory. It had a grim familiarity, albeit one he hadn't encountered for many years.

At that moment the door of the cottage opened and the uniformed figure of a police constable emerged from within. Tall in his helmet, he towered over the men before him.

'Good lord!' Helen gasped in astonishment. 'It's *Will*!'

Will Stackpole was the village bobby at Highfield, where they lived.

'What on earth's he doing over here?'

Unwilling to hazard a guess, Madden simply shook his head.

But already he felt the chill of premonition.

*

THE CHILD'S NAME was Alice, Will Stackpole told them. Alice Bridger. She and a friend had set out shortly before midday to walk to the neighbouring village of Craydon, little more than a mile away, along a path bordering the road that linked the two.

'They were going to have lunch with a friend there and then all three of them were going to a birthday party later.'

Catching sight of Madden and Helen as they got out of their car, the constable had left the group of men and crossed the road at once to speak to them, his forehead grooved with worry. He had made no secret of his relief at seeing them.

It seemed that Alice, recently turned twelve, and her friend, a girl named Sally Drake, had got only halfway to their destination when Sally realized that she'd forgotten to bring the birthday present her mother had wrapped for her that morning – it was a box of home-made fudge – and had dashed back to Brookham to fetch it, leaving Alice at a point on the path where it ran alongside a stretch of densely forested land known as Capel Wood.

They had agreed that Alice would wait for her there, Sally said later, but when she got back – after not more than ten minutes – there was no sign of her friend. Thinking she must have decided to continue without her, Sally had gone on to Craydon herself, only to discover that Alice hadn't arrived at their friend's house and no one had seen her.

'The family rang the Bridgers and Fred walked over to Craydon himself, looking for his daughter,' Stackpole told the Maddens. 'He's the dairy manager on a big farm hereabouts. Anyway, they were going to ring the local bobby when they remembered he was away on leave, so they got in touch with me, since I was next nearest. That was three hours ago.'

As the constable was speaking, thunder rumbled in the distance. Meanwhile, the men gathered across the road had turned to watch them and Helen saw that their glances were directed towards her husband. Before their marriage Madden had been a policeman himself – a Scotland Yard inspector – and his name and reputation were widely known in the area.

'There's been no shortage of volunteers wanting to help,' Stackpole said, mopping his brow. With the approach of the storm the air had grown still. 'We've been up and down the road, searching the fields on either side, and the wood, as well, but there's no sign of the lass. All we found was her gift.'

'Her gift?' Helen asked.

'The present she was taking for the birthday child. A pair of mittens wrapped in coloured paper. It was lying in a ditch by the path, near to where the other girl left her.'

Helen glanced at her husband. Madden had shown no reaction so far. He'd simply listened. 'Where are the Bridgers?' she asked.

'Fred helped with the search, but he's gone to join his wife now. Some of the women have been keeping her company. That's their cottage.' The constable gestured behind him. He wiped his brow again. The strain of the past three hours was beginning to show.

'Has her doctor been notified, Will? Brookham's in David Rowley's practice, I think.'

'He turned up half an hour ago and gave her a sedative. Then announced he'd be on the golf course, if needed.' Stackpole's lip twitched.

'He won't be there much longer,' Helen remarked as lightning streaked the advancing clouds, followed by another rolling boom of thunder. 'I'll go and see her myself.' But increasingly uneasy, she stayed where she was, her arm linked with her husband's, unwilling to leave him now.

'Is there anything I can do, Will?' Madden spoke for the first time. He, too, was aware of the glances being directed at him. He had already nodded to one or two of the men whom he knew by sight.

'Thank you, sir, but I've rung Guildford and they're sending reinforcements. It looks as though we'll have to widen the search area.'

'What about detectives?' Madden's scowl was unconscious. It signalled his concern.

'I've asked for them, and I'm told a couple of plain-clothes men are coming.' Stackpole grimaced in turn as he caught the other man's eye. 'Ah, there's nothing worse in this job, is there, sir? Nothing so bad as a child gone missing. All we can do is put out the word to other stations and keep looking.'

Distressed though she felt, Helen was relieved to hear that her husband wouldn't be needed. She pressed his arm. 'I'll go and see how Mrs Bridger's doing,' she said, but just then her attention was caught by something she saw on the other side of the road, and she paused. The front door of a cottage near the end of the row had opened and a sandy-haired man had come outside. He was looking about him in an agitated manner.

'Isn't that Dick Henshaw?' she asked. 'He and Molly used to live in Highfield. She was a patient of mine.'

Stackpole glanced round, and as he did so the man caught sight of him and hastened in their direction. 'That's Dick, all right.' The constable frowned. 'Now what's this about, I wonder?'

He moved away and the two met in the middle of the road. Taller by a head, Stackpole had to bend to listen to what the other man was saying. They stood like that for perhaps two minutes while Madden and his wife watched from beside their car.

Abruptly, the constable wheeled and came striding back to them.

'It seems I'm going to need your help after all, sir.' He spoke to Madden in a low, controlled voice, but there was no disguising the urgency of his manner.

'What is it, Will? What's happened?' Helen's fingers tightened on her husband's arm.

'I'll tell you in a moment, Miss Helen. But could you come with me now, both of you? Just move away quietly. I don't want that lot over the road getting wind of this.'

Accompanied by Henshaw, they walked up the lane to the end of the line of cottages and then, following the constable's lead, joined a path that went around the back of the houses. As soon as they were out of sight of the men, Stackpole halted.

'Run along and tell Molly we're coming, Dick. And mind you keep this quiet now.'

He waited for Henshaw to move out of earshot. But Helen couldn't contain her anxiety.

'What is it, Will?' she whispered. 'What's this about?'

The constable shook his head in frustration. 'I can't say for sure. All I know is there's an old friend of yours sitting in Molly Henshaw's kitchen and he's acting strange.' He eyed them meaningfully. 'It's Topper,' he said.

Helen's eyebrows rose at the name. She glanced at her husband. 'I didn't know he was back. We've been expecting him for weeks. I was starting to get worried.'

'Has he seen the girl?' Madden asked urgently.

'That's just it, sir. I don't know . . .' Stackpole's face was grim. 'There's some business about a shoe. Molly'll tell us more. But the thing is, he's gone silent. She can't get a word out of him. Now you know old Topper. One sniff of a police uniform and he'll close up tighter than a clam. So what I was wondering, sir, is would *you* try? See if you can get him to open up.'

As he waited for an answer, thunder boomed out again, louder than before, and the afternoon light dimmed still further.

'I'll try if you want me to, Will,' Madden said, after a pause. He sounded dubious. 'But you've got the wrong person.' Smiling, he glanced at his wife. 'Helen's the one to ask. If he'll talk to anyone he'll talk to her.'

2

'THANK GOODNESS you've come, Will.' Molly Henshaw's plump, motherly features were flushed with distress. Before Stackpole had even unlatched the gate she appeared at the back door of the cottage, with her husband behind her, and came hurrying across the bricked yard to meet them. 'I can't keep old Topper sitting still any longer. He's all for running off. Dr Madden . . . !' Her face lit up when she saw Helen and she bobbed her head in greeting.

'Molly, dear! How are you? What a dreadful business this is.' Helen took her hand. 'Have you met my husband?'

Molly Henshaw's reply was drowned in a clap of thunder. Stackpole glanced anxiously at the heavens.

'Quick now, love, before we go inside – tell us about this shoe. Did Topper give it to you?'

'*Give* it me?' She appeared not to understand the question.

'Of his own accord?' Madden spoke for the first time, and she stared at him as though she had not yet taken in his tall, commanding presence.

'Oh, I see what you mean – yes, sir, he did.' She nodded vigorously. 'He knocked on the door – it must have been half an hour ago – and I asked him in. We know Topper, Dick and I.' She nodded to her husband beside her. 'He's been coming to these parts for years, usually in the summer. If there's something needs doing in the garden he'll lend a hand, otherwise I'll just give him a meal and a cup of tea. He never says much. Sometimes you don't get a murmur out of him. But he likes to sit here with us. I reckon he knows he's welcome.'

'The shoe, Molly,' Stackpole urged her.

Mrs Henshaw bit her lip. She wiped her hands nervously on her apron. 'I could see he was bothered about something as soon as I opened the door, but I wasn't surprised, not with all the fuss going on. I brought him inside and right away he went and sat down in the corner. Then I noticed he was carrying something in his hands, both hands, and when he held them out to me I saw what it was . . .'

'A child's shoe?'

She gave the barest nod.

'Do you know that it belongs to Alice?'

'Oh, no, not for sure.' She swallowed. 'But Jenny Bridger brought her a new pair only the other day. Alice came and showed them to me. They were shiny black with pearl buttons on the straps, just like the one Topper brought.'

'But he wouldn't say where he'd found it?'

'No, nor anything else.' Molly Henshaw dabbed at a teary eye. 'So I gave him a cup of tea to keep him occupied and ran outside to look for Dick.'

'We'd just come back from the fields, Will, and I saw Molly waving to me.' Her husband took up the story. 'She told me what had happened and I went in to see

Topper myself, tried to get him to talk. But it were no good. He wouldn't say a word. So I came to fetch you.' Noticing the tears that were coming down his wife's cheeks now, Henshaw put his arm around her shoulders. 'There, there, old girl,' he said gruffly. 'Don't take on now.'

Stackpole caught Helen's eye, his glance bright with urgency.

'Molly, dear, could we go inside now?' She pressed the hand she was holding. 'I need to see Topper myself.'

THE ROOM LAY in shadow, the only illumination coming from a shaft of dull grey light entering through the back window. It fell on the kitchen table, where a child's shoe, black and shiny, showed starkly against the scrubbed wooden surface.

Surveying the scene from the doorway, Helen heard the murmur of Stackpole's voice. It came from the hallway at the front of the cottage. He was speaking on the telephone to the Surrey police headquarters in Guildford. Madden stood behind her in the narrow passage, out of sight of the shabby figure seated on a straight-backed chair in the far corner of the room. She felt his reassuring hand on her shoulder and reached up to press it with her own. Then she crossed the room to where Topper was sitting.

He showed no awareness of her approach. Well into middle age, or perhaps past it – his white-stubbled cheeks were deeply grooved – he sat slumped in the chair with his chin resting on his chest and his hands loosely linked on his knees, seemingly oblivious of his surroundings. Like others who'd encountered the old tramp in the past, Helen knew him only as Topper, a name that derived from his hat, a battered piece of evening headgear, cracked at the brim and missing half the crown, but given a jaunty, individual air by the addition of a cock pheasant's tail feather stuck in a red velvet band. The manner in which he wore the hat – square, and pulled down low – gave it the appearance of a permanent feature, and he was seldom seen without it. Dressed in a black cloth jacket over striped trousers, his feet were shod in heavy boots, worn down at the heels and tied with a combination of string and broken shoelaces.

'Hullo, Topper,' she said softly.

At the sound of her voice he lifted his head. She drew up a chair beside him.

'How have you been?'

He gave a slight shrug, but made no other response.

'Are you well?'

He nodded. A smile came to his lips, and he fixed her with a look of shy affection.

'We missed you at harvest time. Why haven't you come to see us?'

'Was coming . . .' The muttered words brought a faint gasp from the doorway behind Helen where Molly Henshaw had appeared and was watching them. 'Had to meet Beezy first . . .'

'*Beezy?*'

The tramp nodded again.

'Who's Beezy? Where were you meeting him?'

Topper's grey eyes lost focus. He looked away.

Helen regarded him in silence for a few moments. Then she took his left hand in hers. 'Let me see your arm.' She pushed up the sleeve of his jacket and then the threadbare flannel shirt beneath it, revealing a fresh scar fully six inches long running from the top of his wrist up the back of his sunburned arm towards the elbow. She ran her fingers lightly over it.

'Look, Molly,' she said over her shoulder. 'That's where Topper cut his arm last year. He was helping us with the haymaking and his scythe slipped. I had to sew him up.'

'You fixed it . . .' The old tramp chuckled. He brought his eyes back to hers. 'You mended old Topper.'

'It was a nasty cut, but it's healed well.'

Still holding his hand in hers, and continuing to stroke his arm, she spoke again. 'You were right to bring the shoe, Topper. But we need very badly to know where you found it. Can you help us?'

The fingers she was holding stiffened and she saw the fear in his eyes. His glance shifted and went past her shoulder. She looked round again. Madden had come quietly into the room with Molly Henshaw. Stackpole's uniformed figure hovered in the doorway behind them, and when Topper caught sight of it his eyes fell. He slumped lower in the chair.

'Now none of that,' the constable rumbled. 'You know me, Topper. There's no need to take on.'

Helen turned back. 'The shoe,' she said in a low voice. 'Where did you find it? You *must* tell me, Topper. Please . . .' She had kept hold of his hand, and after a moment she felt renewed pressure on her fingers. When she bent closer he whispered in her ear.

'What was that?' She struggled to hear his husky murmur. 'Did you say Capel Wood?'

Behind her, Stackpole stiffened in the doorway. 'We've already looked there,' he muttered to Madden. 'Is he sure?' he asked Helen.

'*Capel Wood?*' She repeated the name clearly and looked into the tramp's eyes for confirmation. He nodded. 'Would you take us there?' she asked. 'Would you show us where you found it?'

A tremor went through his body and his grip on her fingers tightened. He shook his head violently.

Helen studied his face for a few moments. Then she leaned close again. 'Whereabouts in the wood, Topper?'

Silent at first, he simply stared at her. But then, as though drawn by her steady gaze, he bent forward and whispered to her once more.

Helen glanced behind her. 'By the stream, he says . . .' She rose and came over to him. 'Will, this is going to take a long time, and I'm not even sure how much more I can get out of him.'

A scowl crossed Stackpole's features. 'Sir?' He addressed Madden. 'Could we have a word?' The two men went out into the passage. The constable gestured. 'What do you think, sir? Should I try and squeeze him harder?'

Madden shook his head. 'Helen knows him better than anyone. You'd be wasting your time.'

'By the stream . . .' Stackpole grimaced. 'It's not much to go on. And we've already been there. There's a path that runs alongside it. It goes through the wood. I took some men and we walked the length of it, calling her name. Once you get off it you can't see three feet in front of you.' He shook his head in despair. As he glanced at his wristwatch, a flash of lightning lit the dim passageway for an instant, and the answering peal of thunder set the windowpanes in the kitchen rattling. 'Well, those detectives from Guildford will be here soon. Better wait for them, I suppose . . .'

His glance seemed to suggest another course of action, however, and Madden responded to it. Despite the formality of address which the constable insisted on maintaining towards him, they were friends of long standing.

'No, we can't do that, Will. We must get out there right away. I think Topper found more than a shoe.'

3

THE FIRST FAT DROPS of rain splattered the windscreen of Madden's car as he turned off the paved road onto a rough track that ran through hedgerows and over-hanging trees around the dark flank of Capel Wood. The dull grey afternoon light had changed to a deep leaden gloom. Black, swollen clouds were racing in from the west.

'Won't be long now,' Stackpole predicted, squinting up through the glass. He glanced behind him at the roll of canvas lying on the back seat as though to reassure himself of its presence there. It was Madden who'd suggested they bring it with them.

'I don't know what we'll find, Will, but you may need to cover the area.'

The piece of tarpaulin had been provided by Dick Henshaw. He'd used it to patch a hole in the roof of his cottage the previous year when a number of shingles had blown off in an autumn gale. While he was fetching it from the garden shed Helen had come out of the kitchen to talk to Madden.

'I *must* go and see how Jenny Bridger is. I won't say anything to her about Capel Wood.' She eyed her hus-band unhappily, upset to see him becoming involved. Madden's life as a policeman lay in the distant past, and it was one she did not wish to recall. To the constable she added, 'You'd better keep an eye on Topper, Will. He'll slip off if he gets the chance.'

Stackpole had charged both Henshaws with this duty and cautioned them to say nothing to the neighbours until the reinforcements from Guildford arrived.

'I don't want word of this spreading. Not till we've gone over there and seen what there is to see.'

'Please God you find her,' Molly Henshaw had murmured as they departed.

The hope – it was more of a prayer – that the child might be no worse than lying injured and in need of succour had lent speed to their preparations, but glancing at Madden's expression as he steered the car down the narrow, rutted lane, Will Stackpole felt they shared the same grim premonition as to the girl's fate.

'We'll be taking the same route Topper took, will we?' Madden's low voice was barely audible over the sound of the car's motor as they ground along in bottom gear.

'Yes, sir. If he was heading for Brookham he'd have come into the wood from the other side and walked through it on the path, the one that runs by the stream. It leads straight to Brookham.'

They'd debated taking this same path themselves, following Topper's route in reverse and walking up to the wood from the hamlet. But the likelihood of being caught in the open by the advancing storm had persuaded them to use the car instead and they had driven along the road to Craydon for half a mile before turning off it close to the point where Alice Bridger had last been seen.

As the track they were on now continued to circle

the wood, the hedgerows on either side dropped away and they saw to their right a wide, open field where a herd of Friesians stood close together, their sturdy black and white bodies barely visible in the dying light. Although the rain continued to fall in isolated drops the storm was fast approaching and a number of cows were already lying down in anticipation of the deluge that was about to break on them.

Their way ran close to the wood now, the spreading branches of oak and chestnut brushing against the side of the car, the road making a slow bend to the left which they followed until they came to a circular patch of dried mud where the track petered out and where two hay-stacks shaped like beehives stood close together beside a wooden fence bordering a field beyond.

As Madden brought the car to a halt he glanced at the dashboard and saw they had covered just over two miles since leaving Brookham. He got out and briefly inspected the ground around them. The bare strip of earth showed only the deeply engraved ruts made by cartwheels at some earlier date.

'Are you thinking someone might have brought her here?' Stackpole asked. 'Come the same way we did?' He'd climbed out of the car himself and was putting his helmet back on.

Partly shielded by the haystacks, the spot where they'd ended up looked out over empty fields with a distant vista of tree-clad hillocks.

'It'd be a quiet spot,' the constable observed. 'Nobody working in the fields on a Sunday. No reason for anyone to come here.'

'It's possible.' Madden shrugged. 'But we'd only be guessing. Let's get moving, Will. There's no time to lose.'

The constable donned his cape, then retrieved the roll of tarpaulin from the back seat of the car, tucking it under his arm. He pointed ahead of them to a line of willows and low bushes that wound across the field towards the tree line.

'There's our stream, sir. It runs clear through the wood and comes out on the other side not far from Brookham.'

The two men set off, with the constable leading the way, forging a trail through knee-high grass around the outskirts of the wood until they came to the stream. A pathway was visible running alongside it on the further bank and they crossed to it by means of a fallen log. Thunder crashed all around them and they hurried to seek the shelter of the forest. When they got there, Stackpole stepped aside off the path.

'You lead the way, sir. Your eyes are better than mine.'

Madden went ahead and soon found himself in a zone of twilight cast by the dense canopy of foliage, which deepened as they moved further into the trees. Rain pattered on the leaves overhead, but did not reach the ground, which remained dry. A layer of damp leaf mould underfoot muffled the sound of their steps.

The path continued to run parallel to the stream, which was visible most of the time, disappearing only briefly behind tree trunks or overhanging branches. Madden kept his eyes on it, knowing that Topper must have come this way himself since he was heading for Brookham and that whatever he had found would not be far from the water.

'How big is the wood, Will?' He spoke over his shoulder. 'How long will it take us to walk through it?'

'Twenty minutes, at least. It's a fair size.'

Half that time had elapsed, and so far they had seen nothing of note, apart from a set of stepping stones in the stream which they had passed and which Madden had inquired about. Stackpole told him they connected with a secondary path that ran down to the road between Brookham and Craydon.

'So Alice Bridger could have walked into the wood?'

Stackpole nodded. 'Or been brought. I came that way myself with the men when we searched up here earlier.'

Not far beyond this point the path changed direction, crossing the stream by a second set of stepping stones and then apparently taking a course away from the brook into the depths of the forest. Madden halted.

'Topper said *by* the stream . . .'

The constable came up to his shoulder. He saw what Madden meant. 'They only separate for a short distance, sir. The path and the stream. They join up again a little further on.'

Madden shook his head, unconvinced.

'No, I want to stay by the water.' He peered downstream, but his view was impeded by thick undergrowth and overhanging trees. The rain was steadily increasing in volume and the thunder boomed louder overhead. Madden stood for some moments, hands on hips, looking about him. Then something caught his eye and he switched his attention to the brush lining the path, studying the ferns and low, stunted bushes that filled the spaces between the tree trunks.

'Look—!' He went down on his haunches. The constable peered over his shoulder. 'Someone left the path here, or rejoined it.' Madden indicated a fern that had been broken at the base and, near it, a slender oak sapling bent askew. 'If Topper was following the stream rather than the path he might have come this way.'

'But why would he do that?' Stackpole was puzzled. 'It's hard work pushing your way through that.' He gestured at the dense underbrush.

'I've no idea.' Madden bent lower to scan the ground, hoping to find some trace of a footprint, but the damp mould was too loose to hold an impression. He stood up. 'Will, I'm going to carry on down the stream on this side. You stay on the path. If what you say is right, we should meet up further on.'

Had the circumstances been different, his words might have brought a grin to Will Stackpole's face. Without realizing it, Madden had reverted to his old role, taking charge. He was behaving like the police inspector he'd once been.

'I'll do that, sir. Call out if you see anything.'

The constable waited until his companion had moved into the underbrush and then continued along the path, crossing the stream on the stepping stones and following the course of the footway, which left the brook initially, but then bent back so that it was running parallel to it again, only further from the bank than before. He found that, although he could still hear the rushing water, his view of it was blocked by the intervening trees and a screen of tangled bushes.

'Will?'

'I'm here, sir.' Stackpole halted. Madden's voice had reached him clearly from the other side of the stream. He wasn't far off.

'Someone's come this way, all right . . . there's a trail of sorts . . .'

Stackpole shifted the roll of tarpaulin from one arm to the other. He waited for a moment, then walked on, but after only a few paces he heard the other man call out again.

'What kind of clothes was she wearing, Will? What colour were they?'

The constable thought. 'She had a blue skirt on, sir. Blue skirt, white blouse, black shoes.' Dry-mouthed now, he waited anxiously.

'I can see a bit of thread caught on a bramble. It might be blue . . . it's difficult to see in this light . . .' Madden's voice trailed off. But he called out again, suddenly, 'No, wait! There's something else!'

Stackpole stood riveted to the spot, awaiting Madden's next words. Ears pricked, he stared at the dense wall of greenery blocking his view of the stream and presently fell into a half-trance which was abruptly shattered when a bolt of lightning ripped through the low clouds overhead, followed almost instantaneously by a tremendous clap of thunder.

The air about him seemed to shiver and he caught a whiff of ozone. Curiously, the patter of rain drops on the leaves above had diminished in the last few seconds, but the sky continued to darken. It was as if the elements were gathering themselves to unleash an assault, and the constable felt a comparable coiling of forces within him, a rising tide of agonized tension that cried out for release.

'Will?'

'Sir!'

'You'd better get over here!'

The sharpened note in Madden's voice caused the hairs on the back of the constable's neck to rise, and he caught his breath.

'You won't get through those holly bushes, Will. Better to go back to where I left you and come the way I did.'

'What is it, sir?' Fearful of the answer, Stackpole's voice was choked. 'Have you found her, then . . .?'

The few seconds it took Madden to reply seemed to stretch into an eternity. Then at last he spoke.

'Yes, I've found her, Will.'

He said no more. But his voice told all.

IT WAS ONLY BY chance that Madden had spotted the body.

Earlier, picking his way through the brush and clinging brambles, his attention had been focussed on the abundant signs that one or more people had come by this route: snapped twigs and ferns bent back and flattened marked the rough passage that had been forced through the undergrowth.

The disturbance seemed recent – some of the broken twigs were green, with the sap still wet in them – and had probably occurred within the past few hours. Closer study might have told him more, but there was no time to linger and he had carried on downstream until his attention was caught by the piece of thread, which was snagged on a bramble at waist height. This he had paused to examine, but such was the gloom brought on by the approaching storm he'd been unable to determine its colour with any certainty and had decided to leave it where it was.

All this time he had kept the stream in view, though his glimpses of it were intermittent and hampered by the thick brush that clung to the banks. But a few steps further on a sudden break in the bushes gave him a clearer sight of the water. He found he was standing at the edge of a small rectangle of leaf-strewn turf bordering the stream, whose opposite bank was hidden by the overhanging branches of a willow tree behind which an unbroken wall of holly bushes, a little higher up the bank, formed an impenetrable barrier.

Sheltered from rain and sun by the spreading branch of an oak tree, it struck Madden as being a tranquil spot and he was surveying an irregular ring of stones, much overgrown by grass, which lay at one end of the rectangle, wondering whether they'd been placed there by human hand, when his eye was caught by another object on the ground, closer to where he was standing.

'No, wait!' he had called out to the constable. 'There's something else!'

What he was looking at was nothing more than an oak leaf, and it had taken him several moments before he realized why his gaze had suddenly become fixed on it.

The colour, dark brown in the dreary light, was starting to run.

He'd bent down on his haunches at once and picked it up delicately by its stem. The patina coating the leaf's surface had been smeared by falling raindrops; the dry crust was reverting to its liquid form. There was no doubt in Madden's mind as to what it was.

Looking around then, he saw other bloodstains; other leaves bearing the telltale marks. The green grass, too, was spattered with tiny rust-coloured flecks.

Backing into the bushes a little, Madden went down on his hands and knees and brought his face even lower so that he could examine the ground minutely, and it was while he was in that position, like some hound questing on a scent, that he saw, protruding from beneath the drooping willow branches across the stream, at the same level as his eyes were now, a sock-clad foot.

Next moment lightning split the sky above him and the thunder came crashing on its heels. Before the last echoes had died away, Madden had scrambled to his feet, torn off his socks and shoes and waded through the cold, ankle-deep current to the opposite bank. Parting the trailing willow fronds he found the body of a young girl lying on its side on a narrow ledge. Without hope he bent down and felt for a pulse in the thin white wrist that rested on her hip. There was none. She was dead. He had called out then to Stackpole.

During their shouted exchange, Madden's eyes remained busy. The position of the body, wedged beneath an overhang in the bank and screened by the drooping branches, indicated that the killer had meant to conceal it. And it might have remained hidden longer, he thought, had a piece of the ledge on which it lay not crumbled away and fallen into the stream below, causing the girl's foot to slide down into view.

Was that how Topper had found her? Had he taken the shoe off her foot? It seemed unlikely.

The cause of death would be determined later by medical examination, but judging by her blood-soaked hair, which covered her face as she lay, she appeared to have been struck about the head, and the evidence pointed to the assault having taken place on the blood-stained grass behind him . . .

Coolly, Madden continued to compile his mental notes, aware that he was acting from habit, doing something he hadn't done for many years, but had once been trained to do, keeping his emotions separate from the process of observation. But his poise deserted him a moment later when he drew aside the matted hair to look at the girl's face.

'Dear God!' A gasp of horror escaped his lips.

No stranger to violent death, he'd seen more than one murder victim cruelly battered and during two years spent in the trenches had been witness to unspeakable injuries: he'd seen bodies rent and flayed and blown to pieces. But nothing in his experience had prepared him for the sight of Alice Bridger's face, beaten flat to a red pulp on which no trace of a human feature remained. As he stared at it in disbelief he heard Stackpole's voice calling to him from close by.

'Am I getting near, sir?'

'Keep following the stream, Will.' Somehow Madden

found his voice. 'You'll come to me. And hurry. It's going to pour in a minute.'

As he spoke, thunder boomed out again like a great bass drum and the rain grew heavier. Madden glanced uneasily at the stream in which he stood. The ledge where the child's body lay had been carved out of the bank by the water on some earlier occasion and there was no telling how fast it might rise again in the cloudburst that now threatened. Quickly he bent again to study the corpse, noting its position, attentive to details.

The pale blue skirt bunched about the girl's hips was smeared with blood, as were her white thighs. Livid marks that were turning into bruises showed on her small bare buttocks. The water where he stood was littered with loose stones and rocks and Madden supposed that one of them might have been used as a weapon. If so, it would be washed clean by now.

Studying the position of the body, he realized that he was able to observe the full effect of the damage done to the girl's face because her head was twisted around at what he saw now was an unnatural angle. It seemed likely that her neck was broken.

Was this how she had died? He hoped so. The thought that she might have been alive and conscious when the stone was raised above her head was close to unbearable.

'Ah, Christ . . . no!'

Madden looked behind him. Will Stackpole's tall figure had appeared through the bushes on the far bank. Water dripped from the constable's heavy blue cape. His glance dwelt on the pathetic huddled shape revealed behind the drawn willow branches.

'What did he do to the lass?' He pointed. 'Is that her face?'

'Yes, it's been smashed in. God knows why.' Madden let the branches fall, hiding the corpse from sight. Pale beneath his helmet, Stackpole stood rooted. He seemed unable to take in what he'd seen. 'There's blood on the grass over there, Will.' Madden gestured. 'You'd better keep off it. That's probably where she was killed. And raped, by the look of it.' The words he chose, as much as the harsh tone in which they were spoken, served to jerk the constable back to a state of awareness. He listened to what Madden was saying.

'We can either protect that patch, or try to cover the body. But we can't do both.'

Nodding that he understood, Stackpole looked up at the sky. Although the rain was increasing steadily, the full force of the storm was yet to break on them. He took the tarpaulin from under his arm. Unable to make up his mind, he looked from where the body lay to the grass at his feet and back again. A sudden gust of rain blew a shower of raindrops into his face.

'What do *you* think, sir?' His glance was pleading.

Madden scowled in reply. 'Well, the stream's bound to rise, so we may have to move the body.' He paused, turning the problem over in his mind. 'Let's cover that piece of grass,' he decided.

While Stackpole busied himself unrolling the canvas, Madden recrossed the stream, pausing to collect an armful of stones from the river bed which the two men then laid at the corners of the spread tarpaulin on which the rain now drummed steadily.

'The Guildford police won't find their way here. I'll have to go and fetch them.' Madden had to shout to make himself heard above successive peals of thunder, meanwhile struggling to put on his socks and shoes again, balancing first on one foot, then on the other. After standing for so long in the icy water he'd lost all feeling in his toes. 'Keep an eye on that stream, Will. You won't get much warning once the water starts rising.'

He waited a moment longer to look around him, torn between the need for haste in summoning the detectives and the equally urgent task he had set himself of searching for any clues left behind by the killer, evidence that might be destroyed or washed away in the storm, which now broke in earnest upon them. As Madden stood there, shivering in his drenched tweed jacket, a curtain of rain descended and in a second he was immersed in a mist of spray and falling drops as water poured through the flimsy canopy of leaves above him.

Caught there in the downpour his eye fell again on the ring of stones he'd noticed earlier. In the last few minutes an answer had occurred to him to a question he'd been asking himself since entering the wood and he looked around now for other indications that might confirm it. His inspection of the rain-blurred scene had hardly begun, however, when he was interrupted by a yell from Stackpole. Madden glanced up in time to see the constable plunge into the stream in his boots. Just as he'd forecast earlier, the level of the water had risen with alarming speed and Stackpole was already knee-deep in the frothing torrent, struggling to keep his footing while he tore off his cape.

'Hand her to me, Will!'

Madden was at the bank in a moment, and stood poised and ready as the constable tugged aside the screen of willows and lifted the body of Alice Bridger from the lapping water, wrapping her slight form in his cape and turning unsteadily to hand the bundle to Madden.

Even encased in the heavy waterproof material the child's body was a negligible burden. Backing carefully so as to avoid stepping on the tarpaulin, Madden laid her on the ground beside the piece of canvas. The cape fell open as he did so and he was stricken once more by the sight of the girl's ruined features. Hastily he covered her again.

Stackpole, meantime, had clambered out of the stream and stood shaking himself like a dog as the water cascaded off his helmet. He walked daintily around the piece of turf, trying not to leave footmarks in the soggy grass, and joined Madden at the edge of the bushes. The two men looked at the rushing water, which had now flooded the ledge where the body had lain and was already dangerously close to overflowing onto the bank where they stood beside the spread tarpaulin.

'Looks like we may lose the lot, sir.' Stackpole squeezed water from the cuffs of his trousers, which clung to his sodden boots.

'No, I don't think so, Will. It's passing. See!' Madden pointed up at the sky, which was clearing fast. The rain, too, was diminishing noticeably, and without warning it stopped. Sunshine broke through the thinning clouds, bathing the woods and the swift-moving stream in soft evening light. The silence around them was filled with the sound of dripping water. The constable fished a handkerchief out of his pocket and mopped his face.

'You were going to look for those detectives, sir?'

'Yes. In a moment.' While they'd been standing there Madden's mind had returned to the problem he'd been wrestling with earlier. Casting about, his eye had lit on a birch tree which stood outside the ring of bushes, its pale trunk partly screened by the undergrowth. He gestured towards it. 'I just want to go and have a look at that.'

Mystified, the constable followed his lead and they worked their way round the ring of grass until they reached the birch, where Madden crouched down, parting the branches of a laurel that was growing wild beside the bank.

'Yes! There . . . Look, Will!'

Peering over his shoulder, Stackpole saw that the trunk had been scored by grooves etched into it, strange runic designs carved with a knife or some other sharp instrument.

'Those were made by tramps. This is one of their camp sites. *That's* why Topper left the path. He was coming here . . .' Madden shifted on his haunches. He gestured with his thumb behind him. 'That ring of stones on the ground over there – that's where they light their fires. You can't see it now because the grass has grown over. But look at these marks . . . that one's Topper's.'

Squinting, the constable made out the shape of a cross carved into the trunk surrounded by a crude circle.

'It's a calling card. A sign he was here. Just like those others.'

Stackpole ran his fingers over the faint, spidery furrows. 'But they're old, sir, not one of them done this summer, I'd say . . .'

'Except for this one . . .!' Madden indicated a design cut into the trunk somewhat lower down than the rest. It showed a triangle with a line drawn through it.

'That's fresh, all right,' Stackpole acknowledged. He peered at it more closely. 'The bark's only just been stripped. The wood's still white. Why, it could have been done today . . .'

'It probably was.' Madden rose from his crouch. 'Topper told Helen he was due to meet someone hereabouts, a man called Beezy, another tramp, by the sound of it. That could be *his* mark.'

'You mean, he may have been here earlier, this Beezy?' Stackpole looked from the scarred trunk to where the girl's body was lying, wrapped in his cape. His face changed as the significance of what he was saying became clear to him.

Madden nodded. 'He was here, all right, by the look of it. But the question is, where is he now?'

4

CALLED OUT before dawn the next morning by the midwife on a maternity case, Helen did not get back to the house until after nine. Twenty minutes earlier Will Stackpole had rung with news he'd obtained by telephone from the police in Guildford which Madden recounted to his wife while they ate a late breakfast in the sun-filled dining room.

'They haven't had the pathologist's report yet, but there seems no doubt she was raped and strangled. The police surgeon confirmed what I thought: her neck was broken. That's how she died.'

The signs of a sleepless night Helen saw in her husband's face took her back more than a decade. It had been another murder case, the brutal massacre of an entire household in Highfield itself, in the summer of 1921, that had brought them together, and Madden's frown of worry was a grim reminder of those dreadful days.

'What the pathologist will make of the damage to her face I don't know. It looked deliberate to me.'

'*Deliberate?*'

'Systematic. I only glanced at it, but it seemed to me he'd set out to destroy her features. To obliterate them.' Madden set down his cup. 'Her father was shown the body this morning. He broke down, poor man.'

They'd been late getting back from Brookham the previous night. Darkness had fallen before Madden returned from Capel Wood and Helen had wanted to take him home and get him out of his wet clothes. She'd spent the intervening hours herself in the Henshaws' kitchen, keeping Topper company, but had twice visited the Bridgers' cottage, where the missing girl's mother had fallen into a restless sleep from the sedative she'd been given earlier. Mr Bridger had refused Helen's offer of similiar relief. She'd discovered him sitting in the darkened parlour with neighbours, a short, stocky man with thinning hair, his pale features racked by unspoken fears. Alice was an only child, she'd learned.

'I heard there were some policemen come from Guildford and now they've gone off somewhere?' Bridger had accosted her eagerly when she'd looked in. 'Do you know anything about that, Dr Madden?' His eyes had pleaded with her for an honest answer, but Helen could only prevaricate.

'Not really, Mr Bridger, but I'm expecting my husband back soon. He's with Constable Stackpole. They may have some news for you.'

In the event, Madden had returned in his car alone, leaving Stackpole with the two detectives, whom he'd encountered on the outskirts of the wood and guided to the murder site. At their urgent request, he had telephoned the Surrey police headquarters to arrange for a pathologist and a forensic team to be dispatched to Brookham without delay with an ambulance and more uniformed officers equipped with lamps and torches so that a search of the wood could begin at once.

'What about the Bridgers?' he had asked Helen then. They were standing close together in the small hallway of the Henshaws' cottage, where the telephone was. 'What have they been told?'

'Nothing, so far as I know.' Shocked by the news her husband had brought from Capel Wood, Helen had wanted only to get him home. Sensing his intention then, she had put a staying hand on his arm. 'Leave it to the police, my darling. It's not your business any longer.'

But Madden had refused to be shaken from his course. 'They *have* to be told,' he'd insisted. 'They can't be left in ignorance. It's not right. Who knows what time the police will get back?'

So she had taken him to the Bridgers' cottage, leaving him in the kitchen there to wait while she went in search of the murdered girl's father, wishing there was some way she could ease the burden he had taken on himself. A few minutes later, standing alone in the back yard, Helen had watched through the lighted window as her husband spoke words she could not hear and had seen the other man clap his hands to his ears as though in agony and lay his head like an offering on the table before him.

Catching Madden's eye now, she smiled, hoping to dispel his dark mood. 'What's happened to Topper?' she asked. 'Are the police still holding him?'

'He spent the night in the cells at Guildford. Only by invitation, mind you – they'd no right to detain him – but it seems to have loosened his tongue. He told them all he knew and they let him go this morning. He's been ordered to appear at the inquest on Friday.'

'Will he do that?' Helen looked sceptical.

'I doubt it. To quote Will, he'll more likely be in the next county by then. Unless he drops in to see you, of course.'

'I'll be hurt if he doesn't.'

Her words brought a smile to Madden's lips, just as she'd hoped they might, and they laughed together.

The old tramp had first come into their lives several years before, knocking on the back door one summer afternoon, another in the legion of homeless: tramps, vagrants, men of no fixed abode in the language of the law courts, whose numbers had swelled vastly with the years of the Depression. The Maddens' cook, Mrs Beck, had standing orders to offer food and drink to these wanderers whenever they presented themselves. Whether or not she admitted them to her kitchen was up to her, but Helen had returned that afternoon from her rounds to find Topper seated at the table, with his hat beside him and his bundle on the floor at his feet, busily plying knife and fork under Cook's approving eye. He had risen to his feet when she entered and made her a courtly bow.

'A proper gentleman, this one, ma'am.' Mrs Beck had purred her approval.

Ordering her own tea to be served in the kitchen, Helen had sat with the old man, eliciting little more from him than his name and some account of his recent journeyings, but finding herself drawn to the dusty, travel-stained figure with his absurd attire. Although he told her nothing of himself – either then, or later – she'd been moved by the sound of his soft voice and by his gentle manner. His grey eyes, seeking hers across the table in fleeting, timid glances, had spoken of pain and loss; of some past to which he could never return.

His meal done, she had given him directions to their farm, with a note to her husband. Topper had stayed for a week, helping with the harvest and sleeping at night in a corner of the barn. On the morning of his departure Mrs Beck had found an old jam jar on the back steps outside the kitchen filled with pink campion and the yellow buds of St John's Wort, picked from the hedgerows. Tucked beneath it was a scrap of paper bearing a roughly pencilled message: *For the lady*.

She had presented them to Helen at the breakfast table with a smile. 'Looks like you've made a conquest, ma'am.'

'What did Topper tell them?' Helen asked Madden now.

'He said he came into the wood from the same side we did – from the fields – and left the path to get to that camp site I told you about. Most of these old tramps have hidden spots tucked away, places where they can lie up for a while. They like to keep them secret, especially if they're on private land. Capel Wood belongs to the farmer Bridger works for. Topper told the police he'd been using the site for years. When he got there yesterday he spotted the shoe lying on the bank across the stream. Then he saw the girl's foot.'

'It's a wonder he didn't run off at once.'

'He easily might have,' Madden agreed. 'He must have felt terrified. But instead he collected it and brought it to Brookham. It was a brave thing to do.' He smiled at his wife again.

'How have the police reacted? Do they believe him?'

'Oh, I think so. But they wanted to know more about this man Beezy. According to Topper they met at a dosshouse in London last winter. Beezy's usual summer base is Kent – he finds hop-picking work there. But this year for some reason he decided to join up with Topper and come down to Surrey instead. They were moving in our direction: Topper told the police you were expecting him. "Mustn't let Dr Madden down," he said.'

'Quite right, too.' Helen nodded approvingly.

'However, Beezy fell ill while they were doing some odd jobs on a farm near Dorking. He caught bronchitis and was laid up for a week in the barn there. The farmer's wife took care of him. Topper moved on – he'd heard of some work going in Coldharbour – but they agreed to meet up again this weekend. Topper gave him directions to Capel Wood and told him how to find the camp site.'

'But he never got there, did he? Beezy, I mean?'

'Ah, but he did.' Frowning, Madden put down his coffee cup. 'I saw his sign at the camp site.'

'His *sign*?'

'A lot of these tramps have their individual marks. They carve them on trees at meeting spots.'

'Oh, I know about those.' She nodded. 'Topper's is a circled cross. Go on.'

'I noticed several cut into the trunk of a birch tree by the camp site, but only one of them was fresh: a triangle with a line drawn through it. According to Topper, that's Beezy's mark.'

Helen absorbed this information in silence while she refilled their cups. 'So if Beezy was there *before* Topper found the girl's shoe, that must mean he's a suspect,' she said.

'He's bound to be, I'm afraid.' Madden scowled at the tablecloth in front of him. He lifted a hand to his forehead where a faint, jagged scar, the souvenir of a shell blast from the war, showed white against his sun-burned skin. Unaware that he was signalling his concern to his wife, he touched it with his fingertips. 'Topper's in the clear himself, you'll be glad to hear,' he went on. 'He got a lift in a lorry from Coldharbour to Shamley Green yesterday afternoon – the police have already spoken to the driver – and couldn't have reached Capel Wood before three o'clock at the earliest, which was hours after Alice Bridger disappeared.'

'The very idea!' Her tone of scornful dismissal brought the smile back to Madden's lips. Nevertheless she saw there was still some unspoken worry on his mind and would have questioned him further if his glance hadn't shifted just then to the open window behind her.

'Look – there's Rob.' Madden gestured with his coffee cup. 'Has he been up in the woods?'

'He left the house when I did.' Turning in her chair, Helen followed the direction of her husband's gaze across the sunlit terrace, down the long lawn to the orchard at the foot of the garden, where their ten-year-old son, clad in shorts, was just then emerging from the trees, swinging a policeman's lamp in his hand. 'He told me Ted Stackpole was going to show him a badger's sett he'd discovered. The boys thought if they got there before dawn they might see the cubs.'

Madden grunted. He watched as the small figure made its plodding way up the lawn. 'They'll have to stop doing that for the time being.' He spoke regretfully. 'We can't have them wandering off into the woods alone. Not for the moment.' He caught Helen's eye. 'I'll tell Rob about the murder when he comes in. And Lucy, too. There's bound to be talk in the village. Better they hear it first from me.'

5

ALTHOUGH BROOKHAM was only five miles distant, the drive along narrow country lanes busy with farm traffic was a slow one and it took Madden the best part of twenty-five minutes to reach his destination. An unmarked police car parked on the grassed verge by the line of cottages signalled the presence of detectives in the hamlet. They would likely be there for some time. Unless established procedures had changed much since his day, Madden knew that with a crime of this nature all the inhabitants would have to be questioned. The police would want to know their movements and to discover whether any strangers had been seen in the vicinity.

His own return to Brookham was unplanned; a surprise, even to himself. Although he had talked only briefly with the CID men sent from Guildford the day before, he had promised them a statement, and already that morning, before breakfast, had written out a full account of all he had seen and done from the moment he and Will Stackpole had set foot in Capel Wood. That completed, there was no reason for him to go back. The statement could have been forwarded to Surrey police headquarters.

But enough of the old policeman still dwelt in John Madden to ensure that he wouldn't rest satisfied. A nagging sense of duty, the feeling of a job half done, had dogged him since leaving Brookham and he'd spent sleepless hours reviewing the facts surrounding the girl's disappearance and recalling to memory every detail of the murder scene.

Morning had brought no relief and he'd risen saddled with a feeling of guilt which initially he'd put down to his failure to make proper sense of the evidence that had been presented to him at first hand. Some instinct, honed in past years, no doubt, but still lively, told him there was more to be learned from the murder site than he had so far managed to deduce. But troubling though this realization was, it did not measure up fully to the sense of unease he felt, which seemed to spring from deeper roots and was linked to the hideous image he bore of Alice Bridger's ruined face.

Still, he'd had no plan to involve himself further in what was now a police matter, nor to alter his routine, and had meant to spend the morning at the farm, as he usually did. It was only after Helen had left the house to go to her surgery and he was setting out himself that a sudden impulse had prompted him to change direction and take the road that led across the long wooded ridge called Upton Hanger, beneath which Highfield nestled, and make his way by twisting, hedgerowed lanes to Brookham once again.

WATCHED BY MADDEN, Galloway fished up a sizeable stone from the stream bed and examined it closely, peering over the top of his horn-rimmed spectacles.

Portly, and now red-faced from his exertions, he stood shin-deep in the fast-moving current, wearing fisherman's waders.

'I thought myself he might have used a stone,' Madden remarked from the bank above. 'But then I wondered . . .'

'Wondered what, John?' Peter Galloway glanced up quizzically. He was the senior pathologist attached to the hospital in Guildford. Madden knew him socially through Helen.

'He did such a thorough job on her face I thought he might have used a tool of some kind. A hammer, perhaps?' It was the first time Madden had put into words the thought that had tormented him during the long night: the barely believable notion that the killer might actually have brought with him the means for demolishing a human face.

'As it happens, I think you may be right.' Breathing heavily, Galloway tossed aside the stone he was carrying and then bent down, searching the stream for another. His rumpled tweed suit looked as though it had been slept in. 'I was up half the night trying to decide that very point, based on the available evidence, the pulped flesh, I mean. I could come to no conclusion. So, having first photographed it, I left an assistant with instructions to remove said flesh while I came out here. When I return I mean to examine the bone structure, or what's left of it, to see if I can reach a more precise verdict. Such are the joys of a pathologist's life. Would you mind?' Wearied of his search, he reached out a hand and, with Madden's help, hauled his heavy bulk up on to the bank, where he stood, swaying awkwardly in his hip-high boots, blowing hard. 'I might add, it's the worst case of its kind I've ever come across,' he continued, having caught his breath. 'There was nothing left of her features. Thank God, *those* injuries were post-mortem.'

'I was told she was strangled. That's so, is it?' Madden needed to be reassured, and the other man nodded.

'The cause of death was asphyxiation. Mind you, he broke her neck as well. At the same time, perhaps. Hard to be sure. Rigor was quite well advanced when the body reached me. I would estimate she died between twelve and two, but not later.' Galloway controlled a yawn. 'Since I was coming out here anyway, I thought I'd inspect a few rocks at the site. There appears to be a shape to some of the blows. But my instinct tells me that's a blind alley. A hammer's more likely.'

Madden looked about him. He had come back to Capel Wood to find Topper's secluded camp site a scene of antlike activity with no fewer than four plain-clothes men scouring the small rectangle of sodden grass which he and Stackpole had attempted to cover the evening before and examining the far bank where the body had been concealed. Their labours, directed by Galloway, were overseen by a fifth detective, the senior CID man in charge of the case, who had hailed his arrival.

'Mr Madden, sir! I was hoping you'd come by. Wright's the name. Detective Inspector.'

The two shook hands. They hadn't met before, but Madden's name and face were well known to members of the Surrey force; the other men, too, had paused in their work to greet him, doffing their hats in respectful recognition. They included the two young detectives he'd encountered the previous evening and guided to the murder site.

'There are some details I need to go over with you, sir.' Wright had a confident, bustling air. He was in his early forties, a thin, wiry man with a receding hairline. 'How the body was lying when you found it, for example. Before you and the constable had to shift it. Stuff I'll need for my report and for the inquest. I expect you know what I mean.'

By way of reply Madden had handed him the written statement, which he'd brought with him. 'It's all in there, Inspector. I put down everything I saw before the storm hit us. It'll save time if you read it first. Then, if you have any more questions, I'm at your disposal.'

'Thank you, sir. I'll do that now, if I may.'

Leaving him to read the statement, Madden turned his attention to the scene around him. He had left his car parked by the haystacks, where two police vehicles stood nose to tail, and made his way through the wood, quitting the path at the same place as he had the day before and following the now much-trampled trail through the undergrowth to the murder scene. He still felt there was more to be learned from this spot, though its appearance had changed strikingly in the space of only a few hours. Vanished were the foaming torrent and dark, rain-streaked sky of yesterday. Now the gurgle of the stream hardly reached his ears, drowned out by the joyous clamour of birdsong echoing from the woods all around. The bushes, too, were still, unmoved by the faint breeze that was stirring the tops of the trees.

His gaze came to rest on a leather case that lay open on the ground near his feet. It was half filled with labelled glass jars, the fruits of the detectives' efforts that morning, he supposed. Galloway, catching the direction of his glance, gestured.

'You did a good job with that piece of canvas, John. You and the bobby. Thanks to you both, we can say for certain the assault was carried out here, on this very spot. I've plenty of blood samples from the grass. They'll have to be tested, of course, but I've no doubt they're from the girl's body. Pieces of bone, too. And I've had them collecting pocketfuls of soil' – he pointed out several holes dug in the rectangle of turf – 'they'll go to the government chemist for analysis. She must have lost a lot of blood, and most of it probably soaked into the ground.'

Madden's thoughts had been moving on a parallel course. 'He'd have needed a spot like this, wouldn't he? Secluded, I mean?' For a moment he was distracted by the sudden appearance of a kingfisher which shot by like a blue streak, close to the water, leaving its characteristic *chee-chee* call echoing in its wake.

Galloway, meanwhile, seemed to find the image conjured up by the other man's words distasteful. He grimaced. 'Given what he had in mind, I'd have to agree,' he said. 'Rape. Murder. Plus what he did to her afterwards. No, he wouldn't have wanted an audience for that.'

'I was thinking the same thing, sir.' Wright glanced up from the statement he was reading. 'He already *knew* about this spot, didn't he?'

Madden looked at him inquiringly.

'That tramp, sir. Beezy. We can place him here earlier, before the other one found the body . . . what's his name . . . Topper? That mark on the tree . . .' He gestured towards the birch growing by the bank. 'We've got you to thank for that, Mr Madden. I'm not sure any one of us would have spotted it. Or known what it meant if we had.'

Unmoved by the accolade, Madden frowned. 'You're treating Beezy as a suspect, then, are you?'

'Well, yes, sir . . . until otherwise demonstrated. He's the obvious one. We've had no word yet of any other strangers seen in the area, just motorists driving through the village, the usual Sunday traffic. And though we can't *exclude* it was someone local, I'm inclined to doubt that possibility. Being a Sunday, I think you'll find most of them were at home, and able to prove it.'

'So if there *were* any strangers about, it's unlikely they were seen.' Galloway made the point.

Wright shrugged. He seemed more interested in Madden's opinion, which so far had not been offered.

Galloway persisted. 'Don't you find it peculiar that he'd try to conceal a body at a spot where he'd already left his mark?'

'Yes, I do, sir.' Wright turned to him. 'And, what's more, a place where he was expecting to meet another tramp later. But that's looking at it rationally, and this sort of crime doesn't happen that way.' His eyes returned to Madden's face. He seemed to be hoping for some response from that quarter. 'I can tell you how it *might* have come about,' he went on. 'This Beezy turns up yesterday looking to meet Topper, finds he has time on his hands, cuts that mark to show he's been here, then goes off exploring. Remember, he hadn't been to these parts before. Now you can get to the Craydon road from here easy. There's a way off the main path that runs through the wood to the road and it comes out not far from where Alice Bridger was last seen.' He shrugged. 'I'm not saying that's proof of anything, but it's possible opportunity. He *could* have come on her there, lost his head maybe and attacked her, knocked her out or choked her and then brought her back up here. There's evidence she was carried—'

'Evidence?' Madden had been staring at the ground while he listened. Now his head came up.

'Yes, sir, that bit of thread you noticed caught on a bramble.' Wright seemed relieved to have heard him speak at last. 'It came from her skirt. We matched it. Now, if you recall, it was about waist high on the bush, and that suggests to me she was being carried at that point, since it came from the lower part of her clothing, from her skirt.'

Madden nodded his agreement with this interpretation, but made no further comment.

'Now, as I was saying, he could have brought her back here from the road, this Beezy – back to where he knew they wouldn't be seen. And if that's what happened, then I don't reckon he would have been thinking of any mark he'd made on a tree earlier. That would have been the last thing on his mind. Like I said, you can't expect rational behaviour with a crime of this type. Look what he did to her face, for pity's sake! Isn't that so, sir? You must have come across cases like this in the past.' The confidence had begun to seep out of the inspector's manner as he went on speaking and there was a hint of desperation about the appeal he flung out to Madden, who had resumed his former attitude and was standing with arms folded, eyes fixed to the ground, still giving no indication of what was in his mind.

Observing the Surrey policeman, Peter Galloway drew a measure of grim amusement from the spectacle of his discomfiture. He had known John Madden for a number of years and considered him a rare bird. To an air of natural authority, striking enough in itself, another quality was added that was even more disconcerting: a capacity for silence bordering on the inhuman. Once sunk into meditation, or reflection, he gave every appearance of being deaf to reason or argument. Confronted now by these twin phenomena, Wright was descending into garrulousness.

'And then there's something else you can't ignore, sir, the fact he took off in a hurry—'

'*Did* he?' Once again Madden's head jerked up. 'How do you know that, Inspector?'

'Well, from that old clasp knife of his we found—'

'Clasp knife?'

'Yes, didn't you hear, sir? We picked it up last evening by the stream, not far from here.' Wright's expression changed as he realized he had told Madden something he didn't know. 'It was lying on the ground, wrapped in an old bandana. Must have fallen out of his bundle, or his pocket. Now I can't see that happening unless he was in a hurry and not taking proper care. We showed them both to Topper this morning, the knife and the bandana, and he confirmed they belonged to Beezy.'

'On the ground, you say?' Madden seemed struck by the discovery. 'I wonder how I missed them?'

'Oh, it wasn't the way you and the constable came.' Wright was eager to explain. 'It was the other direction.' He pointed downstream. 'He must have made off along the bank that way.'

'Towards Brookham? That's strange. The other way leads back to the fields.'

'Well, if you ask me, he was in a panic by then and could easily have been confused.' Wright shrugged. 'But all he had to do was get back to the path, and you can do that either way, upstream or down. Once he'd reached it he could have doubled back and left the wood the same way he came in, by the fields.' Wright pointed to the mass of tangled holly bushes on the opposite bank and drew an imaginary line along them with his finger.

Madden had been paying close attention to what he was saying and now he signalled his agreement. 'Yes, that's so,' he conceded. 'I see what you mean, Inspector. He must have done that.'

Sensing he'd finally made a breach, Wright pressed ahead. 'But what's really suspicious, sir, is he's disappeared. We've been searching the neighbourhood since last evening and no one's seen hide nor hair of him. There's no doubt he's made himself scarce, and you have to ask yourself *why*.'

Madden pondered the inspector's meaning in silence. Then he nodded. 'Yes, why? That's the question.'

His sudden change of manner took both his listeners

by surprise, and it was clear from Wright's relieved expression that he felt he had won his point, that his line of reasoning had prevailed at last. Madden's next words only served to strengthen that impression.

'You're right about the tramp, by the way. He *must* be found. And the sooner the better.'

DRIVING TO THE FARM later that morning, Madden had much to occupy his mind, but little chance to explore it. On his return from Brookham he had called in at the house for a moment that nevertheless proved long enough for him to acquire a passenger before he departed again, in the shape of his six-year-old daughter. Lucy had been left in the sole charge of Mrs Beck since breakfast and the Maddens' cook was in sore need of relief.

'Can I play with Belle today?'

Flaxen at birth, Lucy Madden's hair now matched her mother's honey-coloured shade. A tireless child, her fair skin had been golden brown all summer from hours spent playing in the open air.

'I don't know.' Madden spoke over his shoulder to the restless presence in the back seat. 'We'll have to wait and see. She was still coughing on Saturday. She may not be allowed outside yet.'

'Then I'll ask May if we can play *inside*.'

'Don't you mean Mrs Burrows?'

Lucy's last nanny had left them six weeks earlier after less than a year's employment, citing urgent family reasons for returning home to Bradford. Helen had diagnosed a case of loss of nerve. No replacement for her had yet been found and the Maddens were wondering if they could manage their daughter on their own from now on with the help of the household staff. Lucy would be going to the village school soon, and when she started it would take some of the strain off them, Madden had pointed out. 'Off us and on to poor Miss Tinsley,' had been Helen's pessimistic prediction.

'Can we go and see the waggle-taggle gypsies?'

'Raggle-taggle. And don't call them that. They're Mr and Mrs Goram to you.' Her eyes, blue as sapphires, challenged his in the rear-view mirror. 'Yes, we can,' he said, after a moment. 'They're leaving soon, and I want to talk to Mr Goram before they go.'

'What about?'

'Never you mind.'

The dirt road to the farm sparkled with muddy puddles. The land on which it lay, overlooked by Upton Hanger, was little more than a mile from the Maddens' house and less than three miles from Highfield itself. They had bought it from Lord Stratton, a local landowner, soon after their marriage, when Madden had quit his job at Scotland Yard to return to the life he had known as a boy.

Although the rain of the previous day had fallen heavily here, too, he was relieved to see no sign of damage to the lines of late tomatoes flanking the roadway. When he and Helen had acquired the property wheat had been its principal crop. Since then cheap grain from Canada and Australia had driven down prices and like many farmers in the area Madden was devoting more land each year to growing vegetables and fruit, which found a ready market.

As he drove past the brick-built, shingled farmhouse, May Burrows waved to them from the kitchen doorway. She had been May Birney when he first came to Highfield; her father owned the village store. Later, she had married George Burrows, a worker on the Stratton estate, and they had moved into the house which came with the farm, a primitive structure when the Maddens had bought it, but now, with the addition of two new rooms and the installation of indoor plumbing, a comfortable house for a young couple.

Madden had made George his farm manager, though not without a qualm. There had never been any thought that he and Helen might move from the house where they lived: a handsome, half-timbered dwelling, it had been in her family for three generations. But living away from his land, leaving it each evening in the hands of another man, made him feel at times like a gentleman farmer, and he was in the habit of assuaging these periodic bouts of guilt by engaging in the hardest manual work he could find – ditching and hedging, scything grass and baling hay – returning home on those evenings with blistered hands and aching muscles, exhausted but happy, to the raised eyebrows of his wife.

'MR MADDEN, SIR! I was hoping to see you today.'

Joe Goram called out from the steps of one of his caravans as Madden rode into the encampment. A burly, dark-haired man with unshaven cheeks, his face bore a scowl that seemed permanently fixed until he caught sight of Lucy, who was wearing a blue dress with a ribbon in her hair, riding perched on the saddle in front of her father. The gypsies' camp lay at the bottom of the farm beside the stream that ran along the foot of Upton Hanger. Madden had parked his car at the stable yard and ridden down.

'Good morning to you, young missy.' Waving to her, he came down the steps. His broad grin showed he had several teeth missing.

'Hullo, Mr Goram.' She gave him a dazzling smile. 'May I see the puppies, please?'

'Of course, m'dear. They're tied up over there, behind the caravan.'

The little girl slid to the ground and ran off.

'Don't offer her one, Joe, I beg you,' Madden said hastily. 'We've two dogs at home, and one of them's just had puppies herself.'

Dismounting, he shook hands with the gypsy and passed him the reins of the old mare he used for getting about the farm and which Goram inspected with his usual disparaging eye. He'd several times offered to replace it with a better animal from his own string, but Madden, no horseman, had suggested instead that he look out for a suitable mount for Lucy at some unspecified date in the future.

'And don't mention the pony, either. Please. We'll talk about that next time you're here.'

Goram didn't hide his disappointment. 'There's no harm in spoiling them while they're young,' he ventured.

Since this was an argument Madden used himself on occasion, and one on which Helen poured particular scorn, he thought it best not to respond.

Instead, he gazed about him, taking note of the signs of bustle and activity in the encampment. The various members of Joe Goram's family – his wife and two sons, his daughter and son-in-law – were all busy collecting and stowing items in the trio of caravans that were parked at the edge of the clearing in the shade of a beech tree. One young grandson, eyes fixed to the ground, was quartering the area, picking up bits of paper and other rubbish and depositing them in a sack.

'You were hoping to see me, you said?'

'Yes, Mr Madden, sir. We'll be pulling out first thing tomorrow and I wanted to thank you again for letting us stay.'

The gypsies had first appeared four summers before. Joe Goram had presented himself to Madden, greasy cap in hand, and asked for permission to park his caravans on a patch of tree-shaded land by the stream and to graze his horses in the lower paddock, which he must have seen was empty. Over strong objections from George Burrows – gypsies had a well-deserved reputation for being light-fingered, he'd argued, it was asking for trouble to allow them on your land – Madden had agreed to let them remain. In spite of his policeman's conditioning, he clung to the belief he'd grown up with: that people, by and large, behaved according to how they were treated.

In the course of the next few days two bridles and a set of stirrups had vanished from the stables and George had found one of his scythes missing. At the end of the week they had miraculously reappeared in the places where they had been before, and Joe Goram had dragged his elder son, Sam, by the collar into the yard and made him apologize to Madden in front of Burrows and the other two farmhands. Sam, sporting a black eye and a loose tooth, had sworn it would never happen again.

The family had returned every year since, accepting the hospitality that was offered and in return mending pots and pans, sharpening knives and doing other odd jobs about the farm. Madden had grown used to seeing the smoke from their fires drifting up through the screen of oak and beech and to catching the scent of strange spices and aromas wafting his way from their blackened cooking pots.

'There's something you ought to know, Joe. A young girl was murdered over at Brookham yesterday.'

'I heard about it, sir. Mr Burrows told us this morning. Poor lass . . .' The gypsy watched Madden's face closely.

'The police will be questioning people in the area. Tramps in particular, but travellers, too. You may be stopped on the road.'

Joe nodded. His face was impassive.

'I understand you were at the farm all day yesterday?'

'That's right, Mr Madden. I took my boys up to say goodbye to Mrs Burrows. She gave us a cup of tea.'

'Good. I'm glad. You'll have no trouble with the police, then. But if you do, refer them to us. To Mr Burrows or myself.'

'Thank you, sir. I'll do that if I may.' Joe Goram

twisted his cap in his fingers. He could think of no way to repay this man who had shown him such special favour. Who *shook hands* with him when they met.

'There's something else, Joe . . .' Frowning, Madden watched as one of Goram's sons dismantled a clothes line, thrusting the poles into a rack beneath a caravan. 'Have you ever come across a man called Beezy? He's a tramp, a friend of Topper's?'

Goram shook his head. 'I've not heard the name, sir. *Beezy*, you say?'

'It's a nickname, I expect. He was in the Brookham area yesterday, near where the child's body was found.'

'Are the police looking for him, then?' Goram's face was expressionless.

'Yes, they are. They think he might have done it.' Madden paused, considering how to frame his next remark. 'You might hear of his whereabouts,' he suggested.

The gypsy's swarthy features darkened still further. He stared down at his feet. Madden studied him in silence. He had more than an inkling of what was going on in the other man's mind.

'There's no need to go to the police,' he remarked, after a moment. 'Just get word to me.'

Goram's face cleared. He looked up. 'Oh, I'll do that, if you want, sir.' Vastly relieved, he made bold to offer his *own* hand to Madden, who took it at once. 'Anything I hear, you'll hear. You have my word on it.'

6

THE CORONER'S inquest into the death of Alice Bridger, held at Guildford the following Friday, was quickly concluded. As officer in charge of the case, Inspector Wright baldly described the murder scene and outlined the measures already taken by the Surrey constabulary at the start of their investigation. Apart from routine questioning, these were mainly concerned with tracking down strangers seen in the vicinity of Brookham that day.

The presence of a number of vagrants in the general area had been reported and some of them had been identified and questioned, so far without result. The search for the rest was being extended.

'I am authorized to inform the court that we are looking for one man in particular,' Wright stated. 'We expect to trace him and to be able to question him in the very near future.'

Dr Galloway was equally terse. Attaching to Alice Bridger's rape the single adjective 'brutal', the patholo- gist briefly detailed the injuries, internal and external, that she had suffered in the course of the assault, reading from a prepared statement, not looking up, aware per- haps of the presence of Alice's parents in court. The girl had been strangled subsequently and from the amount of water found in her lungs it was likely the killer had also held her submerged in the stream. Her face had been 'badly battered', Galloway said, but provided no further description.

'I'm giving the London press as little as possible to feed on,' he'd told Madden and Helen, encountering them outside the courtroom before the proceedings opened. 'They keep an eye on inquests.'

One of the first witnesses, Madden had testified at some length to the discovery of the body beside the stream. The coroner, a recent appointee, was plainly puzzled by his involvement in the affair.

'Why exactly were you there, Mr Madden?' he inquired.

'I gave Constable Stackpole a lift from Brookham. He felt the wood should be searched without delay, rather than wait for the arrival of the detectives from Guildford.'

'Yes, but why were *you* involved in the search? Surely it's not usual for a member of the public to be engaged to that degree in a police investigation?'

'Not usual at all,' Madden had agreed solemnly, leaving his questioner scratching his head, disgruntled, but none the wiser.

'I thought for a moment he was going to clap you in irons, John.' Silver-haired and in his sixties, Chief Superintendent Boyce, head of the Guildford CID, buttonholed Madden in the street outside afterwards. They were old acquaintances. 'Six months to my pension and we're landed with a case like this! Mind you, at least it's straightforward.'

He waited for a response, but none was forthcoming.

'You don't agree?' Boyce cocked an eyebrow, then turned aside to doff his hat and bow. 'Dr Madden!'

'Mr Boyce . . . how are you?' Helen shook his hand. She had come from talking to Mrs Bridger, the murdered girl's mother, who was standing by the steps to the courthouse in a circle of Brookham villagers, clinging to her husband's arm as though she required its support to remain upright. Bridger himself, white-faced and with a glazed expression, was hardly more steady on his feet. Molly Henshaw hovered in attendance on them both.

'They're close to collapse, the pair of them,' Helen said, taking refuge in her dispassionate doctor's voice. 'He won't like it, but I'm going to write a note to Dr Rowley. He really must take proper care of them.'

During the court proceedings, Madden had noticed Fred Bridger sitting two rows from the front in the public seats. Their eyes had met for an instant and he had felt the force of the other man's anguish as he listened to the flat accounts offered by various witnesses of the circumstances surrounding his child's last agonized moments on earth.

'This man you're searching for,' Helen said to Boyce. 'Is he the mysterious Beezy?'

'He is, and I don't know why we haven't laid hands on him yet.' The Surrey police chief looked glum. 'These tramps know how to lie low, mind you – they've places to hide where we wouldn't think of looking. But all the same, he must show himself soon. He'll need to find food, if nothing else.'

Madden had seen the description circulated by the Surrey police. It had been sent not only to village bobbies in the district but to farmers and gamekeepers as well, and Will Stackpole had brought him a copy of the poster.

Beezy was described as being of middle age, bearded and dressed in rough clothes – words that could be applied to a good many vagrants, as the constable had pointed out. However, he had one distinguishing feature noted by the farmer he'd worked for recently at Dorking: the lobe of his right ear was missing.

'And we haven't seen any sign of Topper either since we let him go,' Boyce complained. 'Wright had to strike his name off the witness list today. I wonder where *he's* got to.'

The suspicious glance he directed at Helen as he spoke these words provoked no reaction beyond the amused smile it brought to her lips.

'Whatever you're thinking, you're wrong,' she declared. 'I haven't set eyes on him since that evening in Brookham, and I haven't the faintest idea where he is now.'

Both statements were true, Madden reflected, though, as an old policeman, he might have been tempted to charge his wife with being less than entirely frank. The previous day their gardener, Tom Cooper, had found a bunch of rose hips and old man's beard bound in a willow branch lying on the grass outside the gate at the foot of the orchard. He'd been somewhat put out to discover, in addition, a crude design scratched on the green paint of the wooden gate – it showed a cross with a circle round it – and had been for taking a brush and a tin of paint down and repairing the damage, until Helen had stopped him. 'Let it stay there,' she'd decreed.

Madden had found the tramp's gesture mystifying until his wife explained it to him.

'He's lying low,' she said. 'He knows the police will be looking for him again. They should have hung on to him while they had the chance.'

'Yes, but since he was here, why didn't he come in and see you?'

'Because then we would have had to decide what to do – whether to inform the police or not – and he didn't want to put us in that position. Mrs Beck was right. He's a proper gentleman, my Topper. But I do worry about him. He's getting too old to be wandering about.'

Boyce, meanwhile, had turned his attention to Madden. 'To get back to what I was saying, John – the girl's injuries aside, *do* you think there's something unusual about this killing?'

Listening to the Surrey policeman, Helen felt a twinge of unease. Well aware of the regard in which her husband had once been held by his colleagues – and not only those at the Yard – she knew that his views would be eagerly sought, particularly in a case as grave as this one. But watching it happen now, she was filled with misgivings.

'Oh, it's shocking, I grant you,' Boyce went on, having failed to elicit an immediate response. 'I've never seen anything like that poor child's face. But ten to one this Beezy will turn out to be the man we want. Or someone very like him.'

'A tramp, you mean?' Madden sounded surprised.

'Well, yes, I suppose I do. That sort of man.' The chief superintendent pursed his lips. 'Look, it's not inconceivable, living the life they do ... tramps ... vagrants ... they lack so much ... they've no opportunity ...' He directed an embarrassed glance at Helen, who'd divined the source of his discomfiture.

'You're implying they're sexually deprived,' she said.

'Well, yes. Since you put it that way.' The Guildford chief sought refuge in his handkerchief. He blew his nose loudly. 'And that sort of feeling can build up, can it not? You get pressure, more and more pressure, and when the dam finally breaks, well, it can be sudden and savage. That's what happened here, I think. Whoever killed that girl lost control of himself.'

'Are you certain of that?' Madden's quiet interjection took both his listeners by surprise. Boyce stared at him.

'What are you saying, John?' he asked. 'What are you suggesting?'

'I'm not sure, exactly.' Scowling, Madden seemed suddenly a prey to doubts himself. 'I don't want to burden you with half-baked ideas.'

'Never mind that.' Boyce frowned in turn. 'Just tell me what you think.' And when Madden remained silent. 'Are you saying I should call in the Yard?'

Helen saw that her husband had been expecting the question. But his reply was not what she had thought it would be.

'I don't see how you can,' Madden said. 'Not yet. You could be right about the tramp. And in any case he has to be found. But I'd make sure the Yard was *informed* about this.' He spoke more confidently now; his mind was made up. 'And I wouldn't waste any time, either, Jim, if I were you. I'd get in touch with them right away.'

THE DRIVE BACK to Highfield was a silent one. Madden's habit of withdrawing into himself when preoccupied was deeply engrained, and Helen had learned from experience to be patient with him.

It had taken her many weeks when they'd first met to learn the details of his past. To draw from him the story of the young wife and baby daughter he had watched die in an influenza epidemic before the war; to hear from his own lips of his subsequent descent into the hell of the trenches, an experience from which he'd emerged so injured in spirit that, until fate cast him into her arms, he had ceased to have any hope or belief in his future.

Long dispelled, these shadows no longer troubled their lives. What concerned Helen now was the irrational fear she had felt at the sight of her husband being drawn once more into a police investigation after so long an absence from the profession. His decision to quit his job and start a new life with her had not been taken lightly. Nor was it one he had ever regretted. If he was allowing himself to become involved now it could only be in response to some deep anxiety, and this realization kept the pulse of uneasiness throbbing inside her.

The happy years they had spent together had been born out of tragedy, something she could never forget. Indeed, the thought was fresh in her mind as they drove through the village, past the green and the moss-walled churchyard and along the straggling line of cottages that led to the high brick wall surrounding Melling Lodge. Leased by a succession of tenants in recent years, it was empty at present and the locked gates and dark, elm-lined drive lent it a mournful air.

Time had dulled the pain of that summer morning more than a decade past when an urgent summons from Will Stackpole had brought her, the village doctor, speeding through those same gates to confront the unimaginable reality of a household brutally slain; her dearest friend among the victims. When she drove by now it was of her husband she was thinking.

Yet the two were inextricably linked. It was the subsequent police investigation that had brought them together, and although the love that had flowered between them had drawn a line under Madden's tortured past, their future together had been dearly purchased. The case, one of the bloodiest in the Yard's annals, had come close to costing him his life.

7

FEELING OUT OF PLACE in his town clothes – he was clad in a grey pinstriped suit and homburg – Chief Inspector Angus Sinclair paused at the edge of the green to take in the scene before him. Quite close to where he stood a cloth banner erected on poles bore the words HIGHFIELD FLOWER AND VEGETABLE SHOW in bold capitals, and beyond it, the broad stretch of grass ringed with cottages was filled with stalls, where the fruits of a long summer were on display.

Vegetables piled high in baskets – beans, peas, potatoes, carrots – rubbed shoulders with swollen marrows, while beside them there were tables overflowing with bunches of late roses and chrysanthemums. Pumpkins, apples, pears, blackberries, nuts, brown speckled eggs – there seemed no end to the variety of items arrayed for inspection and the avenues between the stands were thronged with villagers dressed in their Sunday best.

Searching the crowd, the chief inspector's eye lit on a tall, elegant figure wearing a cream-coloured linen dress and a wide-brimmed straw hat standing beside a table stacked with preserves. He gave a grunt of appreciation. A widower now for several years, Angus Sinclair considered Helen Madden to be the best-looking woman of his acquaintance, and it always gave him particular pleasure to see her.

The long tresses she had worn when he first knew her, the fashion of the time, and a legacy of girlhood, perhaps, had long since vanished, but the chief inspector found consolation in the slender white neck their disappearance had revealed. His spirits, dampened earlier that morning by the pathologist's report and accompanying photographs he'd been obliged to examine at Guildford police station, rose at the sight of her.

But his relief was shortlived. Aware of his approach, Helen put down the jar of honey she was holding.

'I was wondering when you'd appear, Angus.'

Taken by surprise – he'd expected a friendly greeting at the very least – Sinclair stood abashed.

'It's that poor child's murder, isn't it? That's why you're here.'

Struck speechless, the chief inspector sought refuge in action. Bending beneath the brim of Helen's straw hat, he planted a firm kiss on her cheek. The jasmine scent she'd always favoured was a reminder of happier occasions.

'I'll admit I've been at Guildford all morning, talking to Jim Boyce about it.'

'And now you want to see John. Angus, you're not to drag him into this. I won't allow it.' Her dark blue eyes offered no concession.

'*Drag* him in! It was John who found the child's body, for heaven's sake.' Sinclair broke off. The subject was a delicate one between them. He continued in a different tone. 'My dear, I *must* speak to him. Surely you see that.'

The smile he tendered her was conciliatory. But in

truth it was no more than a gesture. Though he had never doubted the strength of Helen's feelings for her husband, he had equally never forgiven her for the part she had played in persuading the man she loved to give up his job with the police and start a new life with her. It still rankled with the chief inspector that an officer as talented as his former colleague should have quit the force, and fond as he was of Madden's wife, he could never quite bring himself to absolve her of responsibility for this loss to the public weal.

'Oh, very well. I see I've no choice in the matter.'

Relenting, she returned his kiss. In spite of their differences, they were firm friends.

'He's here somewhere. Probably over in that tent.' She pointed towards a tan-coloured marquee topped with flags near the back of the green. 'John's had to stand in as chairman of the prize-giving committee this year. It ought to be Lord Stratton's job, but he's managed to come down with gout, rather cunningly.' She paused. 'Do stay for lunch, Angus. We don't see nearly enough of you.'

'I wish I could, my dear.' The chief inspector recognized the olive branch he was being offered and declined with regret. 'Unfortunately, I've an engagement in London. I have to get back.'

'Then you must come down and spend a weekend with us. I'll write and let you know when.'

Her smile brought momentary relief to Sinclair. But then her expression changed and she grew serious again.

'You may think I'm making too much of this, but I know John. He won't turn his back on it now. He feels involved, and that worries me. I can't explain why, but I feel threatened. I know you have to speak to him, but don't let it go further than that, I beg you.'

She looked at him directly, and not for the first time the chief inspector felt the effect of her personality, that particular combination of physical beauty and firmness of will against which he felt powerless. But just as he was about to reply – he wanted to reassure her – they were interrupted.

'Excuse me, sir . . . Mr Sinclair?'

Angus Sinclair's grizzled eyebrows shot up in mock astonishment. He peered down at the eager young face that had materialized in front of them.

'Robert Madden? Is it you?' Despite his forty years on the force, the chief inspector retained the precise accents of his Aberdeen upbringing. 'I can scarcely believe my eyes. You were six inches shorter the last time we met. How are you, my boy?'

They shook hands solemnly.

'Have you come about the murder, sir?' Despite a peeling nose and one scabbed knee, Madden's son managed to convey the earnestness of his inquiry. His frown, the near image of his father's, brought a wistful smile to Sinclair's lips. He and his wife had been childless, to their sorrow. 'It was Daddy who found the body, you know?'

'I'm aware of that.' The chief inspector looked grave.

'The police are looking for a tramp.'

'I see you're well informed.'

'Is Daddy going to help you catch him?' The boy's hopeful expression faded when he saw Sinclair shake his head.

'Scotland Yard's not involved, Robert. The Surrey police are in charge. I just happened to be passing . . .' He caught Helen's eye. 'But since I'm here, I would like a brief word with your father. Do you happen to know where he is?'

'YOU MUST HAVE put a bee in Jim Boyce's bonnet. He rang me on Friday in a lather, right after the inquest. I couldn't get down to Guildford till today, but he came into the office to show me the file. On a Sunday, too!'

'I felt they'd made up their minds too quickly about the tramp. I wanted him to think again.' Madden scowled.

Led by his guide, Sinclair had come on his quarry outside the marquee standing beside a table laden with silver cups and other trophies. The chief inspector had paused for a moment to digest the spectacle of his erstwhile partner, dressed in serviceable tweeds, a soft hat and thick-soled shoes, deep in conversation with a party of similarly attired worthies of both sexes. Catching Madden's eye, he had winked.

'I've just spotted a pumpkin of outstanding merit,' he'd confided as they shook hands. 'Would you like me to point it out to you?'

'What are you doing here, Angus?' Grinning, Madden had declined the bait. 'Is it the Brookham murder? Don't tell me the Yard's been called in already.'

'No, we're not involved. Not as yet. Surrey are handling it. But there are one or two points I'd like to discuss with you. I've cleared it with higher authority.'

'You needed the *Yard's* permission?' Madden was mildly surprised.

'I was referring to your better half.' Sinclair chortled at his own joke. 'Forgive me. I couldn't resist that. I ran into Helen a moment ago, and she spoke her mind, as always. Robert was with her. My word, he's a fine-looking boy.'

The delight that shone on Madden's face when he heard these words was reward enough for the chief inspector, who could remember a time when his old friend's eyes had born a permanently haunted look; when it had seemed that the legacy of the war and the sufferings he'd endured in the trenches would pursue him to the grave.

'How can I help you, Angus? You say you've seen the file?'

Madden had drawn him aside, out of earshot of the crowd milling about in front of the tent, and as he took up his stance, arms folded and head bent, his face masked in the shadow cast by his hat brim, Sinclair was assailed by a painful sense of familiarity, aware all at once of how much he had missed this man's presence by his side these past years.

'I've studied the various reports and read the interviews taken. Based on what I know so far, I'd have to say the tramp's the most likely suspect.'

'So he is,' Madden agreed. 'And they have to find him, in any case. He may turn out in the end to be their key witness.'

'What makes you think that?'

'Why, the evidence, of course.' Madden frowned

under his hat brim. 'It all depends how you read it, Angus. The Surrey police have *their* version. Wright thinks the tramp picked up the child on the road to Craydon—'

'Wright—?'

'The officer in charge. He's a good detective. Sharp. No fool. He reckons the tramp brought her back to the wood and that after he'd killed her and hidden her body he ran off down the stream, wanting to get away as quickly as possible, dropping his knife and bandana in the confusion.'

'And?' Sinclair was listening intently.

'It holds water, as a theory, up to a point. But there's another way of interpreting the facts. You see, Beezy, the tramp, ran off in the wrong direction . . .'

'The *wrong* direction – how do you know that?'

'Because he must have come into the wood originally from the fields. He had an appointment at a camp site by the stream with another tramp called Topper.'

'A friend of yours, I gather.' Sinclair nodded.

'When Beezy fled, it wasn't back the way he came, it was in the opposite direction, towards Brookham, and that doesn't make sense, unless you take Wright's view that he was confused, in a panic, and didn't know which way he was heading.'

'Could there be another explanation?'

'Yes, it's possible he heard someone moving towards him through the bushes. And from the same direction he'd come himself, from the fields. Since he was expecting Topper to arrive, that shouldn't have alarmed him. So if he did run off then – and in the other direction – it could well have been because he saw something that frightened him.'

'A man carrying a young girl in his arms? The killer?' Madden nodded mutely.

Sinclair let out a sigh. The morning was growing warm. He took off his homburg and fanned his face. 'What you say is interesting, John. But supposition, just the same.'

'No more so than Wright's version. All the evidence is circumstantial.'

'Yes, but you can't overlook the fact he's disappeared. This Beezy. Gone into hiding. That's not the behaviour of an innocent man.'

'It's the behaviour of a tramp, Angus. An outcast. I know these men. They've no faith in the courts or our system of justice. It's quite possible he's afraid of going to the police in case he's charged with the crime himself. And he wouldn't be far wrong.'

Sinclair grunted as the shaft went home. 'Very well. But I'm still at a loss. As I understand it, either way the Surrey police must find this man. That's not a job for the Yard. Why did you suggest to Boyce that he get in touch with us?'

Madden was slow in responding. He stared at the ground before him. As the silence between them lengthened, Sinclair felt a premonition growing in him. He knew he hadn't yet discovered the true reason behind the other man's concern. But he thought the moment might be approaching.

'You saw the photographs of the girl's face?' Madden looked up.

'What remained of it. The degree of damage inflicted

is unique in my experience. I can only imagine the killer was in a frenzy.'

'Perhaps. But did you note what a thorough job he did?'

'*Thorough?*' Sinclair showed distaste at the word.

'He set out to obliterate her features. That's what it looked like. This wasn't simple abuse of a victim's body. It was something more. Has it been determined yet what was used in the way of a weapon? I spoke to the pathologist a few days ago and he seemed to think it might have been a hammer.'

'That's confirmed now.' Sinclair nodded. 'I read it in the file. He was able to take some measurements from holes made in the cranium. He believes a common workman's tool was used.' He shot a glance at Madden. 'There's no reason why the tramp shouldn't have had one in his bundle.'

'Agreed. Whereas, if the killer was someone else, someone who picked her up off the road in his car, then the implication becomes quite different.'

The chief inspector took some moments to assure himself he had understood his former partner correctly. He didn't like the direction their conversation was taking. 'You're wondering – if it *was* someone else – why he should have had a hammer with him at all. Supposing that's the case, what does it signify to you?'

'That the assault on her face was planned.' Madden spoke quietly, but his voice had grown tense, and the chief inspector, feeling a sudden chill, glanced at him sharply. 'It was what he had in mind all along.'

Sinclair removed a handkerchief from his lapel pocket

and dabbed at his perspiring brow. The crowd on the green was beginning to converge on the judges' table, spreading in their direction, and instinctively he moved a little closer to Madden, lowering his voice.

'I want to be clear about this. You're suggesting he was following a pattern? That he's done this sort of thing before?'

Madden nodded mutely.

'But surely, if that's the case, it would have come to our notice. A crime of that kind?' The chief inspector scowled in turn. His companion shrugged.

'I can't explain that. But don't forget, he tried to hide Alice Bridger's body. If it hadn't been for the accident of him choosing a tramps' hideout to commit the murder in we might be searching for her still.'

'So you think he might have killed elsewhere without our knowing it . . .' Sinclair brooded on the thought. 'Children do go missing, it's true.'

Madden saw that his argument was gaining ground. He pressed harder. 'The Surrey police can't be expected to pursue a theory of this kind. The tramp's the obvious suspect; they have to keep looking for him. But it's different with the Yard. They can afford to take a broader view.'

'Which is why you urged Boyce to ring us? Yes, I see now.'

An island of stillness in the shifting throng around them, the two men stood silent while Sinclair ruminated. Above the hum of country voices, the sudden wail of a baby sounded a summons. The chief inspector came to himself with a grunt.

'You make a good case, John. I won't say I'm persuaded. Not yet. But half-persuaded . . .? Yes . . . possibly.' He caught the other's eye. 'I'll certainly look into the matter. You can rest assured.'

The smile of relief on Madden's face was testimony to a burden shed, and the chief inspector warmed to it. Helen's words came back to him and he acknowledged the truth of them. Among the many reasons he had for regretting the departure of his old colleague had been the depth of commitment Madden had brought to his work, an impulse born of the sense of obligation he seemed to feel towards others; those whose lives touched his.

It was a rare quality among policemen: a rare quality anywhere.

8

AT TEN O'CLOCK on the Friday following, by prior
appointment, Sinclair presented himself at the office
of Sir Wilfred Bennett, assistant commissioner, crime,
whose responsibilities at Scotland Yard included overall
direction of the Criminal Investigation Department.
Burdened as he was with questions of policy and admin-
istration, Bennett wouldn't normally have dealt with the
matter which the chief inspector wished to raise. But
the absence of his own deputy, who had recently undergone an operation to remove his gall bladder, and who
was now enjoying an extended period of convalescence
following a brush with peritonitis, had dangled an opportunity before the assistant commissioner which he'd been
unable to resist.

'This is quite like old times, Chief Inspector.'

Sir Wilfred had kept the same suite of rooms at the
Yard for more than a decade. His office overlooked the
tree-lined Embankment and the Thames. In the past he
and Sinclair had met there frequently, and Bennett
retained a nostalgia for those days when, as deputy to the
then assistant commissioner, he'd been more involved in
the day-to-day running of the CID. Promotion had
brought him a knighthood and entry into the upper
ranks of the Metropolitan Police, but he wondered
sometimes if he had not lost more than he'd gained.

'I've asked Chief Superintendent Holly to join us. I think it would be a kindness. He told me recently that since being "moved upstairs", as he put it, he'd felt left out of things, a sentiment with which I sympathize.' Sir Wilfred caught Sinclair's eye and they shared a wry smile.

'Isn't Arthur still on holiday, sir?'

'He got back yesterday. But he won't have had a chance to look at the file yet, so I suggest you start by taking us through it.'

The assistant commissioner directed Sinclair to the polished oak table by the windows where he was in the habit of conducting his business conferences: gatherings which these days seemed to involve only tortuous bureaucratic wrangling. As they sat down facing each other, Sir Wilfred observed, not without a pang, his visitor's clear grey eyes and air of alertness. Despite having turned sixty, Angus Sinclair looked like a man who still had an appetite for his work.

There was a knock on the door and the chief superintendent entered. He was a heavy-set man in his mid-fifties, blunt-featured and sporting a suntan.

'Good morning, Holly. Welcome back.' Bennett rose and shook his hand. 'I trust you had a good holiday.'

'Thank you, sir. The weather was excellent. I always say there's no place quite like the Scilly Isles at this time of year.' The chief super's soft burr betrayed his rural origins. For years now the Met had done much of its recruiting in the West Country, considering native-born Londoners too fly and streetwise, too clever by half to be suitable for training as policemen. Sturdy country men with open, malleable minds, on the other hand, were regarded as ideal material, and Chief Superintendent Holly was a prime example of the breed.

'My word, Arthur, you've put on weight.' Sinclair eyed his colleague askance. 'I shall have to speak to Ethel. We must get you on a diet.'

Holly blushed. He was now the senior superintendent on the force and nominally Sinclair's superior. But he could never forget that he had once worked under the chief inspector; had felt the sting of his sometimes acid tongue and striven to earn his approval. It was several years now since Angus Sinclair had declined any further promotion, letting it be known that he was satisfied with the rank of chief inspector. There were five such officers on the Yard's strength and they had something of the cachet of specialists, being held in reserve to handle the most difficult and challenging investigations. Holly was relieved that Sinclair chose to call him by his first name and knew from bitter experience that when the chief inspector wished to correct him he would address him as 'sir'.

'So you went down to Guildford last Sunday, did you?' Bennett had waited until they were all settled before speaking. Pale of face, with dark, thinning hair, he had a quick, decisive manner that mirrored the mind behind it. 'I hope you trod carefully, Chief Inspector.'

'As though on eggshells, sir.' Sinclair opened his file. 'Jim Boyce is an old friend. We agreed to treat my visit as unofficial.'

'I can sleep easy, then, can I? I won't open the newspaper tomorrow and read that Scotland Yard detec-

tives have been prowling the Home Counties uninvited.'
Bennett spoke with a smile. He'd developed a warm
regard over the years for the dapper chief inspector.
They had not only cooperated on cases in the past, they
were also allies in a broader sense, having laboured, each
in his own sphere, to bring the institution for which they
worked into the modern world, a task which Sir Wilfred
had been known to compare with trying to move a
reluctant mule.

Sinclair made no comment, merely lifting an eyebrow
in response. It so happened that the file he was holding,
with its sheaf of neatly typed pages, was the fruit of an
initiative which he and the assistant commissioner had
jointly pursued some years previously. Scotland Yard
now boasted a registry where civilian staff compiled
dossiers of cases from material supplied by detectives,
sparing the latter this time-consuming chore.

'Guildford?' Arthur Holly frowned. 'That rings a bell.
Wasn't there a child murdered in the district recently? I
seem to remember reading something about it in the
newspaper.'

'Yes, a young girl. She was raped and strangled. It
happened while you were away.' Bennett settled himself
in his chair. 'The chief inspector drew my attention to it.
There are aspects of the murder which he feels can't be
ignored.' He gestured to Sinclair, inviting him to
continue.

'It was the nature of the crime, Arthur, as well as the
circumstances.' Sinclair addressed his remarks to his
colleague. 'The injuries inflicted on the child's body after
death were unusually severe. Her face was destroyed,

demolished in fact. After due consideration, the pathologist determined that the killer used a hammer for this
purpose, a stonemason's tool, to judge by measurements
taken of the imprint.'

'My God!' The shock showed on Holly's face. 'I've
not heard of that before.'

'Among the various conclusions one might draw from
such an act, the most disturbing to me is that the assault
appears to have been planned in advance. If he had a
hammer with him, he must have intended to use it. It's
one of the reasons why I believe this crime merits our
attention. There may be more to it than meets the eye.'

Silence followed his words. After a moment's pause,
the chief inspector continued, 'For the present, all I can
tell you is that the Surrey police are actively searching
for a tramp in connection with the assault, a man whose
travelling name is Beezy. He was known to have been
in the wood where the girl's body was found round
about the time she was killed. His description has been
circulated in Surrey and the surrounding counties, and
to the Metropolitan Police, as well.'

'What do we know about him?' Holly asked.

'A fair amount.' Sinclair drew a page from his file. 'I
received this information from Guildford yesterday. His
real name is Harold Beal. He's a Londoner by origin and
once had a job as an insurance clerk. Twelve years ago
his wife died suddenly. He began to drink heavily, lost
his job and finally took to the road. He's been a tramp
ever since, and, like many of them, a man of habit. Until
this year he used to spend his summers in Kent, working
on farms there, returning to London for the winter. He's

been found drunk and disorderly a number of times and has one other conviction on his record. Last year he was convicted in a Canterbury magistrate's court of indecent exposure.'

'Was he, now?' Holly sat up. 'What do you make of that?' And when Sinclair failed to respond at once. 'It's a pointer, isn't it?'

'It could be. But I'm not sure.' The chief inspector eased a muscle in his back. 'Petty sexual offenders are ten a penny, after all. Between unbuttoning your flies in public and what was done to that poor girl, there's a vast distance. An enormous leap.'

'True. But they all start somewhere.' The chief superintendent pursued his point. 'Look at the record of any serious offender, Angus, and chances are you'll find he was once a peeping Tom, or something of the kind.'

'I accept that.' Sinclair nodded. 'But let me tell you a little more about Beal's case. A Canterbury schoolmistress alleged that he exposed himself on a public road while she was walking by with a crocodile of schoolgirls. Beal said in court that he was simply relieving himself and hadn't been aware of their approach. He claimed to be hard of hearing, which seems borne out by the court record. He kept asking for questions to be repeated. On the face of it, I'd say it was a charge that should never have been brought, but the magistrate found him guilty and sentenced him to two months' imprisonment. It's there on the record.' The chief inspector tapped the file with his forefinger. 'I don't dismiss it, Arthur.' He caught the chief super's eye.

'Perhaps that's why Beezy chose to come to Surrey

this year instead of going to Kent,' Bennett remarked dryly. 'Wherever he is now he must wish he hadn't. What does Boyce think? Does he believe this tramp is their man?'

'Not as strongly as he did at first. Not after hearing John Madden's views on the subject.'

'Madden?' Holly's eyebrows shot up. 'How does he come to be involved?'

'He happened to be the one who found the body. He was helping the local bobby search the wood. I had a word with him in Highfield on Sunday.'

'Good man, John Madden.' The chief super rumbled his approval. 'You should never have let him go, Angus.'

'I can't imagine why you think I had any say in the matter.' Stung by the remark, the chief inspector responded sharply. 'It was his wife who persuaded him to quit the force. I don't believe you've ever met her, Arthur.'

'I have,' Bennett chipped in. 'At a dinner party in London a few years back. I remember the occasion well. It was soon after Parliament had agreed to allow women into the civil service at last and I asked her if she was pleased by the vote. "Speechless with gratitude", was her reply, but I don't think she meant it.' He chuckled. 'Dashed fine-looking woman, too ... So Madden saw the murder site? What did he make of it? I take it he doesn't hold with the tramp theory?'

Sinclair shook his head. He tugged thoughtfully at an earlobe. 'Madden's always had a way of seeing things clearly, of seeing through them, or rather beyond them. I used to think it was a kind of sixth sense when we worked together, but now I wonder if it isn't just that he understands what he sees better than most. The meaning of it . . .' He shrugged. 'No, Madden doesn't believe Beezy murdered that young girl. When he saw the child's face, what remained of it, he got the scent of another kind of killer. One that may be much harder to track down.'

'Why so?'

'He thought the damage inflicted on the girl's features was deliberate, the work of a man who might have done that sort of thing before, rather than the aberration of some old tramp who's come across an unsupervised child and suddenly taken leave of his senses. What's more the pathologist's findings tend to support his view.'

Holly scowled. 'I'm not aware of any recent crime that fits this pattern, Angus. Have you found something in the files?'

'No, nothing.' The chief inspector shook his head. 'Not even a hint of a connection, I'm afraid. But that's not quite the end of the story. Something else has come to my attention, a straw in the wind, you might say, but I feel I should share it with you.'

Holly and Bennett exchanged glances.

'Please do,' the assistant commissioner said dryly.

Sinclair eyed his two listeners.

'Three years ago – in July of 1929, to be precise – a twelve-year-old girl by the name of Susan Barlow went missing in Henley-on-Thames. Her body wasn't discovered until this year: six weeks ago, in fact. She'd been presumed drowned in the river – the last sighting of her was near the bank – and her body was recovered from the water. It had got trapped in an inlet under a log which itself was wedged into the bank. Needless to say, the girl's corpse was in an advanced state of decomposition.'

'You're not telling us she'd been raped.' Holly scowled. 'Surely they couldn't know that.'

'Indeed not. Nor whether she'd been strangled, if we're going to compare it with the Brookham crime. Lodged in fresh water, the flesh would have turned into adipocere after only six months. But her face told a different story.'

'Was it damaged?' The chief superintendent's features darkened.

'Beyond question. But not to the same extent as at Brookham, which may be an important point. The nose and one of the cheekbones had been fractured and the skull cracked.'

There was silence for some moments. 'Yes, but a body lying in the water that long ... there might be any number of ways injuries like that could be caused,' Holly growled.

'It's a mystery, certainly,' Sinclair acknowledged. 'One which is exercising the minds of the Oxfordshire police as we speak. I should tell you, too, that we've not been officially informed of this matter. No murder inquiry has been instituted. I heard of it by chance.'

He paused, squaring a piece of paper from his file on the table in front of him, then turned to Bennett.

'Do you know who I mean by George Ransom, sir? He's a pathologist at St Mary's in Paddington.'

'I'm familiar with the name.'

'I bumped into him by chance this week and he told me about the body taken from the river at Henley. He offered it more as a curiosity than anything else, but with the Brookham case fresh in my mind, I pricked up my ears. How Ransom came to hear about it was through a dinner he'd attended, some annual medical get-together. You might think it a curious mealtime subject, even for pathologists, but he happened to be sitting next to the doctor who'd performed the autopsy – an Oxford medico named Stanley – so he got the whole story. Stanley said he was convinced the injuries were caused by blows struck to the face – he marked half a dozen at least from the bone evidence – which points to an assault. He told Ransom the Oxfordshire police were holding back for the moment, looking for another explanation.' Sinclair rubbed his chin. 'I can't blame them. We don't seek out murder, do we?' He glanced at his listeners. 'We look for a natural explanation first. But it's hard to find one in this case, or so Stanley thinks.'

'River traffic?' Bennett shifted in his chair. 'That's a busy stretch of the Thames. Half the year round it's jammed with pleasure craft.'

'A boat's propeller, you're thinking, sir? It would have to be several blows.' Sinclair nodded. 'They've considered that. But Stanley gave it as his opinion that the marks on the bones weren't consistent with the shape of propeller blades. He wouldn't go beyond that.'

'What about a paddle steamer?' the chief super suggested.

'It's the Thames, sir, not the Mississippi.'

Crushed, Holly muttered, 'Still there must be other things that could have caused it. We can't be sure it's murder.'

'No, we can't. That's true.'

'And aren't there two quite separate questions here?' The chief superintendent's tone was gruff. He'd not yet recovered his poise. 'First, was it murder at all? And second, is it connected to the Brookham assault?'

'Quite right, Arthur.' Sinclair sought to soothe his superior. 'And I'm not for a moment insisting that it is. But we can't ignore the common factors in these cases: I mean the ages of the girls involved and the damage inflicted to their faces.' He paused. 'Mind you, there's a problem with the time lag, as well. A gap of three years between crimes of this type is most unusual. I'm having a check made of prison records on the off chance that he may have been inside during this period – that's assuming it's the same man – but I'm not overly optimistic. I'm sure if he'd been arrested for a serious sexual offence we would have heard about it by now.'

He caught the assistant commissioner's eye. 'That's all for the present, sir.'

'Good.' Bennett glanced at his watch. 'I've another meeting in five minutes. But let's see if we can reach some interim conclusions before we part.'

Rising, he went to the window and stood there, hands on hips, gazing out. The other two watched him in silence.

'The tramp's still the key, isn't he? Beezy? We must wait till they find him, I think. Until he's been interviewed, until we know whether he's responsible for the

Brookham murder. The Surrey police are quite capable of handling a straightforward inquiry, if that's what this turns out to be. I don't want the Yard butting in and seeming to steal their thunder. All the same, I want to be kept informed of the progress of the investigation. They've no objection to the interest we're showing, I take it?' He glanced over his shoulder.

'Quite the contrary,' Sinclair assured him. He closed his file. 'After listening to Madden, Jim Boyce is as nervous as a cat. Any hint that the case might stretch beyond his domain and he'll be on the phone to me.'

'Still, you seem unsatisfied, Chief Inspector.'

'Oh, no, sir. Not that.' Sinclair shed the frown his superior had noticed. 'By all means let them search for Beezy. What's more, if he can be shown to have been the killer, I'd be inclined to let the whole matter drop, at least as far as the Yard is concerned.'

'You don't think he could have been involved in the Henley business?'

'Hardly. Beal's a man in his fifties. He's known to have spent these past ten summers in Kent. I can't see him suddenly transporting himself to Oxfordshire.' Sinclair shook his head. 'No, if Beezy's their man, I'd be disposed to let this inquiry lapse.'

'What, then? What's troubling you?'

The chief inspector sighed. 'It's what Madden thinks that worries me. He feels we've only touched the surface of this case: that there'll be worse to come. And if past experience is anything to go by, I have to tell you his instincts in these matters are usually right.'

9

THE MADDENS' HOUSE stood at the end of a drive shaded by lime trees. Alerted by the sound of the approaching car, Helen was waiting in the portico to greet Sinclair when he drew up in front.

'Angus . . . how lovely to see you.'

She was wearing an apron, the sleeves of her white blouse rolled to the elbow, and as they exchanged kisses, the chief inspector was prompted to reflect that in years gone by, when Helen's father was still alive and sharing the house with his daughter and son-in-law, visitors had invariably been met at the door by a uniformed maid: the times were indeed changing.

'Mary's busy in the kitchen helping Mrs Beck,' she explained, as though in answer to his unspoken thought. 'We've been bottling all morning. Come inside. I've got a surprise for you. Franz Weiss is here. He's spending a few days with us.'

'Is he really?' Sinclair's face brightened at the name. A psychoanalyst of note, Weiss had been a friend of Helen's late father. Born in Vienna, but now living in Berlin, he was a man for whom the chief inspector felt not only affection, but uncommon respect. 'I had no idea. How is the good doctor?'

'Well enough, but worried. The situation in Germany's so unsettled. They should never have left Vienna.'

She drew him into the house and they passed through the hall to the drawing room.

'Come outside. He's waiting to see you.'

As they stepped out on to the stone-flagged terrace, a figure emerged from the shade of the vine-covered arbour that stood at one end of it. White-haired, and somewhat stooped now – he was in his early seventies – Franz Weiss paused in his tracks to bow with old-world courtesy.

'Chief Inspector! This is an unexpected pleasure.'

'So it is, sir.' Smiling, Sinclair came forward to shake his hand. 'But the pleasure is mine, I insist.'

Though fully two years had passed since their last meeting – the occasion had been a dinner given by the Maddens when Weiss had been in London for a conference on psychoanalysis – he was pleased to see that the doctor had lost none of his alertness; that his eyes, dark, and crinkled at the corners, shone with the same mixture of intelligence and wry humour which the chief inspector remembered with such pleasure from past encounters.

Their acquaintance went back more than a decade to the police investigation into the murders at Melling Lodge when Weiss, by chance, had been visiting England, and Madden, through his relationship with Helen, had obtained advice from him that later proved critical in tracking down the killer he and Sinclair were seeking. The episode had left a deep impression on the chief inspector, who had come to believe as a result of it that insights offered by the new discipline of psychiatry into criminal behaviour might well prove useful to the police in their work. It was a question he had continued to pursue with the analyst on the rare occasions when they met.

'Are you staying in England long, sir?' he asked. 'I was hoping we might lunch in London next week.'

'Alas, I leave tomorrow to return to Berlin.' Weiss spread his hands in a gesture of regret. His English, though fluent, was marked by a strong accent. 'But we have the whole day ahead of us. I've no doubt we will find an opportunity to talk.'

He turned to Helen.

'The chief inspector's work is a source of endless fascination to me. My occupation, I fear, must seem dry by comparison to his. But he is good enough to pretend otherwise.'

He smiled at his hostess.

'And now, my dear, would you excuse me? I have only been waiting here in order to greet our friend. I must return to my labours. We will meet again at lunch . . . yes?'

With a bow to them both, he left the terrace. Helen's eyes followed his departing figure.

'Franz has been up to London twice to talk to old colleagues of his,' she informed Sinclair. 'Men who gave up their practices in Germany to settle over here. He wants to do the same himself, but there are difficulties. Mina is unwell for one thing. He's not sure she's strong enough to travel.'

'Are things so bad in Berlin, then?'

'Bad enough. And likely to get worse, if you happen

to be Jewish, or so Franz says. He thinks the Nazis will soon be in power. Who knows what will happen then? I do worry about them all.'

Her concern came as no surprise to the chief inspector, who knew that as a young woman she had spent six months with the doctor and his wife in Vienna, learning German, and that they had treated her like a daughter.

He was still seeking for some words of reassurance when she turned away to look out over the garden, and he followed the direction of her glance, taking in the vista of the long lawn, bordered by shrubs and flower beds and backed by the green woods of Upton Hanger. It was a view he'd come to love over the years, one he associated with the many happy hours he had spent in this house.

'John's down in the orchard. He's waiting for you.'

The chief inspector said nothing. With some foreboding, he had sensed a slight change in her manner. The memory of their recent conversation at the village fair was still fresh in his thoughts, and he wondered if he was about to be reminded of it.

'You'll find Lucy with him. But don't be deceived by appearances. She's in deep disgrace.'

'Oh, dear . . .' In his relief, Sinclair allowed a grin to escape his lips.

'You may smile, but it's no laughing matter.' Helen's own expression suggested otherwise. 'On her first day at school last week she poured ink over another child and was made to stand in the corner. A whole bottle, no less. People are kind enough to tell me I was just the same at that age, but I refuse to believe them. Ask John to send her up to the house, would you? It's almost time for her lunch.'

She paused then, and he felt her gaze on him.

'You and he can have your talk. But don't be long, please. And remember what I said.'

'I HAD A CUP OF TEA with Jim Boyce in Guildford on the way down. Not only haven't they laid hands on Beezy yet, they've not had a single report of his where-abouts. Your friend Topper's been spotted, though, in the fields near Basingstoke last week. The local bobby was a bit slow off the mark. He sent a message to headquarters asking for instructions, but by the time the reply came back telling him to pick him up, Topper had disappeared again.'

Sinclair had come on his host jacketless and with his sleeves rolled up, hard at work sawing up an old plum tree. The orchard had long since been picked clean, but a sweet smell lingered in the dappled shade from fruit that had rotted on the ground and the sound of the saw was counterpointed by the higher, more delicate buzzing of wasps, few in number now and seemingly weary as the Indian summer drew to its end.

'Tom Cooper's down with rheumatism,' Madden had explained as he broke off his labours to greet his guest. 'I'm standing in for him.'

Mention of the familiar name brought a smile to the chief inspector's lips. Cooper had been the gardener at Melling Lodge, a minor player in the tragedy that had first brought them to Highfield years before, and a reminder of the smallness of the world to which his old colleague had retreated; and where he had found such deep contentment.

Having relayed the message entrusted to him, he had seated himself on the low stone wall bordering the garden, taking out his pipe and tobacco, and waited while Madden went in search of his daughter, who was playing by the stream nearby, and whose cries of delight as she splashed ankle-deep in the shallow water showed precious little sign of repentance. Presently they returned, hand in hand, and trailed by Lucy's companions of the morning, two floppy-limbed puppies, both wet from paddling with their mistress, and generous with the amount of water they distributed about them as they shook themselves dry.

Prompted by her father, the little girl had paused to welcome their guest. The chief inspector had been offered a damp cheek to kiss along with a smile so dazzling he had felt his heart skip a beat.

'And remember to wash your feet under the tap before you go inside.'

The grave tenderness of Madden's expression as he spoke to his daughter reminded Sinclair with a pang of the loss his old friend had suffered many years before. Of the little girl and her mother whom he'd watched die. It was this double blow, the chief inspector believed, that had driven his erstwhile partner to seek oblivion in the trenches.

Madden had waited until they were alone before speaking.

'Well, Angus . . . What can you tell me about the Brookham case?'

He listened now as the chief inspector, puffing on his pipe, revealed what little result his own inquiries had produced.

'There's nothing in the files, as I say; there's only this business at Henley, which has yet to be established as a murder case. The facial assault points to a connection with Brookham, I grant you, and there's also the fact that an attempt seems to have been made to dispose of the body afterwards. But there are still difficulties in linking the two cases, not least the three-year interval separating them. If it was the same man, what's he been doing all this while?'

Madden grunted. 'I take it you've checked prison records?' He was staring at the ground in front of him.

'In detail. We're satisfied he wasn't inside.'

'Mightn't he have gone abroad, then?'

Sinclair shrugged. 'That's certainly a possibility. But not one I can pursue at present: not until the case is officially in my hands, and even then not without further evidence.'

Grimacing, he knocked out his pipe on the wall beside him and then watched as Madden stood brooding, testing the jagged edge of the saw with his fingertips. Plainly he'd hoped to hear better news, and the chief inspector sighed.

'I'm sorry, John. But without some fresh development, it's hard to see how this matter can be taken any further. All we can do now is wait while the hunt for this missing tramp goes on.'

*

THE FEELING, however irrational, that he had let his old colleague down continued to haunt the chief inspector during the day and was still lodged like a burr in the back of his mind when, with the clock on the mantel striking five o'clock and the shadows in the drawing room deepening, he looked up and saw Franz Weiss standing in the doorway.

'Ah, there you are, Mr Sinclair! I was hoping to find you alone. We have not yet had a chance to talk.'

Smiling, the analyst crossed to where his fellow guest was seated by the fireplace with a book on wild flowers open on his lap.

'Is it true our hosts have abandoned us?'

'I'm afraid so, sir.' Sinclair rose to his feet to receive the older man. 'But not for long. John's gone over to Guildford to collect Robert. He took Lucy with him.' The Maddens' son, an absentee from the household, had been playing that day in a school cricket match. 'Then, soon after they left, Helen was called out to see a patient. You find me holding the fort.'

It was the first time the two men had been alone. Apart from a brief appearance at tea-time, when he had joined the others on the terrace, the doctor had remained in his room all afternoon, working. Apologizing for his absence, he'd explained that he had a paper to prepare which he was due to present at a symposium on his return to Berlin.

'The subject to be discussed will be certain aspects of psychopathology, in particular the treatment of patients who indulge in abnormally aggressive and irresponsible behaviour, a difficult question on which to air one's views these days when so many of one's fellow citizens display little else.'

He'd accompanied the remark with a characteristic wry smile, but his words had struck a chord with the chief inspector, echoing as they did a discussion that had taken place earlier, at lunch, when Weiss had spoken at some length about the situation in Germany and his fears for the future. Though aware from newspaper accounts of the turmoil prevailing in that country, so recently an enemy of his own, Sinclair had listened with dismay as the Maddens' foreign visitor drew a picture, blacker than he could have imagined, of a society racked by civil strife and teetering on the brink of political collapse.

Most disturbing of all had been an account given by the doctor of an assault by brown-shirted storm troopers on a group of communist sympathizers which he had witnessed by chance near his consulting rooms in Berlin. Evidently distressed by the memory, he'd described in vivid images the brazen behaviour of the attackers and their indifference to the bodies of the injured which they'd left lying in the street, their blood drying on the cobblestones.

'When civilized man turns so readily to savagery, one can only fear the worst.' Weiss had fixed his dark eyes on Sinclair as he'd uttered these words, seeing him perhaps as one of the law's guardians. 'What restraints are there left, one wonders? Of what crimes is he capable?'

The analyst had made no secret of his anxiety for his family and his desire, ever more pressing, to quit Germany.

'All the signs are that my people are no longer welcome there. At any rate, not with those whose voices are loudest and whose hands are already reaching for power.'

Perceiving that it was not his Austrian nationality Weiss was referring to, Sinclair had felt a flush of discomfiture, and the memory of it served to check his first impulse now, which was to return to the theme of their lunchtime conversation. He wanted to question the analyst further. But having poured him a drink and seen to it that he was settled comfortably by the fire before resuming his own seat, he hesitated, and it was Weiss, his pale face made bright by the blaze, who broke the silence between them.

'Tell me, Chief Inspector, this case you are dealing with, the one to do with the murdered girl, is it causing you much anxiety?'

Though momentarily startled by the question, Sinclair realized at once that Madden must have discussed the assault with the doctor, something Weiss himself confirmed the next moment.

'I ask because John seemed so concerned when he told me about it the other evening. Clearly it has disturbed him a great deal. We did not discuss it at length. Helen was there, and I sensed she was upset by the subject.'

'She thinks he's too caught up with the case,' Sinclair grunted. He'd got over his surprise. 'She's never forgotten how close he came to death all those years ago. She doesn't want him involved in anything like it again. But John won't let go of this.'

Weiss nodded. 'He sees it as his duty, what he owes to others, something presented to him, which he did not seek, but accepts. Our friend is like the Good Samaritan: he cannot pass by on the other side. It is one of the reasons Helen loves him, of course, why she prizes him so. This makes it difficult for them both.'

The shadows in the room had been deepening while they were talking and Sinclair rose to switch on a pair of table lamps. He added another log to the fire and then watched as a shower of sparks flew up the chimney. Behind him the doctor, too, was gazing into the flames, his eyes clouded with thought. Sinclair returned to his seat.

'What did you make of it, sir? The crime itself, I mean? As you probably know, John thinks this man has killed before.'

'So he said. And I can understand why. One must be cautious when drawing conclusions from evidence that is purely circumstantial, but there are strong indications that this was no ordinary predator,' Weiss said.

'You're referring to the post-mortem assault, I assume?' Sinclair sat forward in his chair, curious now. Weiss nodded.

'The battering of the girl's face was most unusual. Although abuse of the victim's corpse is a common feature in cases of this kind – most often it reflects the killer's contempt for the body that has served its purpose – so deliberate an assault has the appearance of a ritual. One should not overlook the care which this murderer took with his preparations, either. Am I right in thinking he carried the child's body some way to the spot he had chosen for the assault?'

'Yes. Through quite dense undergrowth.'

'To where there was a stream. An important detail. Perhaps he already had a picture in his mind of what was to follow. Perhaps he knew he would have to wash the blood from his body afterwards. If we see all this as part of a pattern, then it is hard to believe this man has not committed similar crimes in the past.'

The doctor broke off. He'd shifted his gaze from the fire and was looking at Sinclair, who sat pondering.

'There's something you don't know, sir.' The chief inspector frowned. 'I only told John about it this morning. We've come across a case that might have a bearing on the Brookham murder. It involves a young girl who went missing three years ago in Henley-on-Thames and was presumed drowned. Recently her body was recovered from the river and it was found that her face had been damaged. In the opinion of the pathologist who examined the remains, the injuries were caused by blows. It's too late to tell whether she was raped, of course, or even how she died, but the facial wounds point to a violent assault of some kind.'

'And you think these two cases might be linked?' Weiss's expression showed interest.

'It's a possibility, certainly, and the only lead we've got. But since there's no other indication a killer of this kind has been active in the past, no trace of him in our files, the odds are against there being a connection. I haven't told you, but the Brookham investigation isn't mine as yet, not officially, it's still in the hands of the Surrey police. However, I expect it to arrive on my desk before long, and when it does I'm going to have to decide how to proceed with the inquiry.'

Sinclair paused. His eyes met the analyst's.

'What is it, Chief Inspector?' Weiss set his glass down. 'Is there something you wish to ask me?'

'It's more of a favour I'm seeking, sir.' Sinclair grimaced. 'You may find it an odd request, but I'm looking for advice of a particular kind which only someone in your profession could offer.'

'And what might that be, I wonder?' Weiss smiled. 'I'm curious to learn.'

The chief inspector hesitated. He cocked an eye at his companion.

'Let's assume John's right – this is a man who has killed before, who may even have been active for some time without our being aware of it. Let's go even further and say the Henley girl was one of his victims. Now, as a rule, sexual offenders tend to draw attention to themselves. They become solitaries. Pariahs. Men who stick out like sore thumbs in the community. Even when we can't charge them, we generally know who they are. So what I want to ask you is this – how likely is it that such a man could have slipped the net? Have managed to disguise his true nature and somehow escaped notice? Is it even possible?'

Sinclair waited for Weiss to reply. The analyst had been gazing into the fire as he listened and it was some time before he responded.

'In most instances, the answer to your question would be "no".' He spoke at last. 'But I must qualify my reply. If this individual exists as you imagine him, then we are dealing with an exceptional case, not simply a compulsive rapist and killer, but a man with sufficient self-awareness to have avoided capture over a relatively long period. To call him a psychopath is only to touch on the problem which such people present to my profession, and if I am to be frank I must tell you that in spite of our best efforts we have yet to achieve any great understanding of them. Generally speaking, psychiatry is concerned with the treatment of neuroses, with patients who are aware of their illness and wish to be cured. But where the darkness of the soul is complete, where all sense of right and wrong is lacking, even the most sophisticated clinical approaches have proved ineffectual. To put the question in simple terms, it seems that criminals of this type are born to be what they become, that their condition is organic and beyond the power of any analyst to treat or decipher.'

The frown on the doctor's face had deepened.

'I am giving you my opinion, you understand, rather than any settled medical judgement. This question is still much debated and we are far from a consensus. For my part, however, I have come to believe that there are those born with a predisposition to commit acts appalling to the rest of us and with natures from which all trace of conscience is excluded. Though childhood trauma can never be ruled out as a factor, it is by no means a constant in these cases, and even when present cannot adequately explain the extremes of behaviour we encounter. In the end we are faced with a mystery to which there is as yet no solution. Indeed, if one were seeking proof of the existence of evil – and this is not a search I have ever undertaken, nor wish to believe in – then one need look no further than these monsters who by rights should not exist outside the realm of our nightmares.'

Weiss paused for a few moments, his gaze returning to the fire. Taken aback by what he had heard, the chief inspector waited for him to continue.

'But we are straying from the question you put to me. Let us return to it.' With a sigh, the doctor resettled himself in his chair. 'We are assuming that this man exists and has been active for a number of years. If so, it is clear that he possesses qualities not usually associated with the type. Self-discipline, for one. Although the savagery of the Brookham murder seems to suggest otherwise, it is possible he has been able to suppress his urges for relatively long periods; that the very ferocity of the post mortem attack is a sign of them having been held in check. I made reference to a ritual earlier, and it may be that this battering of his victim's face is his way of giving expression to the dominant emotion of his life, an impulse he must struggle to keep under control.'

'An emotion, you say?' Alerted by the word, Sinclair's eyes narrowed. 'What do you mean, exactly?'

Weiss bit his lip. He seemed unsure how to continue, and his next words confirmed it.

'There is no certainty here. What I offer is only an idea. But it seems to me that this man is possessed, above all, by a feeling of hatred. That there is no other way to read the Brookham crime. To destroy his victim's face in that manner defies rational explanation. That is, unless one assumes that the sexual attack that preceded it was no more than a prelude to what, for him, was the true climax of the act: this last frenzied assault. If so, then it must be the only way he can achieve satisfaction.'

'But hatred ... I don't understand. Hatred for the *girl*? The chances are he'd never set eyes on her before that day.'

The doctor shook his head. 'The emotion I speak of is not personal. Think of it rather as a sickness of the soul.' He saw puzzlement still written on his companion's face. 'You must not seek to apply normal standards of judgement to an individual such as this, Chief Inspector. He is alien to his species, and if he has survived for as long as we think he has, then it can only have been in the knowledge that every man's hand is against him. In the circumstances, it would not be surprising if his own hostility towards others was intense, nor that it should find expression in a sexual context, where satisfaction is denied him. Why he has elected to prey on children, half-women at best, I cannot say, except that they are weak and easily managed and deviants of his kind are seldom able to deal with this area of life except through violence. But the ritual itself – the battering of his victims' faces – almost certainly springs from some event in his past, perhaps even his childhood, and since he seeks to repeat it, one can only assume that it gave him pleasure. A pleasure to which he returns, time and again. Terrible though this thought is.'

In the silence that followed the crackle of a burning log sounded loud, and the sudden flare in the fire that resulted lent a flush to the analyst's pale countenance.

'But this is mere speculation.' He gestured as though

to dismiss it. 'And we are yet to find an answer to your question – how could such a man have eluded discovery for so long?'

'You mentioned self-discipline.' Sinclair took a few seconds to order his thoughts. He had listened in dismay to what Weiss had told him. 'Perhaps he's been able to bring that quality to other areas of his life. To present some kind of front to the world?'

'Oh, undoubtedly.' The doctor was quick to concur. 'There is no question in my mind that if this man exists, he must be remarkable in his way. Above all, he would have the ability to organize his life, to plan ahead, which is by no means the case with most of his kind. It's quite likely he has sought to disguise himself and to adopt, if not a way of life, then at least habits that would tend to mask his true nature. But even so, it's hard to imagine how he could have escaped detection for so long. Given his difference from others – this beast that lies coiled in him – his very presence in any group would be unsettling, and such individuals normally come to the notice of the authorities. Since this has not occurred, we must look for an explanation, and the long interval between these two crimes may provide us with a clue. Have you considered the possibility that he might have spent time abroad? That he moves about?'

The chief inspector nodded. 'John and I were talking about that only this morning. The trouble is, it's not an avenue I can readily explore. Not until the case is officially in my hands.'

'That is unfortunate.' Weiss gnawed at his lip. 'But

there are other areas worth investigating. The question of his background, for example.'

'His background—?'

'His class, if you will.' He shrugged. 'Correct me if I am wrong, but in this country more than any other a man's social position is thought to define him. Peculiarities of manner or behaviour are often overlooked, particularly among the upper classes, where distinction of rank can sometimes render a man above suspicion. But perhaps I exaggerate . . .' He had noticed the chief inspector's frown.

About to resume, he paused as the sound of the front door shutting came to their ears. Footsteps echoed in the stone-flagged hall. They heard Helen's voice: she was speaking to Mary, the Maddens' maid. The two men caught each other's eye.

'We must conclude, yes?' Weiss spoke in a murmur. 'I have only one more suggestion – it's little more than a thought – but it occurs to me that a murderer of this type might have found protection, or rather anonymity, in some unorthodox way of life, outside the law.'

'You mean he might be a criminal . . . a professional?' Sinclair was momentarily arrested by the notion. But then he shook his head. 'No . . . no, I don't think so. We have many sources in that world. If a killer like this had been at large, we would have heard of it. More than that: he'd have been given up.'

'No doubt you are right.' But the doctor seemed unconvinced. 'Nevertheless, he has managed to survive somehow, and it might be as well if you considered the possibility that he has found some form of employment suited to his nature, one that has served as a disguise and has prevented him from coming to your notice.'

'Suited to his nature! Surely not.' Afraid that Helen might appear at any moment, Sinclair kept his voice low. But he spoke forcefully. 'Just think what you're saying, doctor. This is a killer of children!'

'Yes, of course. But you misunderstand me.' Distressed at the way his words had been taken, Weiss leaned closer. 'I'm suggesting you look at the broader picture. The savagery of his crimes tells us something about the man; something important. This is a creature devoid of all moral restraints: one surely capable of other, equally ruthless acts. Other crimes.'

'I understand what you're saying, sir.' Hearing the sound of approaching steps, Sinclair leaned forward in turn. 'But where does that leave us? What place could he possibly have found for himself?'

'That I cannot tell you.' With a sigh, the doctor shook his head. 'All I can do is urge you not to dismiss the notion.' Dropping his voice still further, he peered at the chief inspector through the deepening shadows. 'We may wish it were otherwise, but the world has a use for such men. It has always been so.'

PART TWO

10

'THIS WILL have to be brief, Chief Inspector. I've a meeting in Whitehall in half an hour.'

Assistant Commissioner Bennett ushered Sinclair to a chair in front of his desk. He took note of his purposeful air.

'You've spoken to your colleagues in Surrey and Sussex, I take it? They're happy about us moving in?'

'Quietly ecstatic would be closer to the mark, sir.' Sinclair settled himself without delay. He'd come in haste from his office. 'This case is going to be the very devil to crack. Nobody seems sure what to do next.'

Before he could say more the door opened and the reassuring bulk and rubicund features of Arthur Holly appeared.

'Come in, Chief Superintendent.' Bennett gestured to a second chair. 'You've heard the news, I imagine?'

'Angus rang me a moment ago, sir.' Holly nodded to the chief inspector. 'So they've found another one? Near Bognor Regis, I understand?'

'That's right. The Sussex police uncovered the body two days ago. The chief constable got in touch with us overnight. This is now officially a Yard case. Mr Sinclair will be in charge from our end and will keep us informed on a regular basis. Where do we stand now, Chief Inspector? Briefly, if you would. There's no doubt, is there, that it's linked to the Brookham business?'

'None at all, sir.' Sinclair had his file already opened on his lap. 'Both girls were raped and strangled, faces destroyed in the same manner in post-mortem assaults. However, there was *one* difference.' He glanced up. 'The body found near Bognor Regis showed traces of chloroform in the lungs. It's presumably what he used to immobilize her.'

'There was no mention of that in the Brookham report.' Bennett frowned.

'No, but I've had a word with Dr Galloway – the pathologist who dealt with the body – and he points out that the killer in that instance drowned the girl as well as strangled her. It's quite possible that any traces of chloroform in her lungs or what was left of her nasal passages could have been washed away.'

Bennett grunted. 'Go on, Chief Inspector.'

'Now, as regards the weapon employed for the facial assaults, Galloway has plumped for a hammer, and I gather the Sussex doctor's of the same opinion. Mind you, *his* cadaver is in rather worse condition.'

'Why's that?' Holly intervened.

'Of course – you don't know, Arthur.' Sinclair turned to his colleague. 'The murder in Sussex *pre-dates* the Brookham killing, by as much as a month. That's according to medical opinion, and it's confirmed by the time of her disappearance, which was late July. Her body was found on the coast near Bognor Regis – the girl's name was Marigold Hammond, by the way. It's a flat, fairly empty stretch of shoreline and the corpse was buried in a shallow grave in a patch of reeds and scrubland, covered with loose earth and pebbles – the beaches are shingled there – no more than fifty yards from the sea. Once again he took pains to hide the body. We were lucky at Brookham. The corpse was found within hours, thanks to Madden.' The chief inspector's face darkened. 'I only wish we'd used the time better. The Surrey police have spent the past month looking for that blasted tramp. What's more they *still* have to find him.'

'Because he might be a witness, you mean?' Holly put the question.

'Exactly. In fact, the more I think about John's reading of the murder site, the more convinced I am that he was right. It's odds on this Beezy actually caught sight of the killer. That's why he ran for it, dropping some of his belongings on the way. God alone knows where he is now. Not in *our* hands, that's for certain.' The chief inspector glowered. He caught Bennett's eye.

'Yes, sir, I'm sorry. *Briefly*, then, all we can say for sure about our killer at this stage is that he's *not* Beezy – who was in Surrey for all of July, moving about within a relatively small area, and who's most unlikely to have had a bottle of chloroform about his person – and that in all likelihood he owns a car. In hindsight, it seems probable that both girls were picked up on the road – one between Brookham and Craydon, the other near Bognor Regis. How he persuaded them to get into his car we can only speculate, but once there he could have used the chloroform to render them senseless.'

As Sinclair paused to clear his throat, Holly interrupted.

'You say she vanished in July, the girl at Bognor Regis. Have the police been searching for her since then?'

'The answer to that question is no, Arthur. Though you may well ask it. The child wasn't even reported missing until a week ago. It's an extraordinary story. Believe it if you can.' The chief inspector shook his head. 'Her parents are circus people. Not performers, her mother runs a sideshow, but they travel all over the south coast during the summer months and they happened to be at Bognor Regis when the child went missing. Except it wasn't recognized as such at the time. She'd had a row with her mother and the man they were living with – the girl's father had gone off some time before, he doesn't figure in this – and announced that she was leaving to go and spend some time with an aunt of hers who worked in another circus that was performing in Eastbourne at the time. It was something she'd done before, apparently, and for much the same reason.'

'*Before?*' The chief superintendent was incredulous. 'And how old was this girl? Twelve or so?'

'No . . . and that's an interesting point.' Sinclair tugged at an earlobe. 'Marigold Hammond was fourteen, but she looked younger. This killer seems drawn to girls before they reach puberty.' He caught Holly's look. 'Yes, I know, Arthur, even fourteen seems too young, but all I can tell you is it doesn't seem to have bothered her mother when she packed a suitcase and announced she was off to catch the bus to Eastbourne.'

'But when she didn't hear from her . . . ?'

'There again . . .' Sinclair shook his head in despair.

'We have to understand . . . these people live their lives differently from you and me. They've no telephone to ring up with, and I doubt they correspond by letter. Mrs Hammond just assumed her daughter had joined up with her aunt in Eastbourne and only discovered six weeks later that she'd never appeared there, at which point she reported her missing. The circus she was with had moved on to Devon by then, but she came back to Bognor Regis to help the police, who began searching right away. It took them a further week to find the girl's body.'

'I'll be blowed!' Holly was speechless.

Bennett cleared his throat. 'What next, Chief Inspector? Where do we go from here? I take it you don't plan to interfere with the Sussex investigation?'

'Oh, no, sir. Nor the one in Surrey. As I said, they still have to find the tramp. We may yet have a witness to the Brookham killing. For the time being our best role would be one of coordination. I plan myself to go down to Sussex tomorrow to talk to the officers conducting that investigation. God knows I don't envy them. The trail must be stone cold by now.'

'What about the Henley angle? The girl whose body was found in the Thames? Do you mean to take any action over that?'

'Yes, I do, sir. Mind you, it's still a sensitive issue. I've spoken to the Oxfordshire police. They're no longer inclined to treat it as a case of accidental death. But they're undecided as to how to launch an investigation, particularly with the body in the state it's in. However, I've been informed confidentially that they plan to open a murder inquiry soon. Once it's official, they'll be only too pleased to accept our help. In the meantime, I've told them we'd like to sniff around discreetly, and they've informed the Henley police accordingly. I'm sending a man down there tomorrow.'

Bennett glanced at his watch. 'I can give you another three minutes, Chief Inspector. Where do we stand with the press?'

'Like us, they're sniffing around, sir.' Sinclair shut his file. 'They didn't make too much of the Brookham murder, thankfully. But with this latest body discovered and the Yard called in, they're bound to take an interest. Still, the subject's not an easy one for the newspapers to handle. Sexual crimes involving children are something we all instinctively shy away from, and their readers are no different. So far, published details concerning the facial injuries have been kept to a minimum, and if my wishes are heeded that will continue. Needless to say, they've no idea yet that the inquiry might stretch back several years. That's something I'd particularly like to keep from them. We'll have to see how we go.'

Bennett nodded. 'Very well. That will do for now.' He rose. 'Gentlemen . . .'

As they walked back to their offices Holly's broad brow creased in a frown.

'Do you really feel it's worth pursuing this Henley business, Angus? The connection seems very iffy to me.'

'Perhaps. But I want to get to the bottom of it, just the same. There's a good chance this man may have been active for longer than we think, and if that proves to be the case, it puts a quite different complexion on things.'

The memory of his conversation with Franz Weiss not long since was still vivid in the chief inspector's mind.

'Well, I wish you luck.' They had reached the chief superintendent's office and he paused at the door. 'Who are you sending down, anyway?'

'An officer I've had my eye on for some time now, a detective sergeant.' Sinclair opened the door for his superior. 'Come to think of it, he did his first serious work under Madden. John thought very highly of him.'

'I'm duly impressed.' The chief super's deep laugh rumbled in the corridor. 'Now all I need to know is his name.'

'Why, it's Styles, of course.' Sinclair smiled broadly. 'Billy Styles. I thought you'd have remembered that, Arthur.'

11

THE TRAFFIC that morning was light, and Billy was glad of it. The old Morris he'd been allocated from the Yard's car pool had tired gears and a tendency to stall. Not that he was complaining, mind you. Still clear in his memory were the days when motor cars provided for the use of detectives had been rarer than unicorns.

The very concept of mobile policing hadn't taken hold in the Met until the early twenties. The first patrols had been restricted to bands of uniformed police who'd been ferried around the capital – stopping at prearranged points to telephone headquarters – in a pair of vans bought second hand from the RAF. Some wag had dubbed them the 'Flying Squad' and the name had stuck. Now a fleet of wireless-equipped cars roamed the streets of London day and night and the roof of Scotland Yard spouted a forest of aerials.

All that notwithstanding, the job Billy had been assigned wouldn't normally have called for a car. He could just as easily have taken the train to Henley. But Chief Inspector Sinclair wanted him to have freedom of movement when he got there.

'Don't pay too much attention to what the local police tell you,' he'd advised the sergeant. 'They've got some explaining to do. Nose around on your own if you can.

Bear in mind, if it's the same man he would have had a car.'

The summons to report to the chief inspector's office had come out of the blue, and Billy had responded to it with alacrity. After a dozen years with the Met he could look back on a varied career during which he'd been involved in a wide range of investigations.

None, however, had approached the drama of the Melling Lodge case, and Billy had never forgotten the nerve-racked weeks he had spent in the company of the then Inspector Madden as they'd searched for a savage murderer.

The inquiry had been conducted under Sinclair's leadership, and, ever since, Billy had nursed the hope that the chief inspector might hold him in some special regard. Whenever they met, as they sometimes did, in one of the corridors at the Yard, the older man would pause for a word, and Billy retained the feeling, which dated from their very first meeting, of being perpetually weighed in the balance of Angus Sinclair's steady flint-grey gaze.

His greeting when he'd arrived in Sinclair's office the previous day had been warm.

'Sergeant! It's been a while. How are you?' Sinclair had risen from behind his desk to shake Billy's hand. 'I spent last weekend with the Maddens. John was asking after you. I trust you keep in touch.'

'Oh, yes, sir.' Billy had taken the chair indicated. 'I go down and see them quite often.'

Sometimes for a whole weekend, just like the chief inspector had done, he might have added, though on the first such occasion Billy had been so nervous at the prospect of a dinner party his host and hostess were giving that evening he'd barely found the courage to present himself in the drawing room beforehand, and it had taken all of Helen Madden's skill in the art of gentle teasing to restore him to his usual cheery self.

'You're not married, are you?' Sinclair had inquired. 'Or am I mistaken?'

'Not entirely, sir. Engaged, as it happens.' Billy grinned.

'Well, well! Congratulations.' The chief inspector leaned forward and they shook hands formally. 'What's the young lady's name?'

'Elsie Osgood, sir. We met when I was posted to Clapham for a spell last year. She owns a small dress shop down there. We're getting married next spring.'

'I wish you both well.' Sinclair regarded the younger man benignly. Then his expression changed. 'You've heard about Madden finding that child's body, I take it?'

'The Brookham killing? Yes, sir. It was all round the Yard.' Billy straightened in his chair. He guessed he was about to learn the reason for his summons. 'And now there's been another one, I see. Down Bognor Regis way.'

'Quite right. That's why you're here. The cases are clearly linked and the Yard's been called in. But there's more to it than that. It's possible the murderer has killed before. At Henley, three years ago. That's where you'll be going tomorrow.'

Billy felt a tingle of excitement. Mention of Madden's name had reminded him of that day, far off, but still fresh in his memory, when the two of them had been sent flying to Waterloo station to catch a train bound for Highfield. He watched as the chief inspector picked up a buff-coloured folder from his desk, then paused before speaking again, as though to underline the importance of what he was about to say.

'This is not only a serious matter, Sergeant. It's one of particular urgency. As I'm sure you know, sexual criminals have a tendency to offend again, and that's specially true when it comes to attacks involving children. The man we're hunting is extremely dangerous. And violent. But what concerns me even more is that he may think he's in the clear, that no one's picked up his trail yet. You'll grasp the implications of that, I'm sure.'

Billy nodded. 'It means, likely as not, he's already on the lookout for another victim.'

'Precisely.' The chief inspector hefted the file for a moment, then handed it across the desk to Billy. 'Most of what we know is in there. Take it away and read it. Then come back in an hour and I'll tell you what I want you to do.'

HENLEY POLICE STATION was situated in a double-storey brick building in the middle of the town, a few minutes walk from the riverside. The desk sergeant was expecting Billy – he'd rung to let them know he was coming – and directed him to an office upstairs where he found a sour-faced plain-clothes man called Deacon awaiting his arrival.

'You'll want to see this, I suppose.' Deacon tossed

him a file across the desk, the papers spilling out as Billy clutched at it. Grey-haired and in his fifties, he seemed put out to discover that they were the same rank, both detective sergeants. Discontent sat lodged at the corners of his mouth, which was turned down in a sneer. 'So they're calling it murder now . . .' His shrug was defiant.

'You don't agree?' Billy held out his packet of cigarettes to Deacon, who shook his head. Noticing there was no ashtray on the desk between them, the younger man pocketed his fags. He wanted to keep this friendly.

'I've got no opinion one way or the other.' Deacon's pale brown eyes were expressionless. 'They can *call* it what they want. But I'd like to see anyone prove it was murder.'

'The injuries to her face, though? Is there any way those could have been accidental?' Leafing through the file, Billy realized he was familiar with much of its contents. Sinclair had obtained a summary from Oxford. He remembered Deacon's name now as that of the CID officer who'd been in charge when Susan Barlow's body had been recovered from the water two months earlier.

'Yes, since you ask.' Deacon sat forward, elbows on the desk. 'She disappeared originally during the month of July. You probably don't know what the river's like in summer. Let me tell you, son. It's chock-a-block with boats. After she drowned, the body wouldn't have surfaced for several hours, probably at night. She could have got knocked about, been hit over and over, and without anyone even knowing it.'

And every time in the face? *Come on!* thought Billy, but he continued listening with the same friendly, slightly puzzled air as Deacon tried to justify himself. Tried to explain how he could have made such a basic error as to mark down Susan Barlow's death as accidental *without stopping to think*.

It was the sort of mistake Billy no longer made himself, and if his older colleague had been more observant he might have noticed an inner stillness in this fresh-faced detective from London as he sat nodding, apparently agreeing with every word Deacon said, taking no exception to the Henley detective's bored, dismissive manner.

Billy dated his coming-of-age from the brief time he'd spent working under Madden. The foundations of his career as an investigator had been well laid then, but by his own reckoning, the most valuable lesson he had learned from his superior was that the work they did could never be just a job. That it was necessary to care.

'I noticed her body was found half a mile upstream from the town. Was that a surprise?'

Deacon's eyebrows, though raised, suggested no such response on his part. Rather, they implied disbelief at what he was hearing.

'Not to me, son. You've got to start from the premise that she fell into the water, but you can take it from me there's nothing unusual about *that*. Not hereabouts. Happens all the time, particularly with kids. The bank can be unstable ... treacherous. You stray too close to it, or start reaching for something in the water, and next thing you know you've tumbled in and the current's got hold of you.'

'Yes, but that *far* upstream ...' Billy wanted to make

his point. 'The Barlow house was, what, less than a mile from the centre of Henley? Even supposing she walked back along the river and fell in somehow, wouldn't her body have been swept down closer to the town itself, or even past it?'

Having gone through the file in London a couple of times, Billy had concluded there was little *mystery* about Susan Barlow's movements that August day. All that was in question, really, was the route she'd taken to return home after running an errand for her mother, who had asked her to slip into Henley and buy some oranges; something she'd forgotten to do herself earlier. The house where the two of them lived – Mrs Barlow was a widow whose husband had been killed in the war – lay on a lane that followed the course of the Thames upstream, running quite close to it for a few miles before linking up with the main road to Reading. It was on the outskirts of the town and the walk to the shops would have taken the girl about fifteen minutes.

Her safe arrival there had been confirmed by the greengrocer who had sold her the oranges. She had left the shop well before half-past eleven with her purchase wrapped in a brown paper packet, having given no indication that she meant to do anything other than return home directly. When midday came and went with no sign of her daughter, Mrs Barlow had walked into Henley herself and spoken to the greengrocer, who confirmed the girl had been there recently. She had then wandered about the town for a little while, asking various friends and acquaintances if they had seen Susan, before returning home herself in the hope that her daughter had reappeared by now. Finding she had not, the distracted mother had finally rung the police and the wheels of an organized search had ground slowly into motion.

It was at that point that the question of *how* Susan had gone home, which route she might have taken, had become crucial. The quickest road back would have been the way she had come, along the lane, but she could also have walked further upstream along the river bank for anything up to a mile and then taken one of several footpaths, all of which connected with the lane, and so returned home by a roundabout route.

That she'd obviously chose this latter alternative was Deacon's contention now. (It was also the answer the police had reluctantly come to three years earlier.) Somehow Susan Barlow must have stumbled into the river during her homeward walk and her body had been swept away by the strong current and failed to surface for some reason.

'Like I say, she could easily have walked a mile up the river and then come across the fields and walked back down to her mum's house. At least, that's what she had in mind, only somewhere along the way she went into the river. After that, there'd be no telling what might have happened with the current. Sometimes bodies get brought down here, other times they get lodged in the bank, like this one did.'

'She was spotted on that riverside path, was she?' Billy still wasn't clear on this point, despite having read Chief Inspector Sinclair's file carefully, and Deacon's reply did nothing to clear up his uncertainty.

'Yes and no. There were witnesses who thought they'd seen her, or someone like her.' He shrugged. 'It was before my time here, but I know we had a description of what she was wearing from her mother. It was a pink dress. But have you any idea of how many young girls are running up and down that path all summer? And how many of them might be wearing pink dresses?'

Billy considered what he'd just heard. It made a difference.

'I'll hang on to this for a little while if I may.' He tapped the folder on his knee. 'But I'd like to go and have a look at the general area now. Would you care to come along?'

'Couldn't possibly, son. I'm due at the Magistrates' Court in ten minutes. And I'm afraid my two detective constables are out.'

'Never mind,' Billy said, taking care to disguise his relief at the news, 'I'll manage on my own.'

'Oh, we can't have that. I've got a PC waiting to show you around. Name of Crawley.' Deacon produced a thin smile. It was his first of the morning.

BILLY TOOK OFF his hat and wiped his perspiring face with a handkerchief. Although the October sun had lost much of its summer strength, his skin felt tender. The pale complexion he'd inherited from his mother, along with her reddish hair, made him prone to sunburn. 'I'm not keeping company with a lobster,' Elsie had murmured to him not long ago as she rubbed oil on his back and shoulders. They'd gone on a day trip to Brighton and were lying in their bathing costumes on the shingle beach. Recalling the softness of her fingers on his skin, Billy felt warmth of another kind flooding into his cheeks. He watched as a pair of swans floated by on the current.

'Is that it, then, Sarge? Are we done?'

PC Crawley stood beside Billy with folded arms, his eyes busy beneath his helmet as a trio of young girls dressed in light rayon frocks, their arms and legs bare, went strolling by. Downy about the cheeks himself, he hardly looked old enough to be wearing a policeman's uniform.

'Not yet, Constable.' Billy didn't need to recall Deacon's smile to realize he'd been handed a lemon. Even by the standards of the Henley plod this young copper was a dim bulb.

He let his gaze wander along the river bank. Close by, on their left, was the flagged terrace of a pub, its tables overlooking the bronze-coloured Thames. Just beyond it a bridge spanned the river, and past that, further downstream, lay the straight patch of water where the famous regatta was held each summer. Billy had come to watch it once with some pals a few years ago. They had spent the day drinking beer in one of the marquees erected for the occasion and cheering with the rest of the crowd as the narrow boats, propelled by flashing oars, shot through the water like arrows.

Most of the holiday activity was centred there, he noted. The regatta was long over, but there were still a few campers in the fields lower down, their tents easy to pick out against the green meadowgrass, while the river, though no longer 'chock-a-block', remained busy with pleasure craft and other waterborne traffic.

Upstream, in the opposite direction, the view was different. They were close to the outskirts of the town, standing on a section of paved path that soon petered out into a dirt footway which continued along the tree-clad river bank. For several miles, according to PC Crawley. Billy had already got the constable to show him the spot where Susan Barlow's body had been taken from the water. He'd been able to do that, though not much more.

'I only got posted here six months ago, Sarge,' Crawley had explained defensively when Billy tried to find out how the original search had been conducted. He'd had to turn to the file for more, and discovered that the searchers had concentrated their efforts on the stretch of river below the bridge, which made sense. That was the direction a floating object would take, after all. It was pure chance alone that had brought Susan Barlow's body to rest on the bank upstream.

Billy had spent some time studying the site, a small cove on an outer bend of the river. The log beneath which the remains of Susan's body had been found was still there, drawn up on the bank now, a piece of rotting tree trunk, stripped of its bark. It was possible to imagine how the current, swinging around at that point, might have carried the body, semi-submerged, into this shallow inlet. Trapped beneath the log, half-buried in the mud, it would have remained unaffected by the subsequent rise and fall of the river. A belt of undergrowth, separating the cove from the path, screened it from sight on the landward side, and its presence there had not been noted until some weeks ago when a couple in a rowing boat had pulled in to the bank and been greeted by the grisly spectacle of the girl's arm, or what was left of it, protruding from the mud.

Assuming it was a case of murder, how had she got there?

Not the obvious way. Not by walking up the river on her own and encountering some stranger bent on rape and murder. Having examined the route carefully, Billy was certain of that now. Though hidden from the water by brush and overhanging branches, the path was mostly visible to the open fields it skirted on its inward side, and these all showed signs of having been used as camp sites during the summer. What was more, it was clearly a well-used footway. Even today, when the holiday season was over, they had encountered two families with small children and had passed a group of hikers camping out in one of the riverside meadows. Billy simply couldn't picture the man – this careful killer – seizing hold of the girl in broad daylight, overpowering her and dragging her off to some secluded spot, all the while with the danger of discovery hanging over him.

No, it couldn't have happened that way.

'Come on, Crawley.'

Billy turned his back on the river and led the constable up a flight of shallow stone steps and across a small gravelled garden, bordered by flower beds, to the lane where he'd left his car. This was the same road Susan Barlow had taken when she'd walked into Henley to buy her packet of oranges; and the one she'd used to get home, too. Or so he believed now. Only she'd never got there.

He paused on the pavement, looking up and down the narrow lane. A picture was forming in his mind, and the image wasn't pleasant. He saw the girl in her pink dress, with her brown paper packet clutched in her hand, walking in the shade along the grassed verge. He saw the car drawing up quietly behind her . . .

What words had he got prepared, the smooth-tongued stranger? What invitation had proved so irresistible that Susan Barlow had been persuaded to climb into the car and join him in the front seat? Billy scowled at the thought.

'Are we going back to the station now?' Crawley asked hopefully. 'It's getting on for lunch-time.'

An hour later the constable's stomach was rumbling with hunger and Billy, too, was unsatisfied. He was beginning to think Deacon might be right. There was no way of proving that Susan Barlow's death had resulted from murder.

Sinclair had warned him of the likelihood that his journey would be wasted. 'These old cases have gone cold, I'm afraid. We'll be lucky if we find anything new. But keep an eye open for any similiarities to the Brook-ham murder.'

Billy had started from the supposition that Susan Barlow had been a victim of opportunity. There was obviously no way the murderer could have known she would be walking into town that morning. But he must have been hunting, all the same, Billy felt, on the lookout for prey, and that argued he'd had somewhere in mind to take any child who fell into his hands. Given where the body was eventually found, it meant he'd already reconnoitred the river bank and found some spot upstream where he could park his car discreetly.

Returning to his own vehicle, Billy had spent the next sixty minutes with an increasingly unhappy Crawley exploring the winding, tree-shaded road that led to what the constable assured him had been Mrs Barlow's cottage. He already knew that the bereaved mother had moved away, unable to bear the associations which the place held for her. Pausing only briefly, he'd continued driving along the lane, noting several spots where a car might have been driven off the road and parked under cover of trees and bushes, but none which seemed to offer the kind of privacy that the killer would surely have wanted.

Billy took it for granted that the girl must have been rendered unconscious, chloroformed perhaps soon after she'd got into the killer's car (if that was what had happened). Her abductor could hardly have driven his passenger past her own house without provoking some reaction on her part. But *where* had he taken his captive?

As he pondered this question, Billy's eyes kept flicking towards the mileage indicator. They had already covered two and a half miles since leaving the town centre.

Not back to Henley, certainly. So it must have been beyond the Barlow cottage. But while this fitted the facts, such as they were – the girl's body could easily have floated some way down the river before coming to rest on the bank – Billy just couldn't picture the killer taking her any great distance.

Quite apart from the urgency of his desire, he must have been aware of the danger she represented for him. It didn't matter whether she was conscious or not, every moment she spent in his car placed him in dire peril and he would have wanted to do what he had to do as quickly as possible, so as to be rid of her damning presence.

Billy's glance went back to the dashboard. *Three* miles now. According to the map he'd studied before setting out, they would shortly be linking up with the main road to Reading. It was far enough. He looked for a place to turn round and noticed a signboard on the road ahead. It bore a name – Waltham Manor – printed in gold against a green background, and below that, in smaller letters, the words 'Members Only'.

'What's this, then?' he asked, braking to turn onto a strip of dirt road. Ahead of him he saw a pair of gates standing open in a high stone wall.

Constable Crawley, who hadn't said a word for the past half hour, though his stomach had been audible, now produced a sound that in other circumstances Billy might have taken for a snigger.

'Constable?'

'It's a sort of club, Sarge. They call themselves gym . . . gymnos . . . gym somethings . . .' He was quaking with suppressed laughter.

'What are you trying to say?' Billy demanded. *Christ!*

Where did they find them? 'What sort of club? What do they do?'

Crawley let out a hoot of laughter. 'They take their clothes off . . .' he gurgled.

'You mean it's a nudists' club?'

The constable nodded, wordless now. His downy cheeks had turned bright red.

Billy stopped the car and stared at him. He shook his head, then started to reverse, intending to back onto the paved road, but at once felt a heavy drag on the steering wheel.

'Bloody hell!'

They got out. Just as Billy suspected, the front near-side tyre had punctured on a sharp stone. A few moments later, having opened the boot, they made a further discovery.

'There's no jack,' Crawley announced.

'Brilliant deduction, Holmes.' Billy kicked the flat tyre in frustration. He was thinking of the long drive he still had back to London. 'Come on . . .'

Beyond the gates of Waltham Manor, where a sign warned them this was private property and trespassers would be prosecuted, an elm-lined drive led to an imposing stone mansion with a handsome portico. A further sign, marked 'Reception', directed them to a gravelled parking area at the side of the house from which point a long white paling fence was visible.

'Is that where they take their clothes off?' Billy asked. There were only a dozen or so cars in the parking lot. Business must be slack, he thought.

The constable nodded. 'There's a lot of ground fenced in at the back of the house. You can't see in from any side. When they started up they used the whole garden, I was told. But then the local lads began shinning up the wall to peep over, so they had to build that fence.' He emitted his peculiar hooting laugh. 'Now everything goes on inside there and they've let the rest go.' He nodded towards the parkland further off, where the bushes had grown into tangled thickets and the grass, uncut, was knee high.

A brick path at the end of the parking area led to a door in the side of the house. Billy opened it and was startled to see a young man, apparently wearing nothing, sitting at a long table in the middle of the room, reading a magazine. He glanced up as they entered, his bored expression changing to one of consternation at the sight of Crawley's uniform.

'My name's Styles. Detective Sergeant Styles.' Billy showed him his warrant card. 'We've had a puncture outside your gates and we've got no jack. I was wondering if someone here could help.'

'I'll have to ask Dorrie,' the young man said, getting to his feet; he was, after all, wearing bathing trunks. 'Just a mo . . .'

He disappeared through a door at the back of the room, leaving them alone.

'Cor! What do you think of that, Sarge?' Crawley was grinning from ear to ear.

Billy ignored him. Instead he turned his attention to a framed scroll got up to look like parchment that was hanging on the wall behind the table. Headed *The Gymnosophist's Creed*, it went on for several paragraphs.

The door opened and a young woman entered, wearing a white linen robe, belted at the waist and reaching to her knees. She had short brown hair, fashioned into rolls at the back of her neck, and a quick, birdlike glance.

'Hullo, boys. What's the problem?' She grinned, as though to excuse the familiarity.

Billy explained their predicament again.

'Sergeant, is it?' Smiling, she eyed him with interest.

'Yes ... Styles. And this is Constable Crawley.'

'My name's Doris ... Doris Jenner.' She held out her hand to Billy and as she did so her gown fell open and one of her breasts, quite bare, was revealed for a moment. Unflustered, she covered it swiftly. 'Sorry about that ... you get careless working here.' She remained smiling. 'It's a jack you need, then? Mr Rainey would have one – he's the manager – but he's out at present. Tell you what, I'll see if one of the members can help. Wait here.' Her glance shifted for an instant to the constable, beside Billy, and she smothered a laugh. Then she turned and went out.

Billy looked at the young PC. He was staring after her, mouth hanging open, face the colour of a ripe tomato.

'For Christ's sake, Constable!' Billy's patience snapped. 'Pull yourself together. Haven't you seen a naked woman before?'

'No, Sarge, I haven't.'

'Bloody hell!'

A minute later Doris Jenner returned with a set of keys and they went outside into the parking area where she retrieved a jack from the boot of one of the parked cars. Billy handed it to the constable.

'Off you go. Change the tyre, then bring the car up here.' He felt a compelling need to dispense with the other's company, if only for a quarter of an hour.

'What, me, Sarge?'

'Yes, you, Crawley.' A sudden suspicion struck Billy. 'You can *drive*, can't you?'

'Yes, of course.' The young man was affronted.

'Get on with it, then.'

Hands on hips, Billy watched him stride off, boots crunching on the gravel. He turned to find Doris Jenner observing them with a crooked grin.

'How'd you get landed with that one?'

Unable to think of a fitting response, he changed the subject. 'You wouldn't have such a thing as a cup of tea, would you?'

'Of course, Sergeant. Come inside.'

She led him through the outer room, where the young man in the bathing trunks had resumed his place at the table, into an adjoining office furnished with a desk and some easy chairs grouped around a low table. The walls were hung with paintings showing men and women as God made them dancing in the open air or stretched out on the grass in decorative poses.

'Nymphs and shepherds,' Miss Jenner said drily, cocking an eye at them. 'Make yourself at home. I'll be back in a minute.'

Billy used the time she was away to run through in his mind the results of the day's inquiries. They were scant. He felt he could report to Sinclair with some assurance that the circumstances surrounding Susan Barlow's death were suspicious enough to warrant further investigation. But beyond that he could only offer speculation unsupported by evidence.

'Is this your first time in a nudists' club?' Doris Jenner had returned with a tea tray and a plate of biscuits. She declined Billy's offer of a cigarette, but pushed an ashtray over to his side of the glass-topped table.

'Yes, but I've read about them.' Billy reached out for his cup. 'I thought the fad was dying out.'

'It is.' She'd seated herself opposite him, modestly drawing the robe tightly around her, but tucking her bare feet up on the chair so that Billy found himself gazing at a pair of rosy knees. There was a teasing look in her eye and he was glad he wouldn't have to report this encounter to Elsie Osgood, who had a jealous streak which he didn't take lightly. 'A couple of years ago the parking lot would have been packed. We were turning people away. I give them another year at most.'

'Have you been here since it opened?' Billy lit a cigarette.

She nodded. 'I was working in an office in Henley when I heard they were looking for staff. It's not a bad job, if you don't mind taking off your clothes.' Her crooked grin displayed the tips of her small, pointed teeth. 'Well, most of them. Only the members strip down completely.'

'I didn't know that.' Biting into a piece of shortbread, Billy returned her grin. The thought of Constable Crawley's hunger pangs aroused no tremor of remorse in him.

'So what brings the law up this way?' She put down her cup.

'Routine inquiries.' His comic policeman's voice brought a bubbling laugh from her lips. 'It's true, though.' He went on in more serious vein. 'A young girl disappeared in Henley a while back, and her body's only recently been recovered from the river. We're trying to establish her movements, based on where it was found. It's no easy job. She went missing three years ago.'

Doris Jenner was gazing out of the window. Her eyes had grown misty. 'Poor kid ... I remember when it happened ... Susan ... Wasn't that her name?'

'You've got a good memory.' Billy was impressed.

'Not really ... it was something else, something that happened to me that day ... or rather it *didn't* ...' She smiled mischievously. 'Now don't get me started, Sergeant.' She reached across the table for his cup and refilled it.

Billy waited for her to go on. He was enjoying their conversation. There was a flirtatious edge to her manner that flattered his male vanity. 'Go on,' he prompted.

'You don't want to hear about it.'

'Maybe I do.' He was half-flirting himself, but his words held a germ of truth. One of the reasons he was a good detective – quite apart from the skills he'd acquired – was a basic curiosity in his nature. He was interested in people – why they were who they were. He didn't have to force himself in that direction. It came naturally.

And he listened as he always did, out of habit now, as he had once observed John Madden listen.

Doris Jenner collected herself in her chair. Her brown eyes twinkled. 'All right, then. But remember – you asked.' Her glance was provocative. 'It all has to do with a boyfriend I had then – his name was Jimmy. He was a member here. That's how we met. Jimmy lived in Birmingham, but he used to drive down every Saturday in a big fancy car. You couldn't mistake it, and I used to sit at the desk outside and watch for him through the window.' She smiled, her eyes hazy with reminiscence.

'We never let on, of course. The staff's not allowed to fraternize with members. But I always had Sundays off and when I'd finished work on Saturdays I'd leave on my bike as usual and cycle down the road to Henley, and after a few minutes Jimmy would roll up behind me in his big car and we'd load my bike into the back and off we'd go!' She laughed. 'I thought he was going to marry me, I really did ... he'd sort of *hinted* at it ...' She stretched her arms and sighed.

'Well, anyway, that particular Saturday I sat there at reception all morning waiting for him to turn up and he never did. I kept looking out of the window hoping to see him arrive. Once I thought I'd spotted his car, but it wasn't his, it was someone else's, and I almost burst into tears. I couldn't believe he'd let me down. I'd had my birthday two days before and Jimmy had promised to take me to London that evening. We were going to go dancing. I was sure he was going to pop the question ...' She lifted an eyebrow and shrugged. 'I can laugh about it now, but I'd never been so miserable in my life, and when I went back to Henley that evening I was ready to jump into the river myself. That's when I heard about the girl . . . Susan . . .'

She stared at her hands. Billy sat silent.

'I was living in lodgings at the time and my landlady told me the police had been knocking on doors up and down the street asking if anyone had seen her. She knew the girl's mother, my landlady did. She said although they were still searching in the town, everyone knew the poor kid must have fallen into the river. I went up to my room and lay face down on the bed, and I must have stayed that way for half an hour when suddenly it hit me! There I was, snivelling and feeling sorry for myself, but what that girl's mother must have been going through! And at that very same moment! So that's why I remember that day, because it taught me something.' Her look was defiant.

Billy put out his cigarette. He thought about what she had told him. 'What happened to Jimmy?' he asked.

Doris Jenner rolled her eyes. 'He wrote me a letter full of excuses and said he didn't know when he'd be able to get down again. I made some inquiries and found out he was married. I don't know how he'd managed to pull the wool over his wife's eyes for so long, coming down to the club every weekend, but I never saw him again.'

The door opened and the young man from reception put his head in. 'Your constable's here,' he said.

'Tell him I'll be out in a minute.' Billy kept his eyes on Doris Jenner. He waited until the door had shut, then he spoke to her. 'You mentioned a car, not Jimmy's, another one. Can you tell me more about that?'

'What?' She blinked. 'What are you talking about?'

'You thought you'd seen his car, you said, when you were waiting. But it was someone else's . . .'

'Yes?' She stared at him. Her glance hardened. 'Are you being a copper now?' she asked.

'Yes, I'm being a copper.' He met her gaze.

'Is this about Jimmy? Is he in trouble?'

Billy shook his head. 'No, it's about the *car*. That's all I'm interested in.' He paused. 'You see, you said before that Jimmy had a fancy car. "You couldn't mistake it," you said. But you did. Does that mean you hadn't seen another like it before that day?'

Flushing, she stared out of the window. Her lips had thinned to a hard line. 'If you came here to ask questions, you should have said so.'

'I didn't. It was hearing your story.'

'I thought we were being friendly.' She wouldn't look at him.

Billy sought for a way to heal the breach between them. 'Let me tell you what this is about, Doris.' He leaned forward. 'It's to do with that young girl, Susan Barlow.'

She turned to face him then, a deep flush still mantling her features, but with a glance that was less hostile. 'I don't see how,' she said.

'I need to know if a stranger came and parked his car here that day. Please, try and think back. Tell me exactly what you saw.'

Doris Jenner swallowed. She seemed to be in two minds as to whether or not to respond to his question. But then she shrugged. 'I was sitting at reception, as I said, and I saw what I thought was Jimmy's car drive into the parking area, so I waited, expecting him to come through the door, but he never did. I couldn't understand why – it's the only way into the club – so I went outside and looked for his car and saw what I thought was it parked away down the other end under a tree. I still thought it was Jimmy's. You're right – I hadn't seen another like it – not at the club, nor anywhere else.'

'What make of car was it?'

'Don't know. Can't help you there. It was foreign, that's all I remember.'

'*Foreign?* Are you sure of that?'

She nodded. 'Jimmy was proud as punch of it. Said there weren't many like it on the road. It had lovely leather upholstery.' She laughed cynically. 'Do you know what it smelled of to me? Money.'

'To go back, you saw this car parked at the far end of the lot . . . ?'

'Yes, but there was no sign of Jimmy. I wondered if he'd gone into the gardens, though I couldn't think why. They weren't kept up even in those days. Anyway, in the end I walked down to have a closer look at the car, to make sure it was his.'

Billy shifted slightly in his chair.

'Well, it wasn't.' She shrugged.

'How did you know that? Was it a different colour?'

'No, that was it.' She waved a hand impatiently.

'That's how I made a mistake in the first place. It looked just like Jimmy's. Dark blue. But when I got closer I saw they were different. It was the upholstery. Jimmy's was light brown. This one's was blue. Dark blue, like the chassis.'

'Did you wonder about the driver at all?'

She seemed puzzled by his question.

'Why he never came through reception?'

'Oh, I see what you mean.' She shook her head. 'No, I never gave it a thought. I only had one thing on my mind . . . Jimmy!' She rolled her eyes again.

'So you looked inside the car?'

'Did I?' Her good humour had returned, along with her crooked grin.

'You saw the upholstery. You must have noticed if there was anything lying on the seats.'

'Give me a break, officer.' Her American accent came from the cinema. 'It was three years ago.'

Billy lit another cigarette. He seemed to have relaxed himself. 'Come on, Doris. You can't fool me. What did you see?'

She laughed. 'Not that much. There was a man's hat lying on the passenger seat. I remember that. But I can't tell you what colour it was, or anything.'

'How about the back seat?'

She put her head on one side, inspecting him through lowered lashes. 'Just how important is this, Sergeant Styles?'

'I don't know. I'd have to hear it first, wouldn't I?' He returned her grin.

143

'What if I told you there was a body lying there?'

'I'd say you had a good imagination as well as a good memory.'

She tossed her head, laughing once more. 'Well, it wasn't a body. Just a packet of fruit.'

'Fruit?' Billy went very still. She hadn't noticed.

'Yes, in a brown paper packet, but the packet had split and the fruit was spilled out on the seat. I can see it lying there now.' She was smiling, pleased with herself.

'What sort of fruit?' Billy asked casually. 'Can you see *that*?'

'Of course I can. I've got a good memory, haven't I?' Her eyes sparkled. 'They were oranges. Lovely golden oranges . . .'

12

'BUT WOULD HE really have chosen such a public place to leave his car? In a *nudists'* club?' Chief Superintendent Holly clung to his doubts. 'Surely he would have been spotted there?'

'No, that's just the point, Arthur.' In effervescent mood, Angus Sinclair was inclined to be forgiving towards his plodding superior, who was proving unusually stubborn that day. 'The area the club uses is fenced off. You can't see in *or* out. The killer could easily have driven into the parking lot with the child, left his car there with the other vehicles and taken her down to the lower part of the gardens, near the river, without being seen. They are, and were then, overgrown and untended, Styles says. The Oxfordshire police are searching the grounds now. It's been three years, I know, but they might find something.' The chief inspector switched his gaze to Bennett, who was sitting behind his desk. 'It was a fine, alert piece of deduction, sir. All Styles had to go on was a hint this girl had dropped during their conversation. A lot of people would have missed it. I'll be putting his name down for a commendation when this is over.'

'Yes, yes! And I'll be happy to approve it.' Bennett spoke with uncharacteristic sharpness. 'But all in good time, Chief Inspector. We've still a long way to go.'

The assistant commissioner was in a testy mood. He'd been away for two days, chairing a police conference in Manchester, and had only returned to the capital that morning to find Sinclair's request for an urgent appointment on his desk. Guiltily aware of the mass of paperwork awaiting his attention, Sir Wilfred had summoned the chief inspector and sent a message to Arthur Holly, as well. Much as he wished to keep in touch with the investigation, he was beginning to realize that this piece of self-indulgence on his part meant time stolen from other labours; ones better suited to his lofty station, furthermore.

'So where do we stand now?' Bennett drummed his fingertips on the desktop. He had listened with scarcely concealed impatience to the chief inspector's detailed report. 'Obviously this car is a crucial lead. A Mercedes-Benz, you say?'

'Yes, and since it's foreign-made, there won't be many of them on the road in this country. What's more, we know the model!'

'How's that possible?' Holly asked, with more than a hint of disbelief in his tone. The chief super had recently been placed on a diet by his wife – he'd confessed as much to Sinclair – and the regime seemed to have had a dampening effect on his spirits. 'I can't believe this girl told Styles *that*.'

'No, but she gave him the name of her old boyfriend,' Sinclair countered cheerfully.

In contrast to the other two, he was in a capital frame of mind. This sudden break in what had promised to be the most intractable of investigations had come out of the blue. 'A Mr James Stoddart, of Birmingham, and he's already been interviewed by the police up there, at my request. He no longer has his car. He had to sell it when his wife threw him out a year ago – it seems *she* had the money. But, my goodness, does he cherish the memory of it!' The chief inspector's chuckle was hard-hearted.

'Now, it turns out that particular model, the one Stoddart owned, was offered for sale in this country for the first time in 1929. I have that from the Mercedes representatives here – they're located in Mayfair – along with the details of the car.' He took a sheet of paper from his file and squinted at it. 'Six cylinders, two hundred and twenty horsepower, overhead-valve ... it can do up to one hundred miles an hour, would you believe? There's a photograph of it, too.' He slid a glossy print across the desk to Bennett. 'I'm having that reproduced and circulated in the Brookham area in case anyone remembers seeing it. Someone with an interest in motor cars. There are always a few of them around, and it's unusual enough to have been noticed.'

Sir Wilfred had been studying the picture of the sleek, long-bonneted saloon. 'It certainly looks a rather fancy piece of machinery,' he conceded. 'Not something for the average motorist, would you say?'

'Not at the asking price!' Sinclair smiled wolfishly. 'It sells for a little over two thousand pounds.'

Holly's gloom lifted momentarily and he whistled. 'You're right, Angus. There can't be many of them around.'

'No, and the advantage for us, of course, is that we only have to check purchases made between the spring of 1929, when the car came on the market here, and that summer, when the Barlow child was murdered. The Mercedes people are sending me a list of them this afternoon. It's not a long one . . .' He paused to reflect. 'Of course, it's quite possible the man we're after no longer owns the car he had then. He may be driving something else now. But it makes no difference. If his name's on *that* list, we'll get to him.'

'Yes, I see. This really is quite extraordinary.' Bennett was recovering his enthusiasm. 'If necessary, *everyone* on that list could be interviewed.'

'They could,' Sinclair agreed. 'But I doubt that'll be necessary. We can probably eliminate a good number, for one reason or another, right from the start.'

'How will you approach the others?' The assistant commissioner was eager now to know more. 'You haven't got that much to go on, after all. A car with a packet of oranges in the back . . . ?'

'To start with, we'll simply ask them to account for their movements.'

'*Three years ago?*' Arthur Holly came to life with a growl of disbelief.

'No, *no*, sir . . .' Sinclair strove to keep a curb on his impatience. He wondered if it really was hunger that was dulling the chief super's wits that morning. 'All I'll want to know initially is where they were and what they were doing on those dates in July and September when the girls were murdered at Bognor Regis and Brookham. If any of them says he can't remember, well, we'll have a special word with *him*.'

Holly rumbled unhappily.

'What's the matter, Arthur?'

'You can't haul innocent citizens off the street and interrogate them, Angus.' The chief super set his jaw. 'Not in this country.'

'Do you think I don't know that?' Stung by the remark, Sinclair reddened. 'But since you've raised the question, let's examine it. To begin with, there'll be no question of an *interrogation* until I'm morally sure we've found the man we're after. And while it's fair to say the information we need to identify him may soon be in our hands, knowing who he is could be one thing, and proving it another. Unless some hard evidence comes our way, we're going to be faced with a problem of bricks and straw. How to make a case against him. In that event, we may be forced to take the only path left to us, which *is* interrogation.'

Sinclair directed his gaze at Bennett.

'These men do crack,' he said firmly. 'We've seen it before. Hammer away at that front they've erected long enough, and sooner or later it splinters—'

'Yes, quite. But surely that's a decision we can take later.' Bennett had become increasingly restive while the chief inspector was speaking. Aware of other, pressing demands on his time, he'd kept glancing at his watch. 'We must concentrate on what's to hand. Let's trace the owner of that car first. Then we can decide what to do next.' Picking up a pencil, he drew a pile of documents towards him. 'Will that be all, Chief Inspector?' He looked down.

'Not quite, sir.'

Nettled at being cut off so abruptly, Sinclair made no

haste about closing up his file. 'There's one further step I'd like to take. But I'll need your authorization.'

Alerted not only by the words, but by the tone in which they were uttered, the assistant commissioner looked up sharply. 'What is it?' he demanded.

'I want to send a telegram to the International Criminal Police Commission in Vienna. I'd like them to check their records for us.'

'Now, wait a minute!' Sir Wilfred put down his pencil. 'The International Commission! What the devil have they got to do with this?'

'Perhaps nothing, sir.' The chief inspector carefully folded one well-pressed trouser leg over the other. 'But we are still faced with the problem of what this man, this killer, who is not a tramp and almost certainly owns a motor car, was doing between the summer of 1929 and the end of last July, when he raped and murdered Marigold Hammond. It's almost unknown for a sex criminal of this type to remain inactive for so long. We've checked prison records of known offenders and come up empty-handed. One other possibility is that this man was abroad during that time. If so, he may well have killed one or more children in some other country. If that is the case, we *must* obtain that information.'

'Come now, Chief Inspector . . .' Bennett had returned to drumming his fingertips on the desktop. 'You know as well as I do what our policy towards the commission is. And that's a *government* policy, let me remind you. We have as little to do with it as possible.'

'Nevertheless, we are members of the organization, are we not?' Sinclair affected an air of puzzlement. 'It seems a shame not to take advantage of the connection. After all, their international bureau maintains an up-to-date list of known sex criminals in Europe, together with their modus operandi, and keeps track of their movements.'

'I'm well aware of that,' Bennett snapped. He looked at his wristwatch and winced. 'The fact of the matter is, the commission's a creature of the Austrian government. It's staffed solely by Austrian police officials. There are grounds for believing it operates as an intelligence arm of the Austrian state.'

'Really?' The chief inspector appeared taken aback. 'Strange that none of the other member countries – there must be thirty of them by now – seem to hold that view. But then they don't enjoy our special advantages, do they, sir?'

'And what might those be?' The assistant commissioner's voice had taken on a dangerous note; his pale cheeks were becoming flushed.

'Why, that as British policemen we're privileged to belong to the finest force in the world and have nothing to gain or learn by associating with a pack of foreigners!'

'*That will do!*' Bennett brought his fist down hard on his desk.

'Angus!' Arthur Holly wagged a disapproving finger at his colleague. 'Now calm down, the pair of you,' he added, for good measure.

Red in the face, Bennett rounded on him. 'Don't you tell *me* to calm down, Chief Superintendent!'

Holly regarded him with an unruffled gaze, and after a moment the assistant commissioner collected himself.

Blinking, he sat back in his chair. 'I've not heard any advice from your quarter for a while,' he remarked spitefully. 'Haven't you got an opinion?'

'Yes, sir, as a matter of fact I have.' Holly cleared his throat. 'Normally speaking, if it was a question of turning to a pack of foreigners for help, I'd be the first to vote against it.' He grinned. 'But in this instance, I think Angus might have a point. It's the motor car, isn't it?'

'The motor car, Chief Superintendent?' Bennett eyed him with suspicion.

'Mobility, sir.' Holly made his rumbling sound. 'That's what I'm talking about. It's the curse of modern policing. Time was when a safe was cracked or a house robbed, you could put half a dozen names into a hat and be sure one of them was responsible, because they were the ones that lived in your manor. But not any longer. Now that every flash villain has a motor car, there's no telling where he'll do his next job.' He looked at them both. 'And isn't that the problem we're dealing with here? As far as we know this man has killed three girls: one in Oxfordshire, and two down south, but in different counties. So whatever else, he moves around. What's more he owns a car – we know that, too – and a damned great tourer by the sound of it. Why shouldn't he have gone abroad for a while? We can't ignore the possibility.' He turned to the assistant commissioner. 'Sir, until we can positively identify him, I feel we should cast our net as widely as we can.'

'Well said, Arthur!' Sinclair beamed. 'I couldn't have put it better myself.'

His face flushed, Bennett looked from one to the

other. Glancing at his watch, he groaned. 'My God! Look at the time!' He rose, pointing a finger at Sinclair. 'Very well. You may draft a telegram to Vienna. You may *not* send it before it's been shown to me. Is that clear?'

'Perfectly, sir.' Sinclair's smile was benign.

Without a word Bennett strode to the door. Holly waited until he had heard it slam behind them. Then he stretched, glancing sideways as he did so. 'Sailing a little close to the wind, weren't you, Angus?'

The chief inspector grunted. 'Bennett's a good AC. We're lucky to have him. But we must see he gets his priorities right. Government policy be damned! What matters here is that this man is found before he kills again.' He smiled at his superior. 'By the way, thank you, Arthur. I wasn't expecting you to come to my aid.'

Holly sniffed. 'You always were too sure of yourself.'

Chuckling, Angus Sinclair accepted the reproof with good grace.

'I meant to ask earlier' – the chief super rose – 'what are you doing with Styles now? Are you keeping him on the case?'

'Yes, I am.' Sinclair got to his feet as well, and they went to the door. 'In fact, I've sent him down to Guildford and told him to nose around. It's true, this lead with the car may crack the case for us, but you never can tell, and I don't want to tread water in the meantime. Brookham's the most recent killing, the freshest if you like, and I want to have someone down there on the spot. I've another reason, too, but this is between you and me, Arthur.'

'What do you mean?' Holly eyed him.

'I've told Styles he needn't feel shy about picking John Madden's brains if the opportunity presents itself. John's got a rare instinct for this kind of case and I want to know what he thinks.'

'I see nothing wrong with that.' The chief super was still puzzled.

'Perhaps not. But I'm doing it in a rather underhand way. I can't involve John directly. Helen would have my hide if she found out. But Styles's position is different. His tie with Madden goes back to the time he worked under him, and he's a friend of the family; what's more, Helen has a soft spot for him. I'm hoping she'll allow him some latitude when he comes to call.' Sinclair scowled. 'But I've a nasty feeling I'm walking on eggshells.'

13

Driving cautiously over the bumps and ruts, Billy drew up outside the farmhouse. He got out of the car, narrowly avoiding stepping into one of the copper-coloured puddles that had appeared in the dirt road following last night's rain. He had hardly set foot on the path leading up to the house, however, when he was stopped in his tracks.

'Don't bring your muddy shoes into my kitchen, Sergeant Styles.' May Burrows stood with folded arms in the doorway ahead of him.

'Hullo, May.' Grinning, Billy came to a halt.

'You'll see a pair of mats by the gate just behind you. Wipe your feet first, then you can come in.'

'I'm looking for Mr Madden,' he told her.

'Thought you might be. He's over in the stableyard with the others. They're loading the hogs today.' May's sharp tone was belied by her smile. Once, many years before, Billy had had to take a statement from her. A callow detective constable then and unsure of his authority, he'd tried to bully her, and May had never let him forget it. 'You'll find Belle and Lucy there, too. You can tell them their tea'll be ready in five minutes. Come in and have a cup yourself, if you like.'

'Thanks, May. I will.'

Making a smart about-turn, Billy set off for the

stableyard, skipping over the puddles as he went. Urban to the bone, on his rare visits to the countryside he had come to distrust simple-sounding rural terms, many of them, he believed, designed expressly to deceive ears such as his. But 'loading the hogs' sounded straightforward enough, and so it proved to be.

On reaching the arched entrance to the yard he found a scene of bustling activity within. Two farmhands armed with sticks were prodding a young porker across the cobbles towards an open lorry which stood in the centre of the space, already half-filled with squealing pigs. Fascinated, he watched as the men dropped their sticks, grabbed hold of an ear each, and then, with their other hands clasped beneath the beast's belly, heaved it up and onto the back of the vehicle. Neither of the pair had noticed his arrival, and nor had George Burrows, who was standing by the gate to the sties, controlling the flow. Someone else had, however. A small figure in blue with mud-stained legs and hair that shone gold in the sunlight came flying across the cobbles towards him.

'*Billy!*'

The little girl flung herself without fear into his arms, trusting him to catch her. He whirled her around in the air before putting her firmly back down again.

'Hullo, Lucy!'

'What are you doing here?'

'Just visiting . . .'

Their friendship had been sealed on one of Billy's weekend visits to Highfield when Lucy Madden had discovered, in the course of a walk they had taken in the woods together, that not only was the sergeant unaware of the existence of chiffchaffs, he didn't even know the difference between a shrike and a shrew. Never having encountered such ignorance in an adult before, she had taken instant pity on him and made him the object of her special attention ever since.

'Come and see the hogs.' She dragged him by the hand over to the lorry. 'They're going to slaughter,' she informed him with relish.

'Slaughter?' Billy eyed her doubtfully.

'Yes, there'll be lots of blood.'

George Burrows, apple-cheeked and sturdy, waved a welcome. His dark-haired daughter Belle stuck shyly to his side.

'Is Mr Madden about?' Billy called out to him.

'Yes, he is . . .' Madden's voice came from beyond the gate where George was standing. He emerged from the darkness within, brushing straw from his trousers and stamping mud from his boots. 'Billy, how nice to see you. I heard you were in the neighbourhood. Helen and I were hoping you'd find time to look in.'

They shook hands – or tried to. Lucy was unwilling to relinquish possession of the one she was holding, so Billy was forced to offer his left to Madden's grip.

'Billy's come to visit us.'

'Don't you mean Sergeant Styles?' Her father looked at her askance.

'No . . . *Billy!*' She swung on his arm.

'I've been stuck in Guildford, sir, catching up on all the details. But I managed to get over to Brookham this afternoon, so I thought I'd stop in on my way back. I'm hoping to see Will, too.'

Before glancing down at his daughter's golden head, Madden caught the younger man's eye.

'Mrs Burrows said to say your tea's ready in the kitchen, Lucy,' Billy told her. 'Yours and Belle's.'

'Aren't you coming, too?' She clung to his hand.

'In a minute.'

'Run along now, darling,' Madden said. 'Both of you. Go and fetch Belle.'

They waited until the two little girls had left the yard, hand in hand. Then Madden spoke again, 'I understand you've got a lead at last. Mr Sinclair rang me earlier this week. He said they've been given a list of names in London they're working through, and the killer's may be among them. He also said it was a feather in *your* cap.'

Madden's grin of congratulation made Billy flush with pleasure. 'I had a piece of luck, sir. The chief inspector sent me down to Henley last week. Did you know a girl's body had been taken from the river there?'

'Mr Sinclair told me that some time ago. But I'd like to hear the whole story.' Madden clicked his tongue with impatience. 'It'll have to wait till later, though. I'm just off to pick up Rob. He's been spending the afternoon with a friend in Godalming. You'll stay for dinner, won't you?' Taking the sergeant's pleased smile of acceptance for granted, he went on, 'That'll give us time to talk. But walk me to my car now. Tell me briefly how things stand.'

Only too happy to oblige, Billy embarked on a swift summary of his visit to Henley, relishing the grunt of approval he received when he explained how he'd come to hit on the idea of the killer making use of the car park at Waltham Manor. The esteem in which he held Madden had never lessened. Nor had he forgotten the debt he owed to his old mentor under whose once stern eye he had learned some of the most important lessons of his life. (And not all of them having to do with being a policeman, either!)

'So he picked her up by chance. He couldn't have known she'd be walking along that road. But he knew where to take her, all right.' They had paused at the entrance to the yard. Madden's scowl took Billy back a decade. 'I can't make up my mind about this man. At first I thought he must have seen the girl at Brookham and come back looking for her. But I doubt that now.' With a sigh, Madden glanced at his watch. 'Billy, I have to go. What was that you said about seeing Will Stackpole?'

'I rang him earlier and told him I'd be looking in here. He said he'd try and come by.'

'Good! Stay and have a cup of tea with May. You can talk to Will when he arrives. Then come over to the house.' Madden walked briskly to where his car was parked. Smiling, he called back to Billy. 'You could do me a favour and bring Lucy when you come. She'll count it a treat to have a ride with *you*.'

'YOU OUGHT TO hear Will on the subject of the search the Surrey police are making for that tramp, sir.' Billy grinned. 'He says they haven't got the first notion how to go about it.'

Madden's grunt was enigmatic. Crouched before the fire, he prodded the blaze with a poker. Lit by only a pair of lamps, the drawing room lay in shadow.

'He says they don't know the countryside, most of them, and don't understand how these tramps can disappear if they've a mind to.'

Adding another log to the flames, Madden rose, brushing off his hands. He stood tall in the firelight, looking down at Billy, who was seated in an armchair. 'It's not like searching for a man in a town or city,' he said. 'There you go to his family and friends, or his accomplices, if he has any. You scour his neighbourhood. These tramps never stay long in one place, and once they decide to make themselves scarce, it's hard to know where to begin looking for them.'

'Will said, most likely he's been getting help from other vagrants, other tramps.'

'He's right.' Madden seated himself across the hearth from Billy. 'Mind you, if Beezy had killed that girl, and they knew, they'd have given him up by now. Or at least not protected him. He'll have needed food, of course, and that means someone's been getting it for him. Topper, most likely. If you ask me, they've joined up again. I've tried to get word to him.'

'To *Topper*, sir?' Billy was all ears. 'How could you do that?'

'A lot of these vagrants call at Helen's surgery: she let it be known a long time ago that they could get medical treatment from her if they needed it. I've sent messages by one or two asking Topper to get in touch with us. So far without result.'

Billy took a sip from his glass of brandy. It had been a day of many pleasures. Earlier, he had spent an hour at the farmhouse chatting to May Burrows while she strung beans in the kitchen. Looking at her pink, composed face, he'd remembered the teenage girl with bobbed hair whom he'd once had to question; now May was a young matron with two children of her own, the younger, a baby boy, still in his cradle.

She had seated him at the table where the two little girls were still occupied with their tea, a generous meal in the Burrows household, containing elements of both breakfast and supper in it, and where Billy had had no choice but to submit to the maternal instincts of Lucy Madden, which had taken the form of pressing on him spoonfuls of her soft-boiled egg and morsels of thickly buttered toast steeped in honey.

Later, another old friend had put in an appearance. Will Stackpole had cycled over from the village and Billy had spent some time discussing the case with the constable, whom he had first met years before, during the Melling Lodge investigation.

The autumn evening had been drawing in by the time he'd driven down the avenue of limes, clothed in yellow leaves now, to the Maddens' front door, where Helen had been waiting to relieve him of Lucy's still-voluble presence, returning with her half an hour later, bathed and clad in pyjamas, to say her goodnights, a process which the little girl managed to prolong by a series of well-honed stratagems, causing her brother, who was trying to do his homework, to roll his eyes in despair. Finally, Helen had lost patience.

'Lucinda Madden! That will do. Say goodnight now to Sergeant Styles.'

'He's not Sergeant Styles. He's *Billy!*'

While Madden was helping his son wrestle with a problem of arithmetic, Billy had wandered outside onto the terrace and stood for a while gazing out over the garden at the dark woods of Upton Hanger, lit by a thin sliver of moon that evening, remembering a visit he'd made earlier that year when the air on this very spot had been sweet with the mingled scents of jasmine and roses. Now, only the faint smell of burning leaves reached him.

Helen had soon returned from putting Lucy to bed and before long it had been Rob's turn to be dispatched upstairs. To his bitter disappointment: he was sure his father and Billy were going to discuss the Brookham murder and had hoped for an opportunity to eavesdrop on them.

With the children safely in bed, Helen had taken the two men in to dinner, where the conversation had turned to the subject of Billy's forthcoming marriage. The Maddens were yet to meet his fiancée, and Helen was insistent that this oversight be repaired.

'It's time you brought Elsie to see us. Lucy must be made to accept the situation.' She could seldom resist teasing the sergeant, whose regard for her husband, though it touched her deeply, sometimes made him tongue-tied in their presence. 'You do realize she thinks you belong to *her*. I hope she won't feel rejected now.'

Once dinner was over, however, and with the excuse of a heavy day ahead of her, she had bid them goodnight, saving her last words for their guest.

'I won't ask what you and John are going to talk about, though I can guess. And welcome as you always are, Billy, dear, I sense a hidden hand behind your visit today. You can tell Angus Sinclair I'm not deceived.'

On which note, and with Billy speechless in his chair, she had left them by the fire.

The younger man stifled a yawn. He still had to drive back to Guildford – he'd taken lodgings in the town – but there was a question he wanted to put to his host before leaving.

'You said earlier, sir, when we were at the farm, how you thought at first the killer might have seen the Bridger girl before – marked her out, as it were. I know you changed your mind, but what made you think that in the first place? If you don't mind my asking . . .'

'No, I don't mind, Billy.' Madden smiled, as though in acknowledgement of this sign that the habit of paying careful attention had taken such healthy root in his protegé. 'In fact, the whole business puzzles me. I've been trying to make sense of it. Let me explain . . .'

Billy sat forward, doubly alert now.

'At first I thought it a strange coincidence when I found Alice Bridger's body that the murderer had hit on a tramps' camp site to commit the crime. It only occurred to me later it was much more likely he knew about the spot in advance. He carried the girl's body through thick brush in order to get there. The odds were against him having come on it by accident. That's what made me think he might have had her in mind as prey, that he'd already scouted out a place nearby where he could take her.

'But later I discarded the idea. It implied he must have been hanging around Brookham for some time before, waiting for his opportunity, and there was simply no evidence to support that. No reports of strangers lurking in the neighbourhood that day, or the days preceding. I decided he must have been driving through the village, just as we were, and came on her by chance. But that left the first question unanswered ... how did he find his way to the tramps' site?'

Scowling, Madden rubbed the scar on his forehead. Noting the familiar gesture – and aware from times past of the depth of preoccupation it signalled – Billy smiled to himself.

'Do you see what I'm saying? He's not a pure hunter of opportunity, this man. He only acts when he's pre-pared.' Madden's scowl deepened. 'From what you've told me, I'd guess that at Henley he'd already inspected the manor grounds, perhaps that same day, and knew he could take any victim he picked up there. As for Bognor Regis, I'm familiar with that piece of coastline where the girl was abducted. There are long stretches of reeds and scrubland along the shore. No shortage of cover, I mean, and I'll wager he knew it.'

'And it must have been the same at Brookham – that's what you're saying,' Billy broke in. 'He only picked her up because he knew there was a place nearby he could take her. That spot by the stream.'

'If his behaviour's consistent, that seems to be the case,' Madden agreed. 'But it means he must have been in Capel Wood earlier, for some other reason, and I've been rack-ing my brains, trying to think what it might be.'

Billy thought for a moment. 'He could be a hiker, sir. The countryside's full of ramblers.'

'Yes, I'd thought of that.' Madden shook his head. 'But it still doesn't explain how he found the *tramps'* site. It's not a spot you'd stumble on by chance. He'd have had to leave the path, for one thing, and that's no easy matter. The undergrowth's dense. Discouraging. No, he'd have needed a *reason*, as I said, a particular purpose.' Madden scowled. 'That's what's been puzzling me. How *did* he find it? What took him there in the first place?'

14

It was nearly two o'clock before Sam Watkin got to Coyne's Farm that Friday. Earlier, he'd been delayed in Midhurst making his weekly report to Mr Cuthbertson, who'd been held up himself by a talkative client, forcing Sam to sit outside his office for half an hour or more, twiddling his thumbs.

He'd used the time to write out a report in his notebook of the work that would have to be done at Hobday's Farm, over Rogate way, where he'd been earlier that morning. One of the chimneys on the farmhouse had come down since his last visit, smashing the roof tiles beneath it and leaving a hole as big as your head which went straight down to the room below, where the floor had been damaged. The repairs would have to be done before the next rains came, which might be any day now – the spell of fine October weather they'd been enjoying for the past few days couldn't last – and if the owners didn't want a deteriorating property on their hands, they'd better do something about it quick.

Such, at any rate, was the news that Sam eventually gave to Mr Cuthbertson after he was shown into his office, a pleasant, airy room that looked out over the old Market Square onto St Ann's Hill. Mr Cuthbertson had rubbed his chin.

'Oh, they won't be pleased to hear this.' He'd caught Sam's eye and they'd both chuckled. 'They do so hate paying out money.'

The banks, he meant. The ones that owned so many pieces of property hereabouts now. The terrible slump in prices in 1929 had led to foreclosures left and right. Sam himself had been among the victims. He'd owned a small farm, part of what had once been a large estate just the other side of Easebourne, bought when he'd come back from the war. With the help of a loan from the bank, of course. Well, that had gone.

But he'd been luckier than most. It had been Mr Cuthbertson, of Tally and Cuthbertson, a firm of estate agents in Midhurst specializing in farming land, who'd been charged with handling the business and in spite of the painful circumstances, which had ended with Sam and his family having to move out bag and baggage, all their belongings piled onto a cart drawn up in the yard, and which by rights ought to have turned them into enemies, they'd somehow managed to hit it off and Sam had departed with Mr Cuthbertson's offer of a job in his pocket.

What he was paid to do now was keep an eye on the farms in the district which the firm had on its books. Farms that were for sale, but attracting no buyers, not in present conditions. The Depression had bitten deep into the country and farmers had suffered along with everyone else. It was a matter of hanging on if you could and hoping for better times. Sam spent his days driving from one property to another, inspecting buildings for any damage and keeping an eye out for undesirable trespassers, gypsies in the main, and moving them along where necessary.

Mr Cuthbertson called him 'our factor' when he introduced him to clients. 'This is our factor, Mr Watkin.' It made Sam chuckle. He'd been a lot of things in his time: farmworker, stable lad, a boxer in a fairground booth for one whole summer; and a poacher on the side. He'd even been an officer, to his eternal wonder. Having somehow survived two years in the trenches, he'd still been alive and kicking when the powers-that-be began their policy of promoting from the ranks. Lo and behold, Sam Watkin had found himself a second lieutenant! A 'temporary gentleman', as the saying was then. The phrase still brought a smile of derision to his lips.

After the war he'd considered emigrating to Canada, or perhaps Australia, but Ada Witherspoon, daughter of the landlord at the Dog and Duck in Elsted, had said, 'Well, you can go where you want, Sam Watkin, but don't expect to find me waiting here when you get back.' So they'd ended up buying a farm instead, and now he was a factor, and if you asked Sam what he thought about life he'd have said there was no sense to it that he could see, none at all. It was just one darned thing after another.

The business of the roof had been quickly settled. Mr Cuthbertson had told Sam to get hold of a workman if he needed one, but to see to the repairs himself. There was no point in calling in a firm of contractors. They'd only charge the earth.

There being little else for them to talk about that day, Sam had soon been on the move again, returning to his van, which was parked in the square below. He'd bought it second hand from the Post Office a few years back and painted it dark green, a colour he liked. It was perfect for rattling around in, and for hauling the tools and other odd bits and pieces he needed for his work.

Perfect for Sally, too, his old labrador, who went everywhere with him. The thump of her tail on the van's floor had greeted him when he'd climbed in behind the wheel. Sal liked to lie in the back, curled up on her blanket, snoozing; waiting till it was time for a walk. Or, better still, a snack. Greediest dog alive, Sam always said.

'We'll run over to Coyne's Farm now,' he'd told her, as they set off. 'Could be we'll have a spot of lunch when we get there.'

But another delay had been in the offing.

Soon after he'd turned off the Petersfield road, in the direction of Elsted, he'd run into some roadworks. A gang of men was engaged in widening a stretch of the paved surface, a job that must have begun in the last few days, since they hadn't been there the last time Sam had come this way. The crew were at their lunch break when he arrived, sitting in a line on the bank, leaving one of their number to direct traffic. The patch of road where they were working had been narrowed to the width of a single vehicle and this fellow was controlling the flow from both directions, using red and green flags to warn approaching traffic.

Sam had eyed him with some interest, and given the signal to proceed, had drawn up beside the shabby figure.

'What, ho, Eddie!' he'd exclaimed.

'Crikey!' A bristly face had peered in at him through the opened window. 'Is that you, Sam?'

Eddie Noyes was the chap's name and the last time Sam had seen him he'd been lying face up on a stretcher with the front of his tunic soaked with blood and his eyes wide with shock. At Wipers, it had been. Eddie had got his ticket home that day. He hadn't returned to the battalion.

'What are you doing over this way?' The reason Sam had asked was because he knew Eddie came from another part of Sussex – from Hove, down on the coast, if he remembered right – but as soon as he spoke he'd wished he hadn't. It was obvious, after all, what a bloke was doing when you caught him in workmen's clothes with a two-day stubble on his chin waving flags on the edge of a public highway. He was taking any job he could find. Things were that hard still.

But Eddie hadn't been ashamed to talk about it. (This was after Sam had pulled to the side of the road and sat down with him on the bank, one of Eddie's mates having volunteered to direct the traffic.) He'd lost his position as a salesman for a paper-manufacturing company the previous year – the firm had gone bust – and hadn't been able to find another. Just odd jobs from time to time, this stint with the road gang being one of them.

He was still living in Hove, he said, taking care of his old mum and his sister, who had lost her husband in the war. Money was short – Eddie had shrugged – but they managed. His only problem with this job he had now was he couldn't get home at night – it was just too far – so he was having to bunk with some of the other men in the shed they'd put up to house their equipment. He had grinned then. 'It takes me back, Sam, I can tell you. I've known shellholes more salubrious.'

Sam's first impulse had been to put his hand in his pocket, but he'd checked himself. You couldn't offer money to a chap who'd won the Military Medal. Who wasn't more than an inch or two over five feet, but would stand up to anyone.

'You must come and have a meal with us, Eddie. Just let me warn Ada first. She'll want to put a spread on for you.'

He'd wished he could have offered him a bed, too, but for one thing they were living over at Halfway Bridge now, on the other side of Midhurst, which wouldn't suit Eddie at all, and for another there simply wasn't room in their cottage, what with the kids growing up and Ada having gone into the business of making frocks for friends and neighbours, turning what passed for their parlour into a sewing room filled with patterns and tailor's dummies.

But the image of Eddie lying wedged with the other men like sardines on the floor of a builder's shed bothered him – it didn't seem right – and even before he'd reached Coyne's Farm he'd come up with a solution.

'See what I mean, Sal? This would suit Eddie down to the ground. It'd be warm and dry and there's plenty of hay to make a bed with.'

Standing in the cavernous barn, Sam held forth to an audience of one. A sociable chap by nature, he found the solitude of his working days something of a burden and had fallen into the habit of treating Sally as his confidante.

'No problem with fresh water, either. There's that tap in the yard outside. I tell you, this place is made for him.'

It was Coyne's Farm being so near to where Eddie and his mates were working that had put the idea into his head. The turn-off to the farm was only half a mile further on, though in fact Sam never went that way himself, the muddy track having fallen into disrepair since the place was abandoned. Not wishing to risk the suspension of his old van on it, he would stop some way short of the turning at a spot where the paved road was crossed by an ancient footpath that led over a low saddle in the wooded ridge behind Coyne's Farm into the valley where it was situated.

This path – it was called Wood Way, and according to the guide books dated from before Roman times – ran as straight as an arrow down one slope of the valley and up the other side before vanishing in the rolling contours of the South Downs, which rose only a short way off to fill the horizon.

It marked the boundary of Coyne's Farm, and to get there all you had to do was walk down the path until you came to a gap in the hedgerow beside it, slip through that, cross an apple orchard and a kitchen garden, and – hey presto – there you were in the cobbled yard behind the house, with the barn not thirty paces away at the other end of it. Eddie's barn!

Sam had timed his walk. It had taken him twelve

minutes on the dot from where his van was parked, and on the way a further thought had occurred to him. Just a bit past the gap in the hedge a fork off the main path led across the adjoining fields to a small village, more of a hamlet really, called Oak Green, where Eddie could buy whatever provisions he might need. Not that Ada wouldn't see to it that he'd have most of what he wanted.

By the time Sam reached the yard he'd made up his mind to speak to Mr Cuthbertson on Eddie's behalf. It wouldn't be right to do it behind his back – just move Eddie in without saying anything. But he didn't think his employer would have any objections to his scheme.

Coyne's Farm was a choice property – one of the best on his books, Mr Cuthbertson always said. Being right on the edge of the Downs, it was fine sheep-rearing land and had been profitably worked until a couple of years back when the owner had died. Having no sons to take over from him – his two boys had been killed in the war – he'd left the farm to a nephew of his wife's, but this bloke, who owned a dairy farm outside Petersfield, was only interested in selling the place, which was why it was on the market.

Mr Cuthbertson had told Sam that he expected to get a good price for it one day, once things had picked up again, and that the present owner had already turned down a couple of prospective purchasers on his advice because their offers had been too low. The opportunity of having a reliable man on the spot, in residence so to speak, would not be one he would turn down.

The barn stood at one end of the yard and at right

angles to the house, which was built of patterned brick in a style popular in the region. A lofty wooden structure, it had been used as a storeroom when the farm was abandoned and its doors were kept padlocked as a deterrent against intruders who might otherwise be tempted to rifle its contents.

Sam had a key to the padlock, and having drawn the bolt, he'd flung both doors wide, flooding the dark interior with light, displaying the stacks of hurdles used for temporary fencing, essential for sheep-raising, which lined both sides of the building for most of its length. Where they ended, towards the rear of the barn, the empty space was filled with a variety of objects, including furniture from the house, draped with canvas to protect it from rain coming through the roof, and an assortment of farm implements stored in crates and wicker baskets. At the very back, in one corner, an old pony trap stood with its shafts upraised like the arms of a soldier surrendering.

It was to the opposite corner that Sam had made his way and where he'd spent some minutes clearing an area of the earth floor. Seizing hold now of a pitchfork that was sticking out of a wicker basket, he began raking together the old hay that was still scattered about underfoot and pushing it into a mound.

'See, this'll be his bed,' he told Sal, who'd accompanied him into the barn and was watching his activities with mild interest. 'Eddie's bound to have a bedroll with him if he's sleeping rough, and this'll do for a mattress underneath.'

During the months of his stewardship he'd explored

the stored treasures of the barn and he remembered having seen one or two articles that might come in handy now. Finished with the pitchfork, he went in search of them and presently returned dragging an old Victorian washstand behind him with an enamel jug and basin balanced precariously on its marble top. A second expedition netted a pair of oil lamps which Sam examined and found to be in good working order.

Then a further idea occurred to him and he turned to a large mahogany wardrobe which stood nearby draped in canvas. He'd looked inside it once, he recalled, and unless memory deceived him ... Pushing back the folds of canvas from the doors, Sam tugged them open.

Yes, there it was!

The gleam of a mirror shone in the dark recesses of the cupboard. Formerly attached to the inside of one of the doors, it now stood loose, propped against the back. Sam hauled it out and bore it in triumph over to where he'd prepared Eddie's bed. He leaned it against the wall beside the washstand.

'He's got to be able to comb his hair in the morning,' he said to Sal, by way of explanation. 'All the comforts of home. That's our motto.'

Pleased with the outcome of his efforts, Sam examined his own reflection in the looking glass, grinning at the way the cracked surface distorted his homely features, giving an extra twist to the broken nose he'd had these past twenty years, a souvenir of his days as a fairground mauler.

One thing was certain: Ada hadn't married him for his looks.

'You're no oil painting, Sam Watkin.' She'd told him that often enough. 'But you're a good bloke.'

Sam didn't know if he was a good bloke or not, but he felt warmed by the thought of what he was doing for Eddie, who'd looked older than his years when they'd sat together on the bank a little while back. Just worn out. As though life had been grinding him down.

Christ, times were hard.

'THERE, NOW. That's better.'

Sam lit his pipe and leaned back with a sigh. Their lunch had been unusually delayed that day. But the cheese sandwiches Ada had packed for him had gone down a treat, while the bit of cold sausage and biscuit he'd set aside for Sal had been equally well received. She was stretched out on the ground beside him now, fast asleep, muzzle twitching, chasing rabbits in her dreams.

Even when he'd finished with the barn, he'd still had his regular tour of inspection of the house and outbuildings to make and it had been close to three o'clock before they'd quit the yard and walked up the hillside to the wooded ridge behind the farm. Struggling up the slippery slope, Sam had chuckled to see what heavy weather his companion was making of the climb.

'That's what comes of overeating, my girl.' Fat as butter she was.

Once they got to the top the going had become easier. Here the ground underfoot was cushioned by generations of fallen leaves, the still air rich with the stored scents of summer. Sam had paused to admire the dust motes dancing in shafts of sunlight piercing the canopy of foliage overhead. He loved the woods. They took him back to his boyhood, a time of innocence, in his mind, before the war, when the world had seemed different. To his poaching days, which even now seemed blameless, when he'd been a lad working on a farm up near Redford, and would slip away of an evening into the twilit forest.

Brushing through a stand of ferns, they had roused a cock pheasant, the sudden frenzied beating of its wings making them both start. Sally's excited barking had shattered the deep silence of the trees.

The place where they'd finally settled, under a tall beech at the edge of the wood, was a favourite spot of his. From here he could see the whole valley spread out before him backed by the deep folds of the Downs, whose grassy crests still glowed with the fading light of afternoon.

'The blunt, bow-headed, whale-backed Downs.'

Sam was fond of quoting Kipling's line, which he'd first heard from his eldest, Rose, who'd learned it herself at school. Now, whenever his eye fell on the broad green hillocks he thought how like giant sea creatures they were.

It wasn't only the farm buildings he had to watch out for. Mr Cuthbertson wanted him to keep an eye on the land as well and from where he was sitting he was able to cast his gaze over a wide area, westwards in the direction of Elsted and east as far as the red roofs of Oak Green.

That day the valley seemed deserted. The only figure he spotted was that of a lone man and he was some distance off, on the bare crest of the ridge opposite, gazing up at the sky through a pair of binoculars.

Sam shifted his own gaze to the stream that ran down the centre of the valley, searching for telltale wisps of smoke, any signs of a camp fire in the straggling line of willows and tangled bushes that marked the course of the waterway. Not surprisingly, the empty farms had become a magnet for tramps and Mr Cuthbertson had told him to keep them away as far as possible and at all events to make sure they didn't try to take up residence in any of the buildings.

He had a point, too. Once the weather turned chilly and they began to light fires for warmth and not simply for cooking there was the danger they would set fire inadvertently to whatever barn or stall they'd taken shelter in.

Sam had his own way of dealing with the problem. Whenever he came across any of these vagrants he would stop and chat with them for a while, letting them know in a friendly way that there was someone keeping an eye on the property. They were welcome to pause for a bit, he would tell them, so long as they did no damage, but not to linger unduly; not to make themselves at home. Above all, they were to keep away from the farm buildings; otherwise a charge of trespass might follow.

It wasn't a part of his job he enjoyed. Quite a number of the tramps were known to him, familiar faces from years back. He regarded most of them as decent men down on their luck and more often than not these meetings ended with Sam the poorer by a florin or two.

The gypsies were another matter, sullen and closemouthed when their paths crossed, the hostility in their eyes rooted in some centuries-old soil of resentment. Whether this arose from their own natures, from the manner in which they lived, or from the way they were treated by others – by people like himself, if it came to that – was a question Sam had never resolved, and for want of any satisfactory answer he'd fallen back on a brisk, no-nonsense front when dealing with them. But the business left a bad taste in his mouth and he was always relieved when it was over and he saw the backs of their caravans receding.

He glanced at his watch. It was a quarter to four.

'Come on, Sal. Time we were off.'

Tapping out his pipe, he rose, but had to wait while Sally levered herself up, groaning as she did so. Poor old girl. Rheumatism was starting to get into her joints. He hoped it wouldn't reach the stage when he'd have to put her down. He wasn't sure he could bring himself to do it.

'Off we go, then.'

The quickest way back to his van led along the ridge to the saddle where the path ran. They soon reached it and Sam paused for a moment to cast his gaze down the length of the footway. He was thinking how easy it would be for Eddie to walk over here after work.

'*Sally!*'

The high-pitched cry came from behind them and he looked round. A young girl dressed in a gymslip and carrying a school satchel was hurrying up the path towards them from the direction of the road. Sam waved to her.

'Look, Sal – there's your friend.'

Sally, whose eyesight wasn't all it had once been, seemed unconvinced. She let out a speculative bark. Then her tail began to wag.

'Oh, Sally! Didn't you recognize me?' The girl came up to them. Shedding her satchel and her white straw hat, she went down on her knees and threw her arms around Sal's neck.

Sam stood over them, grinning. 'I thought we'd missed you today,' he said.

Nell was her name. Nell Ramsay. She lived in Oak Green, but went to school in Midhurst, returning on the bus every afternoon. It had been early spring when they'd first bumped into her on Wood Way and since then she and Sal had become bosom pals.

'I'm sorry, Mr Watkin. I should have said good afternoon to you first.' Smiling, she looked up, brushing the dark hair from her eyes.

'How've you been, love?'

'Very well, thank you.' Though she talked posh, she had no airs at all and during the course of the summer Sam had found himself beguiled by her simple manner and the openness with which she talked to him whenever they met. Truth to tell, she reminded him of his own Rosie, who was a year younger, and fair to Nell's dark, but had the same eager expression in her eyes. The look young girls got when they were on the brink of womanhood.

Thanks to her lack of shyness, he already knew all about her – and her family. They had moved from Midhurst to Oak Green three years before, Nell had told him, but her father continued to work in the town as a chartered accountant and drove her to school every morning. Up until this year her mother had always fetched her in the afternoons. But since turning thirteen – Nell was the youngest of the Ramsays' three children, her two brothers being at university – she'd been deemed old enough to make the journey on her own.

'I was saving up a biscuit in case we met, Sally. But I'm not sure I ought to give it to you now. You're getting so *fat*.'

At the word 'biscuit' Sal's ears had pricked, and now, as though under the spell of her moist brown eyes, Nell reached blindly into her satchel and brought out a ginger snap, which was quickly disposed of. Sam could only shake his head and sigh. Greediest dog on earth.

'I'm sorry, I've got to dash today.' Nell searched for her things on the ground. 'Aunt Edith's coming to tea and Mummy doesn't want me to be late.' She planted a kiss on the silky head beside hers and stood up. 'Good-bye, Mr Watkin. Goodbye, Sally.'

Grinning, Sam waved a farewell to her and then watched as she went hurrying off down the path, hoisting her satchel onto her shoulders and clutching at her hat. He turned to leave, but had to pause once more, finding Sally firmly planted on her haunches behind him, busy scratching behind one ear. Or trying to. It was a struggle to reach the awkward spot these days and she was putting all her effort into the task.

'Come on, old girl. I'll do that for you.'

But though he gave her a good scratch, it failed to produce the desired result, and as soon as he'd finished

she went back to what she'd been doing before, leaving
Sam no option but to wait until she was ready to move
on.

He glanced down the path again and saw that Nell
was well along it, approaching the fork that would take
her to Oak Green.

Then he noticed something else. The bloke he'd spotted earlier, up on the ridge opposite, across the valley.
The one with the fieldglasses. He was still there.

Sam had taken him for a birdwatcher. There were
plenty of them around, particularly in the summer, and
it was easy to spot them. They were forever scanning the
heavens, sometimes making notes of what they saw. But
whatever this bloke was looking at now, it wasn't a bird.
He had his binoculars trained on the valley below him,
which was strange, Sam thought, since there was nothing
there to see. Nothing of interest.

Unless it was the sight of Nell's figure hurrying across
the open field away from the path towards the red roofs
of Oak Green, her white hat bobbing up and down like
a flower carried on a stream.

15

'VANE? *PHILIP* VANE?' Bennett stared at the chief inspector with incredulity. 'Are you serious?'

'Perfectly, sir. Do you know him?' The photograph which Sinclair had just withdrawn from his file remained in his hand.

Bennett gestured impatiently for it and he handed him the glossy print. Procured from a magazine archive, it was a studio portrait of a man in his forties with narrow, well-bred features composed in an expression of boredom. Elegant in evening dress, he wore the ribbon of some decoration about his neck. The assistant commissioner stared at the picture for a moment, then nodded.

'That's Vane,' he acknowledged. 'We've met several times.' He looked at the chief inspector, then glanced at Holly, who was sitting beside him. The dull autumn light coming through the windows of his office gave a leaden tinge to their faces. 'Have either of you any idea who he is?' he asked in a neutral tone.

'Never heard of him, sir.'

While Holly's reply had been prompt, Sinclair took his time responding. Warned by their superior's manner, he chose his words carefully. 'I'm aware that he works at the Foreign Office,' he said. In fact, he was a good deal better informed than that about the individual in question, but seeing the look in Bennett's eye, he realized it might be wise if he kept this intelligence to himself, at least for the time being.

'Oh, there's a little more to him than that, you know.' Bennett's tone was silky, but the chief inspector did not fail to catch the warning note in it. 'Vane's a specialist in European affairs, quite a senior figure.'

Sinclair contrived to look impressed.

'He lunches at the palace, what's more. Did you know that?'

'I did not, sir.' In the circumstances, the lie seemed permissable.

'Yes, and he shoots at Sandringham.' Bennett's gaze was penetrating.

'My word!' Holly whistled. 'Is this the chappie with the car, then?'

Bennett ignored him. He kept his gaze on Sinclair's face. The chief inspector had come to this meeting, arranged at his request, in a state of some tension. Now he spoke bluntly.

'With respect, sir, the question here is not whether Philip Vane is well regarded at the Foreign Office – I'm sure he is – nor even if he's on the palace's guest list. The issue's a simple one. Is he, or is he not a murderer?'

Bennett drew in his breath sharply and the chief inspector braced himself for the explosion he could see was coming. Having spent half a lifetime working on the fringes of Whitehall, he knew only too well what effect even a whiff of scandal could have on those in high office. But he'd been surprised all the same by the sharpness of his superior's reaction and for an uneasy moment he wondered if there was even more at stake here than he'd supposed.

Bennett, meanwhile, was struggling to retain his poise. He spoke in a controlled tone. 'Apart from the fact that he owns a motor car of this make, have you any reason to think he might be?'

'Sir, all I have at the moment is information—'

'Can you really think a man like Philip Vane guilty of such bestial crimes?' The assistant commissioner interrupted him, staring. 'In all honesty now, Chief Inspector?'

'Why, I have no *opinion* one way or the other.' Sinclair took care to appear scandalized by the suggestion. He saw he'd stumbled into a minefield. 'What I *must* emphasize, though, is there's every likelihood the man we're seeking has an unusual background. Otherwise we'd have caught him by now. And no one can be excluded simply because of his position. His class . . .'

Franz Weiss's words on the subject had returned to the chief inspector's mind while he was speaking.

'That said, all I'm interested in at present are facts. Let me tell you what I've learned.' He'd already opened the file on his knee and he continued before Bennett could interrupt him again. 'Vane purchased a Mercedes-Benz of the relevant model in June, 1929 – you'll recall the Henley child disappeared in July of that year. In October he was posted to the British Embassy in Berlin where he remained until July of this year, when he was recalled to London.' Sinclair looked up. 'We've been puzzled by the long gap between the earlier case and the Bognor Regis murder, which occurred in late July, and we've discussed the possibility that the killer might have been abroad during that time.' He lowered his eyes again. 'Oh, by the way, the reason he bought a Mercedes rather than a British-made car was precisely *because* he was going to Germany. He apparently thought it would be easier to get the vehicle serviced and repaired there.'

Silence fell in the office. Holly looked at them both. The assistant commissioner had turned pale. When he spoke, the anger in his voice seemed barely in check. 'Have you been making inquiries about Vane among his colleagues and friends, Chief Inspector?'

'Good heavens, no. He's a public servant, sir. This is all a matter of record.' Sinclair tapped the file on his knee. 'As is his purchase of that motor car.'

'And his reasons, his *personal* reasons, for buying a German-made machine? Were those on the record?'

'Gossip, sir. Common knowledge.' Sinclair retained his composure. 'His name was on the list the Mercedes people sent us. It's the only one we haven't checked. In the normal course, I would probably have spoken to him already if he wasn't out of the country at present. But I'm assured he'll be back shortly.'

'It's as well for you that you didn't,' Bennett said quietly, causing Angus Sinclair's eyebrows to shoot up in amazement. 'I'm warning you now, Chief Inspector. *Take care*. If this blows up in your face, there will be hell to pay. And, as of this moment, you are treading on very thin ice.'

'Am I, sir?' Angered himself, Sinclair met his superior's heated gaze coolly. 'Well, so be it. As of this moment Philip Vane is a suspect. He must be asked to give a detailed account of his movements on the relevant days in July and September and to provide supporting evidence, if possible.'

'And what explanation do you propose to offer him for this intrusion into his private life?'

'None, unless he asks for one, in which case I'll tell him the truth.'

Bennett breathed deeply. His pallor had receded, but in its place twin red spots had appeared in his cheeks like warning signals. He stared at the chief inspector, blinking rapidly.

Holly cleared his throat. 'While you're thinking about that, sir, there's something else you might consider doing.'

'What's that, Arthur?' It was Sinclair who put the question. His gaze remained locked to the assistant commissioner's.

'We could keep an eye on him.'

'Put a *tail* on Philip Vane?' Bennett gave vent to his feelings, bringing his fist down hard on the desktop. 'Are you out of your mind?'

'No, sir. Quite rational, I believe. Hungry, though.' Holly smiled ruefully, easing the strained atmosphere just a little. 'But until you decide whether or not Angus is to talk to this fellow, where's the harm in keeping a watch on his movements?'

'Out of the question. Is that clear?'

'Then may I suggest a compromise?' Sinclair intervened without allowing a pause. 'Vane still owns that car. It's garaged here in London. What I would urge, sir, and very strongly, is that the *car* at least should be kept under surveillance until further notice. If Vane leaves the city in it, he must be followed.'

Wearing the look of a man forced to swallow a dose of cyanide, Bennett nodded. 'Very well. I'll agree to that. But no more.'

'And then there's the matter of the interview.' Sinclair refused to let the issue rest. 'I'm requesting your authorization to speak to Philip Vane, and at the earliest possible moment. If he's in the clear, so much the better. We can strike his name from our files.'

The assistant commissioner sat hunched in his chair, his lips drawn together in a thin line. 'I'm forced to remind you that you have no *evidence* against this man.'

'I'm aware of that, sir.'

'Yes, but do you truly understand what it is you're proposing to do? It's not simply a question of Vane's position at the Foreign Office. He has powerful friends and supporters in other quarters.'

'I'm sure you're not suggesting those are reasons why we shouldn't interview him, sir.'

Bennett's lips whitened in anger. Holly looked anxiously from one to the other, wondering if he should intervene. He was becoming concerned for his friend.

'I want to think this matter over.' The assistant commissioner spoke in dead tones. He was making an effort to remain calm.

'Quite, sir. But not for too long, I trust.' Sinclair was relentless.

'Chief Inspector! You've made your point. Don't labour it!' Bennett glared at him. 'I'll see you both at five o'clock. That will be all.'

The two men rose and left the office in silence. No sooner had they passed through the anteroom and gone out into the corridor than Holly seized the other's arm.

'What's got into you, Angus? Are you pushing for an early pension, man?'

'*He lunches at the palace. He shoots at Sandringham!*'

Holly saw he'd been deceived by his friend's icy demeanour inside Bennett's office. The chief inspector's cheeks were flushed with anger. His flint-grey eyes, normally cool, threw off sparks.

'Calm down, for goodness sake,' he urged. 'You've gone at this like a bull at a gate. It's not like you. Give Bennett some time to think it over.'

Grim-faced, Sinclair waited in silence while two detectives walked by them in the corridor. He responded to their greetings with the briefest of nods.

'He's looking for a way out of this. You'll see – he won't let me near Vane.'

'Now you don't know that.' Holly shook an admonishing finger. 'Give the man a chance. Anyway, we'll know soon enough. Five o'clock, he said.'

But they didn't have to wait that long. Fully an hour before the time set, Sinclair received an urgent telephoned summons to return to the assistant commissioner's office. Hurrying down the stairs to the corridor below, he caught sight of the chief super, a trimmer figure after his weeks of dieting, walking briskly in the same direction.

'What now, I wonder?' Sinclair had caught up with

him in the anteroom. They waited while Bennett's secretary reported their arrival. 'I wouldn't have thought our lord and master was in any hurry to get this settled.'

The chief inspector had come psychologically prepared to resume the struggle – he was determined not to yield on the issue – but he saw at a glance as they entered the office that the situation had changed. Bennett, paler than usual, was seated at his desk. The unnatural brightness of his gaze, as he looked up, hinted at some recent shock undergone. His face wore a look of deep anxiety.

'Sit down, gentlemen, please.'

Obeying, Sinclair noticed a stack of telegram forms lying on the desk blotter. Bennett had been looking at them when they came in, and now he turned his attention back to the shallow pile, leafing through the pages for several seconds, before raising his eyes once more and regarding them both.

'Since we met earlier, I've received a message in response to the request we sent to the International Police Commission. You'll recall we asked them for any information they might have relating to crimes similiar to the ones we're investigating.'

'Have they a record of such cases in Vienna?' Sinclair couldn't contain his eagerness for the answer.

'Yes . . . I imagine so . . . now.' Bennett hesitated. 'But this telegram comes from Berlin. It was sent to me by Arthur Nebe.' He glanced up and met Sinclair's eye.

'Nebe?' Holly struggled with the unfamiliar pronunciation.

'Your namesake, Arthur.' Sinclair kept his gaze on the

assistant commissioner's face. 'He's the Berlin police chief, head of their CID.'

Bennett swallowed. His voice had become a little hoarse. 'Nebe was informed of our request by the commission. He asked them to let him respond to it directly, citing "special circumstances" . . . It's not clear from his message what those might be.' The assistant commissioner bit his lip.

Sinclair allowed his eye to stray to the window where darkness had already fallen. Lights in the buildings across the river showed only faintly. The mist that had been gathering all day was thickening into fog.

Bennett went on, 'It appears the German police have had a number of cases similiar to ours under investigation for some time. Nebe doesn't say how many, but reports that they cover a two-year period starting in late 1929 . . .' He looked up and caught Sinclair's glance once more. 'Yes. Quite. That fits the period of Vane's posting to Germany.'

The chief inspector was silent. He felt no sense of triumph, only sympathy for his superior, whose ordeal was just beginning.

'Nebe didn't know, until he learned from Vienna, that we had comparable cases under review here.' The assistant commissioner had turned his attention back to the telegram. 'He suggests that our two police forces should cooperate in this "exceptional matter" – that's a quote – and says he's dispatched an officer to London "to inform you fully on the investigation being carried out in Germany and to offer any assistance he can".

Considerate of them, in the circumstances. My God, I wonder how much they know. How much they've guessed.' Bennett shook his head despairingly. 'This man's on his way. He'll be in London tomorrow.'

He laid the telegram forms aside. Shutting his eyes, he rested his chin on his hands and sat like a statue, unmoving, for some time. As the silence lengthened, Holly cast a questioning glance at Sinclair, who put a finger to his lips and shook his head.

Bennett opened his eyes. 'I owe you an apology, Chief Inspector.'

'Not at all, sir. I'm as shocked as you are.' Even as he made the required response, Sinclair was uncomfortably aware of how closely Philip Vane fitted at least one of the imagined portraits sketched for him by Dr Weiss during their discussion at Highfield. A man protected by his position, able to cover his tracks.

The assistant commissioner straightened in his chair. 'Let's turn to practical matters. On no account should Vane's name be allowed to get out until we've had a chance to talk to him. Do we agree on that?'

'Wholeheartedly, sir.'

'You say he's abroad?'

'I was told he was away on government business. I didn't inquire further. He'll be back next week.'

'Good. By then we'll have heard what our German colleague has to tell us and know better where we stand. But we'd better brace ourselves for the worst. It may well be that responsibility for these crimes lies at the door of a senior government official, and that among his victims are nationals of a country to which he was accredited. Needless to say, it's not a situation we've ever had to deal with before. But deal with it we must. Gentlemen . . .'

Bennett stayed in his chair, but raised a weary hand in farewell as the other two rose to leave. Pausing at the door, Sinclair looked back and saw him start to leaf through the telegram forms again. He was struck by how much the assistant commissioner's face had aged in the past quarter of an hour.

16

'KRIM ... KRIMIN ... ?'

Arthur Holly squinted at the piece of white paste-board Sinclair had just handed him. Although it was only a little past two o'clock, the lights in Bennett's office, including his green-shaded desk lamp, were all switched on. Outside, the blanketing fog pressed up against the windowpanes, reducing what little illumina-tion came from the sky to a dull, uniform glow, the colour of dishwater. Less than twenty-four hours had passed since their last gathering.

'*Krim-in-al* ... ?' Holly scowled. The word he was struggling with – *kriminalinspektor* – was one he had not encountered before and he was having difficulty working his way through the seemingly endless syllables.

'He's a German police inspector, Arthur.' Sinclair came to his rescue. 'A copper, just like us.'

Holly snorted, unimpressed. Since their last meeting the day before he'd had second thoughts on the wisdom of permitting any foreigner to share their deliberations on so delicate an issue – doubts which he'd expressed to Sinclair in private a little while earlier. The fact that their visitor was a German – or 'hun', as the chief super preferred to put it – only made matters worse.

'Probs ... Prost ...' Now he was struggling with the name. 'Probst! That's it. Hans-Jo ... Hans-Joa?'

'Hans-Joachim Probst! For pity's sake, Chief Superintendent!' Bennett's patience snapped. He'd been on edge all morning.

'Thank you, sir.' Unruffled, Holly rose and returned the card to his superior's blotter. It had arrived a few minutes before, dispatched from the reception desk with the news that its owner was waiting in the lobby below. Bennett had ordered him to be shown upstairs to his first-floor office immediately.

Nebe's emissary was late – they'd been expecting him all morning – but through no fault of his own. Fog in the channel had delayed ferry sailings, and when Sinclair telephoned Victoria station it was to learn that the Berlin train would not be arriving until after one o'clock. At twenty minutes past the hour Inspector Probst had rung to announce his arrival. Forgetting that the fog would also reduce the speed of taxis to a crawl, Bennett had sent for Holly and Sinclair at once and the three of them had been sitting in his office twiddling their thumbs ever since.

Observing the assistant commissioner now, Sinclair took note of his troubled glance and pale aspect. He wondered what kind of night Sir Wilfred had passed. His own had been far from tranquil. No policeman could contemplate the arrest of a senior government official without trepidation: one, moreover, who had entrée to the highest social circles in the land. Given the terrible charges that might soon have to be laid against Philip Vane, the case had all the hallmarks of a nightmare in the making. It would have to be watertight. On that score the chief inspector had no illusions.

The backlash from a botched prosecution would be swift and merciless. And of the three of them, the assistant commissioner had the most to lose.

There was a light tap on the door. Bennett's secretary put her head in. 'The German gentleman's here, sir.'

'Show him in, please, Miss Baxter.' Bennett rose, and the other two followed suit. As their visitor entered, the assistant commissioner came around his desk and offered him his hand. 'Inspector Probst?'

'Sir Wilfred!' They shook hands, Probst accompanying the action with a stiff bow. He was in his late thirties, with fair, curling hair that receded from a high forehead. Slight of build, he wore a suit of an old-fashioned cut and a shirt with a high, stiff collar. Both his manner and appearance had struck Sinclair as being fussy and schoolmasterly until the two men were introduced, when the chief inspector found himself looking into a pair of eyes as cool and watchful as his own, yet not without a trace of humour in their blue depths.

Alerted, he observed their visitor closely as Bennett ushered him to the conference table. The initial impression of stiffness and formality the inspector had given was soon dispelled. In fact, considering that he had just made a long, tiring journey and had now to handle a difficult brief before strangers – and in a language not his own – Probst's self-possession was remarkable. While the others seated themselves around him he calmly undid the straps of his briefcase and took out a thick file, tied with black tape, which he laid on the table before him.

'Before we begin, Inspector – may I offer you some refreshment? Coffee? Tea? Something to eat, perhaps?'

Bennett had taken the head of the narrow oak table and placed Holly and Sinclair on one side of him, facing Probst. Far from composed himself, the assistant commissioner fidgeted nervously in his chair, glancing out of the window into the fog, as though seeking inspiration there, in contrast to their visitor, who unhurriedly ordered the papers in his file as he waited for the proceedings to start.

'Thank you, Sir Wilfred. I had lunch on the train. A glass of water will be sufficient.' With a smile and a nod Probst reached for the carafe that stood on the table and poured himself a tumblerful.

'May I say at the start how relieved I am to find that you speak our language so fluently.' Unwilling to come to the point, the assistant commissioner continued to seek an excuse to prevaricate. 'Otherwise, I'm afraid I should have had to send for an interpreter, something I would much rather not do, given the circumstances.' He cast a significant glance at the inspector, perhaps hoping to learn in advance whether the shocking discovery made by the Yard's representatives was already known to their colleagues in Berlin. Probst's discreet nod in response, however, shed no light on the matter, one way or the other.

'You are kind to compliment me on my English, Sir Wilfred, but the credit must go to a lady in Berlin, a Miss Adamson, from Durham. For years I used to visit her twice a week, and it's thanks to her that I'm familiar with the works of Sir Walter Scott and Robert Louis Stevenson, all of which I read to her from cover to cover. A pleasure for me, you may be sure, but perhaps not for poor Miss Adamson, since they appeared to be the only books she used for this purpose and she had many pupils.'

Sinclair noticed, with amusement, that it was their visitor who was endeavouring to put his hosts at their ease.

'But you might be interested to know where I first learned the language,' Probst went on. 'It was in a prisoner of war camp. Quite early in the war – it was in 1915 – I was blown sky high . . . that is the correct term, is it not, "sky high"?' His blue eyes twinkled. 'I awoke to find myself in a British field hospital and spent the rest of the war in a camp near the city of Carlisle, learning not only English but basket-weaving and brick-laying, as well. Rarely have I spent my time more *usefully*, before or since.'

This long discourse seemed to have had the desired effect on Bennett, Sinclair observed. The assistant commissioner sat with his chin cupped in his hand, listening attentively. A glance at Holly, on his other side, revealed a different picture. Apparently the sight of a foreigner – and a hun, at that – spouting the King's English with such aplomb had taken the chief super unawares. Sheer disbelief was stamped on his blunt features.

Bennett resettled himself in his chair. 'To business, then.' He turned to Probst. 'Herr Nebe informed us in his telegram that you have been investigating a series of murders in Germany that may well be linked to similiar crimes under inquiry here. We should be very interested to hear about those, and anything else you have to tell us.'

Probst dipped his head in acknowledgement. 'I have come armed with all the relevant information, Sir Wilfred. The murders I'm about to describe have a distinct "signature", one you may find familiar. Should that be the case, we are ready to offer any assistance we can in bringing this man to justice. I speak not only for my superiors in Berlin, but for the Bavarian police as well.'

'The *Bavarian* police?' Bennett was taken aback.

'Yes, two of the murders I'm talking about were committed there. The other four were in Prussia. They took place in a period of a little over two years between December 1929, and April of this year, since when there have been none reported: none, that is, until we received word of your inquiry to the international commission.'

'So there have been *six* in all?' The assistant commissioner was still coming to terms with the grim figure.

'Six, yes ... though there may have been more.' Probst lifted his glance to theirs.

'Why do you say that?' Holly spoke up.

'For two reasons, Chief Superintendent. Firstly, this murderer hides the bodies of his victims afterwards, or attempts to. Our belief is he aims to leave a cold trail – to be well away by the time the body is found. So it may be there are other corpses still awaiting discovery.' Probst shrugged. 'Are there young girls missing, then, you ask me? Children unaccounted for? Sadly, the answer is yes, but the reasons for this are many, and not necessarily connected to this or any other criminal case.' The inspector paused, his brow creasing in a frown.

'I'm sure you're all aware that my country has been through difficult times since the war ended. First, there was the collapse of our currency, next the Depression. We have had reparations to pay. All this is reflected in our political situation. German society has been disrupted, and one effect has been the breaking-up of families. We have seen begging . . . young people cast out on the streets. I need not go on. If this man was seeking victims unlikely to be missed he could hardly have chosen a better hunting ground than Germany in recent years.'

'Yes, quite, Inspector . . .' Bennett stirred uneasily beneath the Berlin policeman's cool, unaccusing gaze. 'But could you not give us some *details* about these murders? We need to decide whether they resemble our own cases.'

'I believe they do.' Probst's reply was prompt. 'Even from what little we have gleaned from your inquiry to Vienna, it seems almost certain we are dealing with the same killer. But I will let you decide this, Sir Wilfred.' While he was speaking the inspector had produced a pince-nez of antique manufacture from his lapel pocket, which he donned now as he consulted the papers from his file, the gold-rimmed lenses, perched on the bridge of his nose, lending further colour to his schoolmaster's air and making him seem older than he was.

'The victims in Germany have all been young girls, aged between ten and thirteen. None had reached puberty. Rape and strangulation occurred in each case and were followed by an assault on the victim's face in which, according to our pathologists' findings, the same weapon, or an identical one, was used by the killer.'

'A hammer, would that be?' Sinclair put the question in a low voice.

'Yes, an ordinary stonemason's tool.' Probst looked up. 'It is the same with the victims here? Your query to the commission was not specific on that point.'

Before Sinclair could respond, Bennett intervened. 'Our conclusions are very similar to yours. I think we can say there's every likelihood we're looking for the same man. We have two cases under investigation here. More of those later. Continue, if you would . . .' He caught the chief inspector's eye.

Probst bent to his file again. 'What evidence we have been able to gather leads us to believe the children were picked up, usually on a road, and taken by car to the murder site, which presumably had been selected in advance. In the first two instances, the girls appeared to have been either choked or stunned into submission prior to the sexual assault. But in the four subsequent cases traces of chloroform were discovered in the lungs of the victims.'

The inspector looked up. 'This evidence of a refinement in the killer's technique, if I can put it that way, seemed particularly sinister to us, as no doubt it will to you. As policemen we are well aware of how dangerous such men become once they develop a method in which repetition predominates.'

He paused, moistening his lips, and then spent the next few moments rearranging the papers in his file. Observing him, Sinclair realized that the Berlin policeman's dry, precise manner was to some extent a mask:

that although engaging in a bald recital of facts, he was in reality deeply disturbed by what he was telling them.

'Our first two killings took place in Prussia, neither of them very far from Berlin itself.' Probst resumed his account. 'The third occurred in Bavaria, in the Munich region. Unfortunately, the connection between these three murders was not noted at once. As I'm sure you know, Germany has no unified police force, nor any central organization like Scotland Yard, which can coordinate inquiries. The states and *Lande* act on their own account. Regrettably, we have been slow in exchanging information.

'However, with the fourth and fifth murders, which were again in the vicinity of Berlin, it finally became clear that we were looking for a single killer and since then the Prussian and Bavarian authorities have been cooperating closely. And it was the sixth murder, in April this year, also in Bavaria, that provided us at last with a lead of some substance. Though I fear that whatever advantage we gained has turned out to be at your expense.' He favoured his listeners with a wry look.

Bennett frowned. 'I take it you mean this man has now transferred his activities to England?'

'Yes, to us it seems likely that the inquiries we set in motion may have forced him to seek his victims elsewhere. But even here the situation is unclear.' Probst tapped the table once more. 'There is a mystery surrounding this man.'

In the silence that followed this remark the long drawn out, mournful note of a foghorn sounded from the river below. Sinclair sensed Bennett's growing discomfiture at the direction the conversation was taking. He stepped in.

'A lead of substance, you said. Tell us about that, Inspector. What happened with the last murder? In Bavaria, was it?'

'Yes, the victim in this case was the child of a farmer in the Allershausen district, north of Munich. Her body was found in a wooded area not far from the main road. The crime came close to being witnessed. A woodcutter's wife was walking through the forest and heard the child's cries, followed by the sound of heavy blows. Guessing that some act of violence was taking place, she was on the point of running back to her house to seek help when she heard someone approaching. Terrified, she hid herself, lying face down, too frightened even to lift her eyes as whoever it was went by. When it was quiet again, she looked up and saw the figure of a man a little way off. He was on his knees, with his back to her, bending over a stream that the woman had just crossed herself. He was naked from the waist up.'

'*Naked!*' Arthur Holly came to life with a growl.

'He had taken his shirt off . . .' The inspector hesitated. 'One must understand this woman's state of mind at that moment. Complete terror would not be too strong a term to describe it. She saw only that his arms were spattered with blood and that he was washing himself off in the stream, both his arms and his chest, though of course she couldn't see his front.'

'Nor his face, either, I imagine?' Sinclair sensed, rather than heard, Bennett's faint sigh of relief at that point.

'No, alas! A moment later she ducked her head down

again and remained like that, unmoving, until she heard him coming back along the path where she lay, hurrying, but not running. Only when she was sure he was no longer anywhere near did she get to her feet and run back to her own house, which was a mile away.' Probst looked up and caught Sinclair's eye. 'When we received a report of this incident from the Bavarian police – I mean those of us in Berlin who have been concerned with this investigation – we felt despair. It seemed a golden opportunity to identify our man had gone begging. But in fact the woman saw more than she realized.'

The chief inspector grunted. 'I've known that happen,' he remarked.

'Under repeated questioning by Munich detectives this woman was able to add some crucial details to what she had first said. Interestingly, from the start she referred to the man she saw as a "Herr" – a gentleman, if you like – and finally it came out that the reason she thought so was because of his clothes. She had caught a glimpse of his jacket, which was on the ground beside him, with his shirt, and also his shoes, and they must have impressed her as being of good quality.'

Probst raised his hands in a weighing gesture. 'It wasn't much to go on, but the detectives went to work all the same. Since the murder took place near a main road – in fact, it's the most direct route from Munich to Berlin – they assumed the killer had been travelling on it when he came on his victim. But in which direction? North or south? If he was going south, to Munich, there was little chance they could track him down. He would soon be swallowed up in the city. But heading north, the situation was different.' The inspector paused. 'Remember, by this time we had linked these crimes and we knew that the murderer must have spent a good deal of time during the past two years in and around Berlin. So it was reasonable to assume that if he drove north after killing the girl he was in fact returning to the capital.'

Probst took a deep breath. His long day seemed finally to be catching up with him and he took a handkerchief from his pocket and dabbed his brow.

'One of the Munich detectives had an idea. Since the murder had occurred between ten and eleven in the morning, why not drive north along the Berlin road for two hours and then look for likely places where the killer might have stopped for lunch? This they set out to do. Hotels, inns, restaurants. All within a twenty-mile stretch of road were covered and the same question was asked in each place: did anyone remember a well-dressed man eating on his own that day?

'And it didn't stop there. Police notices were placed in newspapers asking any motorist who was on the road that day to come forward. The same thing was done in Berlin. When I tell you the response was overwhelming, you may perhaps be amazed, though you should not be.' Probst's blue eyes glinted behind his spectacles. 'We Germans are a law-abiding people. Overly so, some might say. Appeals from authority seldom fall on deaf ears. A considerable number came forward not only to report their own presence on the road that day but to inform us of others they had noticed and remembered. In this way we were able to form a surprisingly full picture of who was eating in these various establishments and to eliminate most of them by cross-checking. We were left with a handful of men who remained unidentified and who had not come forward of their own accord. Of these, one in particular caught our attention.'

The inspector paused to take a sip of water. Bennett glanced automatically at his watch. The sound of foghorns had continued intermittently during the long recital they'd been listening to, the plaintive notes sounding from near and far, echoing up and down the busy river.

'This man had been noted by several of our voluntary witnesses who had eaten lunch at a roadside hotel near Nuremberg. He was reckoned to be in his forties, and had sat alone at a table in a corner reading a book while he ate. Neither the waitress who served him nor our other witnesses were able to give a satisfactory description of him. This wasn't surprising, however. Unusual features are sometimes remembered: a large nose, say, or a scar. But unless we have particular reason to look at a person we generally form only an *impression* of him . . . yes? And the impression of all was that there was nothing out of the ordinary about this man's appearance. He had sat with his head lowered, reading his book. Even the waitress didn't remember meeting his glance. He ordered, ate quickly, paid and left. Our attempts to obtain some sort of picture of his face, using the services of an artist, failed completely. Some of the witnesses were unable to offer any suggestions; others produced images that differed so much, one from another, they were quite useless for practical purposes.

'One thing only about him seemed unusual . . . noteworthy.' Grimacing, Probst nodded to himself. 'It hardly counted as a clue. It was too vague ... too imprecise. And we only returned to it later, after we'd received word from the international commission about your inquiry. It was something the waitress said in her original deposition.' Probst paused. He looked at them keenly. 'Asked where this man might have come from – whether she'd recognized any regional accent in his voice – she said she had not. "He didn't seem to be from anywhere." That was her exact reply, translated from the German. We asked our Bavarian colleagues to question her again, and this time she was a little more specific.'

The atmosphere around the table had grown tense. Alerted by a new note in the inspector's voice, Bennett leaned forward in his chair, his gaze fixed on the German detective's face. Probst had paused once more, perhaps to underline the importance of what he was about to say. Now he continued.

'She said she wondered if he was German at all.'

'She meant he was a *foreigner*?' Sinclair found his tongue before the others. A glance at Bennett showed him sitting sphinx-like. Holly, beside him, scowled.

'Perhaps, though she didn't say so. Not in so many words. The man's German was faultless, you see – at least to her ears. No, we're back with *impressions*. She just had a feeling he wasn't one of us.' The inspector shook his head regretfully. 'Earlier, as I say, we hadn't given much importance to this aspect of her evidence. After all, she seemed so unsure herself. But after news of your inquiry reached us, we had cause to think again.'

Probst removed his pince-nez. He looked at each of

them in turn, his gaze finally coming to rest on the assistant commissioner.

'It's our belief the newspaper campaign we launched caused this man to flee Germany, Sir Wilfred. No murders of the kind we've been discussing have been reported in my country for the past six months. In the meantime, however, it would appear he has become active here. Remembering what the waitress in that hotel had to say, and given that he *chose* to come to this country, rather than another, I submit there is a question we must all ask ourselves: Could this man we are seeking be *English*?'

BENNETT LEANED BACK in his chair, the gold links of his watch chain glittering against his dark waistcoat. As the afternoon wore on and the gloom of the foggy day outside deepened, the lights in the assistant commissioner's office had grown brighter. He stifled a yawn.

'This has been a long day, and we all have much to reflect on. I don't know about you, but I'd welcome a good night's sleep. I suggest we meet again in my office tomorrow morning so that we can lay the groundwork of our future cooperation, before Inspector Probst returns to Berlin.'

Sinclair was relieved to hear Bennett's words. For some time now he'd sat silent, puffing at his pipe, reluctant to take any further part in what he increasingly viewed as a charade. Earlier, there had been a break in the proceedings; the interval had been proposed by Sir Wilfred on the ground that there were one or two unrelated, urgent matters awaiting his attention that couldn't be delayed, a pretext so transparent, at least to Sinclair's eyes, that he'd wondered whether Probst, too, had seen through it.

But the Berlin inspector had accompanied him without comment to a nearby waiting room reserved for important visitors. His choice of refreshment, offered by Sinclair, had proved to be afternoon tea – 'in the English manner', as he put it, with a glint of humour in his blue eyes.

'At Miss Adamson's we always had sandwiches and Madeira cake.'

The chief inspector had informed the staff canteen accordingly (while mentally wishing their guest luck with the result) and then returned swiftly to Bennett's office, where he found the assistant commissioner and Holly sunk in despair.

'*Six* murders, he says! And there may have been more. This is a dreadful business, Chief Inspector.'

With that observation, at least, Sinclair had no quarrel. But he had a bone to pick with the assistant commissioner all the same.

'With respect, sir, why did you tell him we only have *two* on our hands? It's virtually certain the Henley case is connected, and the time factor puts a completely different complexion on the matter.'

'In this instance, "virtually certain" is the operative phrase, Chief Inspector.' Bennett's response had been sharp. It was plain he resented the accusing note in Sinclair's voice. 'Look, they've already guessed the killer might be a British subject. If we tell Probst there was a linked murder in 1929 by a man who then disappeared for three years, during which time a further *six* killings occurred in Germany, he's quite likely to ask himself what kind of individual would be in a position to lead such an existence: living first in one country, then in another, and at home in both. And just as likely to come up with an educated guess that he's a diplomat, or some other accredited person. Until we're sure about Vane, until we've questioned him, I'm not going to allow any hint to surface that the author of these crimes could be a British official.'

'That's a sensible precaution, Angus.' Holly had added his weight to the argument. 'There's no point in jumping the gun. Just think of the implications!'

Sinclair had not forgotten them; nor, it seemed, had Probst. And although the German policeman's point of view, of necessity, differed from theirs, the fears to which he'd finally given expression at the close of the long afternoon were uncomfortably close to those of his British counterparts.

Before that point had been reached, however, and on the resumption of the meeting following the break called by Bennett, the inspector had been given a detailed summary of the current police investigations into the murders at Bognor Regis and Brookham. Primed by Bennett, and under his watchful eye, Sinclair had led his German colleague by stages through the history of the inquiry in Britain, from the discovery of the first body in Surrey to the slow-dawning realization that what they were dealing with was no common sex killing.

'We didn't know what we were faced with until the second corpse was uncovered near the coast, in Sussex. Up till then the search had been concentrated on finding this tramp. I'm afraid the Surrey police were led astray.'

'What made you get in touch with Vienna, if I may ask? Did you have some reason to think this man might have been abroad?'

The question was an obvious one, but since an honest answer would have meant revealing details of the suspected murder at Henley three years before, Sinclair had been forced to take refuge behind a smokescreen.

'No specific reason. But it seemed to us this murderer might well have killed before. There was a finished quality to his crimes: the battering of the faces, the fact that he brought a hammer with him to carry out the job. No record of such a criminal existed in this country, so we thought to look elsewhere.' Glancing at Bennett as he produced this farrago of lies and half-truths, the chief inspector was gratified to see that his superior at least had the grace to blush.

Probst, meanwhile, had been paying close attention. 'It may interest you to hear what one of our leading forensic psychiatrists has to say about these cases,' he remarked. 'A Professor Hartmann of the Friedrich Wilhelm University, in Berlin. He believes that while the killer's sexual desires may have been the original motive for these crimes, the need to assault his victims' bodies afterwards has now become the dominant element of his psychosis, hence the increasingly elaborate ritual he brings to the destruction of their faces.'

Remembering the similar, prophetic judgement he had heard from the lips of Franz Weiss only a few weeks earlier, Sinclair grimaced, but stayed silent.

At five o'clock, Bennett called a halt, and as the chimes of Big Ben sounded faintly, drifting down through the foggy darkness from Westminster, their visitor addressed them for the last time, making an appeal which at least one among his audience found affecting, even if it did not assuage the guilt he felt, but merely added to it. Angus Sinclair took no satisfaction from the knowledge that he and his colleagues had been successful in keeping their darkest suspicions from the *kriminalinspektor*.

'My superiors have asked me to stress the importance they attach to resolving this case as soon as possible. Quite aside from the human tragedy involved, they believe it contains dangers of which we should all be aware. These are the "special circumstances" to which Herr Nebe referred in his telegram to you, Sir Wilfred. Although we don't yet know the identity of this man we are seeking, it's likely he is either German or English. Which, is not important. What matters, we believe, is that crimes of such brutality committed by a national of one country against the children of another are liable to be seen in the worst light, and given the recent shared history of our two nations there may be those, in both countries, who will seek to make the most of an appalling situation. We on our part are most anxious to avoid any such development and I am authorized to offer Scotland Yard the full cooperation of both the Prussian and Bavarian authorities in bringing this man to justice.'

Probst fell silent. But it was clear from his manner that he had not yet finished speaking and the others waited patiently while the Berlin inspector sat with eyes downcast, assembling his thoughts. When he looked up, Sinclair was struck by the intensity of his gaze.

'My ability to speak English is the main reason I was chosen for this mission. But certain of my colleagues, aware that I share their sympathies, were anxious for me to convey the full extent of our concern over this case.' He paused once more, conscious of his listeners' heightened interest. Bennett was staring at him with a fixed look.

'That said, I must make it clear that I have no authority to discuss the matter I now wish to raise, so that what I say must be regarded as a personal opinion unsanctioned by my superiors. I have already touched on conditions in Germany. No doubt you are aware of how unstable our political scene has been since the end of the war. It has not improved in recent weeks. Neither I nor anyone else can tell you what government my country will have three months from now, except to say that it may well be directed by a party whose leaders are without principle.'

'I take it you mean the Nazis?' Bennett put the question, and the other nodded.

'But I make no biased accusation against them. This is a statement of fact. They boast of it. What others might regard as human decency they see as a weakness to be exploited. I cannot say how a police authority run by such men would deal with a situation of the kind we have been discussing. But one thing is certain: much will change in Germany if they come to power, and both I and the people for whom I speak want to stress how urgent we believe it is that this terrible case should be brought to a conclusion before such changes can overtake us.'

He looked at each of them in turn.

'Let us do all in our power to identify this man, and to arrest him and bring him to justice,' he pleaded with them. 'And let us do it *soon*.'

PART THREE

17

'WHAT DO YOU think, Daddy? Have we got a chance?'

'Better than that, I hope.' Madden slowed at the sight of a gang of workmen who were resurfacing the road ahead. The trip to Guildford took less than twenty minutes now, compared with the half hour it had needed when he first came to Highfield. 'We've a good team, I think.'

'Yes, but if we can't get *Bradman* out!'

The gloomy thought reduced them both to silence, a rare event on their journeys together. Madden drove his son to school in Guildford every morning, and already he regretted the day, still mercifully two years off, when Rob would leave to become a boarder at a public school in Hampshire.

'He'll probably be better than ever, playing at home,' the boy predicted pessimistically. They were discussing the prospects of the MCC cricket team on its forthcoming tour of Australia. 'Do you think we'll be able to listen to commentaries on the wireless?'

'I don't know. It's a long way off. And there's the difference in time. You'll be asleep when they're playing.'

'That might be just as well.' Rob caught his father's eye and giggled. Madden grinned in sympathy. He'd noticed that his son's jokes were beginning to take on a grown-up flavour.

'What's happening about these murders, Daddy?'

'Why are you asking me?'

'I read in the paper the police think they were done by the same man. Why haven't the police arrested anyone yet?'

'I've no idea.'

'Doesn't Mr Sinclair tell you anything?'

'Why should he? I'm not a policeman any more.'

Robert Madden's sigh was laden with reproach. How his father could voluntarily have abandoned the profession of *detective* – and a Scotland Yard sleuth, at that – to dwindle into a mere farmer was a mystery greater than any, and the fact that most of his schoolfriends agreed with him came as no consolation. Some had even hazarded the view that his parent must be mildly touched.

'Why don't you ask Ted Stackpole?' Madden suggested, referring to the Highfield constable's son. 'He may know something.'

'He doesn't. He says the Surrey police are still looking for that tramp.'

'Well, there you are, then.'

AWARE THAT HE'D not been entirely straightforward with his son, Madden drove back to Highfield deep in thought. Despite what he'd said he'd been hoping to hear from Sinclair, to learn whether any progress had been made in the case.

He continued to be gnawed by anxiety, a deep-seated unease that dated from the moment he had come on the corpse of Alice Bridger and seen her shattered face. The image had stayed in his mind and was linked with earlier memories of the war and the horrors he had witnessed then. Though he knew the feeling was irrational, it seemed to him that with the child's murder and disfigurement a door had been opened once more into the world of savagery and barbarism which bitter experience had taught him lay just outside the frail fabric that bound ordered society.

Try as he might he could not shake free of his fears and increasingly he found the quiet rhythms of his life – rhythms dearly bought and cherished – disturbed by unanswered questions, and by the thought of the killer who still walked free.

More distracted than usual that morning – with the autumn ploughing at hand, he wanted to clear up the paperwork that had accumulated on his desk – he was late getting away from the farm and returned to the house for lunch to find Mary, their maid, impatiently awaiting his arrival in the hall.

'Mrs Beck would like to see you, sir.'

'See *me*?' Madden was nonplussed. The household staff were Helen's business. However, she had driven up to London that morning on a shopping expedition and would not be back until late afternoon.

'Yes, sir. She's waiting for you now.' Mary Morris's brown eyes bore a suspiciously innocent look. Her smothered smile hinted that there was mischief afoot.

Alerted, Madden made his way to the kitchen where he discovered their cook standing before the back door with folded arms, as though to bar it. She wore a defiant expression.

'There's a person says he wants to see you, sir.'

'A person, Mrs Beck?' Madden deposited the parcel of butter and eggs he'd brought from the farm on the kitchen table. 'Who is he?'

'I didn't take his name, sir.' Cook's voice was heavy with disapproval.

'*Where* is he?'

'Outside, in the yard.'

Tossing her head in a gesture of disdain, she moved away from the door, and Madden went past her to open it. One glance at the shabby figure sitting slumped on an upturned barrel by the kitchen garden gate, and all was made clear to him. Over the years, and at the insistence of her employers, Mrs Beck had come to accept the occasional presence of tramps and vagrants in her kitchen. But she drew the line at gypsies!

'Hullo, Joe.' Smiling a greeting, Madden stepped out into the yard, and as he did so, Goram looked up. 'What brings you back to Highfield?'

'BEEZY, YOU SAY? Are you sure? Is it him?'

'Ah, well, that's the trouble, sir.' Goram rubbed his bristly chin. 'I can't be *sure*.'

They sat facing each other across the kitchen table, the remains of a veal and ham pie and an array of empty cider bottles between them. Two hard days on the road had put an edge on Joe Goram's appetite.

'We're camped in Dorset, sir, t'other side of Bland-ford. I managed to get one or two lifts on the way, but mostly I've had to walk.' He'd told Madden this while they were still outside, in the yard, and it was plain to see from the leaves and twigs clinging to the gypsy's twill trousers and the grass stains smearing his grimy, collarless shirt that he'd been sleeping rough. Madden had brought him out a cake of soap and a towel to clean up with.

'We'll go inside in a moment and have something to eat. You look done in.'

His words had caused the gypsy's scowl to lift for a moment as his face split in a gap-toothed grin. 'I reckon I'd better stay where I am, sir. That missus won't have me in her kitchen, I can tell you.'

'Oh, yes, she will.'

Madden's brave words had soon been put to the test. It had taken all of the ten minutes Joe had needed to make himself presentable before Cora Beck could be convinced of the seriousness of her employer's suggestion and persuaded to lay the kitchen table for two. That done, she had taken leave of the scene, with an injured air, asserting that there was a mountain of ironing awaiting her attention in the laundry.

Goram had already indicated that he bore news and Madden had asked why he hadn't telephoned the information to him.

'Can't say I've ever done that, sir.' Joe had scratched his head. 'Used the telephone like. Never had cause to. No, I thought I'd better come myself.'

He'd got a lift into Highfield that morning, he said.

'I looked in at Dr Madden's rooms, but she weren't there.'

'She drove up to London early today.' Madden had

seated his guest at the table. Seeing Joe eye his knife and fork warily, he had swiftly cut their pie into pieces and picked one up himself in his fingers. 'Do you need to see her, Joe? Are you unwell?'

'Oh, no, sir, I'm fine.' The gypsy flushed. 'It were something else. I had a message for her from Topper.'

'*Topper?*' Madden's eyebrows rose at the name. 'Have you seen him?'

'Aye, just three nights ago. We were sitting round the fire and he walked in out of the dark. I didn't know it were him at first.' Joe chuckled. 'He weren't wearing his hat.'

'Did he know you were camped there?'

'Must have, sir. It's the same place we stop at every year. There's a farmer there lets us use his field. Anyway, old Topper asked if I could get a message to Dr Madden for him.'

'What message?'

Goram's face darkened. 'He made me promise I'd keep it a secret,' he muttered. 'But I reckon I can tell you, sir. He said to say there was someone with him who was sick and needed help. *Mortal* sick was how he put it.'

'And you reckon that could be Beezy?' Madden leaned forward, his elbows on the table.

'Well, like I say, I can't be *sure* . . .' The gypsy grimaced. 'But it could be, couldn't it?' He eyed Madden anxiously. 'What do you think, sir?'

'I think you're right. It's him. I had a feeling they'd got together again. What did Topper say, exactly?'

'That as soon as Doctor Madden came over I was to

send one of my boys to Boar's Hill. That's where Topper is now. It's not far.' The gypsy's scowl grew deeper. 'He was that sure she'd come.'

'He was right.' Madden snorted. 'But he's out of luck. She won't be back till later.' He glanced at his watch. 'Blandford, you say. That's a good three hours away. More if we hit fog. Did Topper tell you what was wrong with his friend?'

Joe shook his head. 'You know what he's like, sir, the old sod. Two words is all you get from him, three if you're lucky. He just said the man was sick and needed help. Didn't stay more than a minute, either. Just took some food the wife gave him and was on his way.'

Madden pondered the problem. 'We may have to get this man into hospital, whoever he is,' he remarked, speaking the thought aloud. His mind was already made up. 'I'm going to drive you back, Joe,' he announced. 'But you'll have to show me the way to Boar's Hill when we get there. Are you game?'

'I reckon so, sir.' Goram displayed his gap-toothed grin again. Eased of his burden at last, he leaned back in his chair and belched. 'Long as I'm with you.'

'And I want to thank you for what you've done. It was good of you to come all this way to speak to me.'

'I said I would. Anything I heard, you'd hear. I gave you my word.' The gypsy flushed as he spoke, and Madden bowed his head in grave acknowledgement.

'I know you did, Joe. I've not forgotten it.'

*

'HE SAID TO bring the *lady* when she came.' The pale, bearded face was dim in the darkness. 'Didn't say nothing about two *men*.'

'I'm Dr Madden's husband. She wasn't home when Topper's message reached me.' Though he had a lamp with him, Madden kept it out of the man's eyes. Behind him, Joe Goram clicked his tongue with impatience. 'It said he needed help. That's why we're here.'

Topper's envoy had been waiting for them, rising silently from a thicket as they approached, and Madden had had a brief glimpse of greasy locks beneath a torn cloth cap before the man ducked away from the light in his face. Looming against the night sky behind him was a dark protuberance in the land covered with trees and tangled bushes which Joe had already identified as Boar's Hill.

Still short of their ultimate destination, it had taken them many hours to reach the spot, their journey from Highfield having been slowed first by low-lying mist on the road, then by the fading light of late afternoon.

Before leaving home, Madden had scribbled a brief note to Helen, telling her what little he knew himself and saying he hoped to be back before dawn. She would not be pleased to hear that he had involved himself in the case once more, he knew, but he hoped the appeal Topper had sent them would persuade her he'd done the right thing.

Helen would in any case be collecting Rob from school on her way back from London, and since Lucy was spending the afternoon with Belle Burrows, he had had to do no more than ring May and ask her to take charge of their daughter until relief arrived. His final act before departing had been to collect his policeman's lamp – a souvenir of his days in the force, since appropriated by his son – and to prevail on the long-suffering Mrs Beck to put together a packet of sandwiches and a thermos of tea for them.

'Mr Goram asked me particularly to thank you for lunch. He says he's seldom eaten better.'

The variety of emotions struggling for release on their cook's flushed face had lightened the moment of depart-ure, and Madden had smiled to himself as he glanced at his companion, who by now had given in to exhaustion and was snoring beside him on the passenger seat, his head slumped on his chest.

They had left Highfield soon after two o'clock, but it was six before they crossed the River Stour, having driven through Hampshire into neighbouring Dorset. As they passed through the market town of Blandford Forum, Joe had awoken with a grunt, startled to find himself in a moving vehicle and close to the point from where he'd set out two days before.

Soon, following his passenger's directions, Madden had left the Dorchester road and for the next two miles had had to pick his way along narrow, hedgerowed lanes, his headlights probing the darkness ahead, until they came to a turn-off onto a muddy track that led to the gypsies' encampment.

While he'd warmed his hands on the chipped mug of tea which Goram's wife, a large woman, swarthy like her husband, and sporting a gold earring, offered him, Joe had sketched out the problems that still faced them.

'It'll take us a good half-hour to walk out there, sir. Can't get no closer with a car.' For his own part, Joe had turned his back on traditional refreshment in favour of a bottle of gin from which he was taking measured pulls, having first offered it to his guest. 'Topper said there'd be someone looking out for us. We'll just have to hope that's so.'

Another potential difficulty had been occupying Madden's mind, meanwhile. 'We may have to carry Beezy, or whoever it is, back with us. Bring a knife with you, Joe, in case we need to cut poles for a stretcher.'

His proposal had been welcomed by the gypsy, if not for the reason suggested. When Madden returned from retrieving his lamp from the car he found Goram and his sons examining a pair of cudgels which had made their appearance from the storage lockers underneath the caravans drawn up around the camp fire.

'What do you want with those?' he had asked.

'Thought we'd better take them with us, sir. One knife's no good between two of us.' Joe swung the stick he was holding, making it whoosh through the air. 'It's got a name, Boar's Hill . . .'

'A *name*?'

'Yes, it don't belong to no one, see. It's wild land . . . common land.' The gypsy glowered. 'There's rough men out there, sir, or so I've heard. Aye, and some of them wanted by the police.'

'No matter. We're not taking weapons with us.' Madden was adamant. 'Leave the sticks behind.'

Though he felt no fear, once they'd set off into the

inky blackness beyond the circle of light cast by the fire, Madden quickly lost all sense of direction and had to trust to his guide as he stumbled over rock-strewn slopes and through sharp gullies, finding in the deep quiet around them an eerie reminder of the night patrols he had once made in no-man's-land, when the darkness might be lit at any moment by a flare overhead and the silence broken by a sniper's bullet.

Presently they had glimpsed the darker outline of Boar's Hill ahead of them, and after Madden had flicked his lamp on and off several times, hoping it would be recognized as a signal, Topper's messenger had materialized.

'Been waiting here all day,' he grumbled. 'You'll not be welcome, neither one of you.' He had been shuffling his feet in indecision for some time. Now, without warning, he turned on his heel and strode off, calling over his shoulder as he did so, 'Well, come if you're coming.'

They followed him up the hill along a barely marked trail in the brush, and soon the canopy of leaves overhead blocked out whatever light might have come from the sky. While their guide seemed to know his way blindfold and Madden had his lamp, Joe Goram was forced to follow behind in near darkness, and his curses were audible.

'Bloody tramps, bloody nonsense . . .'

At last a glimmer of firelight appeared through the trees ahead and the hillside levelled off into a flatter area. As Madden took stock of the scene, the figure in front of him halted.

'Stay here now. Don't move.'

Not waiting to see if his order was obeyed, he continued on towards the firelight. Breathing hard, Goram caught up with Madden and they stood listening as sounds of an altercation broke out ahead of them. Men's voices were raised in angry argument.

'Come on, Joe.' Madden, too, had lost patience. 'Let's get this over with.'

They moved on and after only a few paces pushed their way through the bushes into an open space of flattened earth, roughly circular in shape. A fire was burning in the centre of the ring and around it were a crowd of perhaps a dozen bearded and dishevelled men, their guide among them, engaged in fierce debate. Some were on their feet; others were seated on stones scattered about the fire; all seemed to be shouting.

As Madden stepped into the circle of light, silence fell. Hostile faces were turned in his direction and a low mutter ran through the group, growing in volume. One of the seated figures rose, a burly man with grizzled hair, wearing a soiled sheepskin belted at the waist. He advanced on them, wielding a heavy stick.

Goram reached for the knife in his pocket. He was poised to intervene. But Madden forestalled him.

'*Put that down!*'

His voice cracked out like a whip above the hubbub and their aggressor stopped in his tracks. The others fell silent.

'Put it down, I say.'

Tall in his coat and hat, and quite motionless, Madden stood where he was. He made no gesture, but after a moment the man lowered his club and moved away, muttering, to rejoin his companions by the fire. The murmur of voices resumed.

Joe Goram watched open-mouthed. He'd been told Madden's history, but had never fully accepted it. Now he'd had the proof before his eyes. *'That were a copper's voice, all right, if ever I've heard one.'* Grinning, he whispered the words to himself, and thought of the tale he'd have to tell his sons later.

Madden, meantime, was looking about him. 'I'm here to see Topper,' he called out in clear tones. 'Can any of you tell me where he is?'

There was no response. The muttering continued.

'He sent a message to my wife, asking for help—'

'Your wife?'

The voice came from the shadows that lay at the edge of the circle, outside the fire's reach. Madden turned his head and saw a tall man, craggy and stoop-shouldered, move forward into the light. Dark, sunken eyes and a strong jaw gave his lean face the stamp of character. His white hair, uncut, was trapped in the collar of an old army greatcoat that fell below his knees. His hands were plunged deep in his pockets.

'Yes . . . Dr Madden.'

A murmur greeted the name. Several heads turned. The white-haired man was silent. He seemed to be absorbing the information.

'Ah, well, that's different,' he conceded, after a moment, speaking in an altered tone. He came closer, offering his hand. 'McBride's the name.' He had a marked Scottish accent.

'John Madden . . .' They shook hands. 'And this is Joe Goram, who showed me the way here.'

McBride turned his dark glance on the gypsy. Despite the turned-up collar of his coat, Madden caught a glimpse of a ragged scar at the base of his neck.

'You were wanting to see Topper? Well, he's asleep now.' McBride nodded towards the shadows from which he'd emerged and Madden made out a blanket-wrapped form stretched out on the ground there. 'Unconscious, more like it.' The Scotsman emitted a dry chuckle. 'He's been up and awake these past two nights. You'll not get much sense from him.'

Madden grunted, registering his disappointment. 'There was someone else I was hoping to talk to,' he admitted. 'A friend of his. A man called Beezy. Is he here?'

A hush followed his words. Madden examined the faces around the fire. When he turned his gaze back to McBride he found the Scotsman's eyes had hardened.

'John Madden . . .' He ruminated on the name. 'I've heard it said you were once a policeman.'

'That's true. But not any more.'

'You wouldn't be doing their job now, would you?'

'It depends what you mean.' Sensing the challenge coming from the other man, Madden sought to stare him down. But the dark gaze met his without flinching. 'I'm aware the police are looking for him. But I doubt it's for murder any longer.'

'We've only your word for that.'

'It's more likely they want him as a witness.' Madden shrugged. 'That's my belief, at any rate.'

'Yes, but all this is *police* business, Mr Madden. I'm asking you again – what's it to *you*?' McBride moved a little away, as though to take the other man in. To see him clearly.

Madden hesitated. He looked at the faces around him. Marked as they were by age and exhaustion – and by something more, a loss of hope past healing – they still showed expectation. It seemed that the words he was about to speak mattered to them. They wanted to hear his answer.

'As I said before, I'm not a policeman any longer.' He had waited some time before replying. 'But I happened to be the one who found the body of the child who was murdered at Brookham, and the memory haunts me. I never believed Beezy was the killer, even if others thought differently, but it's possible he saw something that day. Perhaps the murderer's face. I've been trying to find him in my own way, and I'll continue to do so, come what may.'

McBride grunted. 'Well, there's an honest answer,' he conceded. 'But it's still the law's work you're doing, and Beezy had no cause to help *them*. In their eyes he was guilty as charged.' He peered at Madden. 'Tell me the truth, now. What would his word be worth to you, anyway? An old tramp like him?'

'As much as any other man's.' Madden spoke quietly, but the renewed murmur from the fire showed he had an attentive audience. 'It's you who should explain, McBride,' he went on. 'You say Beezy had no cause to help the police. What are you implying? That all this was nothing to him? That he didn't care if some child was murdered? Frankly, I don't believe you. But if that's the case, let him stand up now and tell me so himself.'

His words brought a sigh from the listeners seated round the fire. McBride lifted his gaze from the flames.

'Ah, well, he can't do that, poor man,' he said softly. 'Even if he wanted to, which I doubt. He did have something to say, though, you're right about that, something to tell anyone with an ear to listen, and it might have been you, Mr Madden. But the sad fact is he died on this spot not three hours ago.'

'THE *DEVIL*'S MARK? What did he mean by that? Didn't he describe the man at all?'

Madden's hopes – initially raised – had quickly been dashed by what the Scotsman had to tell him.

'Oh, he had a great deal to say at the end, poor fellow, but most of it was gibberish. Once we'd laid him down on the ground over there, he never moved.'

McBride nodded in the direction of the fire, burning low now, where most of the men who'd been sitting earlier were recumbent, some propped on elbows conversing in low voices, others snoring, deeply asleep. Seated among them, knees drawn up and head hanging limply between his circled arms, was Joe Goram. The gypsy had joined the group some time earlier, offering what remained of his bottle of gin like a ticket of admission as he sat down. It had gone the rounds and come back to him empty, at which point, having inspected it glumly, he'd settled himself in his present position, prepared to wait patiently until Madden had completed his business.

Before that, McBride had taken Madden to the edge of the clearing, past where Topper was asleep, and pushed aside the ferns growing there to show him Beezy's body. Madden had shone his lamp on the corpse, moving the light slowly up from the cracked boots and canvas trousers, tied at the waist with a length of cord, over the old tramp's torso, which was clad in a torn flannel shirt topped by a buttonless waistcoat, to his bearded face. He had held the beam steady while he bent close to examine the features, noting the missing right earlobe that had been mentioned in the police circular issued earlier that summer.

'I'm not a doctor, but at a guess I'd say he died of bronchitis.' McBride had made no attempt to hurry Madden, holding the ferns back while he made his slow examination of the tramp's remains. 'He had an attack earlier this year, Topper said. Anyway, he coughed and coughed and couldn't clear his chest. In the end he must have suffocated. When it seemed there was no hope of him getting better, Topper had the idea of sending a message to your wife. But by then it was too late.'

Satisfied at last, Madden had turned away from the body and they moved closer to the fire, seating themselves at McBride's suggestion on a pair of flat stones close to where Topper was sleeping.

'We'll share out Beezy's clothes and possessions tomorrow. It's our way. Then we'll bury him.'

Madden shook his head. 'The police won't be satisfied

with that, I can tell you now. They'll want to recover the body.'

'Of course they will.' McBride seemed unconcerned. 'But they know about this place. Once or twice a year we get a visit from the law. You can tell them he'll be in a shallow grave just over there in the bushes, where he's lying now. We'll have moved on by then. A sip of whisky, Mr Madden?'

The Scotsman had produced a bottle from the pocket of his greatcoat and he offered it to his companion. Madden took a swallow from the neck for hospitality's sake before returning it to its owner's hand. He'd been eyeing McBride with some curiosity. Though showing all the marks of vagrancy in his dress and personal appearance, he was clearly a man of some education.

'Each of us has his story, I suppose, though I never discovered Beezy's.' It was as though he'd read Madden's thoughts. 'But I dare say his experience was much like the rest of ours.'

'And what's your story, Mr McBride?' Madden accepted the proffered bottle and took another sip.

The Scotsman chuckled. 'I wondered if you would ask. But I've no great tale to tell. Despite collecting some souvenirs from the war' – his hand went to the scar on his neck – 'I emerged in one piece. But I seemed to have lost some bits of myself just the same. I'm told others had a like experience. Suffice to say the world looked different to me.'

He pulled up the collar of his coat as a sudden sharp breeze blew through the clearing.

'My wife, meanwhile, had set out on a journey. To

Canada, as it happened, and not alone.' He shook with silent laughter. 'But that wasn't the reason I took to the road. No, I set off thinking I would walk for a while, and the walk grew longer. Mind you, I had some help along the way . . .' He tapped the bottle with his finger. 'I made only one discovery. There's an invisible line in our lives, and once it's crossed we can never go back. Invisible, that is, *until* we've crossed it, and then it's all too plain.' He turned his head and regarded Madden in silence. 'But to return to Beezy . . .' McBride straightened, stretching his cramped muscles. 'I know next to nothing about him. This was the first time we'd met. They turned up a week ago – he and Topper – and even then he was in no fit state to hold a conversation.'

'So he didn't speak of the murder at all?' Madden couldn't hide his disappointment. 'He dropped some of his belongings near the scene of the killing, you know. That made me think he might have seen something that caused him to run off.'

'Oh, I dare say you're right about that.' He nodded. 'Beezy indicated as much to me.'

'Then he *did* talk to you about it?' Madden tried to understand what the other man was saying.

McBride shook his head. 'I haven't made myself clear. We had no conversation as such. When Topper went off three days ago to seek out your gypsy friend he asked me to keep an eye on Beezy for him, which I did. I brought him water and tried to keep him warm. He was talking a good deal, but making little sense.' The Scotsman paused, frowning. 'I knew about the murder at Brookham, of course. We all did. And I knew the police had been looking for this man. So I was able to guess what it was he was raving about. He kept speaking of blood . . .'

'Of blood?'

'That was the word he kept repeating. And then there was a man who was trying to wash it off. He wasn't telling me a story, you understand, he was babbling.' McBride looked keenly at Madden. ' "I saw him washing off the blood . . ." He said that many times. "I saw him washing off the blood, but it wouldn't wash off . . . no . . . no . . ." ' The Scotsman mimicked the hoarse, drained tones of an exhausted man. 'He went on that way, repeating himself, over and over, and coughing in between. Then he said something else, in a different voice, and I was struck by it. "He had the devil's mark on him . . ." That's what he said. "The devil's mark . . . I saw it plain." '

'Just that? Nothing more?'

'No. But he said it more than once, and I heard him right. You can be sure of that.' He offered the bottle once more to Madden, who declined with a shake of his head.

'The *devil's* mark? What did he mean? Didn't he describe the man at all?'

Seeing Madden's frustration, McBride had endeavoured to explain. 'You have to understand, he wasn't speaking rationally, he was wandering. But I will say this: I believe he was trying to tell me *something*, to clear his mind of a burden, if you will.'

'Perhaps he told Topper more?' Madden eyed the sleeping form nearby.

'Apparently not. At least, so Topper says. Mind you, that may be because he never asked.' The Scotsman chuckled. He took a long pull from the neck of his bottle. 'A curious character, our Topper, don't you agree? Now there's a closed book...' He mused in silence a while. 'When he arrived here a week ago I took him aside and told him if this friend he had with him was guilty of murdering that child they'd have to leave. We wouldn't have them here. He said Beezy had sworn he was innocent, and he believed him. That was all, but I took Topper's word for it – or rather, I trusted his judgement. I fancy you'd have done the same.'

'I might.' Madden smiled in the darkness. 'My wife would have had no hesitation.'

'At any event, they seemed not to have discussed the matter further. Topper was kept well occupied finding food for them both while Beezy stayed hidden. I gather he was terrified of going to the police. He was sure they'd accuse *him* of the crime. He'd been arrested once before and convicted on a false charge, or so he'd told Topper. He was quite deaf, by the way, poor man, and Topper has less to say than any human being I've ever encountered. I doubt they did much in the way of exchanging confidences. But they were friends. You could tell that. Topper was quite broken up when he died.' McBride shrugged. 'Wake him up if you like, Mr Madden, but you'll get no more from him than I've told you.'

Madden had been considering the question for some time and had already made up his mind. He shook his head. 'Let him sleep.' He rose, stretching. 'Will you tell him something for me, though? Will you say my wife was away from the house when his message arrived? He'll wonder why she didn't come herself. And will you tell him she's concerned for him and wants to see him. It's important you let him know that. She's very attached to him and worries in case he's not well and able to take care of himself.'

'You may be sure I'll pass that on.' Rising in turn, the Scotsman bowed his head as though to seal the pledge. 'Though I must confess to feeling some envy. I don't know how Dr Madden's name is regarded by the world at large, but none stands higher with us.'

'Then I hope you'll pass by Highfield some day so that you can meet her. Our door is always open. Thank you for your help, Mr McBride.'

The two men shook hands and Madden signalled to Joe, who rose from beside the fire, yawning.

'Let me show you the way back down the hill,' McBride offered, but Madden shook his head.

'We'll manage.' Turning to leave, he paused. 'You're sure he was trying to tell you something . . . Beezy? He wasn't simply delirious?'

'That was certainly my impression.' McBride peered at him through the firelight.

'The devil's mark, then – it might be something actual? Something he saw?'

'It might. Or something he imagined.' For a moment the Scotsman seemed unsure. 'All I can say is it seemed real enough to him.'

18

As Probst reached inside the cab to pull out his suitcase, Holly beckoned to one of the porters standing nearby. The chief superintendent had insisted on accompanying Sinclair to Victoria station to say goodbye to their German visitor, who was catching the train and cross-channel ferry back to the Continent.

'I feel I've hardly arrived, and already I must depart.' Pausing in the concourse, Probst let his eyes dwell on the imposing station arch and the busy platforms beneath, as if to record the image. 'I've often dreamed of visiting London. Although Miss Adamson was from Durham she passed a good many years here before coming to Berlin and she used to describe the city to me during our conversational lessons.'

'What took her to Berlin in the first place?' Sinclair asked him.

'She was employed as a governess. When that job ended, instead of returning to England she stayed on and supported herself by taking in pupils. It's entirely thanks to her that I have this fascination with all things English.' He smiled.

'Perhaps you'll come again. If so, and even if your visit's unofficial, please get in touch with me.' Sinclair returned the smile. He'd taken a liking to the younger man, whose pleasant manner hid a mind as sharp as any he'd encountered in his profession. And another quality, too, of which the chief inspector had become increasingly conscious, was one which he would have characterized as moral stature, borne without display and far removed from the easy cynicism that accompanied so much police work. Observing the Berlin policeman, he'd been reminded of Madden, whose name had come up between them, and who in any case was much in his thoughts that morning.

Even before he'd sat down to breakfast the telephone had rung at his flat in Shepherd's Bush and for the next twenty minutes he'd been glued to the instrument, listening while his old partner described his night's adventures and revealed what he'd learned at the tramps' gathering.

Prior to the final meeting he'd scheduled with Probst he had paid a hurried call on the assistant commissioner, but found him in a less than generous mood.

'Sir, this is a piece of solid evidence, one we can pass on to Berlin.' Sinclair had felt a renewal of his earlier frustration. 'Correct me if I'm wrong, but it is cooperation I'm meant to be discussing with Probst.'

'Spare me your sarcasm, Chief Inspector.' A series of sleepless nights had deepened Sir Wilfred's normal pallor. Dark shadows dwelt beneath his eyes. Sinclair had felt a momentary pang for his superior, who was clearly suffering the torments of the damned as the hour of their meeting with Philip Vane drew nearer. The Foreign Office had rung the previous evening to confirm their appointment and fix the time: it was set for three o'clock that afternoon.

'This isn't going to point him in Vane's direction, sir.

In fact, it's not even evidence we could ever use in a court of law. It's pure hearsay. Whatever the old tramp saw, he can't tell us about it now. He's dead.' Sinclair had kept a rein on his temper. 'But it's one way of being sure that we're after the same man, the German police and ourselves. That woman in Bavaria, the woodcutter's wife, must be questioned again. Remember, she saw the murderer naked from the waist up.'

'But only from behind . . .' Bennett was becoming interested, in spite of himself. 'What if this "devil's mark" was on his front? Always supposing it wasn't a figment of the tramp's imagination . . .' He put down his pencil. 'What's Madden's view?' He cocked an eye at the chief inspector. 'Does he think it's worth pursuing?'

'He wasn't sure until he heard what his wife had to say on the subject.' Sinclair chuckled. 'Forgive me, sir, but Helen Madden takes a dim view of John involving himself in what she sees as police matters. When he got home – it was two in the morning – he found her waiting up for him. He'd left her a note, of course, but that hardly sufficed, and he was made to sit down and tell her the whole story there and then.'

The chief inspector tugged at an earlobe, still smiling in recollection at Madden's account of the inquisition to which he'd been subjected in the early hours.

'The funny part is, the original message was meant for *her*, and had she received it, knowing Helen, she would have gone off without a second thought. As John pointed out, for all the good it did him . . .' The chief inspector chuckled. 'Anyway, once she'd calmed down she became interested in his tale and when he got to the bit about the tramp's deathbed ravings she offered an explanation for them. Or a possible one. She suggested it might have been a birthmark he'd seen.'

'A birthmark! On the killer's face or body?'

'Yes, but of a particular kind.' Sinclair consulted his notebook. 'The medical term is haemangioma. What you and I would call a port-wine stain. It's strawberry coloured and can be large and disfiguring. Helen Madden believes it's quite possible that's what Beezy was talking about. The man was washing the blood off himself, but the mark remained. It could well have *looked* like blood ... blood that wouldn't come off. And to answer your question, sir, Madden's of the opinion it's a solid lead. Even though the tramp was delirious, he kept repeating the same words. He had *something* on his mind, all right. And there seems little doubt he witnessed the murder, or at least its aftermath ...'

'So you think we should tell Probst about it?' Sir Wilfred no longer seemed so opposed to the notion. 'Very well. At least it will keep our German colleagues occupied. You realize this whole business may come to a head this afternoon?' He shot a piercing glance at Sinclair.

'Only too well, sir. But in the meantime we should continue conducting the investigation in a normal way. The Surrey police have been informed of Beezy's revelations – Madden rang them first. They're putting the Sussex force in the picture and will see to it that the Dorset police retrieve the tramp's body. It's only right we should tell the Germans about it, as well.'

*

THE CONCESSION WRUNG from the assistant commissioner had made Sinclair's final meeting with the Berlin policeman more agreeable than those that had preceded it, when he'd had to guard against giving any indication that Scotland Yard had any information about the case it was not prepared to divulge. Indeed, once or twice, detecting what he thought might be humour in the inspector's cool, unrevealing glance, he'd wondered whether Probst had guessed as much. If he'd been surprised by the unusually detailed accounts offered him of the investigations currently under way – a case of over-egging the pudding in the chief inspector's jaundiced view – he'd contrived not to show it.

'That is most interesting. The connections with our own case are multiplying. I feel we are drawing closer to our man.' Probst had listened raptly to what Sinclair had had to tell him. 'And just who is this John Madden?'

'A former colleague. A fine detective. He took it into his head to become a farmer, though. More's the pity. Connections, you said. What did you have in mind, exactly?'

'Our witness's account of the man removing his shirt seems to be borne out here. Perhaps this is also part of his ritual. The battering he gives his victims' faces would be bound to produce a spray of blood. He's fastidious, perhaps. Or just practical.'

'The birthmark – if it's a birthmark – could be on his face.'

'Not if he's the man who was seen eating lunch in that roadside hotel. A mark like that would certainly have been recalled by at least some of the witnesses. No,

it suggests a blood-coloured stain on his body to me.'
Probst had risen from his chair in front of Sinclair's desk
and was pacing up and down. 'He is washing the blood
off his arms and chest – that's where most of it would
fall. The blood comes off, but the birthmark remains.
The tramp could hardly have had a clear view. He must
have been in hiding . . .'

'Yes, it's established he was deaf, so it's likely he
didn't hear the murderer approaching until he was
almost on him. He'd have had to find what cover he
could in the undergrowth.' Sinclair was catching some of
his visitor's enthusiasm for the hunt. 'And then there's
the question of the stream . . .'

'Ah, yes . . . the stream.' Probst paused in his pacing
to cast an eye on the chief inspector. 'He chooses these
places with care, it seems, and there's always water
nearby. He's quite cold-blooded in his approach, no
matter how frenzied he may become later. This is a man
of unusual self-control.' The inspector brooded. 'Is this
a way we can track him down, do you think?'

'By his birthmark, you mean? If he has one.' It had
taken Sinclair a moment to catch up with the other's
train of thought. 'Difficult, I should say.'

'Yes . . .' Probst examined his own proposition,
frowning. 'After all, who does a man take his clothes off
for? His wife or mistress, certainly. But we doubt this
killer has either.'

An image of Philip Vane's thin, mask-like features
came into the chief inspector's mind at that moment.
His discreet inquiries, which had not ceased during the
days they'd had to wait to secure their interview with

him, had revealed that the man was a bachelor. Recollection of this fact now caused an involuntary spasm to cross his face. It went unnoticed. Probst was still wrestling with the question he'd raised.

'His doctor, perhaps?'

They got no further in their speculations. Glancing at his watch, Sinclair saw that it was time to leave and five minutes later they were joined in the lobby downstairs by Arthur Holly, who had indicated his desire to accompany them to the station.

AT VICTORIA, the chief super disappeared for a few minutes and returned with a selection of newspapers and a bar of chocolate which he pressed on their visitor.

'Something for the journey, Inspector.' He seemed intent on making up for any shortcomings in his earlier behaviour towards their guest. 'It's been a pleasure to have you with us.'

He ushered Probst aboard the train and waved a last goodbye to him through the carriage window.

'Quite an impressive fellow, I thought.' Holly watched as the train pulled out of the station, sealing his words with a quiet rumble of approval. 'For a foreigner, that is.'

It was a large concession on the chief super's part, but one that failed to register with his companion. Sinclair's thoughts, not without trepidation, were already on the call that he and Sir Wilfred Bennett would be making at the Foreign Office that afternoon.

*

'CHIEF INSPECTOR ... come in.' Bennett gestured to a chair in front of his desk and Sinclair sat down, curious to know why he'd been summoned. Their meeting with Vane had been set for three o'clock and he'd been expecting to meet his superior down in the lobby fifteen minutes before the hour so that they could make the short trip to Whitehall together. Instead, he had received a message saying the assistant commissioner wanted to see him before they set out. It was now a quarter past two.

'I've something to say to you ...' Bennett rose. Gesturing to Sinclair to remain seated, he went from his desk over to the windows by the conference table, where he stood, hands on hips, looking out into the grey November day. 'I realize you feel I've been unnecessarily obstructive where Philip Vane is concerned ... no, there's no need to deny it.' He waved away the instinctive protest that came to the chief inspector's lips.

'Your attitude was quite understandable. I should have felt the same in your position. But there are issues at stake here of which you're unaware and on which, up to now, I've not felt in a position to enlighten you.' He looked directly at Sinclair. 'However, the situation has changed. Since we're to speak to Vane together, it's necessary that you should know what I know ... or at any rate suspect.' He bit his lip. 'But this must remain between us, and that includes the chief superintendent. I've told him I don't want to overwhelm Vane with numbers – that a deputation of *three* from the Yard might seem like an attempt to cow him. But in fact I have another reason, and I can only hope he hasn't taken offence.'

Sinclair smiled. 'Arthur's not given to taking offence, sir. The word equable might have been coined to fit him.'

'How very true . . .' Sir Wilfred's smile eased the tension between them for a moment. Turning from the window, he came back to his desk and sat down. 'Not everything one learns in government comes through official channels, Chief Inspector. Some things are not written down, or even communicated directly. One picks them up from hints dropped in conversation. Do you follow me?'

'Up to a point, sir.' Sinclair sat still.

'As I think I mentioned, I've met Philip Vane on a few occasions. I've also heard his name mentioned . . . in some unexpected quarters. Naturally, I was curious, and I asked questions . . .' He shrugged. 'Answers were not forthcoming. But hints were dropped . . .' Bennett cleared his throat.

'My reluctance to see him dragged into this inquiry doesn't stem only from a desire to avoid any scandal,' he said. 'I can't give you chapter and verse, Chief Inspector. I can only tell you what I strongly suspect: that Vane's job at the Foreign Office is not what it seems. In reality I believe he's a senior intelligence officer.'

19

'MR VANE will see you now.'

The young man rose from behind his desk in the anteroom and went to an inner door. The very epitome of diplomatic tact, he had apologized gracefully to Bennett and Sinclair when they'd arrived for the austere conditions of his tiny office. Taking their hats and coats, he'd invited them, again with an apology, to sit down in two straight-backed chairs of civil service issue while he reported their presence to his superior.

It was the first time the chief inspector had set foot in the Foreign and Colonial Office and his impressions thus far had been fleeting. The marble-floored entrance below had been imposing enough, as were the uniformed commissionaires who received them. But once their identities had been established and the purpose of their visit determined, a clerk had been summoned to escort them upstairs to the second floor. There, a series of corridors, thinly carpeted, and on which their footsteps echoed dully, had led to an unmarked door where their guide had paused, knocked softly and then ushered them inside.

During the few minutes they'd had to wait before being admitted to Vane's presence Sinclair had had the leisure to go over in his mind the tangled trail that had brought them to this encounter. Bennett's last-minute revelation of Vane's likely true occupation hadn't materially altered the situation, at least as far as he was concerned, though he could well understand the consternation it might arouse in other government circles.

His own duty was clear to him. But he was able to extend a degree of silent sympathy to his chief as they sat side by side in silence. The strain of the past few days was clearly stamped on Sir Wilfred's drawn features and his slight frame seemed bowed by the weight of worry he bore. Sinclair was aware that the assistant commissioner might have done more to avoid being entangled in the interview they were about to conduct, with its consequent threat to his career. His own direct superior, the Metropolitan Police Commissioner, had been informed of what was afoot, and, perhaps recognizing a poisoned chalice when he saw one, had taken no steps to intervene. Had Bennett wished to, however, he could have drawn him, and others, into sharing a portion of the risk he now faced. Instead, he'd chosen to grasp the nettle alone, and the chief inspector admired him for it.

Vane's secretary, if that was what he was, opened the inner door and then stood back to allow the two Scotland Yard officials to enter the office beyond. Looking onto an inner courtyard, it was more spacious than the anteroom, but still modest in size and decorated with a spare elegance that seemed to reflect its occupant, who rose from behind a polished desk, bare of ornament, to receive them.

'Sir Wilfred . . . it's been a while since we last met.' Philip Vane bowed slightly, but made no move to come around his desk to greet them.

'How are you, Vane?' The assistant commissioner kept his tone neutral. 'May I introduce Chief Inspector Sinclair. He's a senior officer in the CID.'

Vane's eyebrows rose a fraction as he gestured towards a matched pair of chairs, which Sinclair was unable to identify as to style or period, beyond recognizing that they had certainly not issued from any government warehouse. The chief inspector's attention had strayed only momentarily from the figure seated behind the desk, who remained standing until his visitors were seated. Of medium height and sparely built, his thin, aristocratic features had been faithfully reproduced in the magazine picture obtained by the Yard; but what the photographic image failed to convey was the poise and confidence of its subject. He seemed in no hurry as he waited for them to settle and if his expression betrayed mild boredom with the occasion, Sinclair assumed it was no more than a cultivated air. He'd already detected in Philip Vane a certain kind of Englishman, common enough in the upper ranks of society, with whom, thankfully, he had little to do, either in his work or his private life.

'The CID?' Vane allowed a hint of curiosity to show on his face. 'Not Special Branch? Well, you've got me wondering, Sir Wilfred.' He sat back in his chair, surveying them both. 'What is it you wish to see me about?'

'One of our current investigations.' Bennett's reply came promptly, as though he wished to give himself no time to reconsider. 'Or rather a series of investigations that are being conducted by the police in this country under the guidance of Scotland Yard. It goes without saying that we wouldn't be here now if the matter were not a grave one, nor if there was any way of resolving it without approaching you personally. With reluctance, I've concluded there is not. In short, we require your assistance.' He looked directly at Vane. 'If you're agreeable, I'll now ask Chief Inspector Sinclair to explain in more detail.'

'Chief Inspector?' Vane turned his hooded gaze on the other man facing him. He appeared quite at ease.

Angus Sinclair opened the file that lay on his knee. Although perfectly familiar with its contents, he liked to have it with him and was not above using it, as he did now, to create an artificial pause while he pretended to sort through some papers. He looked up.

'The investigations Sir Wilfred referred to concern a series of brutal murders committed in this country over the past few years. The first took place in 1929. A further two have occurred more recently, during the past summer. The victims were all young girls, children, either just in their teens or younger. They were raped and strangled. A common element in each of these crimes was a post-mortem assault carried out by the killer on his victims' faces. In the two most recent attacks he battered them to pulp.'

The chief inspector had kept what he thought were the most telling words till last, and he was disappointed to see no trace of a reaction from his listener.

'Continue.' Vane shifted slightly in his chair.

'It's the first of these killings I want to discuss with you. It took place in July 1929, but because the victim's body was thrown into the Thames and not recovered until recently, it has only just been recognized that a crime occurred. Nevertheless, we've been able to determine with some certainty what happened that day. Briefly, a twelve-year-old girl was picked up by the murderer and taken in his car to the scene of the crime, which was a nudists' club called Waltham Manor, just outside Henley, in Oxfordshire. Despite the lapse in time, we've also been able to identify the make of car which the killer used. By good fortune – ours, at any rate – it turns out to have been a foreign-made machine, rare enough on our roads, and we've succeeded in pinning it down to a model that only went on sale in this country in the spring of that year. The list of those who purchased such a car in that period is short and we've had no trouble tracing them.'

'What make of car are you talking about?' Vane spoke in a dead voice. His eyes were fixed on the chief inspector.

'A Mercedes-Benz saloon.'

'You're aware that I own one, of course?' He remained expressionless.

Sinclair nodded.

'Purchased in the same period we're discussing, too.' Vane put a hand to his chin. His glance hadn't wavered. 'And on that basis alone, you feel justified in considering me a suspect? In *questioning* me? Please, Sir Wilfred . . .' He held up his hand as Bennett made to speak. 'Let the chief inspector answer.'

'No, Mr Vane. Not on that basis alone.' Cool as he hoped he might sound, Sinclair was aware of the sudden increase in tension between them; it was almost palpable now. And despite the deep well of experience he had to draw on in confrontations of this kind, it was all he could do to maintain a calm exterior. 'From the moment these crimes came to our attention – I mean both the earlier and the more recent ones – we've been puzzled by the long gap in time separating them. Only lately have we acquired information that might possibly explain this. I emphasize the word *possibly*. Inquiries of this kind are largely a matter of eliminating suspects. That's what we're trying to do here.' Just for a moment the chief inspector's nerve had failed him, but Vane gave him no credit for this fractional retreat; nor respite.

'Forgive me if I express some doubts on that score, Mr Sinclair. I think you came here with quite another object in mind. But you were saying – indicating, at any rate – that you had further reason to regard me with suspicion. Pray tell me what it is?' His manner had become glacial.

'By all means.' Angered by his own momentary weakness, Sinclair met the other man's icy gaze without flinching. 'Following inquiries abroad, we have now been informed that a series of murders similar to the ones I've described are currently under investigation by the German police. These crimes fit into a very precise span of time: the first occurred in December 1929, and the sixth and last in April of this year. We are aware that you were posted to the British Embassy in Berlin during that period. Indeed, the coincidence is striking, at least from our point of view. You went to Berlin in October of 1929, did you not? And returned to England in early summer this year?'

So complete was the silence that followed his words, the chief inspector was able to pick up the whirr of a pigeon's wings in the courtyard outside. Vane's eyes remained fixed on him. But his gaze had turned glassy. Aware that the man had suffered some kind of shock, Sinclair waited for him to speak. He'd already formed the opinion that Philip Vane was not an individual who would break easily; nevertheless, his response, when it came finally, proved to be a disappointment.

'What is it you wish to ask me, Chief Inspector?' Apart from moistening his lips, he appeared calm. 'Specifically, I mean?'

'Initially, I should like you to account for your movements on two separate days this summer. July the twenty-seventh and the eighth of September.'

Vane nodded as though the request was a perfectly normal one. 'Those, I take it, would be the days on which the two most recent murders were committed?' He spoke in a toneless voice and Sinclair could read nothing in his face.

'Yes, sir. The first was in Sussex, at Bognor Regis. The second near a small village in Surrey.'

Vane rose abruptly and went from behind his desk to a satinwood library table in the corner of his office where a number of framed photographs stood among piled volumes. From one of these stacks he took a slim book bound in red leather which he brought back with him.

'The twenty-seventh of July, you say . . .' Standing, he riffled through the pages without haste.

'Yes, sir. And September the eighth.'

As Vane bent his head Sinclair stole a glance at Bennett beside him. The assistant commissioner's gaze was fixed on the figure at the desk. His slightly widened eyes hinted at the stress he, too, was under.

'The twenty-seventh was a Saturday, I see. I stayed in town that weekend, which is unusual. I had some work to do, I recall now. I've no engagements listed. In all likelihood I spent the day at my flat – it's in the Albany, though I dare say you know that – and dined at my club. To anticipate your question, Chief Inspector, dinner apart, no, I don't believe my movements can be confirmed by anyone. I would have given my man the weekend off. I always do when I stay in town.'

There was a pause as Vane flipped through the pages. Sinclair continued to observe him, narrow-eyed. He still couldn't read the man. But he felt increasingly that he was playing a game, performing some kind of charade.

'September the eighth was a Sunday. I spent that weekend with friends in Hampshire, this side of Winchester. I can give you their names if you like. Surrey, you said ... where the other murder was committed ... not that far away, then. And I left before lunch on the Sunday to drive back to London.' Vane shut the diary and sat down. 'Hardly an alibi, is it?'

He might have seemed unconcerned – he'd continued to speak in a flat voice throughout – were it not for his finger which began to tap on the desktop in front of him. To the chief inspector it signalled anxiety. Yet he had the curious impression that he and Bennett had become irrelevant to whatever was going on in Vane's mind. Indeed, from the way his eyes strayed to the window just then he appeared to have forgotten their presence. The light in the courtyard outside was fading.

'The murder you were telling me about earlier – the one that took place near Henley – can you give me a date for that?' He spoke in a drawling voice, his tone bordering on the insolent. But his eyes, when he turned their way again, told a different story, the fixity of his stare reflecting some inner turmoil still under tight control.

'Yes, of course, sir. But I wouldn't ask you here and now to account for your movements so long in the past.' It had just occurred to the chief inspector that what the other man had been doing these past few minutes was playing for time.

Vane shook his head impatiently. 'The date, man.'

The change in his manner was startling; Sinclair's eyebrows went up in surprise. 'The eighth of July,' he replied, after a pause.

Vane slid his hand beneath the rim of his desk and a bell sounded faintly in the outer office. The door opened behind them.

'Peter, would you find my personal diary for 1929 and bring it in, please.' Not troubling to look up, he sat staring at his desk and they waited in silence until the young man from outside appeared with an identical book bound in red leather which he laid in front of his superior.

'Thank you. That will be all.'

Before the door shut Vane had the book open and the other two watched while he found the page he wanted. He sat staring at it for a long time. Sinclair glanced at Bennett again and caught his eye. When he turned back

Vane's head was still bent over the page, but now he was nodding, as though in confirmation of something he already suspected. He flicked through a few more pages, going backwards and forwards in the diary. Again he nodded.

'The girl was killed on the eighth, you say. The day before that I travelled from Oxford to Birmingham to stay with friends before continuing on to Scotland, where I spent the rest of July and the first week of August. Naturally, all that can be confirmed.' He shut the book.

Struck speechless by the revelation, Sinclair sat blinking. It was several moments before he could find his voice. 'You were in the Oxford area then?' He could think of nothing else to say.

'Yes, on holiday. I was a guest of Sir Robert Hancock and his wife at their place near Woodstock. He's a colleague of mine. You're welcome to check my story with him.' Vane's tone had altered. To the surprise of the other two, he'd shed his hostile manner. But as though to confuse them still further, he showed no sign of relief at having cleared himself. If anything, the indications of anxiety he'd displayed earlier had intensified. His finger had resumed its rapid tattoo on the desk in front of him. Eyeing him closely, the chief inspector sensed indecision behind his strange behaviour.

'I don't mean to question your word, sir, but did you travel to Birmingham, and to Scotland, in your car?'

For the first time Vane seemed to find difficulty in formulating a reply. 'No, Chief Inspector,' he answered finally. 'I did not. I went by train.'

'You left it garaged in London?'

The question hung in the air between them until it became clear, for whatever reason, that Vane was not going to respond to it. His gaze had turned inwards, and once again the chief inspector felt that his thoughts were elsewhere.

Bennett stirred, breaking his long silence. 'These questions *must* be answered,' he insisted.

Still Vane said nothing, and it was clear to Sinclair that something extra would be needed to shatter the wall of obduracy they were faced by. When he spoke again, it was in a sharpened tone, his crisp consonants lending stark emphasis to the words he chose.

'Sir, the investigation we're engaged in is unique in my experience. This man has killed nine children. Nine that we *know* of. He was described to me by a man who should know as a monster. Scarcely human. I see no reason to question this judgement. I only ask you to consider what's at stake. If there's anything you can tell us – any small fact—'

'*Chief Inspector! I beg you!*'

Vane's anguished cry caught Sinclair off balance, and he stared back dumbstruck. It was the last thing he'd expected to hear.

'There's no need to go on. I *see* what's at stake. But the situation's not what you think. I'm not *protecting* anyone. I want to help you, believe me, but I fear we're too late.'

*

THE FOLDER, DUN coloured, was marked across one corner with a broad red stripe. Vane had placed the file on
his desk a few moments before, and the chief inspector's
eye hadn't strayed from it since. Earlier, he had watched
him retrieve it from a safe housed in a teak cupboard
at the back of his office, using a key selected from
a ring that was attached to a metal watch chain he
wore. Some minutes had passed since his outburst, but
although he'd quickly regained control of himself, apologizing to them both, he was unable to disguise the
effects of the strong emotion he'd just experienced,
which showed itself in his pallor and the jerkiness of his
movements. At the same time, his attitude towards them
had changed. Gone was the air of cold superiority to
which the chief inspector had taken such exception when
they first arrived. Anxiety marked his behaviour now
and he seemed more human.

'We've only met socially, haven't we, Sir Wilfred?'
Vane glanced up from the file, at which he'd been staring.
'I wonder if you're aware of the particular position I fill
here at the Foreign Office?'

'Aware . . . no. At least, not officially.' Bennett
allowed himself a slight smile. His relief a few minutes
earlier on realizing this was not the man they were
seeking after all had been noted by the chief inspector,
who'd been seeking for some image with which to
enshrine the glow of revelation emanating from his
superior's pale, but no longer stricken countenance: St
Paul's encounter on the road to Damascus sprang to
mind. 'But I admit to having been curious about you,

Vane. I've made some inquiries – and received guarded answers. I told Mr Sinclair earlier today that I believed you were engaged in intelligence work.'

'Did you, indeed?' Vane's elegantly raised eyebrow was a mark of his returning poise. 'Well, that clears the air, at any rate.' He looked at them both. 'We're all senior officials accustomed to the need for discretion. But I must stress that much of what I'm about to tell you is for your ears and these walls only, and in the event of it becoming public would almost certainly be denied. More to the point, none of it may be used in any future case for the prosecution. Do you foresee a problem there?'

Bennett seemed unsure. He glanced inquiringly at the chief inspector.

'None that I can think of,' Sinclair replied. With the climactic moment approaching, he strove to maintain an appearance of calm himself. 'As far as the police are concerned, this is a murder case, pure and simple. No connection with intelligence work would be admitted by the prosecution, I'm sure, and if the defence tried to drag it in, there's always the resort of in camera proceedings. Of course, I can't speak for what might happen if the killer were brought to trial abroad.'

'Then let's do our utmost to see if we can prevent that.' Bennett's tone was dry. 'Please continue.' He nodded to Vane, who squared the file on the desktop before him, as though ordering his thoughts.

'I'll start by giving you some background,' he said. 'Of necessity, this must be limited to what I believe you need to know. I assume it comes as no surprise to either of you that the Foreign Office should be involved in intelligence gathering. Traditionally, this has always been so, even now when a secret service exists in departmental form. I was earmarked for this work a while back and in recent years Germany has become my special area of responsibility.' He paused, as though picking his words with care.

'There are various sides to intelligence gathering, but I'm referring now to just one of them: a category of persons whom we use to acquire certain kinds of information and to carry out particular assignments. Agents, in short – or spies, if you prefer – professionals who are expert in the field of espionage and employed for that purpose. The British services have at their disposal a number of such men – and women. They're engaged mainly to carry out functions of a questionable nature that no diplomat or other government official could afford to be associated with.'

Again he paused, this time to raise his eyes to theirs.

'I regret to have to tell you that the man you're seeking is one of these.'

'An agent employed by this country?' Sinclair wanted to be clear on the point. Vane nodded.

'Would you give me his name?' Seeing the other hesitate, the chief inspector spoke quickly. 'I warn you now you have no right under any law to withhold it.'

'No, it's not that. You don't understand.' Vane shook his head. 'Of course I'll give you his name. But which? He's gone by so many. To us he's known as Wahl, Emil

Wahl; that's how he appears in this file.' He tapped the folder before him. 'But his real name is Gaston Lang. That's what he was christened.'

'Lang, you say?' Sinclair opened his notebook. As he reached for the pen in his pocket, he saw Vane shake his head.

'Write it down if you wish, Chief Inspector, but it'll do you no good. Of all the names Lang might be using now, I can assure you it's the one he'll never go by again.'

'HE'D BEEN WORKING for us for many years by the time I met him – that was in the summer of 1929. But his association with our intelligence branch goes back to the war, and it's important you know how this came about.'

Vane eyed his two listeners.

'At that time British intelligence had an outstanding agent working for them, a Swiss called Ernst Hoffmann. He was based in Geneva and through him and his various contacts and sub-agents we were able to obtain an extraordinary amount of valuable information from inside Germany. Lang was his secretary.'

Vane frowned.

'We knew little about him. Apparently he grew up in an orphanage. Nevertheless, in spite of what could only have been the most limited schooling, he'd managed to catch the eye of Ernst Hoffmann and by the time our people got to know him he'd mastered several languages as well as other skills which his employer must have deemed necessary for his education.'

His raised eyebrow hinted at a meaning not apparent in his words.

'Hoffmann was an art dealer, by the way: it was a genuine business, and he used it as a cover for his other activities. He was already working for us before the war and during that period he used Lang as a courier and go-between to keep contact with his agents in Germany.

'So he was well-placed to help us when war broke out, but in 1917 he died – quite unexpectedly, he had a heart attack while sitting in a cafe – and Lang was left to take over his work. With gratifying results, at least as far as our people were concerned. Hoffman's death had thrown them into a panic and they were only too pleased to discover that this young man was able to carry on in his place, and just as effectively.

'However, about a year later, in the spring of 1918, he turned up without warning in France and made his way to the British sector of the front, in the north, where he reported to our intelligence branch. He had a curious tale to tell. He said he'd been identified as a British operative by German counter-intelligence agents in Switzerland who had succeeded in falsely incriminating him with the Swiss police. He'd only narrowly escaped arrest and had managed to slip across the border clandestinely into France.'

'*Incriminating* him?' Sinclair seized on the word. 'As a spy, do you mean?'

Vane shook his head. 'He was being sought for murder. The victim was a young girl.'

'Good lord!' Bennett couldn't contain his astonishment.

Beside him, the chief inspector's eyes had narrowed. 'And they *believed* him? These so-called intelligence officials?'

Vane shrugged. 'It would have been difficult, if not impossible, to check the truth of his story. The world of agents, of spies, is a murky one at best. It wouldn't have been the first time one of them had been discredited in this manner. And the war was still going on, remember. He told them more. He said there'd been an attempt made on his life engineered by these same Germans in conjunction with two Swiss detectives who were in their pay. After a struggle he'd managed to escape, leaving one of the detectives dead. Stabbed. He carries a knife.'

'So now there were *two* murder charges against him.' Sinclair could hardly trust himself to speak.

Vane saw the look on his face. 'Try to understand how the situation must have appeared to our people. The war was being fought as fiercely as ever. No one guessed it would be over in a few months. Lang had brought a great deal of valuable information with him. He was the only person who knew the details of Hoffmann's net-work in Germany. The names of *his* agents. At that particular moment he was of immense value to the Allied cause.'

'So? What happened?'

'Lang disappeared. He was never heard of again. Emil Wahl, a citizen of Belgium, appeared in his place.'

'With all the proper credentials, I suppose?'

Again Vane shrugged. 'I can only repeat, this was a special situation. These things wouldn't happen if wars weren't fought.'

'No, Mr Vane, I must correct you.' The chief inspector's voice was tight with anger. 'These things wouldn't happen if certain people did not choose to place themselves above the law. What those men did was condone one crime and commit another. It's a disgraceful story. Disgraceful, do you hear me?'

Bennett gestured with his hand, trying to calm his colleague. But Vane showed no disposition to take offence. Rather, his rueful shrug seemed a tacit acceptance of the verdict delivered. With a sigh, he went on.

'At this point I should mention that although Lang had worked for us in a number of European countries, because of this wartime episode – or his version of it – he'd never been posted to Germany. However, after a dozen years the danger of exposing him again to their counter-intelligence section was felt to have diminished, and he himself raised no objection to being sent there.

'It was decided to bring him to London first, something which had never happened before, but a sign, if you like, of the value that was placed on his services. In certain quarters, at least.' Vane's face was expressionless. 'Our first meeting was at a restaurant with others present and I took the opportunity to fix a second appointment with him. This would be for the briefing he would need before setting off for Berlin. Since I didn't want him appearing at the Foreign Office, and since I was about to go on holiday anyway, I arranged for us to meet outside London.'

'Had he been in England long?' Sinclair had recovered his poise. 'I'd like to get some idea of his movements.'

'I gathered he'd been here for several weeks and had

visited different parts of the country. He'd wanted a holiday before taking up his assignment. I can't tell you where he went, but I know he's a birdwatcher – it's in his file. He's something of an expert, I believe. It's one of the few things we know about him.'

'Thank you.' The chief inspector inclined his head. 'You were saying you'd fixed a second meeting with him?'

Vane nodded. 'I'd arranged to stay with these friends of mine outside Oxford, and since I was due to travel north myself on the seventh, I'd settled with Lang that we should meet the day before. He'd agreed to take the train up to Oxford and said he planned to spend a night or two at an hotel there before returning to London. I picked him up at the station and took him to a pub in Woodstock where I'd booked a private room for lunch, and where I gave him a detailed briefing.'

He broke off, and sat staring at the desktop in front of him. As the silence grew longer, Sinclair and Bennett exchanged glances. It was a minute or more before the other man looked up. His eyes showed the same unfocussed glaze as before.

'I won't pretend I wasn't curious to know him. Up till then he'd only been a name to me. But I was aware of his reputation and I approached the prospect of our meeting with caution.' He paused once again. 'I don't suppose I need tell you that the qualities required for the kind of work Lang did for us are . . . quite special. It's not a profession for the squeamish. But even so, there are limits . . . or there ought to be.' Vane tapped the buff folder before him. 'Unfortunately I can't show you this.

I'd be in breach of the law. But there are things in it you would find shocking. At least I hope so. They certainly were to me. If I were asked to characterize it I would say it was not so much a record of a man without scruple, as one without moral sense. So you'll understand when I say I had considerable misgivings at the thought of working with him. Nor did this meeting of ours offer much in the way of reassurance.'

He mused for a moment, as though in recollection.

'It's not easy to describe the effect he had on me. In many ways he's quite ordinary. Soft-spoken; almost diffident in manner. And the business side of things went without a hitch. I found him quick to grasp what I was telling him, exceptionally so. Nothing needed to be said twice. But it was as though there was a barrier between us. Something real, but transparent, like a pane of glass. And he was on one side of it and I was on the other and there was no connection between us. No human bond. Thinking about it afterwards, I realized this feeling I had sprang from his glance. His eyes. They were quite dead.'

Vane reflected on what he had said. Then he shrugged.

'It must have been later, when we were driving into Oxford, that I made some reference to my car. It was new, as you know, and I'd bought it because I thought it would be easy to maintain in Germany and less noticeable than a British-made vehicle would have been. It so happened a minor problem had developed with the gears and I must have expressed some irritation over the fact that I couldn't now drive up to Scotland the following day, as I'd intended, but would either have to leave it in a garage in Oxford, or find some way of getting it back to London, so that the necessary repairs could be made while I was away.

'Whatever it was I said, Lang offered to deal with the matter. He said he planned to spend a day or two in the Oxford area, but would willingly drive the car to London for me after that. The worst of it is I so very nearly refused his offer, and for no other reason than that I'd taken such a strong dislike to him. But my reaction seemed out of all proportion, so in the end I let him have it. If only I'd followed my instincts!'

Visibly upset, he stared out of the window where lights could be seen burning in other windows across the courtyard.

'What happened? Did he pick her up on the road?' He spoke without looking round.

'Yes, in Henley. She was running an errand for her mother. The shops were only a mile away.'

With a sigh, Vane turned to face them once more. He seemed paler than before. 'The car was delivered to my garage in London, as promised. By the time I returned from Scotland, Lang was already in Germany establishing himself. I took up my own posting in Berlin in October. It was more than two years before I saw him again.'

'Despite the fact you were there all that time?' Sinclair was incredulous.

'Yes, but that was by arrangement, you see. It wasn't intended we should meet. Lang's assignment was in the area of political intelligence and his orders were to recruit and control agents, to run them, as it were, and to forward their reports to me. Naturally it was important he should have no contact with our embassy in Berlin. My own position was nominally that of a senior attaché with responsibilities in the economic field and I made sure our paths didn't cross. He reported to me in writing.'

'Did his duties take him to Munich, by any chance?' Sinclair asked the question.

'Most certainly.' Vane hesitated. He bit his lip. 'Look, there's no reason I shouldn't tell you what Lang was doing for us in Germany, provided you remain discreet about it. His specific brief was to cultivate contacts in the Nazi party. It's something we've been slow to get on to. Like others, we've tended to dismiss them as rabble. Now it looks as though they may form part of the next government. Or, God forbid, end up running it.

'Lang was sent to Berlin with the assumed character of a representative of an Austrian textile firm. His job was to insinuate himself into party circles with the aim of identifying individuals who might prove useful to us. It's a delicate business, one he'd shown himself to be highly skilled at. He had an eye for picking out the kind of people who could either be bought or persuaded to cooperate by other means, not all of them savoury, and which I'll leave to your imagination.' Vane grimaced. 'Suffice to say he was quite ruthless, something we'd taken note of in the past.

'We'd so arranged it that the firm he was supposed to represent had business ties in Munich and this provided him with an excuse to go there and hang about the beer halls, so as to make his face known.' He noticed the glance that passed between his visitors. 'Why? Is that significant?'

'To us, yes.' Sinclair nodded. 'Two of the murders I've spoken of took place in the Munich region.'

Vane absorbed the information with a frown. He made no comment. 'Well, so much for our plans. Now I'll tell you what occurred. For the first year or so everything ran like clockwork. Lang went about his work with his usual efficiency. In due course he joined the party and having identified various figures whose acquaintance might yield dividends later began to cultivate them. He lent money to several. All was proceeding according to plan. But then, midway through the second year, his work began to fall off. The change was gradual, but quite marked. His reports became irregular – something unheard of, he was methodical to a fault – and when they reached me showed signs of diminishing activity on his part. I remonstrated with him in writing several times, without effect, and was beginning to think a face-to-face meeting between us might be necessary when I received a message from him asking for just that. He wanted to see me urgently.'

Vane made a gesture of weariness. 'There was little I could do but agree, and so we met at a small hotel in the country, outside Berlin, where he told me he wanted to cut short his assignment and leave Germany. He gave as his reason his growing suspicion that he'd been identified once more as a British agent. He insisted he was in danger and said he could no longer carry on with his work.'

'*When* was this?' Sinclair broke in. 'Can you be precise?'

'Early in June of this year. Does that tell you anything?'

'Yes, the last in the chain of murders occurred in April. The Bavarian authorities got a lead from it and with the Berlin police mounted a campaign to identify the killer. They used the newspapers among other means. Lang must have been aware of that.' Sinclair paused, curious. 'What did *you* make of his behaviour?' he asked.

Vane shrugged. 'As regards his being exposed as one of our agents, I was far from convinced. After all, his activities weren't directed against the state. But something was amiss. He was clearly under strain.' He hesitated, gnawing at his lip. 'I won't pretend I had any sympathy for him. I found him no less alien than before. But I couldn't discount the possibility that he might be cracking up, and immediately following our meeting I got in touch with London and it was decided we should withdraw him, temporarily at least. He let it be known he'd been called back to Vienna on some pretext and left Berlin.'

'But came to England?' The chief inspector was listening closely.

'Yes, we brought him back here discreetly. We wanted to keep him under our eye until it had been decided what to do next. I took the opportunity to return to London myself. I had my own views on the subject and every intention of airing them.'

'And where was Lang while all this was going on?'

'In a clinic near Lewes, in Sussex. It's a place we have

a . . . connection with. He was told to take it easy for a few weeks. We arranged for him to receive treatment while he was there.'

'For what, precisely?'

'The doctors found he was suffering from nervous exhaustion, which came as no surprise. We'd seen other agents react to the pressures of their work in similiar ways. It's a hazardous profession, after all. But I was more interested in what their psychiatrist had to say, a man called Bell. It was clear he was fascinated by Lang. In his very first report he described him as an unusual patient, one whose personality he found disturbing, but difficult to penetrate. Opaque was the word he used.'

'Was that all he had to say?' Sinclair frowned.

'At that stage, yes. And since he didn't take issue with the more general diagnosis, Lang was treated simply for strain. He was encouraged to relax. On the advice of the doctors we'd provided him with a car and I understand he spent time driving about the countryside.'

'Did he, indeed?' The coolness had returned to Sinclair's manner. 'Well, I dare say he found occasion to pass by Bognor Regis. One of the two murders I mentioned took place near there, as you may recall.'

Vane's face stiffened. But he said nothing. After a moment, he continued. 'In due course we received a full report from the clinic which included Bell's observations. Though still guarded in his views, what he had to tell us was alarming. He said he had little doubt Lang was suffering from some acute psychological disorder and cautioned us to be wary in our dealings with him.'

'For heaven's sake!' Bennett struck his thigh in impatience. 'Couldn't he have been more specific?'

'I certainly thought so. So I rang him up to see if I could discover more, but he merely repeated what he'd said earlier: that Lang was someone we'd do well to keep at arm's length. I then asked him point blank if he thought he was normal, and he replied that wasn't a word people in his profession liked to use, and that in any case he didn't want to make a categorical judgement since the patient in this case had been unwilling to submit to a proper examination.'

Vane smiled grimly. He caught the assistant commissioner's eye.

'Having cleared his conscience, however, if that was what he was doing, he then informed me that various aspects of Lang's behaviour had given him cause for concern, telltale signs he called them, and one more than any other which he termed "a lack of adequate emotional response", a condition most psychiatrists regarded as being inaccessible to treatment. Extreme detachment from the consequences of one's actions might be another way of putting it. Those who displayed its symptoms frequently felt no guilt or responsibility for what they did, he said, adding it was one of the classic signs of a psychopathic personality.'

'I'll be damned!' Bennett was bereft of words. Sinclair, on the other hand, seemed unsurprised.

'And what effect, if any, did that have on your colleagues?' he asked. 'Were they taken aback?'

'It depends what you mean.' Vane eyed him. 'Some of

us were shocked, certainly. And since I was the person who'd had to deal with him it fell to me to press the case for dispensing with his services. Using Bell's words as ammunition, I insisted that he was a man we could no longer trust and that it was time to cut our ties with him for good.' He laughed harshly. 'I thought I'd made a convincing job of it, but I soon learned better. My arguments cut no ice with those that mattered; nor, it seemed, did the views of some psychiatrist. I was reminded that Lang was one of our best agents with a long record of achievement behind him. As for his flaws of character, they were no more than one might expect from one engaged in so dubious a profession.'

He turned away to stare out of the window. It was some moments before he resumed. In the interim Sinclair and Bennett exchanged glances. But neither felt inclined to speak.

'I dare say you won't find it easy to stomach what I've told you.' Vane addressed the darkness outside. 'You may even wonder how such an individual came to be employed by our intelligence service. I mean, quite apart from the issue of these bestial crimes. I can only answer by giving you the arguments of those who promoted his career in the first place and have championed him ever since. They would say the world was changed by the war in ways the people of this country have yet to grasp. Put simply, it's grown savage – there's no playing by the rules any longer – and men like Gaston Lang, and the uses they can be put to, are just a symptom of that change. It's not a view universally shared, not yet, but one that's likely to gain favour if present trends continue.'

He turned to face them again.

'Where were we . . .? Yes, Lang's future. Well, that was quickly settled. It was decided to send him back to Berlin. His claim to have been unmasked as a British agent had been found to be groundless. We'd been able to obtain independent confirmation of that. Accordingly, he was summoned to London, reminded that he had an obligation to us and instructed to return to Germany without delay and resume his assignment.'

'And how did he respond? Did he accept the decision?'

'He seemed to. He raised no objection, at any rate. But watching him, I was reminded of our meeting at Woodstock and it struck me more strongly than ever that I had no idea who he really was or what was going on in his mind.'

Vane pondered his own words. He shook his head.

'However, it appeared that matters had been settled. Lang returned to Lewes to pack and prepare for his departure. We were expecting to receive confirmation of his travel plans. Instead, two days later, what amounted to a letter of resignation reached us through the post. He said he'd reviewed his position and decided he could no longer continue in our employment. He was returning to Brussels – that's where he was based – and would leave the car we'd provided him with at a garage in Dover. Where, incidentally, it was recovered later. Inquiries made at the ferry ticket office revealed that a man answering his description had booked a cross-channel passage the day before.'

'Was that all? Are you telling me no attempt was made to stop him, or bring him back?' Sinclair was disbelieving.

Vane shrugged. 'Whatever hold we might have thought we had on him, there was little we could do, in fact. You can only lead a horse to water, after all. We couldn't force him to work for us. And there was another consideration. Lang knew a good deal about our intelligence activities; the last thing we wanted to do was antagonize him. All in all, it was thought better to let sleeping dogs lie.'

'So you had no further contact with him?'

'None whatsoever, though we've tried to get in touch with him. We mean to continue with the German operation and there are aspects of it that need clarifying. But there's been no sign of him in Brussels – or anywhere else on the Continent where we might have expected to catch up with him.'

'Hardly surprising, given that it's clear he remained in England.' The chief inspector made no effort to hide his chagrin. 'This man has made fools of you, Mr Vane. You and your confounded colleagues. Do you see what he's done? He got you to spirit him out of Germany, leaving no trace behind. That's twice you've saved his miserable skin.'

'I'm only too aware of that, Chief Inspector.' Vane held his accuser's gaze without flinching. But his remorse was plain.

'I need some dates from you, sir.' Sinclair sought to keep a rein on his temper. 'When did he enter the clinic, and how long was he there?'

'He arrived from Germany towards the end of June and disappeared in the middle of August.'

'The Bognor Regis killing occurred in late July, when he was still a patient, then. But the Brookham murder was in September, long after he was supposed to have gone home. Why did he choose to stay in this country? Can you tell me that? And more important – where do I look for him now? How do I find this man?'

VANE SAT BACK with a sigh. The strain of the long afternoon showed in his pale features. Across the desk, Bennett glanced at his watch. For the past few minutes the assistant commissioner had been trying to attract his companion's attention – he wanted to bring the meeting to a close – but Sinclair's gaze remained fixed on the photograph which Vane had taken from his folder a short while back and handed to them.

An ordinary snapshot, it showed a man clad in a black coat and homburg, standing before some anonymous backdrop – the wall of a building, perhaps. As though caught off guard, his eyes had widened slightly at the moment the photograph was taken, appearing like two black holes in the white of his clean-shaven face. Otherwise expressionless, Gaston Lang stared back at the camera.

'That's the only one we have of him, I'm afraid.' Vane

had been apologetic in making his offering. 'As you can see, he wasn't expecting it. He's not a man who likes to have his picture taken.'

He had added a description of their quarry which the chief inspector had noted down.

'He's in his early forties, of average height, lean and fit. Wiry. He struck me as being stronger than he looks. But his appearance is nondescript: brown hair, brown eyes and with no scars or other identifying marks.'

'What about a birthmark?' Sinclair spoke bluntly. 'We understand he might have one. He was seen half-naked by a witness to one of his murders.'

'I don't know about that . . .' Vane frowned. 'But wait a minute . . . he must have had a full medical examination at the clinic. We insisted on it.'

He opened his file and sorted through the contents.

'Yes, here it is . . .' He picked out a sheet of paper and studied it. 'Well, I never . . . you're quite right. It's on his upper chest. A large haemangioma.'

He glanced up at Sinclair, nodding.

'What else? Can you think of anything out of the ordinary? Any peculiarities he possesses?' The chief inspector's tone remained cool. Although he'd made an effort to moderate the sharpness of his manner, his anger remained unabated. To his way of thinking, it was a sorry tale they'd been treated to.

'Apart from the fact that he speaks English with an accent, none. He'd be easy to miss in a crowd. Up close, though, it's a different matter. That curious quality I spoke of – a sort of lifelessness – it's unsettling.'

On the crucial question of Lang's likely whereabouts, Vane could offer only cautious advice.

'It's been three months since he disappeared. What his intentions were is anyone's guess. Almost the only thing of any value I can tell you is that he's probably changed his name. He won't be Emil Wahl any longer. He'll be busy covering his tracks.'

'Can you be sure of that?' Bennett had questioned the assertion. 'As I understand it, the German police haven't actually identified the man they're after. And there's been nothing in our press to connect the two sets of cases.'

'Perhaps not. But his actions tell a different story. You've only to look at the care he took to make us believe he was returning to the Continent. Isn't that the reaction of a man who in his own mind at least is already on the run and trying to throw any pursuers off the scent?' Vane frowned. 'That said, other aspects of his behaviour seem quite irrational. I'm thinking of those two murders he committed after he got here. They go against all reason. Surely he must have been aware of the danger of drawing attention to himself?' He had glanced at Sinclair as he spoke, perhaps hoping for enlightenment, but the chief inspector's only response had been to repeat the question he'd put earlier.

'What interests me is why he chose to remain *here*. Why not go?'

It appeared Vane had been pondering the same riddle. At all events he'd replied without hesitation. 'If you want my opinion – and it's no more than that – it's because he'd already made up his mind not to return to Europe under any circumstances. That's where he could expect to be found if any large-scale search for him was launched. His stamping ground, if you like. It was safer for him to remain in England, at least in the short term.'

'The *short* term?'

'Yes, he wouldn't stay here for long – at least, that's my guess. It's not a country he'd feel at home in. Given his situation as he sees it, he'd be bound to look further afield for a place of refuge. Somewhere his face isn't known. On another continent, perhaps. And he's had ample time to make whatever preparations he might have thought necessary.' With a sigh, Vane shook his head. 'I can only repeat what I said earlier. I fear we're too late.'

The chief inspector had grunted at his words. 'For what it's worth, I'm inclined to agree with you,' he said. 'But that's not an assumption I can make at this stage.'

Now he gestured with the snapshot he was holding.

'I'll take this with me, if I may. I want to circulate it, along with a description of Lang.'

'Please do. And I promise to comb through this file for any information that might be of use to you.' Vane tapped his folder again. He watched as the chief inspector tucked the photograph in among his papers. Bennett had already risen to his feet.

'I shall have to inform my colleagues of this meeting.' Vane rose himself. 'I'd better warn you now, they won't take kindly to what I have to tell them. The thought that Lang might be brought to trial in open court will start all sorts of alarm bells ringing. Some may even reach *your* ears. I do urge you again to tread carefully in this matter.'

He had addressed his last remark to Sinclair, who had not yet got to his feet. Too late he saw his mistake. The chief inspector's face had hardened.

'I'll be frank with you, Mr Vane. I've no sympathy whatever for your colleagues, or their anxieties. It does occur to me, though, that they might feel differently if they were given some idea of what this investigation will involve. I take it Lang's supporters are among them?' He looked up.

Vane nodded.

'Including those who protected him originally? The ones who shielded him from the Swiss police years ago?' Sinclair's glance had grown cold.

'Some of them – yes.'

'Good. Then you might start by telling them that sexual criminals of Lang's type are every policeman's nightmare. They kill at random, you see, individually their victims mean nothing to them, and this absence of any link makes them among the hardest to track down. All they seek is opportunity.'

The chief inspector closed his file.

'It's a fact men like him appear to act from compulsion – a psychologist would certainly tell you so – they can't stop themselves, which may account for those irrational aspects of Lang's behaviour you mentioned. As time goes by, whatever inhibitions they feel, even those prompted by caution, seem to grow weaker, with the result that intervals between attacks tend to shorten.'

Sinclair rose to his feet. He began to button his coat.

'I'm sure your colleagues will feel concern when you point out to them that more than two months have passed since that child was murdered at Brookham, a long time as these things go, and that wherever Lang is now, here or abroad, the chances are he'll be looking for a fresh victim.'

The chief inspector paused. His listener had turned pale.

'Unfortunately, you'll also have to tell them there's nothing I, or anyone else, can do about that. Except pray he hasn't found her already.'

20

THE WEATHER had cleared at last – it had been raining
for several days – and after a bite of lunch in Midhurst
Sam Watkin drove out to Hobday's Farm, near Rogate,
to see how the roof he'd fixed was holding up. He'd
done the work himself in the end, resetting the chimney
and replacing the smashed tiles. He'd also patched up
the floor below with a couple of new bricks and was
pleased to find the inside bone dry.

'Do you see that, Sal? I reckon I could hire myself
out. Repairs and decorations.'

They had paused only long enough to admire his
handiwork. Once he was sure all was well, Sam had
climbed back into his van. He had another errand to run,
one that had nothing to do with his job, but was every
bit as important. At least that was Ada's opinion.

'Now be sure and pass by Coyne's Farm, Sam. I want
Eddie to have this extra blanket. The nights are getting
colder. I've wrapped up a pork pie for him, too, and a
bit of cheese and a bar of soap, if he needs one. You see
he gets them.'

Though it was a Wednesday, and not one of the days
he usually went to Coyne's Farm – those were Tuesdays
and Thursdays – Sam didn't mind going out of his way.
His plans for making Eddie's life a little brighter had
succeeded beyond his best hopes. There was something

about his old wartime pal – dignity, perhaps, the way he held himself in spite of hardship – that appealed to women; to their motherly side. (Or so Sam reckoned.) It had certainly worked with Ada. And she wasn't the only one.

The day after their encounter he'd picked up Eddie at the roadworks and brought him home to supper, as he'd promised. On the way over he'd given him the good news about the empty barn at Coyne's Farm and how Mr Cuthbertson had agreed to let him sleep there if he liked.

'Could I really, Sam?' Eddie's face had lit up like a boy's and Sam had realized then how much he must have hated having to bunk down in that cramped shed with the other men.

Next day he'd collected him again after work and taken him up the path that led over the ridge to the farm. He'd shown him the gap in the hedge that gave onto the orchard and the walled kitchen garden. Beyond lay the farmyard where the barn stood. Sam had unlocked the double doors.

'Here – you keep this.' He'd tossed Eddie the key to the padlock. 'It's a spare. Be sure and lock the doors each morning when you go to work. I told Mr Cuthbertson you'd keep an eye on the place.'

On his way from Rogate now he paused at the roadworks long enough to tell Eddie about his mission and to say he'd leave the stuff Ada had sent for him at the barn.

'It's kind of her, Sam, but she shouldn't. I've got all I need now. *And* more, thanks to you. Can't you tell her?'

Though he was dirty and sweating – he'd been working with a pick at the side of the road, lifting stones – Eddie's face was split by a wide grin. He looked a different bloke.

'*You* tell her, Eddie. I wouldn't dare.' With a wink, Sam drove on.

He hadn't far to go. The crew was advancing along the road and now was much closer to the point where it was crossed by Wood Way, and where a gravelled space for parking had been cleared. In summer, at the weekends, it was sometimes packed, since many ramblers left their cars there to walk out onto the Downs. That day there was only one other vehicle in the lot, a car that was parked at the back, half-hidden by the branches of an overhanging oak tree.

Sam left his van at the edge of the area, near the road, and then walked up Wood Way, over the ridge, with Sal at his heels, carrying Ada's bundle tucked under his arm. Though the rain had stopped during the night, the air was still damp and a low grey cloud hung over the valley.

Inside the barn he found a number of spots where the roof had leaked, but none of them over the corner at the back which Eddie was occupying. The first day he had brought him over the two of them had quickly set the place to rights. It was something soldiering taught you – how to make yourself comfortable – and he and Eddie had caught each other's eye and grinned as the same thought had struck them both.

'It takes you back, doesn't it?' Eddie's gaze was already brighter as he inspected his new billet.

They hadn't walked over unburdened, either. Remembering the lamps he'd found, Sam had brought a tin of oil with him, and a small brazier, as well, while Eddie had lugged the bag of coke he would need to build himself a fire together with his own belongings.

'Don't worry, Sam. I'll empty it each morning before I leave. I won't burn the place down, I promise.'

He'd been as good as his word, Sam saw now. (He'd spotted the empty brazier at once.) In fact, Eddie had left few traces of his presence. The mound of hay he used as a mattress was pushed neatly into the corner, but his bedding and the rest of his stuff were nowhere to be seen and must have been stowed away, perhaps in one of the cupboards.

When they'd done all they needed to at the barn, Sam had suggested that they walk over to Oak Green so that he could show Eddie the place, not knowing what a lucky encounter was awaiting them there.

As they reached the small cluster of houses, the door of the village shop had opened and Nell Ramsay had stepped out into the narrow street. Catching sight of Sally, who was ambling along at their side, the girl had let out a whoop of delight and come running up to greet them.

Sam hadn't noticed she was with anyone until he heard a grown-up's voice behind him. 'I can see we're not going to be introduced, Mr Watkin.' A woman had come up and joined them. She was smiling. 'I'm Nell's mother. I've been hearing for months about you and Sally. I'm so glad we've met at last.'

Dark-haired like her daughter, Mrs Ramsay had

offered them her hand, and Sam had seen at once where Nell got her looks from. Those, and the easy way she had with people.

Learning that they had walked over from Coyne's Farm, Mrs Ramsay had insisted that they come back and have tea with her and Nell before returning. Sam had accepted without pausing to consider, and then wondered whether she was aware, as he ought to have been, of how uncomfortable the prospect had made Eddie. (He was still in his work clothes, grimy and unshaven.) But his worry for his friend had been needless.

As soon as they'd reached the house, a handsome, double-storied dwelling a few minutes walk from the village, with a garden that stretched down to the stream, she had shown Eddie to a bathroom, saying, 'You must be longing for a chance to clean up, Mr Noyes. Please don't hurry. We're going to have tea in the kitchen. It's nice and warm there, and Sally can join us.'

She'd guessed that Eddie would feel ill at ease in her drawing room, dressed the way he was, and had dealt with the situation gracefully. Just like you'd expect a lady to. (A proper lady, that was. Not like some Sam could name. The ones who gave themselves airs.)

During the few minutes they'd had to themselves he had explained to her about Eddie. Why he was staying at Coyne's Farm. The reason he looked so down and out.

'He lost his job for no reason, the way people do these days. Bravest bloke I ever knew. They gave him the Military Medal in the war. Now he has to pick up work wherever he can. It doesn't seem right.'

Sam had spoken with feeling. But he'd been surprised by the warmth of Mrs Ramsay's response.

'I do so agree with you, Mr Watkin.'

When Eddie returned – a lot cleaner, but still shy and unsure of himself – she had made a point at once of getting him to talk, asking him where he came from and what his background was. It had amazed Sam to see how quickly she was able to break the ice. Soon Eddie had been chatting away, telling her about his home near Hove and his mother and sister, the one suffering from angina, the other still mourning the husband she'd lost.

Listening to him, Sam had gained a new insight into his old comrade-in-arms, one he might never have been granted if it hadn't been for Mrs Ramsay's gentle probing. What Eddie had gone and done was take on the job of looking after these two women and lost any chance of a life of his own in the process. Sam reckoned Mrs Ramsay had seen that. At any rate, her glance, when it rested on his face, had been full of understanding.

Nor would she listen for a moment when he told her he planned to come over to Oak Green from time to time to buy provisions for himself. 'You can't possibly spend all day working and not have a proper meal at night. Even if I'm not here, Bess will have something hot for you.'

'Course I will, Mr Noyes.' The Ramsay's cook had smiled encouragingly. A plump, red-faced woman, she had listened to their conversation with avid interest. 'Just put your head in the kitchen door. I'll be here.'

Dear old Eddie – he hadn't known which way to

look, what with the two of them fussing over him like mother hens. Neither willing to take no for an answer.

It had been almost dark by the time they left to return to Coyne's Farm. Nell had slipped outside earlier – to show Sally the garden, she said – and they had walked with Mrs Ramsay around the house to the front and watched as the girl raced about in the gathering shadows, with Sal labouring gamely in pursuit.

It was the first time Sam had seen her out of her school uniform. Dressed in a plaid skirt and a Fair Isle sweater she looked more grown up. But the high-pitched cries that rang out over the wide lawn had been those of a child still.

It seemed her mother shared his thoughts. Earlier, Sam had told her about Rosie and Josh, his and Ada's two, and now she glanced at him with a wistful expression.

'They grow up so quickly,' she had said with a sigh.

SMILING IN REMINISCENCE, Sam looked at his watch. It was getting on for four. Nell would be back from school soon. They might meet her on the path.

He and Sally had walked up to the ridge behind the farm after locking the barn. Sam had left Ada's bundle on the broken washstand, where Eddie would see it.

'Pity about that pork pie, Sal,' he'd observed regretfully. 'We could have done with that, you and I. I doubt Eddie'll have room for more than a mouthful.'

Not when he was going over to Oak Green most

evenings for his supper. Initially reluctant to push himself forward, he'd plucked up the courage to put his head inside Bess's kitchen, like he'd been told to, and now he was a regular visitor there. Sam had teased him about it.

'I reckon she's got her eye on you.'

Eddie had just laughed. 'I like going over there,' he'd admitted. 'They make you feel welcome.' Although Eddie's thinning hair and lined face still made him seem older than he was, he'd lost that careworn look. 'I met *Mister* Ramsay the other afternoon. Did you know he was in the line, north of us, up near the coast? Wounded twice, he was. Lucky to get home. And that Nell's a sweet lass. She comes and sits with me in the kitchen when I'm there, asks me all kinds of questions. They're a grand family.'

Sam was happy for his old pal, but he couldn't help wondering if his evenings at Oak Green hadn't made Eddie think about his own life, and the chances he'd let slip by.

'Now, don't get settled, Sal. We're moving on.'

He'd noticed her circling a patch of damp earth, getting ready to lie down. His own gaze had been fixed on the valley: he'd been running his eye along the length of the stream, checking for any signs of life there. At that moment the silence about them was broken by a chorus of raucous cries. Glancing up, Sam was in time to see a pair of rooks go sailing off from the edge of the wood.

When he looked down again he got a surprise: the figure of a man had appeared in the farmyard below; he was standing in the middle of the expanse of cobbles, gazing about him. Dressed in tweeds, he had a pair of binoculars in a leather case slung from one shoulder, and the sight of them rang a bell in Sam's memory.

Wasn't this the same bloke he'd seen on the ridge opposite, across the valley, a couple of weeks back? The one he'd taken for a birdwatcher?

His first assumption was that the fellow must have walked up Wood Way, noticed the gap in the hedge and decided to see where it led. It was something that happened with ramblers often enough. They used the footpath to get to and from the Downs and occasionally strayed onto the farm.

But soon it became clear that the man hadn't got there by accident. Not judging by the interest he was taking in the yard. The first thing he did was go over to a tap that stood against the wall by the back door and turn it on, apparently to check that it was working. Next, he crossed the cobbles to inspect the stalls, walking quickly, disappearing from sight for several minutes as he went inside them.

Watching from above, it occurred to Sam that the bloke must have heard the farm was for sale and had come to look it over. In fact, he was just wondering whether he ought to wander down there and offer his assistance — give him Mr Cuthbertson's name, say — when something happened that drove any notion of a friendly gesture out of his mind.

Moments before, the man had turned his attention to the barn. Finding the doors bolted, he'd begun to fiddle with the padlock, weighing it in the palm of his hand and peering at it closely. Now, under Sam's disbelieving gaze, he took what looked like a penknife from his jacket pocket and began to pick at it.

'*Oi!*' Not sure even if he was within earshot, Sam gave vent to his outrage. 'That's enough of that! Come on, old girl—'

Without waiting for Sal to join him, he marched off down the slope, intending to have a word with the intruder. Ask him what he thought he was up to. Yes, and tell him to keep his paws off other people's property. But once he'd descended from the ridge he lost sight of the tweed-suited figure, and by the time he reached the yard – it had taken him only a few minutes – the bird had flown. The cobbled space stood empty.

'Blast!' Sam looked about him in frustration. He noticed that the gate to the walled kitchen garden was open. Apparently the man had left the same way he'd come.

Pausing only to check that the padlock was secure, he went after him, hastening through the garden and the orchard beyond, then slipping out through the hedge onto Wood Way.

Disappointment awaited him there. He'd hoped to find his quarry close by. Instead he saw that the fellow had already put some distance between them. He was up near the top of the path, approaching the crest of the ridge, walking with long, swinging strides, going like the clappers.

'Oi! You!'

Sam yelled after him again, but with no more effect than before. Either the bloke hadn't heard him, or he chose not to look round.

'*Go on, then. Hop it!*'

Bellowing his frustration, he was distracted just then by the sight of another figure on the path, ahead of the man, which he recognized. It was Nell. Unmistakable in her white school hat and navy blue gymslip, she'd just come over the ridge from the road on the other side, where the bus dropped her. As Sam watched, the two of them passed one another without stopping. A few moments later the man disappeared from sight over the brow of the hill.

Nell, meanwhile, was drawing closer, breaking into a trot as she came to the steeper part of the downslope, waving to them.

'Hullo, Mr Watkin . . . hullo, Sally.'

Breathless, her cheeks apple-pink, the girl arrived at the spot where they were standing and at once collapsed in a heap on the ground. Sally's whines of welcome were rewarded with a hug. Sam watched them, smiling.

'You look done in,' he remarked.

'I am. I almost missed the bus.' Nell spoke between gasps. 'I had to chase it for ages. I've *still* got a stitch.' She clutched her side. 'We were rehearsing for the Christmas pageant. I'm going to be one of the wise men. I have to wear a beard and moustache. Mummy and Daddy'll *die* laughing.'

He waited until she had caught her breath. Then he asked, 'That bloke you passed on the path—'

'The one you were shouting at?' Nell raised her eyes to his. The flush was fading from her cheeks.

'Have you seen him before? Around here, I mean?'

'No, I don't think so . . . why?' She brushed the hair from her eyes.

'I caught him poking about in the farmyard, trying to get into the barn.'

'He must have a guilty conscience. You should have seen the look he gave me.' She giggled.

'Look? What look?' The words brought a scowl to Sam's face.

'Oh, you know . . . just a look.' Nell had noticed his reaction. 'It was nothing . . . really.' She shifted on her bare knees, turning to Sal, who'd been busy for the past few moments sniffing at her school satchel. 'Now what makes you think I've got anything for you?' she asked sternly.

Sal's response was to wag her tail vigorously.

'You don't imagine for one moment there's a b-i-s-c-u-i-t in there, do you?'

The spelt-out word was greeted by a bark of encouragement.

'Oh, all right, I admit it. I do have just the *tiniest* piece of gingerbread still.'

Sam watched as the tidbit was produced – and disposed of. The frown hadn't left his face.

'Oh, Sally . . .! You might at least *pretend* to chew it.' Nell shook her head in feigned despair. She began to collect her things. 'It's been so nice having Mr Noyes come over after work.' She looked up. 'Bess absolutely *dotes* on him. Daddy came and sat with us in the kitchen the other evening. He never talks about the war, you know, but the two of them began to tell each other stories, things that had happened to them, and I just sat there, quiet as a mouse, listening. Mr Noyes says his job will be over by Christmas and then he'll go back to Hove. I don't know *what* Bess will do when he leaves.'

'Eddie's going to miss you all.' Sam helped her to her feet and adjusted her satchel. 'He told me so himself.'

'Did he? Well, we'll miss him, too. Won't we, Sally?' She bent to bestow her customary kiss on the dog's head. 'I do hope he won't just disappear when his job ends, that he'll come back and see us sometime. Goodbye, Mr Watkin.' She favoured him with her mother's smile.

'Goodbye, love.'

He watched as she went off, waiting until he had seen her take the fork to Oak Green. Then he turned and, with Sally at his side, started up the path, heading back to the van.

'Gave her a look, did he?' Sam was still fretting over what Nell had told him. He didn't like the sound of it. Any more than he did the scene he had witnessed earlier. 'Just what was he doing, poking about in the yard? What's his business there, do you reckon, eh, Sal?'

For the life of him he couldn't think of an explanation.

One thing was certain, though. He was going to keep an eye out for this bloke in future. Ask Eddie to do the same. And if either of them caught him sniffing around Coyne's Farm again, they'd give him his marching orders.

In triplicate.

Just tell him to bugger off.

21

'I'LL BE HONEST with you, John. I doubt we'll ever lay hands on him. Even supposing he's still in England, where do we begin? He has no friends, or family, no occupation we'd recognize as such and no ties to any part of the country. His way of life's a mystery. As far as the average British copper is concerned, he might as well be from another planet.'

Angus Sinclair had barely allowed Madden time to greet him and to take his hat before launching into a catalogue of complaints and self-criticism.

'I've just spent the morning telling a group of over-worked policemen I've every confidence a well-organized search will uncover Lang's whereabouts, when I think nothing of the sort.'

The chief inspector had driven to Highfield from Guildford, where a conference of senior detectives from the Surrey and Sussex constabularies had been convened at his request. He hadn't planned on seeing Madden when he'd set out from London earlier that day, but as the morning wore on and his dissatisfaction with what he was doing mounted, the temptation to call on his old friend and colleague – the thought of finding at least one sympathetic ear into which to pour his troubles – had become irresistible. A telephone call to the farm had resulted in an invitation to lunch, a proposal Sinclair had been doubly pleased to accept when he'd learned that Helen would not be with them.

'She's gone over to Chiddingfold to take surgery for a friend.'

The chief inspector had no illusions as to how Madden's wife would react to any fresh attempt on his part to further involve her husband in the inquiry. Furthermore, he wanted to be able to speak freely, something he could not have done if Helen had been present. As it was, his frankness caused even Madden to express some uneasiness on his behalf.

'Should you be telling me all this, Angus? Doesn't it fall within the Defence of the Realm Act?'

'Damn the realm, damn the act and damn British Intelligence, whoever they may be!' Fortified by a stiff whisky, Sinclair's tongue had grown ever freer. 'Thanks to certain individuals who will never be held to account for it, a cold-blooded murderer was turned loose on society years ago and has enjoyed the protection of this country's secret service ever since. Those men knew he was a killer and chose to ignore the fact. If he happens to be arrested abroad, all hell will break loose and we may see some chickens coming home to roost. I pray I may be spared to witness that day.'

The chief inspector's mood had already been soured earlier that week on receipt, from Philip Vane, of the information he'd promised to extract from Gaston Lang's confidential file. Rich though it proved to be in details, it had left Sinclair with the feeling that he'd been handed a bar of soap too slippery to hold on to. Vane had given him a list of the countries Lang had worked in, the dates he'd been in each and whatever aliases he might have used on the various assignments.

'It's like a travel guide to central Europe,' Sinclair had remarked to Bennett and Holly when they went to review progress in the investigation. 'What a busy fellow our Mr Lang has been. No doubt he gave value for money. By their lights, at least. But there's nothing here to show what sort of man he is. It's an empty shell. Where are his habits . . . his foibles?'

'Austria, Czechoslovakia, Hungary, the Balkans . . . hmmm.' The assistant commissioner had browsed through the list. 'What do you mean to do with this?' he'd asked Sinclair.

'For a start I'll get in touch with the police in these countries to see if they have any record of unsolved crimes similiar to ours. They'll already have received our earlier request through the international commission, but I'll make the point that he may have been active for years. Then I'll send that list of aliases to the commission along with Lang's physical description and photograph with a request for them to be broadcast. I mean to spread a net for him all over Europe and beyond. The more people we have looking for this man, the better. The German police should be informed separately; they're entitled to know what we're doing.'

'Yes, but have a care, Chief Inspector.' Bennett's fears had resurfaced. 'I've an idea Vane's sticking his neck out, giving us this sort of information. On no account must we reveal Lang's connection with our intelligence people. We gave him our word, remember.'

'Rest assured, sir, I won't cross that line. Though, as

to words given and received, I doubt that Vane and his brethren set much store by them, except as a means to deceive others.' Sinclair's lips twitched in distaste. 'And we *will* have to offer Berlin some indication of a source for what we tell them. I suggest we attribute it to criminal informants. After all, it's not that far from the truth.'

'Come now . . . aren't you being too severe?' Bennett eyed him. 'God knows I'm not defending the way Lang was handled by our intelligence service originally. But their priorities are different from ours. And their problems quite particular. Let's be grateful *we* don't have to deal with them. You heard what Vane said: there's no playing by the rules any longer.'

'So they would have us believe.' Sinclair's tone was cool. 'I beg to differ.'

Sir Wilfred sighed. He glanced across at Arthur Holly, expecting by custom to receive some support from that quarter, but recognizing at once the vanity of his hopes. The chief superintendent had been informed of the substance of their meeting with Vane. He had listened in silence to Sinclair's account of the interview. Only at the conclusion had he given his view.

'I've always thought accountability was the basis of public service, sir.' Rumbling with disapproval, the chief super had addressed his remarks to Bennett. 'We're given a certain authority, and in return we have to answer for how we exercise it. I see no sign of that here. These men seem to think they can bend the law to suit their own purposes.'

In desperation, the assistant commissioner had

changed the subject. 'Coming closer to home, Chief Inspector, what can be done in this country? I take it you're organizing a search here?'

'Yes, but not with much conviction. The last murder was early in September, so it's been more than two months since we heard from him, if I can put it that way.' Sinclair winced at his own choice of words. 'It's likely he's already left the country. But we can't be sure of that, and we have to act on the assumption he's still here, until proved otherwise. I don't believe that photograph will be of much use. If he's on the run, as Vane thinks, it's odds on he's changed his appearance. But I'm circulating it to the police nationally, along with his description and a list of the names he's used in the past. And I'll have the ports watched, of course.'

'What about the press? Can we use them?'

'No, I don't think so, sir. Not in this case. It would be like opening Pandora's box. There's no telling what might come out. And from a purely practical point of view, it won't do us a blind bit of good. Publishing Lang's photograph and description in the newspapers would simply alert him to the fact that we're on his trail – something he can't be sure of yet. Remember, this is a man who's lived in the shadows all his life. No one knows better how to cover his tracks. I want to keep the hunt for him confined to the police for as long as possible. And I want to concentrate our search in the counties where Lang's been active. There's a chance he may have been staying somewhere in the Surrey/Sussex area. John Madden, for one, thinks so.'

'Madden, again?' Bennett brightened at the familiar name. 'What's he had to say on the subject?'

'A good deal, as it happens.' Sinclair's frown, which he'd worn all morning, lifted for a moment, and the smile that took its place showed a hint of self-congratulation. His ploy of sending Billy Styles to talk to his old mentor had yielded one worthwhile result, at least. 'I haven't had a chance to tell you, but John's made a valuable observation. He believes Lang must have explored the countryside around Brookham pretty thoroughly prior to the murder. How else could he have known where to take the girl? He didn't stumble on that spot by chance. If he's had time to wander about, it suggests he might have been living in the general area. In a hotel or boarding house, perhaps. That's where we'll start. It's a job for the county police forces. I've got a meeting of detectives from Surrey and Sussex fixed for tomorrow.'

IT WAS THIS gathering in Guildford that had darkened Sinclair's mood that morning and sent him in search of Madden. The knowledge that he was being less than frank with colleagues sat ill with the chief inspector and he made no secret of his displeasure.

'They must have known I wasn't telling them all I knew. At the very least, they must have wondered where I'd acquired all this information about Lang's travels abroad.'

'Did they ask what his occupation was?'

'They did. I said I couldn't enlighten them. Still, a man with that many aliases is fairly limited as to professions. I dare say they've put two and two together. All *I* could do was emphasize the *police* aspect of this business. Our only concern was with catching a murderer, I told them, and I laid stress on how dangerous he was, how different from the type of criminal we normally have to deal with.'

'That concerns you, does it?'

They had moved from the drawing room into the dining room, where Mrs Beck had served them lunch, and where the dull grey light of the autumn day, flooding through the windows, lay cold on the white tablecloth. Madden had said little up till then.

'A great deal. He carries a knife, and he knows how to use it. Those poor children he butchered aren't his only victims. He killed a detective years ago and Vane hinted there have been other fatalities in his career. I'm insisting this search is conducted by the plain-clothes branch. I don't want some village bobby trying to feel his collar. They can start by checking with hotel keepers and landladies, looking for single men who fit the description. If an interview's deemed necessary, then at least two detectives must be present. And they're to be on their guard. He'll kill if he has to, if he feels threatened. He's done it before.'

Casting all discretion aside, the chief inspector had then embarked on a detailed account of the visit he and Bennett had paid to the Foreign Office. His discourse took them through lunch and coffee and was still not complete when they wandered outside for some air onto the terrace, to be met by a wave of Scotch mist billowing down from the wooded ridge of Upton Hanger and sweeping up the lawn. Already the orchard at the foot of the garden had vanished, while of the great weeping beech that stood near it, only a few bare branches were visible thrusting up through the curtain of grey.

'So that's where we stand, John. And I'm damned if I know what to do next.'

Madden grunted. Unaware of the frosting of white droplets coating his hair and eyebrows, he had stood listening in grim-faced silence.

'So that birthmark Beezy spotted was real. Have you been able to make use of the information?'

'Not really.' Sinclair shook his head. 'Since the mark's on his chest, it's hidden by his clothing. Still, I've decided to take a long shot. We're having leaflets sent out to all doctors in Surrey and Sussex asking them if they've treated any man with a large wine stain recently – not a regular patient, of course – and warning them that he's dangerous. Helen can show you hers when it arrives, which should be any day.'

The chief inspector had been hoping his old partner would provide some insight into the problems facing him. But Madden had only one suggestion to offer, and that, by his own admission, 'the longest of long shots'.

'I was struck by what Vane told you – about Lang being a birdwatcher. It explains something that's been puzzling me.'

'What's that?' Sinclair dabbed at his damp face with a handkerchief.

'I wondered how Lang had come to know about that

tramps' site near Brookham, where he took the girl. He could hardly have stumbled on it by chance. Now I understand. When I went there the next day the woods were full of birdsong. I saw a kingfisher, I remember.' Madden's eyes clouded at the memory.

'And you think Lang had been there before?'

Madden nodded. 'He must have driven past Capel Wood some time earlier and seen that it was a promising spot. He could easily have explored the stream. When Billy Styles came to see me not long ago we talked about that – about how the killer seemed familiar with the countryside. We wondered if he didn't have a hobby that took him outdoors.' He cocked a white eyebrow at his companion. 'It might be worth following up, Angus.'

'I don't see how.' The chief inspector scratched his head.

'I was thinking of the societies – birdwatchers, I mean. There must be several, in both counties. You could get them to canvas their members, see if they've noticed any unfamiliar faces in the fields, men fitting the description. It might ring a bell.'

Sinclair grunted. He seemed less than convinced.

'Well, it's a possibility, I suppose. And since we're clutching at straws anyway . . .' He caught Madden's eye and grinned. 'I'll tell you what, I'll put Styles on to it. He's been sitting in Guildford twiddling his thumbs.'

They stood in silence while the mist thickened about them. Then a groan issued from Sinclair's lips.

'Damn it, it's not enough. We'll need more than luck to catch this man. Is there nothing else we can do?'

The silence which was Madden's only response

seemed to speak louder than words, and to the chief inspector his dark withdrawn gaze was a confirmation of his own worst fears, to which he now gave expression, his voice harsh with anger at the need he felt to say it.

'Must we wait till he kills again?'

22

DARKNESS WAS FALLING – it was getting on for five – by the time Eddie Noyes left the site, waving goodbye to the McCarthys, Pat and Jimmy, both from County Mayo, but not related, they said, who'd become special pals of his, and acknowledging the raised hands of some of the others as well.

It being a Friday, and the end of their working week, the men had taken longer than usual to gather their tools and put things in order before they departed. Eddie's last duty had been to position the moveable signs at either end of the strip of road they were working on, warning motorists to slow down, that the surface ahead was under repair. Six feet high and set in concrete, they were difficult to manoeuvre, but he had learned the knack of tipping them off centre and then rolling them along until he reached the desired spot.

It hadn't been easy for him at first, fitting in. He'd been marked down by the others as an outsider, someone not used to manual labour, and he'd had to prove himself in the early days by taking on some of the hardest and dirtiest jobs – breaking up the old road surface with a sledgehammer, for instance, or mixing and pouring tar – before they'd accepted him as one of them.

But they were a good set of blokes, a dozen men in all, half of them Irish, and their companionship had reminded Eddie of nothing so much as his time in the ranks. Right down to the foreman, Joe Harrigan, who was a dead ringer for his first sergeant, a black-browed Mick from Donegal, who'd been a right bastard if he was crossed, but had taken care of his men just the same. Dooley had been his name. Jack Dooley. A Jerry mortar shell had done for him at Mons.

Eddie had joined the crew some months earlier when they were working on a bit of road near Hove, where he lived. Hearing they were looking for labour, he'd pitched up on the off chance and been taken on by Harrigan, who'd left him in no doubt as to what would be expected of him.

'You don't look to me like you're up to it,' he'd said bluntly, a remark Eddie had taken to refer to his small stature – and perhaps to the softness of his hands, which the foreman had seized in his own calloused palms and examined critically. 'But I'll give you a try. No favours, mind.'

Having been unable to find steady work since losing his salesman's job the previous December, he'd been ready to jump at anything that was offered. The burden of providing for his mother and sister, who shared the small house they lived in in Hove, weighed heavily on him, and the fear of failing them was seldom far from his thoughts.

Continuing along the road, Eddie had reached the point where it was crossed by the path that led over the ridge to Coyne's Farm. Busy with ramblers during the mild weeks of autumn, it was deserted now that winter was approaching. Looking back, he saw that his workmates had collected their tools and were heading off in a straggling line in the opposite direction, towards the corrugated iron shed a good half mile away which housed Harrigan's cubbyhole of an office, storage space for their equipment and a few square yards of bare earth where those of the crew who'd chosen to save their money and sleep rough, rather than seek cheap lodgings in the neighbourhood – Eddie had been of their number – would spread their bedrolls for the night.

It had been these long hours of darkness, loud with the sound of the men's snoring and their muffled groans, that he'd found hardest to bear. Sleepless in the midst of the closely packed bodies, breathing in the fetid air, he had felt his spirit foundering and it had taken all his resolve to rise each morning and face the new day.

Even so, when the chance to escape this purgatory had been offered him, he'd hesitated, afraid that the others might resent his good fortune. But he found he'd misjudged them. Laughing, they had watched while Pat McCarthy begged Eddie with a wink to spit in his hand in case his luck was catching. As one man they had urged him to make the most of his windfall.

At the thought of how his circumstances had changed since Sam Watkin's unexpected appearance, the grin on Eddie's face grew wider. (The image of a stone dropping into a stagnant pool came to his mind.) He remembered with delight the moment when the green postal van had drawn up beside him on the road and he'd heard the driver's jovial greeting.

'What, ho, Eddie!'

The surge of happiness he'd experienced at that instant

had come from another time – from the very worst days
of the war – when Sam's bent nose had seemed like a
symbol of its owner's pugnacity, his refusal to surrender
to whatever life might throw at him, and in the mud-
choked horror which had become their daily existence,
his spirit, like some ancient tribal magic, had cast its spell
on all around him.

'*What, ho, Eddie!*'

Everything that had happened since their chance
encounter – his move to Coyne's Farm and the kindness
he'd received at the hands of the Ramsay household –
seemed to Eddie like an extension of this marvellous
power his old pal possessed, and his own spirits had
risen in response, giving him fresh heart. Once more
he'd resumed his long struggle to escape from what he
saw as the dead hand of the past, a mysterious force that
threatened always to drag him down.

For years he had suffered from a sense of inertia, a
lack of will that had prevented him not only from living
his life to the full, but also from making proper provision
for the future. Unaware that the malady was one he
shared with other survivors of the trenches, men in their
thousands, Eddie had attributed it instead to a particular
event: he believed it stemmed from the moment when
he'd received the near-fatal wound that had ended his
military career.

He could still recall the impact of the sniper's bullet
when it struck him like an iron fist, piercing his ribcage
and sending splinters of bone into one of his lungs.
Clear, too, in his memory were the minutes that followed. With the voices of the men around him growing

faint in his ears, he had lain staring up at the darkening sky, waiting for oblivion. Knowing he was scuppered.

And even though the conviction had proved false, the memory of it had returned like a ghostly echo when he regained consciousness a few days later in a hospital ward and discovered what had happened to him in the intervening period.

'You're the bloke who came back from the dead,' the doctor in attendance had told him with a grin. 'They'd already loaded you onto the meat wagon when one of the graves party noticed your eyelid twitching. Good thing he did, or by now you'd be pushing up daisies.'

During his slow recovery – for weeks he had lain in a dreamlike state, indifferent to his future, unmoved even by the knowledge that he would not be returning to the front – a mood of fatalism had settled on him that had changed little with the passing years, and which sprung from the belief, already rooted in his mind, that he was living on borrowed time.

HAVING REACHED the crest of the ridge, Eddie quickened his pace. The long twilights of summer were a thing of the past and darkness fell swiftly at this time of year. But the sky had cleared after a spell of rainy weather and a new moon had risen in the past few days that would light his way to Oak Green later.

Shy at first of accepting the invitation that had been extended to him, he had come to delight in the hours he spent in the Ramsays' kitchen, where the warmth of his welcome seemed like a reproach to the melancholia that so often afflicted him.

He even felt in a strange way that he had become a member of the family, part of the household at least, his presence at the kitchen table in the evenings so accepted that when Mrs Ramsay looked in, as she always did, for a few words with him, she would sit down – checking his movement to rise to his feet – and begin talking at once about whatever was in her mind, just as though a conversation they had been having earlier had been interrupted, wasting no time on formalities, but plunging straight into some topic.

Often she would ask his advice, her smile and the open friendliness of her manner putting Eddie so much at ease that he would find himself holding forth on all kinds of subjects, some of them things he knew very little about. Not that it seemed to matter.

'What a good idea, Mr Noyes. I think I'll take your advice.'

Then she would turn to Bess and ask her what *she* thought and the Ramsays' cook, who obviously knew her mistress's ways well, would offer a forthright opinion, meanwhile trying to catch Eddie's eye, so that they could share a conspiratorial wink.

What Sam had said jokingly was true – Bess did seem to have a soft spot for him – but thus far it had manifested itself only by the blushes with which she greeted his arrival each evening, her broad face lighting up like a lantern the moment he popped his head through the doorway. Not knowing quite how to handle this display of affection – the peculiar circumstances of Eddie's life had left him with little experience of women – he'd resorted to treating her as he might a pal, which seemed to content her.

What concerned Mrs Ramsay at present – she had raised the subject yet again only last evening – was whether she ought to continue to allow her daughter to return home from school on her own.

The shortening hours of daylight were one reason why she was thinking of putting an end to the practice, that plus the fact that now that the autumn was almost over and winter approaching, the path Nell took to Oak Green from the bus stop was increasingly deserted.

'I know it only takes her ten minutes, but it's getting so lonely. I really think I ought to put a stop to it – at least until the spring – but Nell won't hear of it. She's at the age when she doesn't want to be treated like a child any longer, and she's managed to get her father to take her part. What do *you* think, Mr Noyes?'

Though Eddie secretly agreed with Mrs Ramsay – most days he didn't see a living soul on the path when he walked back to the barn after work – he was reluctant to say so. From the start of their acquaintance, Nell had behaved to him as though they had known each other for years, confiding in him with a candour that would have made any word spoken behind her back seem like a betrayal of friendship.

And while he recognized that her openness was most likely an unconscious copy of her mother's manner, he found it hard to resist, as he did her gift for living in the moment, a blessing denied him, and perhaps all adults, but one which Nell displayed still with an artlessness that won over all whom she encountered.

Some weeks earlier, when he'd still been shy of accepting the invitation extended to him – he had been to the house only twice, allowing a gap of several days to elapse between each visit – she had walked down the road from the bus stop on her way back from school in order to press him again on her mother's behalf to call on them.

Her message delivered, Nell had lingered to watch the men at work – they were tarring a stretch of road when she arrived – questioning them in her unaffected way, taking it for granted they would welcome her curiosity, which they had, to the point where even old Harrigan had shed the beetle-browed scowl with which he had first greeted the sight of her slim figure darting among the busy men and taken it on himself to initiate her into the mysteries of macadamized roads.

Thereafter the men had watched for her every afternoon, looking up from their work when the bus from Midhurst went by to wave to the smiling face in the window.

'Look, there's Nell,' they would call out. 'Hullo, Nell!'

Earlier that day, when she'd passed by, Pat McCarthy had doffed his hat and bowed deeply, whereupon Nell, giggling, had responded to his salute with a royal wave, making the whole gang roar with laughter.

Chuckling now at the memory, Eddie quickened his pace still further. He was impatient to get over to Oak Green. A fortnight earlier, Mr Ramsay had mentioned that among his clients was a large stationery company headquartered in Chichester, with customers in a number of south coast towns, and that if Eddie wished he could inquire discreetly when the opportunity arose as to the possibility of them employing him as a salesman.

He had since been informed by Mrs Ramsay that her husband was even now engaged in auditing this same company's books and hoped to have some news for him by week's end.

Glancing down at himself as he strode along the path, Eddie's grin grew ever wider. Anything less like a salesman than the figure he cut would be hard to imagine. Filthy from a day's labouring and dressed in his oldest and most threadbare garments, he looked more like a tramp.

But before going over to Oak Green he would stop at the barn to wash and change his clothes. It was something he took pride in now, making himself presentable. He saw it as symbolic of his new-found determination to reforge his life: to free himself from the shadow that had hung over him since the war.

Lately he had begun to wonder if the depression from which he suffered might not be an actual illness, a condition over which he had no control, but for which there might be a cure; thoughts which came to him most often at the end of the day, when, having returned from the warm kitchen at Oak Green, he would ready himself for sleep, first lighting the brazier Sam had given him, then laying his bedclothes on the mattress of hay they'd prepared.

Lying in the cool, scented darkness, in a silence broken

only by the stir of roosting pigeons and the scratching of mice in the straw, he would marvel at the transformation that had taken place in him already: at the spirit of resistance which Sam had helped to spark in him, and the world of small pleasures to which his eyes had been opened since.

With his awareness of both had come a flowering of fresh hope.

SLIPPING THROUGH the gap in the hedge, Eddie hopped over the ditch on the other side and then walked through the orchard where the sweet smell of fallen apples, unpicked since the farm's abandonment, hung heavy in the still air.

The walled kitchen garden was only a few paces further on, and having let himself in through the wooden gate he crossed the weed-filled expanse of old beds by a gravelled path whose borders he could barely make out in the fading light, but which he knew by heart.

Another gate on the opposite side of the rectangular plot gave access to the yard and there Eddie paused for a moment, his eye caught by the sight of the moon, rising like a golden sickle over the looming outline of the barn. The light it cast was still faint, but once darkness had fallen – and that would not be long now – it would offer ample illumination for his walk across the fields.

He went on and had covered perhaps half the length of the yard when it struck him that there was something strange about the barn doors. The gathering gloom, neither night nor day, made it difficult to see clearly, but presently he realized what it was he had noticed. Although the doors were shut, as they should be, the gap between them was marked by a thin thread of light coming from the inside.

Eddie stopped. His first thought was that Sam had dropped in to pay him a visit, but he dismissed the notion at once. Today was a Friday – not one of the days he regularly called at Coyne's Farm, which were Tuesday and Thursday – and besides there'd been no sign of his van in the parking area by the road.

Then he remembered something else. Only a few days before Sam had told him about a near encounter he'd had with a man he'd caught snooping about in the yard. He'd tried to hail him, Eddie recalled now, but the bloke had made himself scarce.

'He was about my size and dressed like a toff.' Sam had scowled as he recounted the incident. It was plain something about it had upset him. 'I didn't like the look of him, or the way he behaved, so if you see anyone like that hanging about the place, tell him to shove off.'

Alert now, Eddie strode across the yard, his boot heels ringing on the cobbles. When he reached the barn he saw that the bolt on the doors had been drawn and the padlock, which somehow had been opened, hung loose from it.

He pulled the doors open and looked inside. There was a light burning at the far end of the barn, but he couldn't see where it was coming from.

'Who's there?' he called out loudly.

Silence greeted his words.

'Come on out. I know you're there.'

Again there was no response. Eddie strained his ears, trying to pick up any sound from inside, but heard nothing. The silence was unbroken.

Delaying no longer, he stepped inside and strode down the broad corridor formed by the hurdles, which were stacked up on either side of him above head height. At the end of this artificial passageway, the rest of the barn's contents – canvas-draped pieces of furniture and odd bits of farm equipment – had been stored haphazardly, turning the area, cloaked in shadow now, into an obstacle course through which he had to pick his way to the back of the building.

There a further surprise awaited him. The source of the light proved to be one of the oil lamps he used himself. It was hanging from a nail in the wood above the corner where he slept, somewhere he would never have placed it himself. He and Sam had agreed that both lamps and brazier should be kept well away from the straw bedding for fear of starting a fire.

Of the intruder himself there was no sign. With the whole of the rear of the barn illuminated, Eddie could see that it was deserted. But if his visitor had made himself scarce, it was plain he had not been idle.

The mound of hay which served him as a mattress had been enlarged to more than double its size and filled the corner. He spied a pitchfork that must have been used for the purpose lying on the floor beside it, the prongs upturned as though it had been dropped in haste.

Eddie scratched his head. At first glance it looked as though whoever had broken in had been seeking a place to spend the night. But that didn't make sense. Or rather, it hardly fitted in with the picture Sam had drawn of the supposed intruder. A toff, he'd called him.

He shrugged. There was no point in racking his brains about it. Clearly the fellow had run off. The riddle would remain unanswered. All he could do was tell Sam what he'd found and leave it up to him to decide what to do next.

Meantime, he thought he'd better check on his own belongings to make sure they were safe. Tidy by nature, he had put his toilet articles in the small cupboard beneath the washstand Sam had provided him with, while his bedroll and spare clothes were stowed away in a tall mahogany wardrobe, stripped of its canvas shroud, that stood handily nearby.

He went to the washstand first, but as he bent to open the cupboard doors he had a flash of intuition that made the hairs on the back of his neck stand up. The sensation was eerie, but not unfamiliar. The selfsame feeling had come to him during the war in the few seconds before he was shot, when he had known instinctively, but too late, that a sniper's eyes were upon him.

He whirled round.

The figure of a man had appeared behind him, as if from nowhere. Half hidden in the shadows, he stood at the edge of the circle of light cast by the lamp, in one of the narrow alleys that led into the piles of stored furniture.

'So there you are!' Angry at being given such a fright, Eddie let his feelings show. 'Didn't you hear me call out?'

The man made no reply. Well dressed, he was wearing a tweed coat with a soft hat of the same material pulled down low over his forehead.

'What's the matter with you?' Eddie's tone sharpened still further. 'Are you deaf?'

This time he provoked a response, though not the one he was expecting. The man moved, coming forward into the light, giving Eddie a clearer picture of his face, which was pale beneath his hat brim and without expression.

'What are you doing here, anyway?'

Eddie scowled. There was something here he didn't understand. It was obvious the fellow had been hiding in the shadows for the past few minutes, not wanting to be discovered. He could easily have slipped away during that time, crept out of the barn and escaped, but instead he had chosen to show himself.

'Don't you know this is private property?' he demanded.

Thus far the man had shown no reaction to the words addressed to him. It was as though he had not been listening. But his eyes, sharp behind gold-rimmed spectacles, were busy. He was studying Eddie closely, examining him from head to toe, and now he spoke:

'Who are you?' he asked. His voice was low and rasping, the accent guttural and foreign-sounding.

'Never mind who I am.' Eddie fairly bristled with anger. The unblinking stare to which he was being subjected had made him conscious of his own appearance: of his torn clothes and unwashed body. It was quite possible the fellow had taken him for a tramp, which would explain his apparent lack of concern at being discovered trespassing. 'You're the one breaking the law. I've a good mind to set the police on you.'

At the word 'police', the man's manner changed. He seemed to stiffen, and as their eyes met for the first time Eddie felt a tingle of alarm. Up till then he'd simply thought the fellow's behaviour peculiar. Now, looking into the slightly sunken eyes, which reflected the lamplight in yellow glints, he sensed something else, something he couldn't put a name to which made the hairs on the back of his neck prickle once more.

He barely had time to take note of his reaction when the man moved again, edging to his right and turning so that the lamp was behind him. To Eddie, the manoeuvre seemed hostile: the light was shining in his eyes now. But he'd faced scenes like this before, a long chain of confrontations starting in his school playground and continuing after he had joined the army, when he'd had to assert himself in the rough society of the barracks. Because he was small, some people thought they could push him around, and he'd learned early on that the only way to take care of yourself was to stand up to them.

'Look, I've had just about enough of you, whoever you are,' he declared roundly. *What was a foreigner doing messing about in someone else's barn?* 'This is your last warning. Either hop it now, or you'll get what's coming to you.'

Suiting words to action, he stepped forward, reducing the distance between them, staring the intruder straight in the eye. Although the fellow hadn't offered him any violence – he'd been standing all this time with his hands thrust into his coat pockets – his attitude had implied a challenge, and Eddie was pleased to see that change now.

The man took a step back, raising his right hand in a gesture of surrender. He turned and began to move away towards the doors. Relieved to see the crisis was over, Eddie relaxed himself. The tension of the last few minutes had kept him on edge, his muscles taut as bowstrings. Now he let them go loose, shifting his weight back on to his heels, and was helpless to react when the man struck.

Without any warning the stranger suddenly wheeled round, bringing his left hand into view and swinging it like a boxer's punch into Eddie's unprotected side. So swift was his action Eddie caught only a glimpse of the knife in his hand before it was buried in his flesh. But the force of the blow made him gasp, and as the blade was withdrawn, then driven in a second time, up beneath his ribs, a pain like nothing he had ever experienced shot through his innards.

He sank to his knees, but was unable to stay upright and fell, like a tree toppling, forward onto his front. All but paralysed by the blows, he thought for a dazed moment he was back in the trenches, lying in the mud after the sniper's bullet had struck him. Then his mind cleared and he realized what had happened, though not why.

The event overwhelmed him. He could make no sense of it. Only one thing was certain, and he knew it beyond question as he lay there unmoving. This time there could be no doubt. He was scuppered for sure.

The floor of the barn was only inches away from his

staring eyes and at the periphery of his vision he was aware of a pair of shoes pointing at him. As he watched, one of them drew back, and then came forward, accelerating. His senses, drowned by the flood of pain that was spreading like fire from the centre of his stomach, barely registered the sharp blow to his side.

He heard a grunt from above, followed by words spoken in a foreign language. Harsh and angry-sounding, they served to jolt him into wakefulness just as his consciousness was fading. Hands grasped at his clothes and the next thing he knew he was being lifted and turned, the barn swinging crazily before his eyes as he rolled over onto his back.

Once more he almost lost consciousness: the surging pain inside him seemed to have no limit. But when his wits cleared – he was staring at the roof now – he became aware of some activity under way not far from where he lay, and by turning his head a fraction was able to make out the figure of his assailant, who had his back to him and was clearing a pathway into the heaps of stored furniture, pushing aside strips of trailing canvas and shifting some of the smaller pieces.

Just past his own feet he could see the pitchfork lying beside the gathered hay, but it was too far away for him to reach, and in any case all physical effort was beyond him.

Or so he thought until he heard the man returning to where he lay and through half-closed lids watched as he crouched to take hold of his legs. It seemed his assailant was bent on dragging his body to some other location, but his first attempt to shift it was thwarted by the boots

Eddie was wearing which prevented him from getting a firm grip on his ankles. Muttering, the man tore open the laces and flung the boots aside. He had shed his coat and hat – that much Eddie could see through the mist of pain that enveloped him – but otherwise was little more than a silhouette against the brightness of the lamp behind him as he took a fresh grip and threw his weight back.

It was the moment Eddie had been waiting for. With what remained of his strength, he jerked his right foot free of the grasping fingers and kicked out with all his might, catching the man flush on the forehead with his heel and sending him tumbling over backwards. His despairing effort was rewarded by a cry of pain as the man rolled free of the upthrust prongs of the pitch-fork, plucking at his back and cursing.

Eddie could do no more. Emptied now and strangely at peace, he watched as his attacker clambered to his feet and, with the pitchfork clutched in his hands and raised to strike, advanced on him.

He prepared himself for the death blow he knew was coming and was determined not to cry out. But at the end he was spared this final test of courage.

As he stared unflinching at the looming form above him his consciousness faded and the light that had shone so brightly in his eyes went out.

23

'I WISH I HAD better news for you, John. Or any news at all. We've been checking hotels and boarding houses, but there's no trace of him.' Angus Sinclair's clipped tones couldn't disguise the weariness in his voice. At the other end of the telephone line, Madden listened with a heavy heart. 'It's still going on, and I'm extending the search to the neighbouring counties. I pray we're not wasting our time.'

More than a week had passed since the chief inspector had unburdened himself at their meeting; they had not spoken since.

'And there's been nothing from abroad?'

'No sightings, if that's what you mean. But the Swiss have been quick off the mark. The Geneva police have confirmed that Lang's wanted there on a double murder charge. It's been so long, the cases had been shelved. But they're anxious to get their hands on him now.'

'Do they know about his connection with espionage?' Madden asked.

'They haven't said so. But they've promised to send us some background on him, so we'll wait and see. We've also been in touch with the Belgian police. Lang – or Wahl, as he called himself – kept a small flat in Brussels. It's been empty since he went to Germany, but he had an arrangement with his concierge to keep an eye on it. She hasn't heard from him in nearly a year. It looks as though Vane was right: he's cut and run.'

'Did they search the flat?'

'They did. No incriminating evidence was found and nothing to indicate what sort of man he was, either, what his business might be. Our friends from the Sûreté were naturally curious as to his background, but I was unable to enlighten them.' Sinclair's chuckle had a hollow ring. 'Two interesting points, though. There've been no killings with his trademark in Belgium. He knew enough to keep his own doorstep clean.'

'Two points, you said—?'

'Yes, they found a number of works of ornithology on his bookshelves. So the birdwatching link is confirmed. I've had Styles making inquiries among the societies, incidentally, as you suggested. Nothing's come of it as yet. But hope springs eternal.' The chief inspector's sigh seemed to suggest otherwise. 'Will you give my love to Helen?'

The call came midway through lunch and Madden was relieved not to have to relate its contents to his wife, who had driven up to London earlier that day in response to an appeal from her Aunt Maud, a lady in her eighties, who had fallen and injured her hip the night before and needed comforting.

Only too conscious of the effect his involvement in the case had had on Helen, his guilt on this account was made heavier by his awareness of the debt he owed her. Having returned from the war a broken man – in his own mind, at least – he knew that the deep happiness he had found, his sense of wholeness restored, came from the assurance her love had given him, and in following her wishes and breaking with his past he had made open acknowledgement of the fact.

But the brutal murder on which he'd stumbled had sounded a summons he'd found hard to ignore. The hunter's instinct, for so long dormant in him, had reawakened and as the weeks passed and the police investigation seemed to draw no closer to its quarry he had realized he would find no peace until the man who had turned Alice Bridger's face to pulp was brought to answer for it.

Like his old chief, he was tormented by one anxiety in particular: that the longer the killer remained at large, the more likely it was he would strike again. But when news of a fresh tragedy reached him at the close of that same day, it came from a quarter he had not foreseen.

'IT WAS MOLLY HENSHAW found him, sir. She'd been taking him his meals each day. After his wife left, that is . . .'

'Mrs Bridger left her husband?' Madden was finding it difficult to come to terms with what Will Stackpole was telling him. The Highfield constable, tall in his helmet, stood like a pillar in the misty driveway in front of the house. Drawn up a little way off was an old Morris with its bonnet raised. Billy Styles was leaning on the mudguard, peering down at the motor.

'Not left, as such, sir. She hadn't walked out on him. But she said she couldn't go on living in that cottage, not with the child gone, not with the memories. So she went off to live with her sister in Liphook. Bridger stayed on. He had his job, I suppose, but even there things weren't going too well. He'd started drinking. Anyway, the farmer he worked for got rid of him not long ago, and after that he went to pieces, Molly said. They were trying to get his wife to come back, or him to leave, but I reckon Jim had his mind made up by then. Poor Molly, though. To come on a man hanging from his own rafters! Now that was wrong ... he should have thought what he was doing ... who it was who'd find him.'

Lost for words, Madden stared at the ground. He had got back himself only a short while before, having fetched Rob from school, in time to receive a call from Helen who had rung to report that Aunt Maud was being difficult and she would not be able to return until the following day. As he put down the phone he'd heard the sound of a car approaching, its engine labouring.

'The Henshaws have got word to his wife. She's coming over. I left Bert Thomas, from Craydon, to handle things.'

Madden shook his head helplessly. In his mind was the memory of the child's body lying sprawled on the bank of the stream while the thunder crashed above. Catching a look in the constable's eye, he saw that they shared the same bitter thought.

'It's never just the victim, is it?' Stackpole's growl came from deep in his chest. 'It's everything else that comes with it, the pain it spreads, the damage it does ... What I wouldn't give to get my hands round that bastard's neck!'

The sound of footsteps approaching on the gravel

made Madden look up. 'How'd you come to be there, Billy?'

'I happened to be at Albury, sir.' The sergeant wiped his oil-smeared fingers on a piece of rag. 'I heard there was some trouble at Brookham, so I drove over . . . and found Will.'

'Bert Thomas had rung me earlier,' Stackpole explained. 'I managed to get a lift in the post van, but there wasn't much I could do when I got there.'

The three men stood in silence for a few moments. Then Madden stirred.

'Come inside, both of you. We'll have a drink together.'

'Not for me, thank you, sir. I ought to be getting back.' Stackpole's glance remained grim beneath his helmet.

'Let me at least run you into the village, Will.'

'If you don't mind, sir, I'd rather walk.' The constable straightened. 'Yes, I could do with a breath of fresh air.' He shook Madden's hand and then clapped his colleague on the shoulder. 'Thanks for the lift, Billy. I'll see you again soon.'

Wheeling about, he strode off down the drive. Madden watched as his figure disappeared into the mist-wreathed darkness.

'Albury?' He glanced questioningly at Billy.

'I went there to see a birdwatcher, sir. Your idea, I believe?' The sergeant smiled. He'd purposely stood apart while the two older men had spoken together, feeling they might want to share their grief in private. But he hadn't missed the agonized expression that had crossed Madden's face when he heard what the other had to tell him.

'Mr Sinclair told me you were handling that line of inquiry. Have you had any luck?'

'Not so far. We've had plenty of reports of strangers spotted here and there, but no one's been able to identify Lang. I've been getting around a good bit, seeing plenty of the countryside.' The sergeant grinned. 'Mind you, I'm not sure I'll be going anywhere in the near future.' He jerked his head in the direction of the Morris. 'The Yard gave me that when I went to Henley. She started playing up this morning. Will and I were lucky to get this far.'

Seemingly oblivious of the thickening mist, Madden stood brooding. 'Stay the night,' he said suddenly. 'No, I mean it, Billy. Helen's away. I'll be glad of your company. So will the children. I'll get someone from the village to look at your car in the morning.'

'Well, if you're sure it's no bother, sir.' The sergeant was pleased to accept the invitation. He knew his old chief wouldn't want to be alone. Not that evening.

'Quite the contrary.' The frown darkening Madden's brow lifted. 'Your presence will be hailed by one and all. Rob has a long list of questions to put to you, I know, and as far as Lucy's concerned, you need only appear in person to make it a red-letter day. She'll be as pleased as punch.'

24

'THERE'S NOT much we can do for the moment, Sal. Except wait and see. One thing puzzles me, though. If Eddie's got a problem, why hasn't he been in touch?'

Fretting, Sam glanced at his watch again. It was after ten and still there was no sign of the client Mr Cuthbertson had asked him to meet. He and Sal had driven out here to Tillington earlier that morning; to a farm just this side of Petworth, which some prospective buyer was showing an interest in.

It was a side of the business Mr Cuthbertson normally dealt with himself, taking customers around properties. But that morning he'd had a dentist's appointment: one he couldn't postpone, either.

'It's a wisdom tooth, Sam, and it has to come out pronto.' Mr Cuthbertson had rung him the previous evening, sounding strange on the phone, as if his tongue didn't fit in his mouth. He said his jaw had gone up like a balloon. 'Hitchens is the fellow's name. I'd have put him off, but he's coming all the way from Horsham, and bringing his wife with him, so she can look over the house. It sounds as though he's ready to make an offer. I don't want to discourage him.'

Sam had assured his employer it would be no trouble, though in fact going out to Tillington that morning was inconvenient, since he usually spent Tuesdays on the other side of Midhurst, visiting properties to the west of the town, including Coyne's Farm.

But he could see there was no help for it and had already decided to adjust his afternoon's itinerary when a new factor had arisen.

'I do apologize for ringing you so early, Mr Watkin – I found your number in the book – but we're a little worried about your friend Mr Noyes. Do you happen to know where he is?'

If Sam had been surprised to hear Mrs Ramsay's voice on the telephone that morning, what she had to say during the next ten minutes had left him scratching his head in bafflement. It seemed Eddie had disappeared. What's more he'd gone off without saying a word to anyone.

'We were expecting to see him on Friday evening, but he never came, and that was strange because he knew we might have some good news for him. You see, Mr Ramsay has mentioned his name to a company he does business with in Chichester and he heard himself on Friday that they were interested in meeting Eddie and might even be able to offer him a job. We were so puzzled by his not appearing, Nell and I, that we walked up to Coyne's Farm on Sunday. There was no sign of him there, and when Nell came back from school yesterday he wasn't with the other men working on the road, so she walked back from the bus stop and spoke to the foreman, a Mr Harrigan, and *he* said Eddie hadn't appeared for work that day and he didn't know where he was.'

Mrs Ramsay had hardly drawn breath as she'd poured

out her story, and Sam had been touched by her concern for his old pal. He did wonder, though, if she wasn't making too much of the situation. It didn't sound that serious to him.

'The only explanation I can think of is that he went home for the weekend – to Hove, I mean – and the fact that he hasn't come back suggests it might be because of some family emergency. Don't you think that's possible? But I want him to know about Chichester. It would mean so much to him if he could find a proper job. I was hoping you might know how to get in touch with him.'

Sam's thoughts had been moving along similiar lines while she was speaking. But first he'd had to explain that he only had an address for Eddie in Hove. The Noyeses had had their telephone disconnected a while back to save money.

'I'll tell you what I'll do, though. I'll send them a telegram. If Eddie's there he'll ring me at home. If not, then either his mother or sister might be able to help.'

He told her he was coming over to Coyne's Farm later – after he'd finished with the Tillington job – and would let her know what he'd found out.

'Would you, Mr Watkin? I'd be so grateful. I just feel worried about him, I don't know why. I have to play bridge this afternoon, unfortunately, but Bess will be at the house. You could leave any message for me with her.'

Mrs Ramsay's call had come just as Sam was leaving and he'd driven the extra mile or so into Petworth in order to send the telegram from the post office there. If Eddie, or his sister or mum, rang in the course of the morning, Ada would take the call.

The more he thought about it, though, the more it seemed likely that Mrs Ramsay was right. Eddie had gone home for some reason and been delayed there. While it was strange he hadn't let the Ramsays know in advance, particularly in view of this Chichester business, he might well have had to leave in a hurry. To catch a bus or train, say.

What troubled Sam more was to hear that Eddie hadn't bothered to inform Harrigan that he might not be turning up for work on Monday. That didn't sound like him. It was clear he was going to have some explaining to do.

'There might be a spot of bother over this,' he advised Sal, who was lying behind him in the van on her bit of blanket. 'But there's not much we can do about it until we know what Eddie's been up to.'

They were parked outside the gate leading into the farm so that he could keep an eye out for the client when he arrived. Last night had been chilly and thick fog had greeted him when he'd set out from home that morning. This Hitchens bloke would most likely be delayed himself coming over from Horsham and in this kind of weather might easily miss the gateway into the farm and go sailing past.

Sam blew on his fingers. He was wishing he'd come out with something warmer than the old corduroy jacket he was wearing. But then he cheered up at the thought that he'd be looking in at home on his way back to Midhurst later in case Ada had heard from Hove and could collect his overcoat before he went out again.

It was a cold day, and unless the fog cleared later, it would stay that way.

25

OUT OF TOUCH since the previous day, Billy rang the Yard after breakfast to report his whereabouts only to discover that Sinclair was not at his desk and that all calls concerning the Lang case were being referred to Chief Superintendent Holly.

'Mr Sinclair went down to Sussex yesterday to see the chief constable. They have to decide how long it's worthwhile going on with this search. He was caught by the fog and decided to spend the night in Chichester. You'd better tell me what your movements will be today, Sergeant. He may want to get in touch with you.'

Billy explained that he was not yet sure.

'My car broke down yesterday, sir. Mr Madden was kind enough to put me up for the night. I'm having it fixed now.'

Summoned by telephone, the village mechanic, a man called Pritchard, had appeared at the house soon after dawn and departed shortly thereafter at the wheel of Billy's Morris, lurching down the drive in bottom gear, promising to report back once he knew the extent of the problem.

Word of Fred Bridger's suicide had already reached London and the chief superintendent spoke feelingly of the tragedy. 'Poor fellow. I hope to God he didn't think we'd failed him. At the very least he must have hoped to see justice done.'

He asked Billy for the Maddens' telephone number. 'I'll ring you there if anything crops up. Oh, and give my regards to John, would you? It's been many years. Thank him for all his help. I dare say he wants to see this devil caught as much as we do.'

Of that there was little doubt. Madden's preoccupation with the case was self-evident and the previous night he had given the sergeant an insight into the foreboding that gripped him.

'There's no point in deceiving ourselves. It's quite possible this man will never be caught. We tend to assume killers like Lang give themselves away. That they can't remain at large in society for any length of time. But he's not like the rest. He would have learned long ago how to cover his tracks. His profession must have taught him that.'

It was Billy's first intimation that his old chief was aware of their quarry's true identity.

'If he disappears now it could be years before the police catch up with him again. He's had all the time he needs to plan a new future. And now he's got the world to wander in.'

It was not until late, when the two men were sitting alone by the dying fire in the drawing room, with the house quiet about them, that Madden had unburdened himself. Earlier, he had seemed only too ready to seek relief from his anxiety in the high spirits which Billy's unexpected arrival had produced in his children, who'd contrived, in the absence of any firm parental word to the contrary, to stay up well past their usual bedtimes.

Just as her father had predicted, it had been Lucy who had taken special delight in the sergeant's presence. Unswerving in her devotion to her chosen friend, she had kept him at her side throughout the prolonged and noisy supper shared by all at the kitchen table, and when it was over had insisted that he accompany her upstairs for the last solemn rituals of her day.

He had stood by while she washed her face and brushed her teeth and before tucking her into bed he had listened to her prayers and heard his own name included among those for whom a blessing was sought.

Looking down at her small, kneeling figure, golden-haired like her mother, and possessing something of the same intensity he had always sensed in Helen, that capacity for fierce attachment, he had recalled the sight of Madden's face not long before as he'd regarded his daughter at the supper table, the tenderness of his expression clouded by another emotion which Billy had recognized as grief, and which had puzzled him until he'd realized that it was not the bright countenance lifted towards his that the older man was seeing at that moment, but the now-empty cottage at Brookham and the lives it had once contained, so savagely destroyed.

FROM HIS BEDROOM upstairs Billy could hear the phone ringing and he wondered if it was Pritchard calling about his motor car. The mechanic had rung an hour before with the discouraging news that not only was there a fault with the Morris's clutch – something the sergeant had guessed for himself – but there was trouble with the gearbox, too.

'I can't see her being ready before this afternoon at the earliest, sir. And even then I wouldn't go too far, not without a proper overhaul.'

Forcibly immobilized, Billy had spent the morning on paperwork, drafting brief accounts of the series of interviews he had conducted among the birdwatching fraternity for the Yard's records. It was a dispiriting exercise. The hunt for Gaston Lang had yielded no dividends to date, and sitting at the window gazing out over the garden the sergeant had found his mood of pessimism mirrored in the drab scene that met his eye outside where lingering fog hid all trace of the wooded ridge beyond the stream and the sky was hidden by a blanket of low cloud.

Nor had his spirits been raised by another phone call earlier, one to which he'd been summoned by Mary, who had come upstairs to knock on his door. Helen Madden, ringing from London to let the staff know her movements, had discovered his presence in the house, and with Madden absent – he was taking both children to school – it had fallen to Billy to break the news of Bridger's suicide to her.

'Oh, how dreadful! That poor family . . .'

Distressed though she was, Helen's first thought had been for her husband.

'This will upset John terribly. He'll feel he should

have done more. You must talk to him, Billy. Make him see it's not his responsibility.'

She had told him she would be back by lunchtime, fog permitting, and hoped he would not have departed by then.

The phone had stopped ringing below and presently Billy heard the sound of hurried footsteps in the passage outside. There was a knock on the door, which opened to reveal the figure of the Maddens' maid, flushed and out of breath.

'You want to watch it, Mary.' The sergeant grinned. They were old friends. 'You'll give yourself a heart attack running up those stairs. Is that call for me?'

'Yes...' Panting, she nodded. 'And you're the one who'd better run. It's a Mr Holly ringing from Scotland Yard. He says it won't wait a moment.'

The telephone was kept in the study. Billy hurried downstairs. As he picked up the receiver he heard the sound of a car in the driveway outside and saw through the window that Madden had just returned.

'Styles here, sir?'

'Ah, Sergeant!' Holly's deep voice rang in his ear. 'Thank God I've caught you. Lang's been spotted.'

'Spotted! Where, sir?'

'In Midhurst. He was treated by a doctor there yesterday. Some injury to his back. It meant he had to take his shirt off and the nurse saw his birthmark. She rang the police this morning and they sent someone round to show her that photograph. She identified Lang beyond question.' The chief super's customary calm had deserted him. His voice boomed down the line. 'I've just spoken to Mr Sinclair in Chichester. He's on his way to Midhurst now and he wants you to join him there.'

While Holly was speaking Billy's eye had fallen on a framed map hanging on the wall beside the desk. It showed Surrey and the adjoining counties. He could see Midhurst marked. It wasn't far, just across the border in Sussex. He became aware that Madden was standing in the doorway, watching him.

'Sir, my car's still out of action.' Billy spoke into the phone, but he caught Madden's eye and gestured with his clenched fist. 'I'll have to go by train.'

'Do whatever's best, Sergeant. But get yourself there.'

The line went dead. Billy jumped up. His heart was thumping.

'That was Mr Holly, sir. Lang's been seen in Midhurst. It was that birthmark of yours.' Billy grinned. 'I've got to get down there right away. Do you know if there's a train—'

He broke off, silenced by the look on Madden's face.

'*Midhurst*, you say?'

The sergeant nodded. He was transfixed by the other's expression: the intensity of his gaze.

'Was he recognized?' Madden spoke quietly.

'So Mr Holly says. It was a doctor's nurse picked him out. They showed her his photograph.'

'Damn the train, then.' The growled words made Billy's hair stand on end. 'I'll take you there myself.'

26

LEAVING HIS VAN in the otherwise empty parking area by Wood Way, Sam walked briskly down the empty road to where the men were working. Driving past he'd hoped to see Eddie's figure among them. There was always the chance his friend had returned overnight. But it had been Harrigan's eye that he'd caught, and the foreman was waiting for him, brawny forearms folded, his brow knotted in a scowl.

'Well, where is he, then? Have you had any word?' The Irishman didn't bother to explain who he was talking about. Behind him the other members of his crew drew nearer so as to hear what was being said. They had just finished surfacing a strip of road and the air was sharp with the reek of hot tar.

'I've no news, if that's what you mean.' Sam saw no point in beating about the bush. 'But I've sent a telegram to his family, in case he's had to go home for some reason. I'm still waiting for a reply.'

He had got back from Tillington a little after noon to discover there'd been no response from Eddie as yet, no message from Hove, and had paused only long enough to bolt down a sandwich and split a piece of cheese with Sal.

'What can have happened?' Now it was Ada who was starting to fret. She'd come out to the van with him when he left, her forehead creased with worry. 'It's such a strange thing to do. Going off like that without a word.'

She was right, of course, Sam could see that. But wasn't it a fact that these apparent mysteries of life usually had simple explanations? Not forgetting, too, that people sometimes behaved in peculiar ways for peculiar reasons. Both possibilities had occurred to him in the course of the morning and he was prepared to take either into consideration.

What he wouldn't accept, though, would have no part of, was the suggestion he could hear coming from Harrigan's lips now.

'I took him for a dependable fellow, someone I could trust.' Burly, and with a moustache that matched his dark eyebrows, the foreman stood glowering. 'Not the sort who'd let you down.'

'Now you've got no cause to say that.' Sam faced him squarely. 'Not till you know the facts.' He was pleased by the murmur of approbation his challenge evoked from the men around.

Harrigan grunted. 'We'll see.' His glance stayed hostile. He seemed unconvinced.

'When was the last time you saw him?' Sam kept his own gaze steadily on the other.

The foreman shrugged. 'Friday evening, knocking-off time, same as usual.'

'Did he mention he had any plans for the weekend?'

Harrigan jerked his head in the direction of one of the men standing nearby, a youngish chap with fair, curly hair and stubbled cheeks. Sam recognized him as a pal of Eddie's. A bloke called Pat McCarthy.

'Nothin' special.' Pat shrugged. 'He said he might join us for a drink Saturday night. There's a pub down in Elsted we go to. But he never turned up.'

'I sent Pat over to that barn Eddie sleeps in when he didn't show up for work yesterday.' Harrigan gestured towards the wooded ridge that ran alongside the road. 'The doors were locked. There was no one around. Isn't that so?' He looked at the younger man, who nodded.

'I hammered on them, and all.'

'Well, that's where I'm headed now.' Sam gathered himself. 'I've a key to the barn.' He tapped his coat pocket. 'I'm going to have a look inside. Then I want to go over to Oak Green. There's a lady there who knows Eddie. She's worried about him, too.'

'Would that be Nell's mother?' Harrigan's face had lost its grudging scowl. Sam saw that his belligerence was only a mask; he was as concerned as the others. 'The lass was here yesterday, asking about him.'

'Yes, it's Mrs Ramsay.' Sam looked around the ring of men. 'I'll be back later,' he promised them. 'We're still waiting to hear from Hove. With any luck I'll have something to tell you.'

He saw the doubt in their eyes.

'Listen, there's bound to be an explanation,' he insisted. 'People don't just disappear. He'll turn up. You mark my words.'

*

'COME ON, OLD GIRL, don't dawdle . . .'

Sam called back to Sally from the crest of the ridge. She was still some way behind, plodding her way up the path. Poor old thing, she was starting to feel the cold; it was getting into her joints. But for once his patience was short.

'Come on . . .'

Not waiting for her to catch up, he set off down the long slope, his gaze turning automatically in the direction of Coyne's Farm, visible now in spite of the mist that still clung to the ground, blurring the contours of the land-scape and bringing a hush to the woods, usually loud with birdsong, through which he had just passed. There was no break in the cloud cover as yet and Sam doubted they'd see the sun that day.

When he came to the gap in the hedge he paused once more, but it was obvious Sal was coming at her own pace. He could see her some distance back up the path, her nose buried in a bank of leaves. Delaying no longer, he slipped through the hedge and crossed the walled garden into the farmyard beyond.

It had come as a shock, talking to Harrigan and the others, to realize what they were thinking. That this bloke who they liked and had counted on, who they'd treated as one of them, had upped and walked off without a word, leaving them to wonder what had become of him. Sam told himself they were wrong – he knew Eddie too well, knew he'd never behave in such a way – but as he strode across the yard to where the barn was he could feel a nervous flutter in his stomach. There was no telling what he might find inside.

Difficulty with the padlock delayed his entry. For a while it seemed jammed, the mechanism refusing to budge, and it took him several tries, pushing his key in and out and jiggling it about, before the spring inside was released and the curved arm sprang open.

Even with the double doors pulled wide the interior remained dimly lit – the grey light from outside provided little in the way of illumination – and by the time Sam had made his way through the stacked hurdles and canvas-covered bits of furniture to where Eddie's quarters were at the back of the barn he found himself enveloped in a leaden twilight.

It made little difference to his mission. What he'd come to seek out wouldn't be in plain sight.

But he knew where to start his search and without pause he went straight to the tall mahogany wardrobe which stood near the back of the building, the same piece from which he'd retrieved Eddie's mirror. Its canvas covering was still drawn back, allowing him to open the doors without hindrance. When he saw what it contained a sigh of relief issued from his lips.

He'd found what he was looking for: Eddie's bedroll. The blankets were neatly stowed on one of the shelves that took up half of the wardrobe. (The other half was given over to hanging space.) His spare clothes were laid out on a separate shelf above.

He hadn't walked out on them. The proof was plain to see. He hadn't gone anywhere.

Except maybe to Hove for the weekend, as Mrs Ramsay had suggested. But there was nothing Sam could do about that. He could only wait for his return and for the explanation of his sudden departure, which he was sure would follow.

Relieved, he lingered for a moment longer to look about him. Now that his eyes had grown accustomed to the half-darkness he was able to make out familiar details and he saw at once that Eddie had been making some changes to his living quarters. His bed of hay had grown to more than double the size of the original mattress he had raked together and made into a rectangular shape so that his bedroll would fit neatly on top of it. Now it spread in a large triangle across the corner of the barn.

And that wasn't all. The mirror had been moved. (The one Sam had salvaged.) Formerly it had been propped against the back wall behind the old washstand so that Eddie could use it when he was shaving. Now it stood in the corner where the bedding was, reflecting the strewn hay in front of it; but little else.

Sam scratched his head.

What was the use of putting it *there*?

Then he thought he saw an explanation, though it was one that brought a scowl to his face. One of the oil lamps he'd found for Eddie was hanging from a nail above the straw bed, and what displeased Sam was that they'd both agreed at the very start, when Eddie was settling in, that it would be dangerous to put it there since it only had to slip off the nail and fall onto the straw beneath for everything to go up in flames: hay, hurdles, furniture, barn. The whole bang shoot!

Yet there it was, just where they'd decided *not* to put it, and the only thing Sam could think was that it had something to do with the mirror, and where it stood now. Positioned as they both were, the light from the lamp would be reflected more widely, illuminating the area where the hay had been gathered. Though why Eddie should want to do such a thing was beyond him.

Sam clicked his tongue with impatience. He was fed up with trying to work out what it meant. If there was a puzzle here, its solution would have to await his pal's return. He was more concerned about the lamp. Should he leave it where it was, or move it to a safer place?

It required only a few moments reflection to persuade him it would be better to leave things as they were. He didn't want Eddie to feel he'd been checking up on him. There was no danger with the lamp unlit. He'd have a quiet word with his chum when he got back.

He turned to go, but as he did so his toe struck something on the floor and he glanced down and saw it was a workman's boot. Another lay near it. Sam sank to his heels and picked them up. They were old and well worn and he supposed they must belong to Eddie. The lace of one of them was broken.

Puzzled afresh, he examined them, looking at first one, then the other, as though the worn soles and scuffed leather might offer up some answer to the riddle he was faced with.

Had Eddie left in a rush? Sam pictured him tearing off his boots, breaking a lace in the process, hurrying to catch a bus or a train. (Yes, but that still didn't explain the problem that had bothered him earlier. How could any summons to depart have reached Eddie, isolated as he was at Coyne's Farm?)

A feeling of unease was starting to grow in Sam; it

was like a cold lump in the pit of his stomach. Something was wrong. The very silence of the barn seemed to hold a secret. It was as though all the little things he had noticed – the mirror, the hay, the lamp – and now the boots, dropped carelessly on the barn floor in a way that seemed at odds with Eddie's natural tidiness, were clues to some mystery he was yet to unravel.

Crouched on his haunches, he scanned the semi-darkness around him, seeking some further sign that might bring enlightenment. Wrinkling his nose at the musty smell coming from the dirt-covered floor, he bent lower to peer beneath the washstand and as he did so he heard a faint sound behind him and felt a warmth on the back of his neck.

With a start he spun round on his heels.

Sal's moist black nose was an inch from his. Her pink tongue touched his cheek.

'Gor blimey! Do you want to give me a heart attack, old girl?' He fondled her head. 'Creeping up on me like that.'

Sal wagged her tail, then turned aside to sniff at something on the floor. He watched as she followed whatever scent it was she'd caught across the dusty, hay-strewn surface back into the area where the furniture was stored.

'Well, that's enough of that.' Sam rose from his crouched position, groaning with the effort. He took a moment to ease the cramped muscles of his thighs. 'We won't find any answers here,' he remarked after Sal's disappearing form. 'It's best we get over to Oak Green.'

He was impatient to ring Ada at home to discover

whether there'd been any word from Hove yet. To find out if Eddie was there, and if not, whether his sister and mother knew of his whereabouts. He still nursed the hope that this whole business could be resolved in a flash.

Taking a last look round, he noticed a pitchfork lying on the floor by the back wall and realized it must have been used by Eddie to gather hay for his now-enlarged mattress. The sight of it stirred Sam to look again at the mass of dried grass stalks filling the corner, and to shake his head in bewilderment.

'It doesn't make sense.'

He spoke the words aloud, then turned to leave, threading a path through the furniture to where the hurdles were stored, whistling for Sal as he went. There was no sign of her when he got there, so he went back, calling her by name.

'Sally! Where are you?'

Peering around, he caught sight of her then at the side of the barn. She was sniffing at something; a long, low object, most likely a chest, covered in canvas like the rest.

'What have you found there? Is that a rat you're after?'

He whistled to her again, but she paid no attention, remaining stubbornly where she was, running her nose up and down the length of the chest, until in the end he had go over there and pull her away.

'We can't hang about here, old girl.' He tugged at her collar. 'There's no time to waste. We have to find Eddie.'

27

Sinclair paused at the open door and surveyed the scene before him.

Close to a score of detectives were crowded into a room that might comfortably have housed half that number. Some had found chairs, but most were either standing or sitting on the edges of desks. In the far corner a space had been cleared and a large-scale map of the town of Midhurst had been propped on an easel. The hum of conversation, loud enough to be heard on the floor above, where Sinclair had just come from, dropped to a murmur as those nearest the door noticed his appearance and that of the officer beside him, a uniformed inspector by the name of Braddock, who was in command of the Midhurst police station.

'Pay attention, everyone.'

Sinclair's companion issued the order in a ringing tone, and silence fell.

'I'll keep the introductions short. For the benefit of new arrivals, this is Chief Inspector Sinclair from Scotland Yard. He's in charge of the investigation into the girls' murders, and it's at his request that we've been conducting a search for this man Lang all over Sussex. According to information received this morning, it now appears likely he's been living here, in Midhurst, or somewhere nearby. From this moment on, Mr Sinclair will be directing the search, and you'll take your orders from him. Sir . . .'

He turned to the chief inspector.

'Thank you, Mr Braddock.' Sinclair nodded to him. He walked briskly to the head of the room and took up a position beside the easel. Stuck to the wall behind him was a copy of the poster that had been sent to all police stations. Taken from the grainy snapshot supplied by Philip Vane, it showed a blown-up image of Gaston Lang's face, the enlargement process lending stark emphasis to the wanted man's features, deepening his pallor and transforming his eyes, slightly widened, into dark tunnels.

'I'll try to keep my remarks brief, as well.' Sinclair faced the assembled detectives. 'While there's every reason to think Lang is in the neighbourhood, it's by no means clear how long he plans to remain. He may in fact already be preparing to depart, and even if he's not, it won't be long before the search we're about to launch will be common knowledge, and he'll know he's in danger. So time is of the essence.'

While he was speaking the door had opened and more men had entered. Keeping a rein on his impatience, the chief inspector waited until the shuffling of feet had subsided. Accompanied by a squad of plain-clothes men, he had arrived himself from Chichester only an hour earlier, his drive across the Downs slowed by the lingering fog. Before leaving he had arranged by telephone with the Sussex chief constable for further reinforcements to be drafted in. Hampered by the same problem that had delayed his journey, they had been arriving in

Midhurst in one and twos, summoned from surrounding towns, filling the small police station with the sound of voices and the clatter of shoes on bare wooden floors. Obliged to wait until his forces were assembled, Sinclair had used the time to formulate a plan, which he was about to reveal.

'Since we've no clue as to Lang's exact whereabouts – and since the hotels and boarding houses in Midhurst have already been checked, like others in the county – it's my intention to search the town itself, to go through it with a fine-tooth comb. Details of that in a moment. First, I'll tell you what we know.'

Again he was interrupted as the door was pushed open and those just inside forced to make way, with a consequent stirring and shuffling of feet. The chief inspector directed a sharp glance towards the back of the room. His eyes widened in surprise as he caught sight of Madden, who just then was edging his way in behind Billy Styles. Blinking, he went on.

'The man we believe to be Gaston Lang presented himself at the surgery of a doctor named Driscoll here in Midhurst yesterday needing treatment for an injury to his back. He arrived near the end of doctor's hours, just before midday, explaining that he was a stranger in the region, a foreigner in fact, and was on a walking tour. His complaint, which the doctor examined briefly before dealing with it, was a small wound on his back, quite a nasty cut, which he'd been unable to deal with himself, since it was too awkwardly placed. In the course of their brief, their very brief exchange – the man was not disposed to converse, Driscoll said – he disclosed that he'd suffered the injury when he'd tripped and fallen over backwards onto a pitchfork that happened to be lying behind him.'

The murmur of disbelief that greeted these words was echoed by the chief inspector's own raised eyebrows.

'Yes, I had the same reaction. But, curiously, Dr Driscoll says that judging by the appearance of the man's back, it was probably the truth. There were two distinct bruises, and a third where the skin had been pierced, all in a straight line. They could well have been caused by the prongs of a pitchfork. How he came by this injury is not a mystery I intend to dwell on. Suffice to say the wound required cleaning and dressing. Driscoll himself was in a hurry – he had a round of house calls to make – and he left the patient in the care of his nurse with instructions to obtain the necessary details from him and to tell him that he would have to return in three days to have the dressing changed. It was at that point that the story took an interesting turn.'

Sinclair let his gaze run over the sea of faces before him until he caught Madden's eye at the back of the room. Taller than anyone else, his old partner stood with folded arms, expressionless.

'Lang – we'll call him Lang – had had to take his shirt off to be treated and the doctor had left him in a screened-off area of his office, where he attended to patients, to get dressed, while he himself departed. He'd had no occasion to see Lang from the front since he'd been lying face down for the operation. But his nurse –

her name's Mrs Hall – caught a glimpse of him while he was putting on his shirt and she noticed that he had a large birthmark on the upper part of his chest.'

The words brought a renewed murmur from his audience.

'As I'm sure all of you know, the man we're after has just such a mark on him. What you may not have been told is that notices have been sent to all doctors in Surrey and Sussex asking them to be on the lookout for any patients previously not known to them bearing a birthmark. The notices started going out last week. Unfortunately, the one addressed to Dr Driscoll only arrived at his surgery with this morning's post. It was opened by Mrs Hall – the doctor himself had been called out earlier that morning on an emergency – and she remembered what she'd seen. Since these notices carried a warning that the man being sought was dangerous, she had the good sense to ring the police immediately, rather than wait for the return of her employer. Mr Braddock himself went over to the surgery to see her along with Detective Sergeant Cole, whom all of you know, I'm sure.'

He nodded to a man standing at the front of the crowd of detectives, and then turned to Braddock, who was at his side.

'Why don't you go on, Inspector?'

Braddock cleared his throat. He was in his fifties, balding, but with the quick glance and vigorous air of a younger man.

'It so happens Peter Driscoll is my doctor and I know

both him and his nurse well. Mrs Hall was a ward sister at Chichester hospital before she came here. She's a sensible, clear-headed woman. When we showed her Lang's photograph she took a good hard look at it and then said it was him, no question about it, though he looked different. He was wearing glasses, she said, and his hair was longer, and combed back in a different style. But she reckoned it was Lang all right.'

'Did he give a name, sir?' The question came from among the packed audience.

'He did. But not his own. Hendrik De Beer was what he put down on the patient's form he was asked to fill out. That's d e and then Beer, like beer, which I dare say you won't forget' – the inspector allowed himself a grin – 'but you'd better write down just the same.' He paused while a rustle of notebooks ensued. 'To anticipate the next question,' he continued. 'Yes, he gave an address, as well, but that was in Amsterdam. As Mr Sinclair said, he claimed to be a tourist of sorts and told Mrs Hall he'd been staying in the area temporarily, but didn't say where.'

He exchanged a glance with Sinclair, who nodded. It was the chief inspector who took up the story.

'I've already arranged for the police in Amsterdam to be contacted, but I'm fairly sure we'll find they haven't heard of him either and that the address he gave there is a false one. He's not Dutch, by the way, he passes for Belgian, but I won't go into his background now, except to remark that he would have been forced to choose a foreign alias while he was here because, although he speaks English fluently, he has an accent. So bear that in mind when you start looking for him, which will be soon.'

'Excuse me, sir.' Another voice came from the crowd. 'How do we know this name he gave the nurse is the one he's using here?'

'Good question.' Sinclair turned that way. 'As soon as Mr Braddock reported his discovery to me – I happened to be in Chichester this morning – we agreed that the first place to check was the post office. If Lang had been residing for any length of time locally – and we've reason to believe he's been in England for some months – chances are he's been using the poste restante service to collect any mail that might have been sent to him. It turned out to be a good guess. Sergeant Cole?'

Sinclair caught the eye of the man standing before him.

'Right you are, sir.'

Cole, a stocky figure in a mustard-coloured suit, turned around so that he could face his audience. Raising his voice, he addressed the crowded room.

'After Mr Braddock had talked to the chief inspector he sent me off to the post office. Nobody there could recognize this bloke Lang from his picture, not at first, but when I mentioned the name he'd given – De Beer – the clerk at the counter remembered it. And then he took another look at the poster and said, yes, it could have been him, though he looked different. The reason he recalled the name was a, because it was foreign, and, b, because he'd been in three times a week, regular as clockwork, for the past month asking if there was anything for him. Which there wasn't, not until last Wednesday, when finally something arrived. A small package, the clerk said.' He glanced at Sinclair, who nodded.

'Thank you, Sergeant.' The chief inspector continued. 'You'll understand now why we think this man has been residing locally, rather than just passing through. However, as I said earlier, he may be about to leave. Our reason for thinking so springs from something he said to Mrs Hall. When told he would have to come back to have his dressing changed, he said he'd be unable to do so because he was leaving to return home, but would see to it when he got back to Amsterdam.'

Sinclair paused. His expression was reflective.

'Now it's true he might have been lying about his departure, except I can't see any reason for it. Why not return and have his dressing changed, if that is necessary? There is nothing stopping him, unless he really is going. And then there's the matter of this item of post he'd been awaiting – with some impatience, it sounds. It looks like his decision to leave may well be connected to its arrival. At all events, I intend to read the situation this way and to assume that we have very little time in which to lay hands on him. Which brings us to the question of means . . .'

He looked about him: once again his eye caught Madden's.

'What we want, of course, is his address, or, failing that, some indication of his movements, where he might have been seen in and around Midhurst during the past few weeks and months. These inquiries have already begun. Three of the four detectives stationed here were

sent out earlier, one to take detailed statements from Dr
Driscoll and Mrs Hall, the other two to visit local estate
agents to inquire about flats or houses let to single men
in recent months. Since we know Lang hasn't been
staying in a hotel or boarding house, this is an avenue
that must be explored. But it's only a beginning. We
must spread our net wide. In the course of the next few
hours you'll be visiting shops and offices, showing
Lang's photograph and trying out the name De Beer on
whoever you meet. It's important that we cover the
town systematically, street by street, and you'll be
assisted in this by Sergeant Cole, who'll assign each pair
of detectives a district to search, and to whom you'll
report, and by members of the uniformed branch, who'll
accompany you. No doubt this will cause some stir, but
that can't be helped. It's the quickest way to achieve
results. And time, as I said before, is of the essence.'

The chief inspector fell silent. But it was plain from
his frown that he had not finished, and after a brief pause
he continued, speaking in an altered tone.

'One final word. I'm aware of the feeling most of you
have that you've not been fully informed: that from the
moment this search was launched, both here and in
Surrey, questions about this man have remained
unanswered. Questions you had every right to ask of
your superiors. I can only apologize to you and say that,
again for reasons I cannot reveal, this has been unavoid-
able. However, there's one point I wish to stress: it
concerns the warning all of you already engaged in this
operation have received regarding the danger Lang poses.
I mean the danger he poses to *you*.'

Once again Sinclair paused, allowing time for his words to sink in.

'It may be that in the course of today, one or more of you will encounter this man, or someone who appears to resemble him, and whom you think might be worth questioning. Should this happen – *be on your guard.*' The words issued from the chief inspector's mouth like the crack of a whip, causing several among his audience to start with surprise. 'Lang isn't just a sexual killer, nor are these poor children his only victims. He's a criminal of a kind none of us has encountered before, one who as likely as not will show no surprise if accosted and may even appear to cooperate. Don't be deceived. He carries a knife, and I can tell you now that he's used it before, on a detective, too, with fatal consequences. Since arrest for him means a certain death sentence, he'll stop at nothing to escape capture.'

The chief inspector's glance was drawn once more to the back of the room, where Madden was standing with folded arms. It seemed to Sinclair that his old partner nodded.

'So I say once more, and I urge you to remember it. *Be warned!*'

THE TELEPHONE RANG and Braddock picked it up. 'For you, sir.' Putting the receiver down on the desk in front of him, he rose, leaving his seat free for Sinclair, and came around to sit beside Madden, who just then was busy reading the detailed statements made by Dr Driscoll and his nurse which the detective sent to interview them had delivered earlier. As Sinclair began to speak into the telephone, there was a knock on the door and a constable came in with a tray on which three steaming cups of tea and a plate of sandwiches were balanced. At a nod from his superior he laid the tray on the desk and went out, shutting the door quietly behind him.

'Thank you, Arthur, that's clear . . . I'll speak to you later.'

Sinclair replaced the receiver. He regarded the other two.

'That was Chief Superintendent Holly. He says all ports have been warned to look out for Lang. We've told them about the changes to his appearance; they already have copies of the poster.'

'What if he's only moving base?' Braddock was on his feet again. He offered one of the cups to Madden, who shook his head; he was busy with the statements.

'It's possible, I grant you. But the odds are he's getting out. Quitting England. He can't fit in here. There's no hiding the fact he's a foreigner. He'll want to be somewhere where he's less noticeable.'

Sinclair began to rise, but Braddock checked him with a gesture.

'You might as well stay there, sir. And help yourself to a sandwich, if you'd like one. It's the only lunch we're likely to get today.' Following his own advice, the Midhurst inspector took one of the cups of tea and slipped a sandwich onto the saucer before resuming his seat beside Madden. 'This piece of mail Lang was expecting . . . what do you reckon it was?'

'Travel documents of some kind, perhaps.' Sinclair

shrugged. He glanced at Madden. 'What do you think, John?'

The unexpected appearance of his old partner had caught the chief inspector off guard and he was still taking stock of its implications, not all of them reassuring to him. No matter what their past connection had been, the presence of a civilian in the midst of a police operation of such delicacy – and secrecy – could hardly be squared with standing regulations, and while Sinclair knew that the rules could be stretched if necessary to include a man of Madden's reputation, he was uncomfortably aware that this was far from being the end of the story.

There was another aspect to be considered, one he could hardly ignore, and which he'd brought up immediately after greeting his old colleague at the conclusion of the gathering downstairs, and learning how he and Styles had come to arrive together.

'Does Helen know you're here?'

Discovering from Madden that his wife had been in town overnight and had not yet returned to Highfield when they departed, and that in consequence he had had to leave her a note explaining their absence, Sinclair had raised his eyebrows in silent comment, while reflecting on the near certainty that when the time came for a reckoning, it would be he who would pay the price. Given the degree to which he'd consulted his former partner in the course of the investigation, he could hardly complain of the situation, however, and the chief inspector was honest enough to admit to the comfort he drew from the familiar figure seated opposite him, whose opinion he was seeking once more.

'Travel documents?' Madden's scowl of concentration lifted for a moment as he glanced up. 'Yes, I should think so, Angus. Papers to support his new identity ... a passport perhaps. He'd know where to get them forged, wouldn't he? Not here, maybe, but on the Continent?'

'Why do you say that?'

Inevitably, the question came from Braddock, who had realized they were speaking of things to which he was not party. The Midhurst police chief had shown no disposition to question Madden's presence. On the contrary, his face had lit up when they'd been introduced earlier and he'd wrung the other's hand.

'I know your name well, sir. I was hoping we'd meet one day.'

But Sinclair saw from his frown now that he felt excluded, and the realization brought him to a swift decision.

'Inspector, I'm going to tell you something I shouldn't. But you must keep it to yourself, now and in the future. As you may have guessed, Lang's no ordinary sexual criminal. In fact, he's been an agent employed abroad for intelligence purposes, and a highly successful one. I've already underlined how dangerous he is, but there's also another side to him we have to consider: his skill at disguising his identity. He's used many aliases in the past as part of his work: it's something he's accustomed to doing. Just as I'm sure he's altered his appearance. It's why we're treating this investigation with such urgency. If he slips through our hands now, God knows when we, or anyone else, will catch up with him again.'

'Christ Almighty!' Braddock's exclamation was involuntary. He shook his head ruefully. 'I was starting to wonder ... and to think, he's been walking around Midhurst for months. I might even have passed him in the street!'

Confirmation of the wanted man's presence in the neighbourhood had not been long in coming following the dispatch of the search teams earlier. Within twenty minutes, word had been sent back to the station that a man answering Lang's description, a foreigner, had purchased cigars in a tobacconist's shop not far from the post office on several occasions. Although the young woman who worked behind the counter there could not identify him positively from the poster, she said he resembled the photograph, adding that she had found him an unpleasant customer.

'The way he looked at me,' were her reported words.

Then, soon afterwards, a second message had been received: the proprietor of a stationer's had recognized the features in the poster as belonging to a man to whom he'd sold sketching supplies – pads and pencils – some three months earlier.

'He remembers the fellow was in again a fortnight ago. They were out of the kind of pads he wanted, but when the owner asked for his name and address so that he could let him know when a new supply came in, this man, Lang, said he was leaving soon to go back home to Holland and would get what he needed there.'

The information had been brought upstairs by Billy Styles, who was assisting Sergeant Cole in the CID room below. As the lunch hour approached, and shops began closing for the statutory break in the middle of the day, the men had been drifting back to the station. Among their number had been the two local detectives sent to inspect estate agents' lists, but neither had returned with any information worth following up.

'They've made very few lets to single men, and none to foreigners.'

'Is that only in town, or on the outskirts, as well?' Sinclair asked the question.

'Both, sir. All three firms have rented cottages on their books, but none recent, and none to any men on their own.'

Sinclair had grimaced on hearing the news and as he looked at his watch now and saw that it was after one, another spasm of discontent crossed his features. It was all very well knowing they were on the right track – that Lang was here, or nearby – but he remained tantalizingly out of their grasp, and the chief inspector was tormented by the thought that the presence of so many police engaged in a search of the town would soon become known and it would not be long thereafter before their quarry had shaken the dust of Midhurst from his heels.

Meanwhile, the lunch hour was on them, and the teams of detectives were returning to the station, their presence signalled by the gathering volume of sound coming from the floor below, voices and footsteps echoing up the stairwell. The chief inspector looked out of the window behind him on to the market square, lined with stalls and busy with shoppers when he'd arrived that morning, but now almost deserted. Turning back, he found Braddock's expectant gaze fixed on him. Madden was still studying the handwritten statements he'd been passed.

'What is it, John? What's the matter?'

Their years together had taught Sinclair to read his old colleague's face. Madden's familiar scowl of preoccupation had been replaced by another expression: a frown, still, but one accompanied by a puzzled look. His fingers had gone to the scar on his forehead.

'This book Lang had with him . . . it's in the nurse's statement . . .'

'The bird manual? Yes, I saw that. What about it?'

As Madden opened his mouth to reply, they were interrupted by the sound of rapidly approaching footsteps in the passage outside, and then, almost at once, by a hurried knocking on the door, which was flung open.

'Sir!' Billy Styles stood before them, panting.

'What is it, Sergeant?' Sinclair looked up.

'Two of the men just back . . . they talked to a chemist . . .' Billy struggled to catch his breath. 'He said Lang was in his shop only yesterday . . . around midday . . . it must have been after he saw the doctor . . .'

'Yes? What of it?' Unconsciously the chief inspector snapped. The look on the younger man's face had sent a chill through him. 'We know he's here . . .'

'It's not that, sir . . . it's what he came in for, what he bought . . .'

Billy swallowed. He caught Madden's eye.

'It was a bottle of chloroform.'

28

WITH A GROAN, Sam put the receiver down.

He'd been staring at the painting on the wall in front of him while he talked: it showed two horses grazing in a green meadow. Not yet ready to move, he allowed his gaze to wander around the small sitting room, which, to judge by the mending basket he saw lying on the sofa, a swatch of blue material protruding from the lid, and a writing desk of delicate design, must be Mrs Ramsay's. His eye was caught by a pastel drawing of a smiling, dark-haired child of one or two. Nell, as a baby, he reckoned.

'Oh, Christ!' The exclamation was wrung from his lips.

Sighing, he got to his feet. Flower-patterned curtains drawn back from a sash window gave a glimpse of the garden and Sam stood for a few moments gazing out at a lily pond whose still surface, like a grey shroud, reflected the lowering sky.

'What now?' He spoke the words aloud, knowing what the answer had to be, but unwilling to face it as yet.

Quitting the room, he walked down the passage to the kitchen, at the back of the house, where Bess, the Ramsays' cook, awaited him. Flushed and anxious, she had been watching for his arrival and he'd seen her red face at the kitchen window as he'd unlatched the back gate. Before he and Sal had crossed the bricked yard, the door had been flung open and Bess's plump, white-clad figure had appeared.

'Oh, Sam, tell me . . . have you any news?'

She'd been instructed by her mistress to show him to the telephone so that he could ring Ada. Back in the kitchen now, he found her shelling peas at the table, and guessed she'd been trying to keep herself occupied until his return. Her face fell at the sight of his.

'Ada's talked to Eddie's sister. She rang half an hour ago. They had a card from him a week ago, she said, but he didn't mention anything about coming home. They don't know where he is.'

'But how can he just disappear? It don't make sense.' Bess's homely features were twisted in distress. She seemed on the verge of tears. Sam could only shake his head.

He'd been pondering the matter, though, turning it over in his mind. The process had started even before he'd arrived at Oak Green. Walking over from Coyne's Farm, blowing on his fingers to ward off the biting cold, which had returned with the fading of afternoon, it had occurred to him that something might have happened to Eddie, either on the way over to Hove, if he'd decided, after all, to go home, or somewhere else. That he might have been hurt in an accident, got knocked down by a car, perhaps, or injured in some other way, and be lying in hospital now. Unconscious, for sure, because otherwise he would have let people know who he was, and the police would have got in touch with his family.

At first Sam had shied away from the thought. He had not given up hope then that the mystery might be solved when he spoke to his wife; that she would have had word from Hove regarding Eddie's whereabouts. But having learned the worst now, he was forced back to his earlier line of reasoning, disturbing though it was. He saw that the nettle would have to be grasped.

'When do you expect Mrs Ramsay home, love?' He put the question gently to Bess. He didn't want to share his fears with her. The poor thing was upset enough as it was. It was clear she was sweet on Eddie, which might be no more than a fantasy so far as his old pal was concerned, but was no less real to her on that account. She was sitting now, staring at the bowl of shelled peas before her, the glint of tears held back shining in her eyes. 'She told me she'd be playing bridge.'

'That's right . . .' Bess came back to herself with a half-sob. She pushed a strand of hair back under her white cap. 'She's gone over to Petersfield. She said she'd try and get back not too late . . .'

Sam grunted. He'd been hoping the mistress of the house would be there, either to share his burden of worry, or, better still, to tell him his fears were groundless. But he saw he'd have to act on his own.

'Can I use the phone again?' He got to his feet. 'Is that all right?'

'The phone? Yes, of course . . . but why?' She looked up, blinking. 'What for, Sam?'

'I'm sorry, lass. It has to be done.' He couldn't keep his concern from her any longer, and with a sigh he reached across the table to pat her on the shoulder. 'We need to know if anything's happened to Eddie. I'm going to ring the police.'

369

29

BILLY HELPED himself to a fish paste sandwich – they were the only kind left – and then refilled his cup from the tea urn. The CID office, which ten minutes ago had been thronged with plain-clothes men, was deserted. Only Sergeant Cole was there, busy sticking coloured pins into the map of Midhurst, marking out areas of the town already covered by the teams of detectives, whose brief lunch hour had just ended and whose assignments now bore an urgency that needed no underlining.

The news Billy had taken in haste to the office on the floor above had galvanized the chief inspector into action. After canvassing both Braddock and Madden for their opinions, and finding they shared his view, he had telephoned Bennett at Scotland Yard with a radical new proposal.

'We have to go public, sir. We must see to it that tomorrow's papers carry stories about this investigation, particularly the fact that we're looking for a foreigner, and giving Lang's description. I hate to do it: I think it'll only scare him off. But better that than he kills another child.'

Billy had stood by the open door watching, his presence seemingly forgotten by Sinclair, who was listening to what Bennett was saying to him, his brow knotted in a frown, his fist clenched on the blotter in front of him.

'Yes, sir, all the national papers, and Mr Braddock and I will deal with local editors here in Sussex.' There'd been a pause while the chief inspector's fingers drummed on the desk. Then he'd spoken again. 'It seems unlikely, I grant you. But one can't read the mind of a man like that. The information has to be taken at face value: we must assume he means to strike again.'

When the call ended a few moments later, Sinclair had turned to Madden.

'Bennett was wondering whether Lang would really choose to endanger himself now, just when he was about to leave. What's your view, John?'

Billy heard Madden grunt. He'd watched as a scowl came over his old chief's face.

'I'm not so sure, Angus. From what Vane told you, it sounds as though Lang is finding it harder to control himself. Isn't that why he had to get out of Germany in a hurry? He's kept a check on himself since Brookham, but it can't have been easy. Now that he's leaving he may feel he can afford to take risks. He may even see an advantage in it. He can leave the police investigating another of these crimes, and searching for the killer in England, while he makes his escape.'

In the silence that had followed, the chief inspector's eye had fallen on Billy, who was still standing by the door.

'Is there anything I can do, sir?'

'Tell Cole from me to keep the men at it. The search goes on as before. Any further sightings of Lang to be reported immediately. They must get word back without delay.'

Billy had already passed the message on and he strolled over now to inspect the map and see how much progress had been made. Like spreading ripples, the circle of red pins was approaching the outskirts of the town and Billy bent close to read names that heralded the start of the countryside beyond: Beggars Corner, June Meadows, Nine Acres, Guillard's Oak. So far he'd found little to do of any use. His position as a Scotland Yard officer set him apart from the others – in their eyes, at least – and he'd been forced to stand by while men who knew both the town and each other well had gone about their business.

And there was another thing bothering him: the memory of the chief inspector's reaction when he and Madden had presented themselves to him earlier that morning. For a moment he'd seemed displeased, or at any rate disapproving, and Billy had felt that Sinclair's censure was directed towards him.

'You say your car's broken down?' The chief inspector had contrived to make the question sound like an accusation, meanwhile glancing across at Madden, who was talking to Braddock. 'Couldn't you have found some other way to get here?'

The thought that his superior might not have wanted to see his former colleague there had never occurred to Billy, and while under normal circumstances Madden's civilian status would have presented a problem, the scene he had just witnessed upstairs between the two men, when the chief inspector had turned to his old friend as naturally as if they were still working together, seemed to contradict any such notion. So what was it all about?

The sergeant was still ruminating on the riddle when he saw the door open and Madden enter.

'Ah, Billy! There you are . . .' He was wearing his coat and had his hat in his hand.

'Are you leaving, sir?' Billy put down his cup.

'Yes, I must get back. This business could take a while. Helen will be worried.' He advanced into the room. 'But there's something I want to do first. Perhaps you could give me a hand. It would be easier if we made it a police matter. Are you busy?'

'Anything but.' Billy grinned.

'I don't want to bother Mr Sinclair. He's got his hands full. He and Mr Braddock are drawing up a statement to give to the newspapers. But there's something that ought to be checked . . .' He noticed that Cole had turned from the map and was regarding him with curiosity. 'My name's Madden, Sergeant.' He went over, offering his hand as he did so. 'I used to be a policeman.'

'I know, sir.' Cole's face was split by a grin. 'The word's gone round the station. We all remember Melling Lodge. Lord, what a business that was!'

They shook hands.

'Sergeant Styles worked with me on that case. We were partners.'

Billy's pleasure at hearing the word was heightened by the glance he received from the Midhurst copper, and his grunt of acknowledgement, grudging though it was.

'Can I do anything for you, sir?' Cole asked, and Madden nodded.

'I need directions.' He gestured towards the map. 'Would you show us where your library is?'

ON THE WAY, Madden explained what was in his mind.

'I think Lang might have called in at the library yesterday. Have you read the statement Mrs Hall, the doctor's nurse, gave? The full statement, I mean? The one she made to the detective Inspector Braddock sent over later?'

Billy shook his head. They were striding across the market square, past an old set of stocks and a pillory, hands plunged into coat pockets against the freezing fog that had gripped the countryside all day. Sergeant Cole had told them the library was only a few minutes' walk away.

'She was asked to recall all the details she could about Lang and she mentioned a book he had with him, on his lap, while he was sitting in the waiting room. He took it into the doctor's office when he was called in and later she noticed it lying on the desk and glanced at the title. It had to do with birds, she said, and she thought the author's name might be Howard, though it was probably Coward. T. A. Coward. His books are well known. *Birds of the British Isles.* We've a set of them at home. They belonged to Helen's father.'

Madden had stopped for a moment to check a sign. Following Cole's directions, they had left the square and arrived at a curving street of timber-framed houses, some of them still with the narrow, glazed windows of an earlier age.

'When I read what she'd said, I wondered what he was doing with it. Lang, I mean.'

Billy scratched his head. 'Well, we know he's a bird-watcher, sir . . .'

'Yes, but I mean what was he doing with it there? At the doctor's rooms?' Madden gestured as they walked on.

'Perhaps he took it along to look at while he was waiting.' Billy still couldn't see what his old chief was driving at.

'That's not what the nurse said. She's an observant witness. She said he had it with him. To me that suggests he'd brought it for some other purpose. But if he was going for a walk in the country later and needed it with him, surely he'd have left it in his car. Driscoll's surgery's not far from here – it's on the Petersfield road. I looked at the map. Mrs Hall locked the door when he left – doctor's hours were over – and she saw him walking off in the direction of North Street. That's the main street. He was heading back to the centre of town.'

'Where he stopped at the chemist's shop,' Billy reminded himself with a shudder.

Madden scowled. 'Yes, but he still had the book with him, that's the point, and I wondered where he went next, and whether it might have been here.'

They had reached their destination, yet another timber-framed dwelling, but this one with a sign on a brass plate beside the door proclaiming it to be the Midhurst Public Library. When Billy tried the door, he found it locked. It was not yet two o'clock.

'You see, there's no reason he shouldn't have joined the library.' Madden blew on his fingers. 'It's not as though the police have been on his trail. As far as he's concerned, using a false name was only a precaution. If he'd wanted to get his hands on any reference books, this was the obvious place to come. He could have been returning one yesterday. After all, he's on the point of leaving. Or so it seems.'

While they'd been standing there, the lights inside the library windows had come on. Billy hesitated a moment longer.

'But would he bother, sir? A man like Lang? Wouldn't he just pocket the book?'

'Oh, no, I don't think so.' Madden was quick to respond. 'His aim in life is to avoid attracting attention. If he did borrow the book, he's more likely to return it than not.'

'So if he's a subscriber, they'll have his name. Or rather, De Beer's. Is that what you're thinking, sir?'

'More than that.' Madden's voice had hardened. 'He'd have had to give an address. And while it's possible he might have left a false one, I'm inclined to doubt it. It's the sort of thing that causes questions to be asked. Eyebrows to be raised. If it comes to light, I mean. No, if he joined the library – and it's a big if – I think he'd have given them his true address. But we'll soon find out . . .'

*

BILLY CHECKED THE index for a second time, riffling through the cards with his fingers, looking at the Bs now.

'It's no use, sir. He's not here.'

He'd already been through the Ds.

'There's no De Beer.'

Madden grunted. He was standing by the desk with folded arms, watching. Billy saw the disappointment in his face.

'Could he have used some other name, do you think?' he asked, but Madden shook his head.

'I doubt it. Going under one false name is difficult enough; it's something you have to keep in mind constantly. A second would only compound the problem. I know Lang's accustomed to doing this, but I doubt he'd take unnecessary risks. And as I said before, he's had no reason to feel threatened.'

Although the library had not yet opened – it seemed that a quarter past two was the appointed hour – they'd been admitted after Billy had knocked on the door, by a woman clutching a pile of books to her chest. Friendly, but harassed-looking, she had given her name as Miss Kaye and told them she was not in charge there, she was merely the assistant to the head librarian, a Miss Murdoch.

'Agatha's away, I'm afraid. She's gone to Chichester for the day to see her mother. The poor dear's not well. I've been left to manage as best I can.'

Slight, with red hair tucked up in a bun at the back of her neck, and green eyes blinking behind spectacles, she'd ushered them through a raised flap in the counter to a desk on which a small wooden cabinet, equipped with drawers, stood.

'That's our index of subscribers. By all means examine it.' The horn-rimmed glasses perched on the bridge of her nose gave her an owlish look. She'd declined Billy's offer to inspect his warrant card. 'But you'll have to excuse me. I came in early to tidy up.'

Madden glanced at his watch.

'I'm sorry, Billy, I've dragged you over here for nothing. I must be off.'

Peering about, he saw Miss Kaye approaching from the direction of the stacks carrying a pile of old newspapers in her arms and he lifted the wooden flap in the counter to let her through. Smiling her thanks, she dropped her burden into a large wicker basket already brimming with waste paper behind the desk.

'Have you had any luck?' she asked.

'I'm afraid not. We've bothered you for nothing. But thank you all the same.' Madden smiled in response.

'Just who is this man you're looking for?' she asked, as Billy rose from the desk. She seemed reluctant to let them leave.

'A foreigner called De Beer,' Madden replied. 'We thought he might have joined the library recently. But his name's not in the index.' He paused, as though reflecting. 'Sergeant Styles has a photograph of him. May we show it to you?'

'Of course.' Eagerly, she turned to Billy, who'd already taken the poster out of his jacket pocket and was unfolding it on the desktop. But after studying it for a few seconds, she shook her head.

'No, I'm afraid not. I don't remember seeing him.' She seemed disappointed at having failed them, and watching her reaction, Billy smiled. It was not the first time he had observed the effect of Madden's personality on a witness, even if his memories of the phenomenon came from many years back. There was some quality his old chief possessed, a gravity, perhaps, some deep well of seriousness, that seemed to draw a response from others. As though they accepted without question the importance of what he was asking of them and the need to help.

'If he was here at all it would have been yesterday, just before one.' Madden smiled at her again, encouragingly, but she shook her head.

'You'll have to ask Agatha, I'm afraid. Miss Murdoch. She was working here, at the counter, all morning. I was mostly in the stacks, putting books away.' She gestured towards the shelves. 'But why yesterday, particularly?'

'We think he's leaving the district for good.' Madden buttoned his coat, nodding to Billy, who had folded the poster and put it away in his pocket. 'He was seen with a book that might have been borrowed from a library. It occurred to me he might have come here to return it, but it seems I was wrong. Thank you again.'

He lifted the flap on the counter for Billy, who nodded his own thanks and followed. As they moved towards the door she addressed them again.

'Leaving, did you say?'

'Yes, we think so . . .' Madden paused. Billy was at his shoulder.

'Then he might have said so . . . to Miss Murdoch, I

mean?' She spoke hesitantly. 'He might have told her he was going away?'

Madden stared at her for a moment. He seemed surprised. 'I didn't think of that,' he admitted. 'I should have. You're quite right – that's exactly what he would have done.' To Billy, he added, 'He'd have wanted De Beer's name removed from their list of subscribers.'

'I asked because if he was here yesterday, and told Agatha that, she would have taken his card out of the index and torn it up. Deadheading, she calls it.' Miss Kaye smiled.

'Yes, of course. I see.' Madden shook his head in chagrin. 'So we're a day too late.'

'Oh, no . . . not necessarily.' Miss Kaye's green eyes sparkled. Her face had lit up. 'If Agatha tore up his card, the bits will still be here, with the waste paper.' She pointed at the wicker basket behind her. 'It's only emptied once a week.'

IT WAS BILLY who came on the first piece. Sifting through a stack of old periodicals, holding up each in turn and shaking it, he was rewarded by the sight of a torn shred of pasteboard, blue-ruled like the cards he'd already seen in the index, slipping out from between the pages of one of them.

'Sir! I've got half of it.'

His eye had fallen on the letters 'eer' penned in a neat hand near the top of the card and right beside the jagged tear. On the line beneath it was the word 'view' and below that the letters 'ane'. At the bottom a single 'd' was visible. He handed it to Madden.

They were both on their knees on either side of a heap of old newspapers and magazines mixed with scrap paper. At Miss Kaye's suggestion, Billy had brought the wicker basket out from behind the counter and tipped its contents onto an empty space on the floor beside the shelves.

'There's more room here.'

Pink in the face with excitement, she had hovered about them until the sound of knocking had reminded her that it was time to open the library and she'd gone to unlock the door, admitting two elderly ladies to whom she'd given a brief explanation of the goings on inside, and who themselves now stood a little way off watching open-mouthed as the two men sifted through the paper.

'Ane . . .' Scowling, Madden turned the letters into a word. 'That could be "lane". And "view" has an apostrophe after it. It must be the name of a house.'

As he put the fragment of card to one side, Miss Kaye gave a gasp. She was standing close beside him, bending down.

'There!'

She pointed, and Madden saw a tiny corner of white pasteboard showing beneath the edge of a sheet of carbon paper. He drew it out. Picking up the other portion of the card, he fitted the jagged edges together. Billy watched with bated breath.

'We'll need to use your telephone, Miss Kaye.' Madden spoke calmly.

He handed the joined sections of the card carefully to Billy who received them with shaking fingers. Hardly able to believe his eyes, the sergeant read what was written on them:

H. De Beer,
'Downsview',
Pit Lane,
Near Elsted.

30

'RIGHT, INSPECTOR. Let's get this over with.'

Sinclair nodded to Braddock, and the Midhurst policeman gave a grunt of acknowledgement. He turned to Sergeant Cole, who was standing a few paces away at the edge of the trees with the others, and signalled with his hand. The sergeant murmured something to the men and they set off down the slope.

'It doesn't look as though he's spotted us,' Braddock muttered. He settled his cap on his head. 'When you hear my whistle, it means we're going in.' He strode off after the men.

Sinclair drew in a deep breath, expelling it slowly. He watched as the men split into two groups, one party heading for the front of the cottage, which was enclosed on three sides by a yew hedge the height of a man's head, the other taking up position at the rear, behind a wooden shed. Eight in number, they included five detectives – the men who had happened to be closest to the station when word of Lang's address had been received – and three uniformed officers. The force had been hurriedly assembled on Sinclair's orders and bundled into a pair of cars. But not before two of the detectives, the most experienced, had been issued with revolvers.

'I've no reason to think Lang carries a gun,' the chief

inspector had told his Midhurst colleagues. 'But I'm not taking any chances.'

Remembering his own words now, he glanced at Madden, who was standing beside him, with Billy Styles at his elbow. Before leaving Midhurst he had requested, and received, from his former partner an explicit undertaking not to involve himself in the police operation that was about to get under way.

'You needn't be concerned, Angus.' Madden had been amused. 'It's the last thing I want. Just show me this man in handcuffs. That's all I ask.'

Reassured, but unwilling to leave anything to chance, Sinclair had found a moment to take the younger man aside. 'You're to stay with Mr Madden at all times,' he'd warned Billy. 'He's not to put himself at risk. Do I make myself clear?'

Coming downstairs from Braddock's office, the chief inspector had found his old colleague waiting in the CID room with the detectives already gathered there. Word of how Lang's address had been acquired had already spread among them, but seemingly unaware of the glances being cast his way, Madden had been standing with folded arms in front of the poster of the wanted man, his gaze fixed on the eerily white face with its staring eyes.

Realizing that only a direct order on his part would prevent him from accompanying them, Sinclair had taken the next best option and suggested they go together in Madden's car, taking Braddock and Styles with them. Travelling at the tail of the convoy, they had driven west out of the town, following signs to Petersfield, but soon turned south onto a minor road that led down a valley overlooked by a long wooded ridge. The address provided by the library's records had not been difficult to locate. Shown as a mere track on the Ordnance map, Pit Lane, as the name suggested, had once led to a chalk quarry, now abandoned. It was at the edge of the Downs, no more than a mile from the hamlet of Elsted.

'One of my blokes thinks he knows that cottage.' Braddock had leaned over from the back seat to mutter in Sinclair's ear. 'He's got a girl in Elsted. They walked past it once. She told him it belonged to some old lady who'd had to move into a home and was up for rent. That was six months ago.'

'Why wasn't it on the estate agents' lists?' Sinclair had wondered.

'Can't say for sure, but she might have advertised privately, in a newspaper. What's this now?'

The inspector had frowned as the cars ahead of them drew to a halt; there seemed to be a hold-up. He was about to get out to investigate when the convoy moved on again and they saw that there were road works in progress. A group of men wielding picks and shovels were standing aside while one of their number waved the cars through. They had stared at the police uniforms visible through the windows.

A mile further on the cars had slowed once more, this time to turn off the paved surface onto a narrow rutted track, unmarked apart from a white signpost on which the name 'Downsview' appeared, accompanied by an arrow. It led over a saddle in the ridge, on the far side of which a cottage could be seen situated a little way down the slope. Brick-built, in the style of the region, it looked out over a wide expanse of rolling pastureland towards the distant Downs, whose green rounded crests were hidden by mist and low-hanging cloud.

The cars had pulled up short of the house, at the edge of the tree line, and Sinclair had climbed out with Braddock to study the situation. At once they had noticed a trickle of smoke coming from the chimney on the tiled roof. Sinclair had given orders for the men to get out and gather at the edge of the trees. As they were doing so a light had come on in the kitchen at the back of the cottage and the figure of a man had been glimpsed through the window.

'We'll enter from both sides, front and back.' At a nod from Sinclair, Braddock had issued the necessary orders to his men. 'No talking until this is over. Not a word – is that clear? When I blow my whistle, move! And you needn't bother to knock. Just get in there and grab him.'

Watching now as the men below moved silently into place, Sinclair felt a quickening of his pulse. A sideways glance at Madden showed him to be equally tense, gazing down, narrow-eyed. The men at the back of the house were already in position; the rest, led by Braddock, were padding along the side of the cottage, heads bowed. Reaching the corner of the hedge, they turned right and disappeared.

'This is it, then . . .' The chief inspector found himself suddenly short of breath. 'Shall we move a little closer?'

Deliberately, without haste, they walked down the grassy slope to where Sergeant Cole and two of the detectives were concealed behind the shed at the rear of the house. The sergeant was peering around the corner. Hearing their footsteps he looked back, eyes bright with anticipation.

'No sign of him.' He spoke in a whisper. 'But the light's still on inside.'

At that moment the silence was split by the single piercing blast from a police whistle. Cole reacted like a greyhound loosed from the traps.

'Come on!' he cried, springing forward.

'LESS THAN AN hour ago – you're certain of that, are you, Mr Meadows?'

Telephone in hand, Sinclair directed his question towards the rumpled figure on the settee. Receiving a nod in reply, he spoke into the receiver, 'He hasn't had time to get anywhere, Arthur. Not to the channel ports, certainly, nor to Southampton. But I want them all alerted ... Yes, I'm aware it was done earlier today. But this is a specific warning. We know he's on his way. And I want it spread wider. Bristol. Liverpool. Anywhere he might take passage from.'

The chief inspector paused to listen, biting his lip as he did so, and then peering at Madden, who was standing with folded arms by the fireplace, a frown etched on his brow. Beside him, Billy Styles knelt on the hearth: he was carefully sifting through the ashes in the still smoking grate, though with little expectation of finding anything. No trace of their quarry, no single piece of physical evidence that could be tied to Gaston Lang, had been discovered so far: not in the sitting room, where they were, nor anywhere else in the house, which still echoed to the tramp of detectives' feet. All they knew for sure was that Lang himself had been there not an hour before. And now he was gone.

'Yes, a Mr Henry Meadows . . .' Sinclair had begun speaking again. He glanced at the man on the settee, who, in the middle of trying to tuck in his shirt, half rose, as though answering to his name. 'He works for a solicitor in Midhurst called Bainbridge. The owner of the cottage is a client of Bainbridge's and he dealt with the lease. It was advertised in a local newspaper. Lang, or De Beer, as they knew him, called at the office unannounced – this was in early August – and made an offer. Apparently Bainbridge wasn't keen on the business – Lang had no references – but after he made a cash offer and agreed to a deposit he let him take it. On Friday Lang rang up and announced he was leaving. Although he was paid up to the end of the year, he didn't ask for any money back. But Bainbridge thought he'd better send out one of his clerks just the same to do an inventory. Meadows says they were supposed to go through it together, but Lang told him when he got here that he was leaving right away and he'd have to do it on his own. My guess is we missed him by half an hour, no more.'

The bitterness of the pill he'd had to swallow showed in the chief inspector's tense expression. Angry and thwarted, he'd needed all the self-control he could muster to deal with the hapless Meadows, who, shocked by the sudden eruption of detectives into the cottage and the rough handling he'd received, had proved to be a witness of limited value.

'This car he left in – what make was it?' Almost before the clerk had recovered his senses, Sinclair had begun pressing him. 'What model?'

'I'm sorry, sir. I really couldn't say . . .'

Fair-haired, and tending towards plumpness, Meadows had been helped to the settee and given a glass of water, but neither had settled his nerves. Discovered in the sitting room by the detectives who'd burst in at the front, he'd been thrown to the floor and pinned there for several seconds, and although it was soon realized he was not their man, the experience had rendered him all but speechless for precious minutes, leaving the chief inspector to pace the sitting room while he waited.

'I've never owned a car, you see. I get about on a bike . . .'

Still gasping, Meadows had paused to fumble with his tie, pulled askew in the struggle, and only belatedly become aware of the glare he was receiving from Sinclair.

'It was black, though . . . the car, I mean. Mr De Beer had taken it out of the garage. He was putting his trunk in it when I arrived, pushing it up on the back seat.'

'His trunk, you say . . . can you describe it? Size . . . colour . . . anything?'

Meadows' fleshy face had turned redder. Near tears, he'd stared back at his tormentor.

'It might have been brown, sir, but I'm not certain. It was just a trunk . . .'

Sinclair had already imparted this information to Chief Superintendent Holly in London, asking that it be passed on to the authorities at the ports, including customs officers. 'The car's obviously a four-door sedan, not that that helps much.'

With a glance at his watch now, he brought their conversation to an end.

'I must ring this fellow Bainbridge, the solicitor in Midhurst, and tell him what's happened. He may have other information. We'll be here for a while. I want a forensic team to go through the place. It looks as though Lang's wiped it clean. But we might find a fingerprint somewhere.'

As he put down the phone, Braddock entered. He'd been to the garage to see if anything had been left there by their quarry. A quick shake of the head told Sinclair his errand had been fruitless.

'There's no need for you to stay, Inspector.' Sinclair reached for his pipe and tobacco. 'You can take the uniformed officers back if you like. But return the car, if you would. We'll need it later.'

Meadows stirred unhappily on the settee. 'What about me, sir? Can I go? I ought to report to Mr Bainbridge.'

'You can do that in a moment, when I ring him. But I want you here just now. You may remember something useful.'

The chief inspector hadn't meant his words to sound harsh, but Meadows flushed on hearing them and his misery seemed to increase. Unaware of it, Sinclair caught Madden's eye and gestured towards the front door, inviting him to step outside into the garden.

'We had him in our hands, John. And now, by God,

we've lost him.' Waiting only for the door to be shut behind them, Sinclair gave vent to his frustration.

'Don't assume that, Angus.' Seeing the distress on his friend's face, Madden sought to assuage it. 'They may still get him at one of the ports.'

'I very much doubt it. He won't try to leave now. He knows we're looking for him.'

'Are you certain of that?'

Sinclair shrugged. 'You heard what Meadows said. He wouldn't wait for a moment. He was getting out.'

Eyes cast down, the chief inspector studied the small patch of garden before them. In the dying light of afternoon, grey as lead, the sodden lawn, bordered by shrubs and flower beds, had a dank, unwelcoming look. He'd been fumbling for some minutes with his tobacco pouch, trying to fill his pipe, but as though defeated by this simple task, he abandoned the effort and thrust both back into his pocket.

Madden grunted. 'So you think he learned about the search going on in Midhurst?'

'It's the obvious explanation, isn't it?' Sinclair grimaced. 'The word would have spread fast enough. Perhaps he was there himself, in town. He's got the luck of the devil, this man.' He shook his head bitterly. 'He's been carrying a bottle of chloroform around with him in his pocket since yesterday. Does that mean he had a victim in mind? Or was it just a precaution? Either way, all I can hope is that we've scared him off. But I can't see him walking into any trap now. Not Gaston Lang. He'll find another place to lie low and wait for the fuss to die down. It'll be up to someone else to catch him. If they ever do.'

Lifting his gaze he stared out over the hedge towards the distant Downs.

'I've no taste myself for the hangman's rope. The practice is barbaric. But there's never been a man I wanted to lay hands on more. Aye, and hoped to see swing. But I doubt we'll set eyes on him now. We've missed our chance, and we won't get another. He's gone for good.'

31

SAM TURNED AT the gate and whistled.

'Come along, Sally. Get a move on, old girl.'

The dog hesitated in the lighted doorway, unwilling to leave the warmth of the kitchen. Behind her he could see Bess's anxious figure. The cook's pink face, even more flushed than usual from the tears she'd shed, radiated distress like an alarm beacon.

'You'll let us know what they say, won't you, Sam?' she called out to him.

'Of course I will, love. What's more I'll get them moving. You can tell Mrs Ramsay that, too.' Sam slapped his thigh. 'Now that's enough of that, Sal. Come on!'

It would be dark in less than an hour and he wanted to get over to the barn again while there was still some light to see by.

'Sally!'

At last she moved, crossing the yard reluctantly, with that shuffling gait which showed her arthritis must be hurting, poor old thing, following him out. With a last wave to Bess he shut the gate behind them and strode off.

Still fuming.

His attempt to ring the Midhurst police to see if they had any news of Eddie had ended in fiasco, his call having been answered by a green young copper – at least, that was what he'd sounded like – one who didn't seem to know what day of the week it was. And when Sam had demanded to speak to someone more senior he'd been told there was no one available just then.

'They're all out,' the bloke had said, reducing Sam to near apoplexy.

'I'm trying to report a missing person,' he'd roared down the phone. 'Someone who might have been hurt in an accident. Don't you have lists?'

If they did, no one had told the young copper about them, it seemed.

'I'll have to ask someone about this,' he'd said, sounding unsure. 'If you could just leave your number, sir . . .'

'Never mind. I'll come in myself.'

Sam had slammed down the phone, then wished he hadn't. No doubt the young copper was doing his best, but it was a fine thing when police stations were left in the hands of babes and sucklings.

And he still had no news of Eddie.

Sam's anger had been fuelled partly by fear. In the midst of making the call to the police he'd remembered something from his visit to the barn. It had sent a chill up his spine.

Eddie's work clothes . . . where were they?

He'd found his boots all right, both of them, lying on the barn floor, as though they'd been chucked there. As if Eddie had been in haste to depart somewhere. He recalled that the lace of one had been broken.

But where were his dirty clothes?

He wouldn't have shed his boots alone, surely. He

wouldn't have set out for Hove, or anywhere else, wearing the same soiled garments he put on every day for work. Sam had seen clean clothes in the wardrobe. But he remembered clearly now that there'd been no sign of the others.

Which didn't mean they weren't there somewhere. (At once Sam had sought for reassurance.) Tucked away in a corner, perhaps, or in the small cupboard under the washstand. But it was something he had to find out – for his own peace of mind, if nothing else. Because if the clothes were really missing, then Eddie couldn't have gone anywhere, which meant something really had happened to him, some accident, and it might have occurred closer at hand than anyone had imagined. In the barn itself, perhaps, or nearby.

Given that the light was fading fast now, he had to get moving, and having ended his phone call abruptly, Sam had hastened back to the kitchen where he'd found that Bess, too, was concerned about the gathering dusk, though for a different reason.

'It's time Nell was back.'

She'd been standing by the window, gazing out in the direction of the path that led across the fields from Wood Way.

'The bus must be late. The days are so short now . . .'

Sam had told her he was leaving, but not why. This was one fear he couldn't share with her.

'Did you talk to the police?' she had asked. When she turned to him he saw she'd been crying. 'Did they tell you anything?'

He'd shaken his head. 'Something's going on at the station – they're at sixes and sevens. I'll have to go there in person. I'll do it on the way home.'

He could see she was hoping he would stay longer. But he already had his coat on.

'Don't worry about Nell,' he told her as he opened the back door and called to Sally. 'I'll keep an eye out for her. I'm going that way.'

He hurried now along the path, glancing up at the grey-shrouded sky and wondering how much longer the daylight would last. He could light one of the oil lamps, if necessary, if he had to make a search, he thought, drawing his coat closer about him. A bit of a wind had got up in the last hour. In time it would blow away the mist and fog, but for the present it only sharpened the biting cold, and Sam was grateful he'd been able to stop at home on his way back from Tillington earlier and collect the coat. It was the same one he'd had all through the war, but better now since Ada had got her hands on it. She'd sewn a good thick lining of padding on the inside and once it was buttoned up, as it was now, it was proof against even the coldest weather.

Sam paused to look back and saw that Sal had already fallen behind.

'Come on, old girl!'

She was having a bad day – it was the cold, stiffening her joints even more than usual – and she was dealing with it the only way she knew how, by not hurrying.

He walked on, quickening his own pace. He could see the top of Wood Way now, where it came through the trees on the ridge, but there was no sign of Nell yet.

He was close to the point where the two paths met, and where a small coppice blocked his view for a few moments. Coming out of it he looked up the path and saw her now, descending from the ridge, her white school hat bobbing up and down, walking fast, half breaking into a run as she approached the spot where the gap in the hedge led to Coyne's Farm.

He waved to her, and she waved back.

Looking round for Sal, he saw she had stopped some distance off to sniff at a bush; taking a breather. Sam grinned. He decided to leave her be. She'd catch up with him in due course.

Turning again, he started up the path . . . then stopped.

There was no sign of Nell. She'd vanished.

Unable to believe his eyes, he stood staring.

Only a moment before she'd been bounding down the path towards him.

Then he realized something else. Peering narrow-eyed through the dusk, he saw there was an object lying on the ground up ahead: a round white shape.

It was Nell's school hat.

He barely had time to register the fact. The next moment the sound of a scream came to his ears. Though faint, and quickly cut off, the cry was enough to break the spell that held him frozen to the spot. And to shock him into action.

'Nell!' He roared out her name in response.

The hat lay by the gap in the hedge, and Sam ran flat out towards it, charging up the path, yelling out her name as he went.

'Nell . . . Nell!'

32

MADDEN BACKED his car onto the chalky track so that
he was pointing in the right direction, then waved to
Billy Styles, who was standing nearby. He wound down
the window.

'I almost forgot. Do me a favour, would you, Billy?
When you get a chance, give Helen a ring and tell her
I'm on my way home. She'll be getting worried.'

'Yes, of course, sir.' The sergeant smiled.

'I don't know where you'll end up spending tonight.
But if you can get back to Highfield, there'll be a bed
waiting for you.'

'Thank you, sir. If not tonight, then tomorrow.
There's that car of mine I have to pick up.'

With a final wave Madden drove off. He had stayed
as long as possible, hoping to the last that some clue to
Lang's whereabouts might be discovered, meanwhile
offering what moral support he could, listening while
Sinclair rang Bainbridge, the Midhurst solicitor who'd
handled the renting of the cottage, but seeing from his
expression even before their conversation was over that
there was nothing to be learned in that quarter.

'Apparently Lang spun him a yarn. Told him he'd
recently returned from Batavia where he'd worked for a
rubber company, and was spending a few months in
England prior to returning to Holland. Said birdwatch-

ing was his hobby and he was writing a treatise on the migratory habits of certain northern European species. Even that wasn't enough to persuade Bainbridge, who'd taken a distinct dislike to him, so he added a line about having lost his wife in the East to cholera and wanting somewhere secluded to mourn her passing. Our friend seems to have mistaken his calling: he should have been writing romantic novels. Bainbridge said he held out till Lang volunteered to rent the place till the end of the year, cash down. It was too good an offer to refuse. His client's a widow who needs the money.'

Sinclair had handed the phone to Meadows when he'd finished, but the clerk had exchanged only a few words with his employer, who'd already been informed of the situation by the chief inspector.

'Mr Bainbridge says I'm to stay as long as you need me sir,' he'd told Sinclair in a tone of resignation after he'd replaced the receiver. 'I'll have to lock up, anyway.'

'You needn't worry about that, Mr Meadows. We'll see to it.' The chief inspector had got over his annoyance with the clerk. He was regretting his earlier harshness. 'You can leave now. You've got your bicycle, have you?'

'Oh, yes, sir.'

'Then you'd better be off. It'll be dark soon.'

'Well, if you're sure, sir ...' Meadows was already looking for his coat and attaché case.

The light was beginning to fade as Madden walked up with Billy to where he'd left his car near the top of the wooded ridge, both of them striding along briskly in the cold breeze that was blowing. Glancing sid-

Billy noted the familiar scowl of preoccupation on his old chief's face.

'Don't worry, sir. We'll get him.'

'I hope so, Billy. I hope so.' Madden had paused by his car, smiling now. 'Well, at least I'll be out of your hair.'

'Sir?'

'It's my impression you've been keeping an eye on me, Sergeant Styles. Did Mr Sinclair give you an order to that effect?'

Billy had grinned, but said nothing.

'Well, you can both relax. I'm on my way.' Madden had chuckled.

Approaching the top of the ridge now, driving carefully over the rutted track, he came on the figure of Henry Meadows. The clerk was pushing his bicycle up the slope, which steepened over the last twenty yards or so. Bulky in his coat, and with the added burden of his attaché case, which was strapped to a carrier on the back of his bike, he was making heavy weather of the climb. Hearing the sound of the car behind him, he moved off the road. Madden drew to a halt.

'Would you like a lift, Mr Meadows? I'm going by Midhurst.'

'Oh, goodness, sir ... thank you.' The doleful look on the clerk's fleshy face was dispelled in an instant. A smile of relief took its place.

'We can put your bike in the back.'

Having done so, they were soon on their way again and within minutes had rejoined the paved road.

'What an afternoon, sir! I still haven't got over it.'

Seated beside Madden in front, with his hat, containing his bicycle clips, perched upside down on his knees, Henry Meadows seemed disposed to relive his experience. 'The men bursting in like that. I don't know when I've had such a shock.' He hesitated, unsure whether to continue. 'Sir, what's he done, this Mr De Beer? No one would say.'

'I can't tell you that, I'm afraid.' Madden glanced at him. 'But you can take it he's a dangerous man.'

Silenced by these words, the clerk swallowed.

'What did you make of him?' Madden switched on his headlamps. Although it was not yet dark, the light was dull and leaden.

'Nothing, sir. I mean, we hardly spoke. He must have known I was coming: he'd left a note on the kitchen table with the keys. If I'd have been ten minutes later he'd have gone. But he never said goodbye or anything; he just drove off.'

'He was in a hurry, was he?'

'Oh, yes . . . no doubt of that.' Meadows nodded. 'He looked at his watch twice, I remember, even in the few minutes we were there together. It was as though he had somewhere to go, somewhere else to be.'

'Somewhere else?' Madden repeated the words. But his attention had shifted to the road ahead where a bus had appeared, blocking their forward progress. He saw a group of men bearing tools on the verge beside the vehicle and realized they had reached the roadworks, where the surface narrowed. The bus was motionless; the driver seemed to be waiting for him to make way.

'There's a parking area just behind us, sir.' Meadows

had noted the problem. 'It's for Wood Way. Ramblers going to the Downs use it.'

Twisting about, Madden saw the space he was referring to and put the car into reverse. When he reached the entrance to the gravelled area, he spun the steering wheel hard and continued backing into it, avoiding a small van that was parked there. The bus had already begun moving forward.

'Sir?' Meadows spoke beside him. He'd turned round in his seat while Madden was reversing and he was still looking back.

'Yes?' Madden's eyes were fixed on the bus as it lumbered past.

'That car of Mr De Beer's ... the one the chief inspector was asking me about. He wanted to know the model, but I couldn't tell him ...'

'I remember ... what about it?' Madden changed gear and they started forward.

'It was just like that one over there.'

Madden put his foot hard on the brake. Turning, he peered through the narrow rear window and saw, on the far side of the parking area, half hidden by the overhanging branch of an oak tree, the vehicle Meadows was indicating. He changed into reverse again and backed rapidly across the area, wheels spinning on the loose gravel. As they drew near the spot, he saw that the car was a black Ford sedan.

'Come on. Let's have a look at it.'

Meadows was on the side nearest and as he opened the door to descend he let out a yelp of excitement.

'It's his! It's the same car. Look – there's his trunk! The one I saw.' He was pointing.

Madden had already seen the object. Brassbound, and bare of any label, it occupied the rear seat. Swiftly, his heartbeat quickening with every second, he tried the doors and found them locked.

'Mr Meadows – get your bicycle out!'

He spoke in a low tone, but the clerk responded as if stung, springing to obey. He dragged the machine from the back of their car, then turned to find Madden standing on the running board of the other car looking about him. His eyes moved in a slow circle; first he peered at the trees bordering the parking area on this side, then swung round to look in the other direction, where the country was more open; finally, he shifted once more on the cramped running board and gazed up at the wooded ridge that ran parallel to the road they'd come on.

'I don't see him.' Madden murmured the words to himself. He turned his glance on the clerk, who was standing nearby, bicycle at the ready, but with the stunned look of one who wasn't sure what would be asked of him next.

'I need your help, Mr Meadows.' Madden stepped down from the running board. 'You must ride back to the cottage as quickly as possible and tell Mr Sinclair – the chief inspector – that De Beer's car is here.'

'Ride back?' If Henry Meadows was dismayed by the prospect, he managed not to show it. The day had been a hard one for him, but now he rose to the challenge.

'Yes, of course . . . I'll go at once.' As he bent to fix his
bicycle clips he heard a hissing sound and glanced up to
see Madden, on his knee, letting the air out of one of the
Ford's tyres.

'You can tell Mr Sinclair he won't be going anywhere.'

'Yes, sir. Right, sir.' In the intervening seconds,
Meadows had shed his coat, tossing it into the back of
the car. Hoisting one plump leg over the saddle, he
mounted the bicycle and moved off, wobbling on the
gravel at first, but then picking up speed.

'And Mr Meadows!' Madden called after him.

'What is it, sir?' the clerk yelled over his shoulder.

'Pedal like blazes.'

MADDEN DROVE HIS car across the gravelled area to the
entrance and left it parked beside the van. Hastening on
foot down the road to where the workmen were assembled, he saw that they were knocking off for the day,
gathering their tools – picks and shovels, mostly – and
putting moveable signs in place. His own hurried
approach had not gone unnoticed, and as he came up,
one of their number, evidently the foreman, a brawny
figure with a thick black moustache, came a few steps
forward to meet him.

'Madden's my name. I was with that party of police
that went by. I dare say you noticed them.' Madden held
out his hand.

'Harrigan,' the other responded. He shook Madden's

hand. 'Aye, I saw 'em.' He spoke with an Irish accent, his tone wary.

'We're looking for the man who was driving that car.' Madden pointed behind him towards the distant corner of the parking area, now almost invisible in the dying light. 'You can't see it very well, but it's there. A black Ford. Did any of you notice him when he arrived? Did you see where he went?'

He scanned the faces of the men who had gathered around while he was speaking. Most of them were rough, none was particularly friendly.

'What do they want him for, then, this bloke?'

The question came from one younger than the rest. He had blue eyes and fair curly hair. Stubble coated his cheeks.

'Murder,' Madden replied bluntly. He looked the foreman squarely in the eye.

'Jaysus!' Harrigan paled, and the men about him began to mutter. The atmosphere had changed.

'I reckon I saw him,' the foreman said. He was planted in front of Madden, his arms folded. ''Twas about an hour ago. He went up the path there.'

Madden followed the direction of his pointing finger. 'Is that Wood Way?'

'I reckon so.' Harrigan nodded.

'Where does it go?'

'To the Downs.' He shrugged. 'There's farms there, too. On t'other side of the ridge. And a village. Oak Green.'

'Have you seen anyone else?'

'Going up the path, you mean?'

Madden nodded.

'A bloke we know called Sam Watkin went over there earlier. It was around two o'clock. That's his van you left your car by.'

'Anyone else?'

Harrigan thought. 'Don't reckon so.' He shrugged again.

With a nod of thanks, Madden turned to leave. He'd decided to wait in the trees by the parking lot, where he could keep an eye on the Ford. But as he moved off he heard the men muttering among themselves.

'Except Nell,' a voice said, louder than the rest.

Madden stopped where he was. He turned.

'Who's Nell?' he asked in a low tone.

'Just a lass.' It was the same curly-haired young man who had spoken earlier. 'She lives over in Oak Green. Takes the bus back from school every day. She was here just a minute ago. We had a word with her.'

'Are you telling me she went up the path?'

The young man paled at the look on his questioner's face. He nodded.

'My God!' Madden stood stunned. 'He's after the girl.'

'What do you say?' It was Harrigan who responded first. He stared at Madden. 'Who's after Nell?'

'That man. He's a killer.' Madden seized his arm. 'Listen to me now. I can't stay . . .'

He turned even as he spoke and begun to run down the road away from them, shouting over his shoulder as he did so.

'The police are coming. You must wait for them. Tell them Lang's up in the woods. Lang . . . do you hear me? Tell them about the girl. Tell them!'

But he was already out of earshot and too far off to hear the single word that was Harrigan's only response.

'Jaysus!'

33

MADDEN RACED up the hill, peering into the woods on either side of the path, looking for any sign of life in their dark depths; listening for any sound. In an agony of mind at the thought of the savage act that might be taking place within a stone's throw of where he was, under cover of the deepening dusk, he called out the girl's name as he ran.

'Nell . . . Nell . . .'

He was hoping to disturb her assailant if they were near, but tormented by the fear that he was already too late: that the horror he had come on at Brookham was even now being re-enacted.

Out of breath by the time he reached the top of the hill, he paused, heart pumping, to take in the wide sweep of country beyond whose outlines were still visible in spite of the dying light.

Before him, the path ran straight as an arrow down the slope, heading for the distant Downs, themselves hidden from view by the clinging mist. To his left were the lights of a village, which he took to be Oak Green, and to his right, some distance off the path, and separated from it by a hawthorn hedge, a farmhouse with darkened windows. Nothing stirred in the fields: the countryside seemed deserted.

He set off again, jogging down the hill, looking left

and right, but after only a few steps he paused, arrested by the sight of an object lying on the path ahead of him. It was some way off still, but he could just make out its white shape in the gathering dusk. Gripped by a sense of foreboding, he ran flat out down the slope, but even before he reached it he knew that his fears had been realized.

Gasping, he picked up the white school hat with its characteristic ribbon. The elastic beneath the brim was broken.

'Nell!' In desperation he shouted out her name again. 'Nell!'

There was no answer. But in a silence broken only by the sound of his own heavy breathing, he heard a faint noise coming from the other side of the hedge and realized after listening hard for several moments that it was a dog's whine.

'Who is it? Who's there?' He called out again, and this time was rewarded by a bark.

Madden tore at the hedge, which at first seemed impenetrable, until he discovered a gap in the dense foliage nearby. Plunging through it, he found himself in an apple orchard; beyond was what looked like the brick wall of a kitchen garden. It had a gate in it.

Again he heard the dog's whine, this time mingled with a man's groan. It was coming from the garden. Madden raced across the orchard and went through the open gate, almost tripping and falling as his foot caught on something. Looking back, he saw a hand reaching up and realized that a man was trying to drag himself out of an old compost pit beside the path. A dog crouched by the lip, whimpering.

'Wait!'

Madden turned to help him, and as he hauled the man from the pit by his arms he saw that his head was wet with blood. But it was his stomach that he clutched as Madden laid him groaning on the ground. Distressed by the scene, the dog, an old Labrador bitch, growled and bared her teeth.

'There, now . . .' Madden calmed her, and then drew her to lie by the injured man, who was still holding his stomach. Pulling open the old army greatcoat he wore, Madden discovered a spreading stain on his shirt.

'Lie still,' he urged him.

But the man tried to resist, pushing himself up. 'Not me . . . not me,' he gasped, struggling to rise, while the dog whined beside him. 'Nell!' He pointed across the garden. 'Nell!'

'Where?' Madden looked in the direction indicated. He could see nothing. 'What's he done with her?'

In a fever to go on, he hesitated. He felt he couldn't leave the injured man. Tearing off his coat, he tried to lay it on the prone figure. 'Keep still,' he pleaded with him. 'You're bleeding.'

But the man wouldn't heed him. 'Not me,' he repeated, desperation turning his words into a cry. 'Nell . . . Nell . . .' His finger continued to point. Madden saw the anguish in his face.

'Don't move,' he said. 'I'll find her.'

Springing to his feet, he raced across the garden and came to another gate, also open. Beyond it was a large stableyard backed by a farmhouse: it was the same one he'd seen earlier from the crest of the ridge.

Breathing heavily, he halted for a moment at the edge of the cobbled space to look about him. Darkness had fallen in the last few minutes, but he was still able to make out a line of stalls to his right, facing the house. Further off, at the very end of the yard, a barn was visible, its lofty roof silhouetted against the moon that was rising behind it. There was no sign of life in any of the buildings.

About to run on, he hesitated, disturbed by something he had sensed rather than seen, a change so slight he was not sure at first whether it wasn't something he'd imagined. The perception had occurred at a moment when the darkness in the yard had seemed to deepen, and as he peered narrow-eyed into the blackness before him he saw what it was: there was the faintest suggestion of illumination coming from inside the barn, a vertical sliver of light at the point where the doors met, so thin it hardly seemed to be there at all.

He leaped forward, sprinting across the yard, his footsteps ringing on the cobbles. Reaching the doors, he hauled the heavy wooden sections open and saw a glow of light coming from the far end of the cavernous structure.

'Gaston Lang!'

Madden roared out the name at the top of his lungs.

'Show yourself!'

Striding forward between piles of hurdles lining the barn on either side, he called out again.

'Lang! Gaston Lang!'

Wanting only to stop what might be in progress beyond the dark, canvas-covered shapes he could see in front of him now; not caring if he alerted the man he had come for, he moved swiftly, hoping to surprise him nonetheless with the speed of his approach. Seeing a way through the heaped objects in front of him he took it, peering from side to side, but taking no other precaution in his haste to reach the back of the barn where the light was brightest.

He came to a tall shape from which the canvas had been thrown back and saw it was a wardrobe. The lighted area at the back of the barn was just beyond and he paused as he reached it, wary now. The illumination, he saw, came from an oil lamp hanging from a nail in one corner above a heap of straw. His gaze swept the area. He saw an old washstand and a wicker basket filled with farm implements; near it was a pony trap standing with the shafts upraised.

Of Lang and his victim there was no sign.

Or so Madden thought, until his glance returned to the lamp and he saw the mirror leaning against the wall beneath it. Reflected in the glass was a sight that brought a cry to his lips.

'Oh, God!'

Half hidden in the hay the body of a girl lay sprawled. The skirt of her gymslip had been pulled up baring her thin white legs.

'No!'

He ran to her side, and, crouching, felt for her pulse. It throbbed faintly against his fingertips. He caught a whiff of anaesthetic on her shallow breath.

'My poor child . . .'

Her face had been turned away from him as she lay

and he saw it was undamaged. When he reached to pull down her skirt he found her white pants in place and the sight of them brought tears of relief to his eyes. Covering her legs, he stooped to take her in his arms, glimpsing his own face in the mirror above as he did so – and then behind it the shocking sight of a half-naked figure that sprang out from the open door of the wardrobe with arm upraised and launched itself across the short space that separated them.

With a cry, Lang struck.

But Madden had seen the hammer descending, and he flung himself to one side, avoiding the blow by a hair's breadth, letting the force of it carry his assailant stumbling past him into the hay where he lost his footing and fell forward, striking his head against the mirror, cracking the glass. Dazed and bleeding from the forehead, Lang dropped the hammer, and the time it took him to retrieve it, burrowing in the hay, gave Madden the few seconds he needed to scramble to his feet. As his attacker turned with arm upraised to strike again, he closed with him, catching hold of his wrist with one hand and with the other seizing him by the throat, and then, with his fingers sunk deep in the other's flesh, shaking him savagely, like a rat, from side to side, the rage that possessed him so great he could readily have torn his head from his shoulders.

Lang struggled to fight back. He was naked to the waist, his body slippery with sweat and with the blood that ran down from his forehead, and he clawed at Madden's arm, seeking to break the iron grip on his throat, striving to free his hand so that he could strike with the hammer again. But his strength was no match for his adversary's and gradually, choking from lack of breath, he sank to his knees in the straw.

Quickly, Madden shifted his position, bending the wrist he was holding up behind the other's back. The hammer Lang held was now trapped between them, and Madden let go of his throat and caught him once more around the neck in a lock with his free arm. Kneeling behind him, he saw their faces side by side in the mirror, his own flushed and straining, Lang's bloody and twisted with pain.

'Let go.'

Breathless himself from the struggle, Madden growled in his ear, but his words had no effect. Lang's only response was to jerk his head back savagely, seeking to catch his antagonist unawares.

'Drop it, I say.'

He tightened his grip on the other's wrist, twisting it further.

The face in the mirror glared at him, and Madden increased the pressure, bringing a cry from his captive's lips.

'Let go, or I'll break your wrist.'

He hoped for some sign of surrender. None came. When their eyes met in the mirror, Lang bared his teeth in a snarl.

With a wrenching jerk of his hand, Madden made good his threat. The snap of sinews breaking was echoed by a piercing scream. The hammer dropped from Lang's nerveless fingers and he collapsed face down in the straw.

His thoughts now all for the child who lay unmoving

behind him, Madden paused only long enough to pick up the hammer and hurl it into the shadows behind him. Quickly checking Lang's body for other weapons, he found a small sheathed knife in one of the pockets of his trousers and he threw it after the hammer. Feeling safer in his mind now, he stumbled over to where the girl lay and bent to gather her in his arms. But he found the task beyond him. Weakened by the struggle he'd just been through, he could only wait, kneeling in the straw beside her, and hope that the trembling in his limbs would stop and his strength would return.

The sound of movement behind him made him look round and he saw that Lang had rolled over and was lying on his back staring up at the lamp which hung from the wall above him. His breath came in hoarse gasps and he was muttering to himself, but in a foreign language which Madden could make no sense of. He bent over the girl once more and this time managed to lift her clear of the straw mattress on which she'd been laid. Summoning up his strength, he was on the point of clambering to his feet, when he became aware that something was happening behind him. He glanced round and saw that Lang had got to his knees. Like a wounded animal he was resting his weight on one arm, while the other hung limp. His pale brown eyes gleamed yellow in the lamplight.

'Stay where you are.' Unsure what the other intended, Madden made his meaning plain. 'Don't come near us.' He felt no pity for the broken figure. But he shrank from the thought of inflicting further injury on him.

While he was speaking Lang had straightened slowly

and now he was kneeling upright, resting on his heels. A red welt at his throat marked the place where Madden's hand had gripped him; below it, spread across his chest, his birthmark showed plain. Bright strawberry in the lamplight, it mingled with the blood that had run down from his forehead. Seeing the state he was in, Madden spoke again.

'It's over, Lang. The police will be here any minute. They know who you are and what you've done. It'll go easier with you if you give yourself up.'

His words brought no immediate response. The yellow eyes remained fixed on his. Sensing the hatred in their pale depths, Madden braced himself for whatever might follow. He watched as the other man licked his bloodied lips.

'C'est fini, tu dis?'

The muttered words were barely audible and before Madden had properly registered them, Lang's expression changed. A grin appeared on his face. Ghastly as a death's head, it flickered across his features. He bared his teeth.

'Bien, alors . . .'

Without warning, and with a sudden convulsive movement, he reached up behind him and unhooked the lamp from the nail where it hung. Using the momentum of its descent, he whirled it around like a plane's propeller . . . once . . . twice . . . and then, with no pause in the movement, hurled it against the back wall of the barn near to where Madden crouched with the girl in his arms. As the glass shattered, his cry pierced the darkness.

'C'est fini!'

At the same instant the hay burst into flames.

With only a moment to react, Madden flung himself from the spot, clutching the girl to him. Together they rolled across the barn, away from the roaring inferno which the piled hay had become in seconds. Fuelled by the spilt oil, the fire pursued them, carried by the straw strewn on the floor. As Madden staggered to his feet he saw the nearest piece of canvas go up in flames and then all was hidden in a cloud of billowing smoke. With only his sense of direction to guide him he stumbled towards where he knew the doors must lie, running at once into a densely packed mass of objects covered in canvas which he'd supposed were there for storage and which formed an obstacle course through which he tried to find a path, holding the girl's body close to his, trying to shield her face from the smoke that already filled the barn and from which he knew they must quickly escape; or succumb to.

The fire itself followed close behind them, and a piece of burning wood falling from the roof beside them served as a warning that it would not be long before the whole structure came down on their heads. But the approach of the flames proved a blessing, too, bringing light as well as blistering heat, and with their help he was able to find his way to the broad corridor he remembered and to stumble between the lines of stacked hurdles already on fire through the wide open doors and out into the stableyard.

Into the blessed, blessed night.

Reeling, his head spinning, coughing up smoke and spit, Madden staggered away from the burning building, and as he did so the sound of raised voices came to his ears and he saw a party of men, one of them with a lamp, issue from the kitchen garden. Only when he spotted the burden they were bearing among them and noticed the dog shuffling in their wake did he remember the man he'd helped from the pit. So long ago, it seemed. Several of the group were already running across the cobbles towards him: he recognized the dark-browed foreman he'd spoken to. But all that was consigned to some distant past.

'Is she safe?' Harrigan's voice rang out above the others. 'Have you got her? Is that the lass?'

They crowded around Madden to peer at the girl, but he could find no words with which to reassure them. A great tiredness had come over him, he wanted to lie down and sleep. But he knew he could not do so as long as the child was his to care for, and he was struggling in his mind with this conundrum – how to resolve it – when his thoughts were interrupted by a sound, sudden and shocking, like the scream of an animal in pain.

'What in God's name . . . ?'

Harrigan swung round, the others with him. Looking back towards the burning barn they saw coming through the doors, staggering, spinning around like some demon conjured from the fiery depths, a shape consumed by flames. Blazing like a torch, it came across the yard towards them, weaving from side to side, hardly human, but still shrieking in agony until all at once the sound ceased and the figure collapsed in a smoking heap from which the stench of burning flesh arose, rank and pungent.

Shocked into silence, the men stared. It was Harrigan who found his tongue first.

'Is that him?' he asked.

Madden nodded. He was swaying on his feet now. 'Do something . . . help him if you can.'

But he turned from the sight himself and moved as quickly as his stiffening legs would take him away towards the line of stalls, where the injured man from the garden had been borne, and where a light already burned. He had felt the girl stir in his arms a moment before and knew he must spare her any further horror.

The others lingered, several of them trying vainly to bat out the flames that continued to lick at the now smouldering corpse.

But not for long. Having watched their efforts for a minute or so, standing to one side, not lifting a hand himself, Harrigan called a halt.

'Never mind that,' he growled. 'One of you fetch some water. Bring it up to the stalls. It'll be needed.'

He cast a last glance at the smoking remains, shapeless now in the darkness.

'Let the bastard burn.'

34

It was late by the time they reached the village, after nine, and Billy asked the two detectives to drop him at the gates to the Maddens' house. They were both with the Guildford CID and he'd spotted their familiar faces at the Midhurst police station earlier. Surprised to see them there, he learned that they'd been investigating a case of robbery at Haslemere, just over the Surrey border, when word of the events at Coyne's Farm had reached them and they had driven down into Sussex to discover for themselves what was going on.

'It's all over now,' he'd told them. 'They'll be bringing Lang's body in soon. But since you're going back to Guildford you could do me a favour and drop me off on the way. If I don't get to Highfield sometime tonight, my life won't be worth living.'

Billy wasn't exaggerating. When the chief inspector had discovered Madden's disappearance from the stable-yard, he'd hit the roof, and it had been Billy's bad luck to be the one in the firing line.

'Do you mean to say you let him walk out of there? In the condition he was in?' Sinclair had been white with anger.

What Billy had wanted to say was that he hadn't let anyone go anywhere. That what with the chaos in the yard caused by the swarm of police and firemen, not to mention the casual onlookers who'd been drawn to the spot and who'd had to be shepherded away, it had been impossible to keep an eye on everything. That he didn't have a crystal ball and there was no way he could have guessed that his former chief would suddenly take it into his head to walk off without a by your leave.

But if a dozen years on the force had taught Billy anything, it was that there were times when all you could do was bite your tongue, and he'd stayed silent.

'Just pray nothing's happened to him on the way, Sergeant.' The chief inspector had been incandescent. 'Just hope he hasn't had an accident, or run off the road.'

He'd ordered Billy to get himself to Highfield without delay, saying that he, Angus Sinclair, wanted to hear before the night was out that Madden had returned home safe and sound, and that in the event of there being any other sort of news to report, the sergeant might well consider embarking on a new career.

'And you might just remind him that leaving the scene of a crime without police permission is an offence punishable by law, and that he ought to know better.'

Which had given Billy something to grin about, at least, as he'd set off.

Not dealt with by the chief inspector had been the question of how he was supposed to get himself back to Midhurst, never mind Highfield, but luck had been on his side and he'd encountered Inspector Braddock in the parking area by the road. Hearing what was afoot, the Midhurst commander had hurried back from the station, and having no immediate need for his car and driver had told the latter he could take Billy as far as the town.

'After that, you're on your own, I'm afraid.'

Whatever doubts Billy might have had regarding his former mentor's surreptitious departure had been removed when he'd spoken to the uniformed sergeant in charge at the parking lot. He'd had a word with Madden when he'd left in his car sometime earlier.

'He asked me to make his excuses to the chief inspector if I saw him. To tell him he felt he had to get home.'

None of which had come as any surprise to Billy when he considered the events of the last few hours. He himself was still shaken by what he'd been through, and could recall the apprehension he'd felt on hearing from the man left behind by the foreman at the roadworks that Madden had set off in pursuit of Lang alone. Leaving the party of police that was assembling behind him, Billy had sped up the path on his own and on reaching the crest of the wooded ridge had instantly seen the huge fire blazing down in the valley, away to his right. Thwarted at first by a hedge that ran alongside the path, he'd eventually found a way through to a farmyard where a sight met his eyes that had turned his blood to ice.

Silhouetted against a blazing barn were two men standing on either side of a smoking shape that lay on the cobbles between them. Even before he'd reached them Billy had known instinctively that what he was looking at were the remains of a human being.

'Who is it?' he'd shouted to them, unable to contain his anxiety. And then, 'Police . . .' when they'd turned inquiring faces his way.

'Some bastard who tried to kill a lass,' one of them had answered him bluntly, a tough looking customer with several days' growth of beard on his cheeks, but a bloke Billy would happily have flung his arms around and kissed.

A few moments later, having been directed by the two towards a lighted stall at the side of the yard, his relief had been complete. There he'd found Madden, his face swollen at the temple and blackened by the fire's ash, and with a burn mark showing on the back of his hand, sitting on the straw-covered floor with a young girl cradled in his arms. Close by them, lying on the cobbles, was another figure, that of a man dressed in an army greatcoat, whose eyes were shut and whose hand rested on the head of an old Labrador curled up beside him.

A group of roughly dressed men stood about them and Billy had had to push his way through to reach his old chief, whose face had lit up at the sight of him.

'Ah, Billy . . . there you are.'

Pale beneath the caked ash, Madden's features bore the stamp of exhaustion. He was in his shirtsleeves and Billy saw that his tweed jacket was wrapped around the girl, whose head rested on his shoulder.

'She's asleep, poor child.'

Billy had offered to take the girl from him, but Madden had seemed reluctant to let her out of his arms.

'Better not to wake her.' His eyes were bright and staring and it was plain from his dilated pupils that he was suffering from shock.

It was at that point that one of the men standing around had drawn Billy aside. A heavy-browed Mick by the name of Harrigan, he'd identified himself as the foreman of the road crew.

'I sent a man down to Oak Green to ring for an ambulance. That was after we found Sam Watkin over there.' He'd nodded towards the figure in the greatcoat. 'Sam was crawling through the kitchen garden, trying to get to the yard. He'd been stabbed. Aye, and knocked on the head. I reckon he tried to save the lass. He'll be all right, though. That coat of his is padded. The knife didn't go in too deep.'

He'd told Billy he and the others in his gang had rushed up from the road on Madden's heels and had got half way to the village before they'd spotted the fire behind them . . . and come pelting back.

'You'll have to ask your fella what happened.' He gestured towards Madden. 'We've not bothered him with questions. You can see he's done in. One thing I can tell you, though – the lass isn't . . . hurt.' Harrigan's cheeks had flushed and he'd looked away in embarrassment. 'You take my drift. She woke up for a moment and told us she was feeling sick, but that was all. Your bloke said it was from the chloroform he gave her. That bastard out there.' The foreman jerked his thumb towards the doorway. 'Well, he won't be doing it to another, will he?'

While they were talking the clatter of boots on the cobbles outside had signalled the arrival of the main police party. The sight of blue uniforms crowding into the cramped stall had seemed to reassure Madden and Billy had coaxed him at last to hand over his burden into the care of a burly sergeant, who had wrapped the child in his coat and settled down with her in a corner.

Madden had struggled then to rise to his feet.

'I don't know what's come over me. Give me a hand, would you, Billy.'

Helped up, he'd appeared unsteady on his legs and Billy had led him out of the packed stall into the yard where the cold air had revived him. Finding an upturned bucket to hand, he'd persuaded Madden to sit down.

'I had to break his wrist, Billy. He wouldn't have it otherwise.'

Slumped over his knees, staring at the ground between his feet, Madden had given a brief, fragmented account of what had occurred to an audience which by now included several of the Midhurst contingent. Not once had his glance strayed to the shapeless, black form, guarded by a pair of constables, that lay still smouldering on the cobbles not far from where he sat.

'It was Lang who set fire to the barn. He must have known he wouldn't survive it. But he wanted to kill *us*, come what may.'

He hadn't yet made sense of the experience, come to terms with it. Billy had seen that. But there'd been no time to talk. Just then the chief inspector had appeared, entering the yard by the kitchen garden, and Billy had signalled to him. Out of breath after his brisk walk up from the road, but already informed by runner of the part Madden had played in the rescue of the girl, Sinclair had stood before them, wordless.

'Ah, John . . . !'

Seeing the state his old partner was in, he'd directed him to sit quietly and wait for transport of some kind to arrive, an order Madden had seemed happy to obey.

Taking Billy with him, the chief inspector had then crossed the yard to examine the remains of their quarry. Lang's smoking corpse lay on its back with one hand raised, the fingers bent. Where the face had been, only charred flesh remained.

'Not something you'd want to show your maiden aunt, is it?' Sinclair's lip had curled in disgust at the grisly sight. 'But a comfort to some, I dare say. No chance of him turning up in the dock.'

Billy had told him what he'd learned from Madden. 'Lang tried to kill them both.'

Sinclair had absorbed this information without comment. Then he'd shrugged. 'I wonder how he came to end up here. I mean at this particular spot.'

The answer hadn't been long in coming. Presently Sergeant Cole had approached them. The Sussex detective reported that he'd been speaking to Sam Watkin, the man found stabbed in the garden, who had information he'd wanted to communicate.

'He says he heard the girl scream and ran to help. Lang was waiting for him just inside the garden wall. He hit him with a hammer and then stabbed him. But the point is he reckons he'd seen him before hanging around the farm, trying to get into the barn, fiddling with the tap outside to see if it worked. And when you consider that this same girl, Nell Ramsay, comes home from school every day at the same time, and by the same route . . . and that Lang's been living not more than a mile away . . .'

Cole had gestured wordlessly.

'But there's more. The reason Watkin was over here

this afternoon was to look for a pal of his who's gone missing. A bloke called Eddie Noyes. He was part of that road gang. Watkin works for an estate agent in Midhurst. He'd fixed for Noyes to sleep in the barn and he'd asked him only the other day to keep an eye out for any stranger he saw nosing about and to tell him to shove off.'

'So it's possible they ran into each other and Lang disposed of him. That would have been in character, all right.' The chief inspector grimaced. 'He wouldn't have wanted his pitch queered. Not if he had the girl in his sights.' He was silent for some moments, reflecting. Then he'd sighed. 'There's a fire engine coming, I take it?'

'Yes, sir. I sent a man down to Oak Green to ring for one.'

'Tell them to search what's left of the barn carefully. Likely as not they'll find another body in there.'

'AMERICA, SIR. BALTIMORE, in fact. That's where he was bound. He'd booked passage on a freighter due to sail from Southampton tomorrow. One of the fellows at Midhurst told me. They broke into his car and found his ticket and a lot of other stuff in a briefcase.'

Billy could tell from Madden's expression that he was having trouble following all this. His old chief's eyes were on matchsticks, as the saying went, and his head was nodding. It was odds on that any moment he would lay it on the kitchen table in front of him and go quietly to sleep.

'By freighter, you say . . .' Madden frowned with the

effort of trying to keep up. 'Not one of the liners. It sounds as though he was taking precautions. Did they find a passport?'

'Yes, they did, sir. French. In the name of Victor Lasalle. There was a file of business correspondence, too, letters and invoices. They made out this Lasalle was an art dealer. Some of the letters were from galleries and the like with fancy letterheads. All forged, most likely, which may explain that package he was expecting. Why it took so long to arrive.'

Billy glanced over his shoulder at the door. He was wondering when Helen would appear. He'd arrived himself ten minutes before, walking down the darkened driveway to the house, where he'd seen Madden's car standing by the front door, and felt relief for the second time that day. The fear that the other man might have suffered some mishap on the way back from Midhurst – that he wasn't in a fit state to drive – had made the sergeant's own journey an anxious one.

Seeing the entrance hall dark, Billy had walked round the side of the house to the kitchen where a light was burning and found Madden sitting at the table before the remains of a meal, alone and nodding.

'Come in, Billy, come in . . .' Blinking, he had half risen. The sergeant couldn't imagine why he was still up. 'Helen's on the phone . . . she's trying to find out for me about that girl . . . if she's all right. And the man who was stabbed, too. I should have stayed, I know. But I had to get home.'

Billy had been grateful for the chance to reassure him.

Grinning, he'd described the eventual arrival of the ambulance, which had occurred just as he was leaving.

'It took a while to get there. There's a road to the farm, but it's in bad condition; hasn't been used for ages. Someone had gone down to Oak Green to fetch the child's mother, and you can imagine the state the poor woman was in. But the girl herself was fine. She'd woken up by then and was more worried about the bloke who was stabbed, Sam Watkin, than anything else. Him and his dog. Turns out they all know each other. So when the ambulance arrived, Nell said she wouldn't get in unless the dog came too. And she stuck to her guns, what's more. They had to give in.' Billy had chuckled. 'She's a fine girl, sir, full of spirit. She won't be put down by what happened to her. You'll see.'

Billy added these last words to his account, knowing they would please his old mentor, and heard Madden grunt in approbation. Then he seemed to hesitate.

'You'll find Helen's upset,' he said, touching the lump on his temple. The size of a pigeon's egg now, and tinted with iodine, it gave Madden's face a lopsided look 'She caught Rob down here, trying to find out what had been going on, and gave him a fearful ticking off. Just bear with her, if you would?'

It was a remark the like of which Billy had never heard coming from Madden's lips before, and he was still wondering what to make of it when he heard the sound of quick footsteps approaching in the passage outside.

'They went to Petersfield, not Chichester . . .' Helen

began speaking even before she had pushed the swing door into the kitchen open. 'I spoke to the doctor who examined the girl. She's quite unharmed. A mild case of shock, nothing more. They'll keep her in overnight . . .'

As she swept into the kitchen her eye fell on Billy and she paused. He'd already risen to his feet, but the words of greeting he'd been about to utter died on his lips when he saw the high colour in her cheeks and the anger in her eyes.

'The man's stab wound is quite serious – he's lost a lot of blood – but it wasn't deep enough to damage any vital organs.' Ignoring Billy, Helen went on speaking to Madden. 'He's also got a fracture of the skull. But the doctor said he's fit and strong and should recover well.'

She stood by the table looking down at her husband. After a moment she reached out, turning his head a little to one side so she could examine the lump on his temple.

'Do you know, I can't remember how that happened?' Madden spoke to Billy through the crook of Helen's arm. 'It might have been something falling from the roof when we were coming out of the barn. But I simply don't remember.'

It came to Billy that what Madden was trying to do was alert him. That his casual tone was an attempt to defuse a bomb that was about to go off. Helen's silence, her refusal even to look at him had left the sergeant puzzled and wondering. Too late he saw what was about to happen.

'*How could you do it?*' Without warning she turned on him. '*How could you let this happen?*'

Billy was struck speechless.

'*I spoke to you only this morning. I begged you to take care of him.*'

'My dear—' Madden tried to check her, but she brushed his hand aside.

'*You had no right to put him in danger. He should never have been allowed to get near this man. Yet you let it happen.*'

It made no difference that her charges were unfair. Fairness didn't come into it. Billy saw that. Her distress, the fury she'd felt on learning of what had befallen her husband, was its own justification. The situation called for a sacrificial lamb, and there were no other candidates present. But he was cut to the quick by her words. Her good opinion had always mattered to him and he knew that the loss of it would leave him forever the poorer.

'I thought I could trust you. I believed he'd be safe as long as he was with you. So tell me, how could this have happened?' She demanded an answer, peering into his face, refusing to release him from her gaze. '*You*, Billy . . . I'm asking *you*. How could you have—'

'*Stop it, Mummy.*'

Cut short by the child's cry, Helen turned. She saw her daughter standing by the door. Lucy's tear-filled eyes had the puffy look of one just aroused from sleep. The cord of her blue dressing gown trailed on the floor behind her.

'Why are you being so horrid to Billy?'

'Lucinda Madden!' Knocked off balance, Helen struggled to recover. 'Go to bed this instant.'

'*No.*'

Defiant, the little girl came forward into the kitchen.

She took up a position in front of the sergeant. Pale with the enormity of her rebellion, she faced her mother. 'Not till you promise,' she declared, her voice quavering.

'Promise what?'

'That you won't be horrid to him any more.'

'And why should I do that?'

'Because he's our friend.'

Helen stared back at her daughter. She seemed in shock, and Billy saw, with a flash of insight, that her anger had been only a disguise, something to cling to. That knowing how close Madden had come to death that afternoon had thrown her emotions into turmoil, pushing her to the edge of collapse. It was with an enormous effort that she gathered herself now and spoke.

'Because he's our friend?' She looked down at the small figure before her, as though in puzzlement. Then a smile came to her lips. 'But of course he is. And thank you for reminding me, my darling. I promise not to be horrid again.'

She stooped and kissed the little girl.

As she straightened, Billy saw that tears had begun to stream down her cheeks. Madden had already risen and he came to her side at once. Taking her in his arms, he drew her away from the table and they stood together, not speaking, but holding each other so closely they might have been one.

Wide-eyed, Lucy looked at Billy for an explanation. The sergeant put a finger to his lips.

'Let's go upstairs,' he whispered in her ear, and hand in hand they tiptoed out together.

Epilogue

It was not until spring of the following year that Angus Sinclair finally closed the file on Gaston Lang and his many aliases. Despite weeks of patient digging little more had emerged to flesh out the figure whose shadowy past, like the single grainy snapshot supplied to the police by Philip Vane, offered no more than an impression of the man behind the mask.

'We've found out all we ever will about him, sir. I think it's time to write finis to the case.'

Sinclair had offered his verdict to the assistant commissioner after Bennett had summoned him to his office, along with Chief Superintendent Holly, so that he could inform them of the contents of a letter which he'd received from Berlin.

'It's full of assurances . . . inquiries proceeding, and so forth . . . but nothing beyond what they've already told us. "Many difficulties have arisen in the course of this investigation and the full truth may never be known." I think Nebe's warning us not to hold our breath.'

Bennett passed the letter across his desk to Sinclair who studied it for a moment.

'*Reichskriminaldirektor.*' The syllables tripped lightly off the chief inspector's tongue. 'There's a mouthful for you, Arthur.' He handed the letter on to the chief super, who was sitting beside him. 'It seems at least one of our

Berlin brethren knows which side his bread is buttered. No surprise there, by the way, sir.' He addressed himself to Bennett. 'There's a good reason why they won't pursue this matter. I've received a letter myself on the same subject. I'll get to it in a moment. But first, let me sum up what we've gathered in the way of information. It's been accumulating somewhat in my absence.'

The chief inspector had only recently returned from Manchester where he'd been engaged for some time in a complicated case of company fraud.

'The Swiss police have delved a little deeper into Lang's background and come up with one rather chilling detail. It certainly made my hair stand on end when I read it.' Sinclair grimaced. 'You'll recall what we learned from them earlier. That he was born a bastard. His mother was a domestic servant in a village not far from Geneva and if she knew who the father of her child was she never said. In any event, she died soon after he was born and Lang was taken in by the village pastor and his wife who gave him their name and raised him as a son along with their own baby daughter.'

'Yes, I remember.' Bennett sipped at a cup of tea. He'd had a tray sent in. 'But later they dispatched him to an orphanage. We wondered why.'

Holly rumbled in accord. 'They were still making inquiries, as I recall.'

'Yes, the problem was they'd lost track of the pastor. Lang, of course, his name was. His wife had died and he'd disappeared from the village. More than that: it turned out he was no longer a churchman; he'd left the ministry.'

'What about his daughter?' Holly frowned. 'She must have known something.'

The chief inspector grunted. He was staring into the cup of tea which he held balanced on his knee.

'That's part of what I have to tell you.' He looked up. 'It's what the Swiss police learned after they'd tracked down Lang. The pastor, I mean. He was living in another part of Switzerland, in a village in the mountains, near Davos. He'd become a recluse, and at first was unwilling to respond to their questions. In particular, he didn't wish to hear any mention of the boy: of the child he and his wife had raised.' Sinclair shrugged. 'However, by degrees they broke down his resistance and in the end he told them the story.'

The chief inspector paused. He appeared to be choosing his words.

'It seems clear to me, reading between the lines, that they didn't understand what it was they had burdened themselves with. The pastor and his wife, I mean. What affliction they had brought into their lives. As the boy grew older they realized he was not like others: that he had neither the desire nor the capacity to make those connections necessary in human society: that he was quite alone in the world and content to be so. But the picture was darker than that. Quite early on they detected a strain of deliberate cruelty in him. He had to be kept away from domestic pets, which he was prone to torture, and also had to be watched when in the company of other small children.'

Sinclair shook his head. 'This is a theme we're familiar with. It crops up time and again in cases involving violent offenders, particularly sexual criminals. Childhood experience is sometimes held to account for this sort of extreme anti-social behaviour. But it's by no means the rule, and would seem to have been absent in this case, where the boy was shown nothing but kindness by his foster parents. Did something happen to him earlier, you may ask – during the months he was with his mother?' The chief inspector shrugged. 'I've no answer to that. In fact, I've no explanation to offer beyond the somewhat chilling observation that as a species we seem to possess a capacity for savagery that defies reason. That these seeds must lie in all of us. And that it's a lesson history teaches us over and over, and which we never seem to learn.'

The chief inspector coughed to cover up his embarrassment. He wasn't sure why he'd said what he'd just said, except that in some way it was related to the talk he had had with Franz Weiss at Highfield, and beyond that to some broader comprehension of which he had not, until that moment, been aware.

'Forgive me. I'm digressing. To return to the earlier point, the pattern of behaviour I've described continued throughout the boy's childhood, which was marked, in particular, by a growing hostility towards his stepsister. There seemed no reason for this, other than the fact that they were thrown together, and not surprisingly, the girl came in time to return the sentiment, and as she grew older made common cause with the other village children, who seem to have been united in their dislike of the boy. He himself, while still quite young, began to pursue a solitary pattern of life, and having developed an interest in birds took to wandering in the countryside, spending long hours away from home.'

The chief inspector sighed. He eyed his two listeners.

'One can only pity the parents in their attempts to deal with this catastrophe that had befallen them. No doubt things would have been different these days. They might have been able to seek help from competent medical authorities. But they lived a simple rural existence and Pastor Lang was apparently of a disposition to treat whatever trials came his way as an expression of God's will; a test of his faith. It seems he was determined to do right by the child. However, a point was reached where the situation became untenable. The boy was twelve and increasingly difficult to control. Perhaps he sensed weakness in his foster parent; a lack of resolution. At all events the Langs decided he would have to go and the pastor arranged for him to be taken in by a church-run institution, an orphanage of sorts, in Geneva. He informed the boy accordingly.

'"He looked at me with his pale eyes and said nothing."'

The change in the chief inspector's tone caught his listeners off guard.

'It's a line from the report the Swiss police sent us. I find it sticks in the memory.' Sinclair glanced at them both. 'His departure was set for two weeks hence. He was assured he would return home for holidays at regular intervals. Still he had shown no reaction. A few days before he was due to go his stepsister went missing. A search was organized and her body was found in a gully not far away. It seemed she'd had a fall and broken her neck. There was some damage to her face: her nose had been broken and her features disfigured.'

'Good God!' Holly was dumbstruck. 'And the boy did it? Is that what you're saying? But why, man, why?'

'For spite? For pleasure?' Sinclair shrugged. 'No one can answer that question, Arthur. No one but Lang. And he took his secrets with him.'

Bennett stared at the blotter on his desk. 'Was the boy questioned about it?' he asked. 'Was he a suspect?'

'Apparently not. He'd wandered off as he often did earlier and returned to be told the news. Or so he made out. Although the police were called in they concluded it was an accident. The girl appeared to have fallen from a height and to have rolled down the gully. There was no evidence of an assault, sexual or otherwise, and no reports of any strangers being seen in the vicinity.'

'But his stepfather, this pastor, thought the boy was responsible?'

'He indicated as much to the police when they tracked him down. Though whether he thought so at the time, I can't say. Perhaps the realization came to him later. In any case there was no proof. Suffice to say, neither he nor his wife ever saw their stepson again. She died a year later and he left the church soon afterwards. He told the detectives who interviewed him that he'd lost his faith and explained why. He said the boy had been born beyond the reach of God's mercy and that since such a thing could not be, or not in the world he'd believed in, he could no longer continue with his ministry. He had ceased to pray, except for death.'

Bennett rose and went to the window. The day was showery and he examined the cloud-covered sky outside.

'What happened to Lang? To the boy, I mean?'

'He was sent to the orphanage, as planned. Interestingly enough, his record there was unexceptional. He gave no trouble and was marked down as intelligent, but unresponsive. Again, he made no friends, and shortly before his sixteenth birthday he absconded. He walked out of the place and was never seen again. We've no way of knowing how he spent the next few years, though it's likely he lived by his wits. Equally, there's no clue as to what kind of sexual life he might have had during these years. Perhaps none. Until the murder for which he was sought, which occurred when he was in his twenties, there was no record – in Switzerland, at least – of any similar unresolved crimes. Mind you, he'd been working for Hoffmann for some time, often as a courier, so it's not to say he didn't take advantage of his trips abroad. For what it's worth, I'm inclined to think that in these earlier years, at least, he was able to hold himself in check. The kind of life he'd fallen into was already dangerous enough. He can't have wanted to add to it. The killing for which the Swiss police sought him may well have been his first. But as I've told you, the information we've received from the various police forces around Europe is sketchy at best. All we can say for sure is that there are a number of unsolved sexual crimes in the countries we know he's visited, some of them not dissimilar to the attacks he specialized in.'

The chief inspector broke off to place his cup of tea,

untasted, on the desk before him. Bennett remained by the window. But he had turned to listen.

'It's tempting to believe that his fixation with facial assaults harks back to the murder of his stepsister, and I've no doubt a psychologist would make much of it. The increasing ferocity of these episodes over the course of time suggests they were gaining a hold on him. Certainly he took more risks. If he hadn't stopped to attack that child near Midhurst last November, he might have escaped. My God! Just imagine him wandering about America! The sheer size of it. Would we ever have caught him, I wonder?'

Holly growled his agreement. A frown had settled on the chief super's face as he'd listened.

Bennett returned to his desk. 'You said you'd received a letter, Chief Inspector. I gather it has some bearing on the German attitude to this investigation?'

'Yes, I have it with me.' Sinclair took an envelope from his pocket and removed several handwritten pages from it. He spread them on his knee. 'It's from Inspector Probst – I'm sure you remember him. He wants all the facts about this case to be made known. That's why he's written to me. It's a letter I'd rather not place in the file. There's no telling what kind of relations we'll end up having with the new order in Berlin once the dust's settled over there – though for my part, I hope they're minimal – but I wouldn't like to think it might fall into the wrong hands one day.'

'I see . . .' Bennett's eyes had narrowed. 'But isn't he taking a risk writing to you behind his superior's backs?'

'A risk, I'm sure. But he's not with the police any longer, so it isn't a question of him disobeying orders. He resigned as soon as the Nazis took over at the end of January. "As a policeman one cannot serve criminals: it is a contradiction in terms."' Chuckling, Sinclair read from one of the pages. 'He doesn't pull his punches, does he? Of course, he wouldn't have lasted in the job. One of the first things the Nazis did when they took over was purge the police. He's amusing on that score, too. Well, perhaps "amusing" is not quite the right word . . .'

The chief inspector squinted at the sheet of paper he was holding.

'"Goering came in person to the Alexanderplatz and shook many hands."' He quoted from the page. '"They say he's good company; jovial; the war hero with the common touch. I looked into his eyes and saw a natural-born killer. How well I know the type."'

Sinclair laid the sheet of paper back on his knee.

'But with regard to the Lang investigation, Probst said they'd continued with it up to the time the government changed hands. Inquiring into his background, that is. Whether or not they guessed that he was an agent he doesn't say. But he describes his past as "murky" and says he was not what he seemed to be: in other words the representative of an Austrian textile firm. In tracing his movements between Berlin and Munich they also discovered his Nazi connections, and it was at this point, or very soon afterwards, that the inquiry was brought to a halt. Whether Nebe acted on his own initiative, or was spoken to, isn't clear. But he seems to have known which way the wind was blowing. Probst says the investigation is no longer being actively pursued; nor will it be.'

There was silence while Bennett absorbed what he'd been told.

'Of course, he joined the party, didn't he? Vane told us that.'

'Indeed he did, sir.'

'And the last thing the Nazis would want is for their reputations to be tarred by a case like this only months after they've taken power.'

'I'm sure that thought occurred to them.'

'So even if they do discover some link to our intelligence service it's unlikely they'd want to air it. Mud sticks, after all.'

'Quite. And there's no prospect of anything more coming out at this end, is there? Lang's background remains a mystery as far as our press is concerned. My impression is they've given up digging. I think your friends in Whitehall can sleep easy.'

'*My* friends, Chief Inspector?' Bennett favoured him with a stony glance.

'A slip of the tongue, sir.'

Sinclair had derived some amusement from the minuet he had just performed with his superior. Not so Holly, who cleared his throat loudly.

'Well, I think it's a damned disgrace,' he said bluntly. 'The whole wretched business. What's worse is, no one's going to answer for it.'

In the embarrassed silence that followed, Sinclair returned Probst's letter to his pocket.

'And we've no cause to congratulate ourselves, either.' The chief super was working up a head of steam. 'There's only one person who comes out of this with any credit: John Madden. I hope you'll tell him that when you see him next, Angus. And thank him from me.'

'I will, Arthur,' Sinclair promised him. He looked at his colleague with affection. 'And sooner than you think. I'm going down to Highfield this weekend.'

A SOLITARY FIGURE WAS standing on the platform when Sinclair's train pulled into Highfield. As he stepped from the compartment, the glint of sunlight on golden hair caught his eye. Helen Madden advanced down the plat-form to greet him.

'John was planning to meet you himself. But the children insisted on an expedition into the woods. They've been cooped up for days with the rain we've been having. They'll come back soaked, I know.'

The showery weather she'd been speaking of had begun to clear at lunchtime and the chief inspector's train had passed through sunlit fields bright with spring flowers.

'The house is packed at the moment. I hope you won't find it too much for you. Franz was so pleased when he heard you were coming down. But you won't see him till this evening. He's been in London all day house-hunting.'

The blue woollen dress she was wearing matched the colour of her eyes, Sinclair noted. The pleasure he took in her company had never diminished with the years and he felt a lightening of his step as she linked her arm in his. They went out to where her car was parked.

'I know you've been away, but it seems ages since we last saw you. I'm afraid it took me a while to get over that dreadful business. I needed time to recover.'

She glanced at him. They were driving past the village green.

'But I've thought of you often, and particularly the day we went down to Midhurst. That family ... the Ramsays ... invited us. Not for the first time, either, poor dears. They wanted to thank John. But I hadn't felt able to face them before. I thought it would be too upsetting. But it turned out to be a lovely day. Mrs Ramsay had organized a picnic for the children on the Downs and they'd also invited the man who was stabbed, Sam Watkin, and his family. It was his friend whose body was found in the burned out barn later. Eddie was his name. But they'd all known him, it seems, and they talked of him with such affection, particularly the girl, Nell, and her mother. They'd been trying to help him find a proper job – the Ramsays, I mean – and John and I could see how upset they still were by what happened.'

She mused in silence for a few moments.

'Afterwards we walked up to the farm. The children insisted on seeing it and Nell told them the whole story. Needless to say, they were spellbound. They wanted to hear all the grisly details. It was poor John who couldn't bear to listen. All he could think of was what might have happened. He knew better than anyone how close it came to ending in tragedy. People who don't know him think he's detached and unaffected by things. It's because of his manner. But he's not like that at all. He's quite the opposite.'

She brushed a tear from her eye, then turned towards him, smiling. 'But I don't have to tell you that, do I?' She touched his cheek with her hand as she spoke, a simple gesture that brought joy to the heart of the chief inspector, who saw that after all he had been forgiven. 'That was a month ago, and it was only a few days later that I went to Germany.'

'Yes, I heard about that from John. He rang me.' The chief inspector became animated. 'You brought Dr Weiss and his family back?'

'I went over to help with the move. It seemed sensible, since I'm the one who speaks German, and I worried that Franz might not be able to manage on his own. You know his wife died?'

'John told me.'

'That was soon after Christmas. And something else dreadful had happened. They have two children, a son studying in America, and a daughter called Lotte, who was married to a university lecturer in Berlin, a young man called Josef Stern. He was active in politics, too much so, perhaps, and in the weeks before the Nazis came to power he got involved in a street battle with some brown shirt thugs and was terribly beaten. He never recovered consciousness and died in hospital. So thank heavens I went. They were both distraught, Franz and his daughter, quite unable to cope, and I took care of everything.

'They had a house on the Wannsee, outside Berlin. It's by the lake and lovely in summer when the trees are in leaf. But we never saw the sun while I was there, just leaden cloud. There's a wall at the back of the house, and on the day I got there I found a Star of David daubed in yellow on it. I had it removed. The next day it was back, and again I made the gardener wash it off. And so it went on, day after day. I never saw who did it: there wasn't a soul about. But each morning the star was there again. I finally got the house cleared and the furniture carted away, but I felt dreadful doing it. John and I spent a holiday with the family there two years ago and all I could think of was how happy they had been.'

She fell silent, and they continued through the village, passing the locked gates of Melling Lodge. Soon they were turning into the familiar drive where the lime trees were green with new leaf.

'Franz is looking for a house in Hampstead. He wants to set up in practice. Lotte will live with him. She has a daughter called Hana, who's six. Lucy's taken a great fancy to her. She has such passions for people, my Lucy. Did you know your Billy Styles is one of her favourites?'

They'd arrived at the front door. Helen's smile had returned.

'He brought his fiancée down to meet us not long ago. Elsie's her name. It must have been trying for the poor girl. Being put on parade is never easy. But to make matters worse, Lucy spent the entire day stalking her like a panther, watching her every move. Heaven knows when she'll pluck up the courage to visit us again.'

*

SHOWN TO HIS ROOM, Sinclair returned downstairs ten minutes later to find his hostess sitting in a garden chair on the terrace, from which vantage point all the colours of spring were to be seen in the beds bordering the lawn and the air was sweet with the smell of honeysuckle.

Some movement was visible in a shrubbery near the bottom of garden and presently a man emerged from it pushing a wheelbarrow. The chief inspector peered in that direction. He was about to speak, when Helen gestured, pointing.

'There they are now.'

Following the direction she indicated, Sinclair caught sight of a pair of darting figures which had appeared, as if by magic, at the very bottom of the garden, flitting through the orchard like sprites, two separate forms that nevertheless seemed joined, since they moved as one.

'Those are the two girls,' Helen explained, seeing the chief inspector's furrowed brow. 'Lucy's on the left. I told her about Hana's father dying and her response has been to keep a firm grip on her. To show her that *she's* there and won't disappear. At least, I think that's how she reasons.'

They watched as the two figures suddenly veered to one side and set off in pursuit of the man with the wheelbarrow who was disappearing at that moment into another part of the shrubbery and whose movements the chief inspector was following with close attention. His observation was interrupted once again, however, by the appearance of Madden, who came striding out of the orchard just then in the company of a pair of young boys, one of whom Sinclair recognized as his friends' son.

'Who's the other?' he asked Helen, shading his eyes. The sun was low in the sky; the afternoon light was fading.

'Will Stackpole's son, Ted. It means a lot to me that he and Rob are such friends. Will's someone I love. He was the first boy who ever kissed me.' She smiled in recollection. 'I was Lucy's age, six or seven. He made eyes at me all one summer. I love seeing them together now, the boys. But it makes me anxious. They keep growing older ...'

'Why should that bother you?'

'Because there's going to be another war.'

She spoke the words in so natural a tone it was a moment or two before the chief inspector registered what she'd said.

'Oh, surely not.' He responded automatically. 'I mean you can't be sure ... so many things can happen ...' He fell silent. She seemed not to have heard him.

'I can't tell you how awful I felt in Berlin.' Helen's eyes were on the figures advancing up the lawn. 'The flags, the uniforms, the strutting. And the never-ending rant. I saw one uniform. It was black. Black from head to toe. The badge on the cap was a death's head. Can you imagine?'

She held her face in her hands.

'I knew then ...'

He said nothing. Allowing her time to recover, he waved to Madden, who waved back, but then gestured to demonstrate some intention on his part, which presently became clear when he and the boys changed course, directing their steps towards the side of the house where the kitchen lay.

'They're going to leave their muddy shoes there. They'll come in the other way.'

Helen ran her fingers through her hair. Next moment the smile was back on her lips and he saw that something else had caught her eye.

The two little girls had emerged from the shrubbery where they'd been hidden from sight and were running up the lawn, still hand in hand, towards them. The fairer of the two whom he now recognized as Lucy held a bunch of yellow daffodils in her free hand. As they ascended the steps of the terrace, Helen rose to meet them.

'For you, Mummy,' Lucy declared breathlessly, thrusting the dripping flowers into her grasp. Well spattered with mud, the pair seemed in haste to continue on their headlong course, but Helen checked them.

'What on earth have you been doing? Just look at poor Hana.'

She spoke a few words of German to the dark-haired child, who replied breathlessly in the same language. Both girls were pawing the terrace in their eagerness to be off.

'It's time for your baths.' Helen turned to her daughter again. 'Mary's waiting upstairs. Take Hana with you. And don't pull her arm off—!'

The warning came too late. Shrieking as one, the two little girls sprang away and as though glued together ran full tilt across the terrace and into the house.

'Introductions will have to wait, I'm afraid.'

Leaving his hostess to shake the water from the bouquet she'd been given, Sinclair got up from his chair and moved to the edge of the terrace. He peered down into the gloaming. The figure he'd noticed earlier was advancing up the lawn now, pushing the wheelbarrow in front of him. The chief inspector could contain his curiosity no longer.

'Who on earth is that?' he asked. 'And what's he got on his head?'

'Can't you guess?' Helen answered in a teasing tone. 'It's Topper. Surely you remember him.'

'I've not had the pleasure of making his acquaintance. But I recall the name well. Am I not right in thinking he was summoned to give evidence at the inquest in Guildford ... and never appeared?' Sinclair turned to regard his hostess. 'Harbouring fugitives, are you, Dr Madden?'

Helen smiled. 'He turned up out of the blue just after Christmas. John set him up in one of the stalls at the farm with plenty of bedding and a stove. Luckily Tom Cooper went down with rheumatism just then. I say luckily, because Topper doesn't like accepting charity beyond the odd meal. So we've turned him into a sort of substitute gardener, and he seems happy doing it.'

She paused. The figure had come to a halt just below the terrace and Sinclair took in the spectacle of the hat with its jaunty pheasant plume.

He watched as Topper removed it and bowed. Helen smiled to him in response.

'Goodnight, Topper. And thank you for the lovely flowers.'

Replacing his hat, he continued on his way without a word, disappearing around the side of the house.

'John says he'll pack up his bundle one of these days and move on, but I hope not. I don't like to think of him wandering around. He's too old. He needs a home.' She was looking at the daffodils in her hand and he saw her brush something from her cheek. 'My hope is he'll find it hard to leave now. He so loves the children.'

'The children?' Sinclair glanced at the flowers she was holding, then at her face, which was turned away. 'Aye ... the children.'

'Oh, dear ...' She made no pretence now about wiping away the tears which had started from her eyes. 'I'm sorry, Angus. I still haven't got over that awful business. I lost my nerve for a while, and I'm not sure I've got it back. I'm afraid of the future. I see dreadful things ahead. Look what's happened to poor Franz and his family. How many others will suffer in the same way? Who will help *them*? It's as though some terrible dark night is about to descend on us all and I want to protect the people I love and care for, but I don't know how, or even if I can ...'

'My dear ...' Seeing her distress, the chief inspector put his arm around her and tried to comfort her. 'It's because you're still upset. These wounds take a long time to heal.'

'Yes, of course ...' She touched his cheek. 'Dear Angus ...'

She collected herself.

'I must put these in water. Come inside, if you like, or stay and watch the sun go down. I love the way the colours of the trees change as the light dies. John will be here in a moment, but I warn you he'll be busy. As soon as the girls come down he'll have to read to them. Lucy's trying to teach Hana English and she thinks having her listen to *The Wind in the Willows* will do the trick. I believe Mr Toad is about to set off in his motor car, so the proceedings might get noisy. But come in soon. I want us all to be together.'

He waited until she had gone inside, then turned to look out once more over the deserted garden, his mind full of what she had said. The day was nearly over and only the topmost trees of Upton Hanger still glinted in the dying light. The rest of the long wooded ridge was already plunged in Stygian gloom, and the chief inspector was not disposed to linger. As he stood there a wash of light fell about his feet from the lamps that were being switched on in the drawing room and he heard the high-pitched cries of the children.

Drawn by the thought of the warmth inside and the many dear faces around, he hesitated no longer, turning his back on the end of the day.

And on the dark night that was coming.

OTHER PAN BOOKS
AVAILABLE FROM PAN MACMILLAN

MARTIN CRUZ SMITH
WOLVES EAT DOGS   0 330 43586 8   £6.99

ARTURO PÉREZ-REVERTE
THE QUEEN OF THE SOUTH   0 330 41314 7   £7.99

G M FORD
BLACK RIVER   0 330 49262 4   £6.99
A BLIND EYE   0 330 42016 X   £6.99

All Pan Macmillan titles can be ordered from our website,
www.panmacmillan.com, or from your local bookshop
and are also available by post from:

Bookpost, PO Box 29, Douglas, Isle of Man IM99 1BQ
Credit cards accepted. For details:
Telephone: +44 (0)1624 677237
Fax: +44 (0)1624 670923
E-mail: bookshop@enterprise.net
www.bookpost.co.uk

Free postage and packing in the United Kingdom

Prices shown above were correct at the time of going to press.
Pan Macmillan reserve the right to show new retail prices on covers
which may differ from those previously advertised in the text
or elsewhere.